A Night Out of Time

Brazos stood at the base of the steps, the eddy of a light ground fog swirling around his boots. The glow from a three-quarter moon shone blue-black upon his hair. His eyes were glittering jewels. Madeline closed her eyes as a wave of longing crashed over her like surf upon the sand in the face of a violent storm. "Are you really here, or have my dreams conjured you up?"

His laugh was mocking as he replied, "I don't know, Maddie. Maybe it was your nightmares."

Moving like a wraith, he stood beside her. His hand lifted and his fingers brushed her cheek. Their gazes met, his burning and hungry. Ravenous. Madeline's filled with yearning.

It was a night out of time. Somewhere deep in her heart she knew that this time, this intensity, this emotion, might never be repeated.

So she kissed him, the touch of her lips as soft as the rose petals in her hand, the whisper of her breath as it mingled with his as gentle as the breeze off the ocean.

Madeline's kiss sparked the flame that had been burning inside Brazos all across the Atlantic. She wasn't his to take, not any longer, but he didn't give a damn.

Also by Geralyn Dawson:

THE TEXAN'S BRIDE

Capture
the
Night

GERALYN

DAWSON

BANTAM BOOKS

NEW YORK • TORONTO • LONDON • SYDNEY • AUCKLAND

CAPTURE THE NIGHT
A Bantam Fanfare Book / December 1993

ISBN 0-553-56176-6

Published simultaneously in the United States and Canada

Bantam Books are published by Bantam Books, a division of Bantam Doubleday
Dell Publishing Group, Inc. Its trademark, consisting of the words "Bantam
Books" and the portrayal of a rooster, is Registered in U.S. Patent and
Trademark Office and in other countries. Marca Registrada. Bantam Books,
1540 Broadway, New York, New York 10036.

PRINTED IN THE UNITED STATES OF AMERICA

RAD   0 9 8 7 6 5 4 3 2 1

For the little beasties who make my life so beautiful—Steven, John, and Caitlin.

I love y'all.

Capture
the
Night

Prologue

He bared his teeth and snarled as the hand reached out to touch him. Straining against the iron shackles, he fought the assault like the animal he'd become, bucking and twisting, the curled and yellowed tips of his fingernails digging into his palms and drawing blood. He threw back his head, heedless of the matted and lice-laden lengths of hair that whipped into his mouth as he loosened a feral roar.

The sound echoed off the dungeon's granite walls, then faded into nothingness as he retreated to that place within himself insulated from the rage and pain, isolated from the degradation.

His body jerked spasmodically when the red-hot blade sliced deep into his breast. His nostrils twitched at the stench of singed hair and branded flesh.

The governor of the prison stepped away and plunged the heated weapon into a nearby pail. A hiss rose from the water, and the Mexican pursed his lips in pleasure. What a wonderful beginning to this next amusement.

He faced the animal chained naked to the wall, noting the bruises, the wounds, and the trace of madness in the eyes. A heavy heat curled in the governor's loins, and as his fingers lifted to trace the filigree and etchings adorning the silver band around his arm, he observed, "It is a shame I have been forced to separate you from your companion. My entertainment lacks that certain edge of one friend watching another's . . . pleasure. Never worry, though. I have devised a new delight. We shall begin this evening." His sinister chuckle echoed off the walls as he added, "Actually, if one is being accurate, it began more than a week ago."

The governor exited the cell, and as he twisted the key in the lock, he grinned in anticipation and said, "Ah, *bestia,* you are still my favorite prisoner. Tell me, are you hungry?"

THE MAN CALLED Brazos Sinclair by family and friends ceased to exist while held in the prison's deepest, darkest cell. For the final eight months of his captivity, a beast roamed the pits of Perote.

Only upon his flight from the fortress did the man, Brazos, surface. Slowly, and with the aid of a beautiful Mexican woman, pieces of his humanity returned to him. As they made their way across the sandy, barren plains at the foot of the mountain range known as the Coffer of Perote, words and language replaced gutteral sounds as his method of communication. He bathed for the first time in years in an icy mountain stream seven thousand feet above sea level. At a village one hundred twenty miles north of Vera Cruz, he stole a razor and shaved away his beard.

When he traded a pilfered Mexican mule for a knock-kneed roan gelding on a South Texas ranch, he wore a gentleman's attire filched from a brothel along the banks of the Rio Grande. Beneath the black frock coat and white linen shirt lay a scar, puckered and ridged from neglect. Beneath the scar, in the hollow where once dwelt a soul, hissed the breath of evil.

The beast lived, patiently awaiting his freedom.

Chapter 1

ANTWERP, BELGIUM, 1855

"*Kidnapping* is such an ugly word," Madeline Christophe murmured, gazing into the angelic face of the infant she cradled in her arms. It was an ugly word for a monstrous deed—taking a child from its parents for the purpose of extortion. That's how the police and the newspapers would label her crime, but they would be wrong.

She had absolutely no intentions of ever returning the child she had stolen.

Madeline was a thief, a talented thief, and she'd been stealing all her life. Her earliest memory was of slipping her hand into a green brocade reticule and silently removing the jeweled hand mirror into which her beautiful stepmother so often gazed. Though only four years old, she had already possessed the delicate touch and dramatic flare that would serve her well in the years to come. That day, however, all she'd wanted was to see for herself just how ugly one must be to merit abandonment by one's mother.

While her beautiful parent had tossed a bag of coins onto a desk at an English boarding school, her scorn-filled voice saying, "See to the loathsome child," Madeline had stared into the mirror and decided it must be the brown eyes and sprinkling of freckles that made her ugly. Mama had sparkling green eyes and unblemished ivory skin.

Now, more than twenty years later, Madeline's eyes remained a velvet brown, and a dusting of freckles had yet to fade from the bridge of her nose. She also still owned the mirror.

Madeline never returned the things she stole.

A biting wind swirled across the wharf, the salty scent of the North Sea mingling with land's dust in a whirlwind that swept over the queue of colonists waiting to board ship. Madeline shivered and tucked the yellow lamb's wool blanket snugly around the sleeping child. Her life had become a whirlwind—cold ashes of lies, betrayal, and death twirling around an aching emptiness. But the barest hint of refuge rode the squall, and she clung to its promise as she advanced a position in line.

On board the *Uriel,* the packet on which Madeline and the baby would sail, final loading of equipment and supplies was under way. Ropes creaked as heavy bundles swung from shore to ship. Dockworkers shifted crates and lowered hogsheads into the hold.

A hand touched her on the shoulder. "Madeline? Madeline, did you not hear me call?"

She turned to see a diminutive woman with a round, smiling face and bright hazel eyes. "Oh, Lillibet, I'm sorry, I only—"

I only forgot the name I'm using, she thought. She must be more careful, mistakes like that could be dangerous. Self-disgust swept through her as she searched her mind for an excuse. One would have thought that the quantity of time she spent during her youth playing roles from beggar-child to princess would have better prepared her to slip into a new identity. But apparently, after twenty-three years as "that poor little orphaned Mary

Smithwick," she needed more than two weeks to accustom herself to the name Madeline Christophe.

In apology, she touched the soft velveteen of Lillibet Brunet's cloak. "It's the excitement of it all—such a distraction. I vow I'd begun to believe the weather would never clear."

"Is that not the truth. Why, these past two weeks have been the longest of my life . . . well, except for the two right before little Thomas was born." Lillibet bestowed a prideful, maternal look upon the bundle nestled in her plump arms.

"He is a precious child, Lil."

Madame Brunet beamed, "Yes, yes, he is. But then, your little Rose is too. Why, in the week and a half that I have been caring for her, I've come to love her like my own. Of course, with a mother like you she's bound to be special. You've more courage than most, continuing with your plans when so newly widowed."

Guilt rolled through Madeline like a North Sea swell. She winced, saying, "It was his dream, our dream. What else could I have done?" She reached for Lillibet's hand and gave it a friendly squeeze. "I'm so thankful that you offered to assist with Rose. I searched desperately for a wet-nurse willing to emigrate, and I'd almost abandoned hope when we met."

Lillibet dropped kisses first on Rose's forehead and then on her son's. "Think nothing of it, Madeline. I'm happy to help. After all, isn't that what the Colonization Society of Texas is all about? Man helping his fellow man for the betterment of all, or in our case, perhaps I should say woman helping woman? The fact is that the shock of your husband's death dried up your milk." She fingered the edge of the blanket framing Rose's face. "I, on the other hand, can easily provide for both my son and your daughter. I would be failing in my duty to my beliefs if I refused to help you."

She shrugged sheepishly and added, "Besides, she's as sweet as spun sugar, and I enjoy her tremendously. I'm hoping some of Rose's good nature will rub off on my little scamp."

Madeline shifted the sleeping baby to her shoulder

and gently patted her back. "Still, I am in your debt, Lillibet. If you'd not agreed to feed Rose for me, we could not have joined the La Réunion colonists. You truly are a kind and generous woman."

Lillibet shook her head, dismissing Madeline's praise. "Now, don't start in again, Madeline. I do not wish to hear it. Besides, I haven't the time. My André has already checked us aboard, and he's waiting in our cabin. I must get back to him before he wonders whether I've changed my mind about sailing."

She giggled, then lowered her voice. "Dearling, I must tell you. André did speak with the captain about changing our assignment from steerage to the cabin next to yours. Madeline, you're such a friend to spare the coin, and especially to do so unbeknownst to my husband."

She huffed. "Men and their silly pride—I think we should outlaw such nonsense at La Réunion. While admittedly, André and I are not nearly as wealthy as most of our fellow colonists, in a true Utopian society like La Réunion, that should not matter." As she spoke, indignation lifted her chin and sharpened her tone. "My André may not have gold like most of the émigrés, but he was the best farmer in the entire south of France. He'll be of much more use to the colony in Texas than will Monsieur Robards, the musician, or Monsieur Correll, the banker, or the hatters or the artists or countless other who are members of the Society!"

Madeline nodded, laying her hand atop Rose's ear. As much as she liked Lillibet Brunet, she wished she'd muffle her voice. "You are right, Lil, André will be central to the success of the colony. It was my pleasure to upgrade your accommodations, so you mustn't think a thing about it. Why, it would be nonsense to have you anywhere but at my side—what with your caring for Rose—not to mention the fact that you've quickly become my very best friend."

As she made the vow of friendship, Madeline realized that she spoke the truth. Suddenly, an intense and unprecedented need to confide brought the entire ugly store to her lips, and she bit back the confession just in time. With her jaw clenched tight, she scolded herself. *Fool, the madcap dash across Europe must have scrambled your brains.*

Why, never before had she entertained such an imprudent notion. Madeline prided herself on her superior intelligence—she could plot and scheme and connive better than anyone she'd ever met. But talking about the baby would be nothing more than stupid. Even alluding to Rose's true identity could lead to disaster.

Madeline had risked too much in stealing this child from Château St. Germaine, and she mustn't allow her own desire for comfort to jeopardize her plan at this critical time. Europe was too small a place in which to hide from one as powerful and wealthy and evil as Julian Desseau.

She swayed beneath the weight of the burden she'd assumed, closing her eyes as fear surfaced. *Is Texas big enough to hide us? Will anyplace be safe? Does Rose have a chance to grow up healthy and happy, or will she forever carry the stigma of her unholy birth?*

"Madeline, are you all right?" Lillibet touched her sleeve. "You're as pale as the mizzen sail. Why don't you sit for a bit. I'll hold your spot in line."

"I'm fine, Lil." Madeline forced a smile. "I was thinking about—"

Nodding wisely, Lillibet finished for her, "The baby's father?"

"Yes, the baby's father." *Well, at least I'm mixing some truth in with the falsehoods.* She swallowed a self-mocking laugh and waved toward the ship. "Now, you go on to your André, Lil. I'll bring Rose to you when she awakens."

Watching her friend make her way aboard the *Uriel,* Madeline sighed heavily. Lying, unlike thievery, stirred her conscience—at least where friends were concerned.

Suddenly, the seabirds' caws and sailors' curses were muted by the angry roar of a man who stood before the gangway. Dressed in a simple, navy blue sailor's jacket over a chambray shirt and denim trousers, he braced his hands upon his hips and glared down at Victor Considérant, the colonist's leader and the man who had chartered the *Uriel*.

"*Mon Dieu*," the stranger shouted in the most horribly accented French Madeline had ever heard. "I tell you I'll do anything, pay anything, to get aboard this ship. I must go home to Texas immediately!"

Madeline frowned as Rose stirred in her arms, disturbed by the man's bellow. Don't wake up, darling, please, she thought. She'd purposely waited for the child's nap time to arrive at the ship—the last thing she wanted was to attract the attention of the hawkers selling their wares around the docks. Memories of a crying infant might linger where danger could follow.

At the gangway, Considérant turned his back on the dark-haired man, whose blue eyes blazed at the insult. Madeline watched the Texan as another couple gave their name to be checked against the manifest.

His jaw hardened as his gaze trailed the boarding passengers. He appeared completely out of place in his surroundings and totally at ease with himself in spite of it. Standing straight as a mainmast and seemingly as tall, he towered over Considérant. He wore no hat; his hair was unfashionably long, a slight curl of black past his collar. He lacked but guns at his hips to fit her image of a Texan, what with his sun-darkened skin, a face set in rugged, though attractive angles, and broad shoulders that stretched the seams of his wool jacket.

He conformed to her picture of a Texan until he turned and caught her staring. Then he looked like any other man whose thoughts more often originated beneath his belt buckle than in his mind.

One corner of his mouth lifted in an appreciative grin as he very deliberately scrutinized every facet of her appearance. Madeline resisted the urge to pat her wind-blown hair back into place and ignored the sudden desire to study him as thoroughly as he did her.

Disgusted with both herself and the stranger, she lifted her chin and looked past him, focusing on a crate marked "Farm Implements and Musical Instruments." From the corner of her eye, she saw him stick his hands in his back pockets and rock on his heels. Tall and broad, he blocked a good portion of the gangway.

"Mr. Sinclair, if you would please move away?" Considérant asked. "Boarding procedure cannot take place with you obstructing our path."

"But we've not finished," the Texan said.

"Wait in line, please."

Madeline groaned as the man called Sinclair sauntered toward her. This is all I need, she thought.

He stopped beside her and dipped into a perfect imitation of a gentleman's bow. Eyes shining, he looked up and said in his deplorable French, "Madam, do you by chance speak English? Apparently, we'll be sharing a spot in line. I beg to make your acquaintance."

She didn't answer.

He sighed and straightened. Then a wicked grin creased his face, and in English he drawled, "Brazos Sinclair's my name, Texas born and bred. Most of my friends call me Sin, especially my lady friends. Nobody calls me Claire but once. I'll be sailin' with you on the *Uriel*."

Madeline ignored him.

Evidently, that bothered him not at all. "Cute baby," he said, peeking past the blanket. "Best keep him covered good though. This weather'll chill him."

Madeline bristled at the implied criticism. She glared at the man named Sin.

He grin faded. "Sure you don't speak English?"

She held her silence.

"Guess not, huh. That's all right. I'll enjoy conversin' with you anyway." He shot a piercing glare toward Victor Considérant and added, "I need a diversion, you see. Otherwise I'm liable to do something I shouldn't." Angling his head, he gave her another sweeping gaze. "You're a right fine-lookin' woman, ma'am, a real beauty. Don't know that I think much of your husband, though, leavin' you here on the docks by your lonesome."

He paused and looked around, his stare snagging on a pair of scruffy sailors. "It's a dangerous thing for women to be alone in such a place, and for a beautiful one like you, well, I hesitate to think."

Obviously, Madeline said to herself.

The Texan continued, glancing around at the people milling around the wharf. "Course, I can't say I understand you Europeans. I've been here goin' on two years, and I'm no closer to figurin' y'all out now than I was the day I rolled off the boat." He reached into his jacket pocket and pulled out a pair of peppermint sticks.

Madeline declined the offer by shaking her head, and he returned one to his pocket before taking a slow lick of the second. "One thing, there's all those kings and royals. I think it's nothin' short of silly to climb on a high horse simply because blood family's been plowin' the same dirt for hundreds of years. I tell you what, ma'am, Texans aren't built for bowin'. It's been bred right out of us."

Brazos leveled a hard stare on Victor Considérant and shook his peppermint in the Frenchman's direction. "And aristocrats are just as bad as royalty. That fellow's one of the worst. Although I'll admit that his head's on right about kings and all, his whole notion to create a socialistic city in the heart of Texas is just plain stupid."

Gesturing toward those who waited ahead of them in line, he said, "Look around you, lady. I'd lay odds not more than a dozen of these folks know the first little bit about farmin', much less what it takes for survivin' on the frontier. Take that crate, for instance." He shook his head incredulously. "They've stored work tools with violins for an ocean crossing, for goodness sake. These folks don't have the sense to pour rainwater from a boot!" He popped the candy into his mouth, folded his arms across his chest, and studied the ship, chewing in a pensive silence.

The nerve of the man, Madeline thought, gritting her teeth against the words she'd love to speak. Really, to comment on another's intelligence when his own is so obviously lacking. Listen to his French. And his powers of observation!

Why, she knew how she looked. Beautiful wasn't the appropriate word.

Brazos swallowed his candy and said, "Hmm. You've given me an idea." Before Madeline gathered her wits to stop him, he leaned over and kissed her cheek. "Thanks, Beauty. And listen, you take care out here without a man to protect you. If I see your husband on this boat, I'm goin' to give him a piece of my mind about leavin' you alone." He winked and left her, walking toward the gangway.

Madeline touched the sticky spot on her cheek, damp from his peppermint kiss, and watched, fascinated, despite herself, as the overbold Texan tapped Considérant on the shoulder. In French that grated on her ears, he said, "Listen, Frenchman, I'll make a deal with you. If you find a place for me on your ship, I'll be happy to share my extensive knowledge of Texas with any of your folks who'd be interested in learnin'. This land you bought on the Trinity River—it's not more than half a day's ride from my cousin's spread. I've spent a good deal of time in that area over the past few years. I can tell you all about it."

"Mr. Sinclair," Considérant said in English, "please do not further abuse my language. I chose that land myself. Personally. I can answer any questions my peers may have about our new home. Now, as I have told you, this packet has been chartered to sail La Réunion colonists exclusively. Every space is assigned. I sympathize with your need to return to your home, but unfortunately the *Uriel* cannot accommodate you. Please excuse me, Monsieur Sinclair. I have much to see to before we sail. Good day."

"Good day my—" Brazos bit off his words. He turned abruptly and stomped away from the ship. Halting before Madeline, he declared, "This boat ain't leavin' until morning. It's not over yet. By General Taylor's tailor, when it sails, I'm gonna be on it."

He flashed a victorious grin and drawled, "Honey, you've captured my heart and about three other parts. I'll look forward to seein' you aboard ship."

As he walked away, she dropped a handsome gold pocket watch into her reticule, then called out to him in crisp, King's English. "Better you had offered your brain for ballast, Mr. Sinclair. Perhaps then you'd have been allowed aboard the *Uriel*."

BRAZOS SINCLAIR PATTED his empty pocket and scowled. What else could go wrong this afternoon? Some little urchin had up and stolen his watch, the one his father had given him the last time he'd stopped by home, the family cotton plantation, Magnolia Bend, for a visit. Hell and Texas, he silently cursed, I've gone as soft as a queen's feather pillow not to have noticed.

Many a time during his trek around Europe had a light-fingered thief attempted to divest him of his valuables, but this was the first time anyone had succeeded. Of course, as distracted as he'd been by the circumstances, a cutpurse could have purloined his pants, and he'd probably not have noticed.

It was time to go home.

Brazos lifted a half-empty glass of brandy from the table in front of him. Staring into the shimmering amber liquid, he wished the tumbler were half full, but life had managed to knock the optimism right out of him. Right about now he needed every scrap of confidence he could muster to force himself to climb aboard that boat.

After his row with the Frenchman he had come directly to the alehouse across the pier from the *Uriel*. Choosing a table by the window, he'd ordered a drink and bent his mind toward figuring a way aboard that boat. Time, seldom a concern in this vagabond existence of his, had become his greatest enemy.

On this side of the Atlantic, that is.

The letter from Juanita lay like a hot brand against his chest. "Salezan," he cursed. Hatred electrified his nerves, and his muscles tensed reflexively at the name. Damasso Salezan, prison governor extraordinaire— thief, sadist, butcher. Brazos felt the black tide rise within him, and he quickly slammed back his drink.

He must get on that ship. Juanita's life was at stake, the children's happiness and safety at risk. He'd put it off a long time—almost two years—but now it was time to go home. Salezan's men had stumbled across Juanita's trail.

Absently, Brazos pressed his jacket's sleeve, feeling for the silver armband he wore above his elbow. Embossed and engraved, the band had originally belonged to a Franciscan priest, his dear friend Miguel Alcortez, before Damasso Salezan had claimed it for his own. Brazos wore it not as jewelry, but as a symbol of his escape from Perote Prison, a reminder of the night when he'd stripped the band from the governor's arm and made a grievous mistake.

He should have killed the bastard then. Now Juanita was suffering as a result of his cowardice.

Why had he allowed the man to live? Brazos didn't know, and Juanita had been unable to tell him. He couldn't remember anything about the months he'd spent in The Hole. Even his memories of the escape and the subsequent return to Texas were sketchy. One particular moment stood out in his mind, however. He could clearly picture himself standing over Damasso Salezan, his fingers itching to wrap themselves around the governor's neck, instead wrenching the silver band from the cowering man's arm and leaving a long, deep gash in the skin.

Brazos remembered the blood and how it had frightened him. The sight of blood bothered him to this very day.

Salezan was the only man alive who could tell him why.

Had that been the reason he'd spared the governor's life? Brazos twirled his glass on the tabletop. Fool, he told himself, you put Juanita at risk for something you've no intention of pursuing.

Going on four years following his escape from Mexico, Brazos was certain of one fact. Whatever evil had occurred in the dungeons of Perote Prison, he was better off not knowing about it. Something told him that the truth might just kill him.

Ordering another drink, he considered his present predicament. For months now, he'd wandered around

Europe, wanting to go home, but too damned scared to do it. Climbing a ship's gangway was like crossing a bridge into hell, to his way of thinking. Sailing brought on the terror—a hard lesson learned on the trip over.

He held up his glass, admiring the warm glow of light shining through the liquid. "And now," he murmured, "when the price of staying here is more than the cost of haulin' my tail aboard a boat for an ocean voyage, I have to run up against the Napoleon of Utopia, Victor Considérant. Grand, simply grand."

Lifting his glass to his lips, he sipped. The drink scorched a delicious fire down his throat. "Mmm," he said, savoring the taste. That's about the only thing he'd miss when he left this godforsaken continent. French brandy was not easy to come by at home. "Maybe I'll take a case with me."

Because he would make it home—somehow. He looked out the window toward the vessels lining the wharf and grimaced. "I'll be on a ship in the morning if I have to steal one and sail it myself."

For some time now, Brazos had absently watched the people go about their business along the quay. Except for the woman, that is. Her he had watched with considerably more interest. Glancing toward the docks, he noticed that the flaxen-haired beauty hadn't moved since the last time he'd looked, all of three minutes before.

Seems he wasn't the only one having trouble getting on board that boat.

She'd tweaked his curiosity when she'd had her own confrontation with Considérant. She'd been the last in line, all alone—her husband never put in an appearance. Brazos had lifted his glass in salute when she'd reached the gangway. He'd almost dropped it when he saw Considérant shake his head forcefully and deny the woman access to the ship. She'd argued; from where he sat, he'd seen her brown eyes flashing. Watching her arms flailing about, he'd worried she'd drop the baby.

She'd talked for the best part of fifteen minutes, her agitated movements sending her full pink skirt to swaying. He'd gotten a good peek at a pair of trim ankles, and her stiff spine showed off a right fine bosom. Nursing women did have a certain advantage in some areas.

The fussing hadn't done her any good, apparently. After dragging herself and her child away from the ship, she'd sat atop a short stone fence and had been staring out at the water ever since.

Maybe I ought to go check on her, he thought. Nah, she didn't need him. He shrugged and ran a finger along the rim of his glass. Half a dozen times he'd seen scurvy-looking sailors or rough-cut men approach her. Half a dozen times he'd risen to go save her, but by the time he'd made the street, the men were gone. "I wonder what she says to them," he muttered into his drink.

"Ah, never mind the woman." He slammed his glass on the table. This was no time to worry about a petticoat. He had to get on that ship. The lives of his loved ones depended on it.

Sighing, Brazos took another sip of his brandy. Perhaps he could stow away and count on the captain's mercy. The hand holding the glass trembled a bit at the thought. But the *Uriel* was the only ship bound for the United States scheduled to sail from Antwerp in the coming week, and he dare not waste any time.

Juanita was in trouble. Now that the governor knew she hadn't accompanied Brazos to Europe, he'd turn Texas inside out looking for her. And to further complicate matters, now Brazos had to worry that Salezan would learn about the children. He could not allow that to happen. Nope, as much as he hated the idea, somehow he'd get aboard that goddamned boat. Tomorrow, he'd sail for Texas.

Then he felt it, that tickle at the back of his neck. He looked around. Behind him, a timid, vulnerable expression on her face, stood the beauty. He arched an eyebrow, the question in his eyes.

Without asking his permission, she took a seat at his table. She settled the baby on her lap and looked at him. "Mr. Sinclair," she said, her voice husky and earnest. "May I ask you a question?"

Brazos nodded.

"Mr. Sinclair, are you married?"

He frowned and shook his head. What was this about?

"I see." She looked down at her lap. He saw her swallow hard, and when she lifted her gaze, he felt as if he were face-to-face with a wounded doe.

"Then perhaps, Mr. Sinclair," she said, "perhaps you would consent to marrying me?"

Chapter 2

The rumble of laughter shook Brazos's shoulders long before it burst from his lips. "Lady," he said, shaking his head, a wide grin on his face, "you'd best stick to speakin' French. You'd have a fit if you realized what you just said to me."

"Mr. Sinclair, I've spent considerably more than half my life in England, and I daresay I've a better command of the language than you. I know very well what I asked."

Brazos's expression abruptly sobered. "There must be an asylum near here, huh?"

Madeline leaned toward him and spoke in an earnest and rational voice, "Mr. Sinclair, I realize this is an unusual situation—" She ignored his snort and continued, "But hear me out, please. I have something you want, and you can provide something I need."

Blue eyes swept her with contempt. "I may want it, lady," he said, clipping his words, "but I've seldom paid for it, and I've *never* married for it."

Madeline stared at him in confusion until slowly,

his meaning dawned, and she flushed with impatience. Gracious, the man's ego knew no bounds! "You misunderstand me, Mr. Sinclair," she said, swallowing a surge of anger. "I'm speaking of the *Uriel*. I have a berth, a private cabin. I'm offering you the opportunity to sail with the colonists tomorrow morning."

Silence stretched between them. Sinclair inclined his head, folded his arms across his chest, and stared at her.

"I'm not doing this very well, am I?" Madeline muttered. The idea had seemed so simple when she'd thought of it. If only she'd had more time to consider the problem, undoubtedly she'd have developed a better plan. But with time as her enemy, Madeline, like any good thief, trusted in her instincts. Her intuition told her to use this man named Sin.

She drew a deep breath and said, "Mr. Sinclair, your assumption that I am a married woman is incorrect. The fact that I am not is at this time causing me considerable trouble. What I am proposing is a *mariage de convenance*, a marriage of convenience. At the last moment, Monsieur Considérant denied me my place among the colonists, solely because I lacked a man with whom I could travel. Your earlier outburst led me to believe that sailing on the *Uriel* was of considerable import to you, and I wondered if we might not come to an agreement."

Brazos's brow furrowed. "Lady, you've got more brass than a church bell. What's your name, by the way?"

"Madeline, Madeline Christophe."

"Well, Mademoiselle Christophe, let's take a walk." Brazos rose and tossed a coin on the table. "Besides, a tavern is no place for a baby."

Outside, the wind had calmed and the afternoon sun warmed the air. Brazos bought a hot loaf of bread from a vendor on the quay, and the aroma reminded Madeline of the kitchens at the boarding school in England. Oh, to be home again, she wished. Then she clutched the stirring child close to her chest and thought, No, this is the only place for me.

Sinclair broke a hunk off the loaf and offered it to her. Madeline declined with a slight shake of her head. He shrugged and took a bite. "Umm, good bakers, these Belgians. You ought to try some. Fresh bread's gonna be hard to find in the middle of the Atlantic."

"We're instructed to bring some with us when we sail tomorrow," she said absently. Then she halted and looked up at him. "You'll do it?" she asked.

"Depends."

Rose's eyes opened, and she began to cry. Madeline shifted the baby to her shoulder, patting the child's back and watching the Texan anxiously.

He scowled. "Here, let me have him." Brazos gently lifted Rose and cradled her in his arms, shoving the bread into Madeline's. "What's the problem, little fella? Smell of that bread make you hungry?" He frowned at Madeline. "You need to find a place to feed this boy."

"Girl. She's on the ship—the nurse, I mean. Rose's wet-nurse. Considérant will have to let her feed her. Oh, dear! Why does everything have to be so complicated?"

"Lady, you've gotta start makin' some sense when you talk. Are you tryin' to tell me that you're not providin' for this baby yourself? You're takin' a woman along to Texas just 'cause you can't be bothered with motherin'?"

"It's not like that—"

"And you folks try to call Texans barbaric. I've heard all about these French *meneurs*, these baby brokers, who take infants from their parents and ship them off to the country to be nursed by a stranger. Hell, I can just imagine a child of mine bein' sent away for two years to live with people I've never even met." Brazos's mouth flattened into a disgusted frown. "We may have our problems in Texas, but at least we take care of our children."

By now Rose's cries filled the air—exactly what Madeline had tried to avoid. Tossing down the bread, she extended her arms to take the baby and spoke through gritted teeth. "I must take my daughter to her nurse. Now. If you can contain your bluster, Mr. Sinclair, would you be so kind as to escort us to the *Uriel*? You and I have yet to settle this matter."

Brazos ignored her outstretched arms, pivoted, and walked briskly toward the ship. Madeline hissed in anger, then followed, almost running to match his long strides.

Before she quite caught her breath, Brazos had brushed past Victor Considérant, asked about and located Lillibet, and deposited Rose in the Brunets' cabin. Then, with a firm grasp on Madeline's arm, he'd marched off the ship and over to a dockside bench, where he plunked her down and demanded, "Talk."

Madeline smoothed the folds of her skirt as she tried to decide exactly what she should say.

Brazos's boot began to tap against the boards. "Listen, lady, I'm not waitin' here all day. Let me hear your story from the beginning."

"Well . . ." Madeline drew a deep breath, then offered him a version of the truth. "I have embraced the philosophies of Charles Fourier. He was a brilliant man who believed that the people of the world wallow in misery because we have failed to follow God's Divine Plan."

"God's Divine Plan?"

She nodded. "Monsieur Fourier discovered the Plan and has designed a way for it to be put into practice. That's what the Colonization Society of Texas is all about. In our colony, La Réunion, happiness will replace misery, unity will replace division, and Harmony will replace Civilization."

Brazos closed his eyes and shook his head. "This is even worse than I had imagined. You folks have about as much sense as my cousin Tilli, and she's been knittin' socks for the family rooster for years."

Madeline replied with the zeal of a recent convert. "La Réunion will be a safe and wonderful place in which to live and raise a family. You'll see, Mr. Sinclair. The colony in Texas will provide a perfect home for my Rose. That's why I am determined to go."

Scowling, she got to the heart of her story. "When I purchased membership in the Society, the agent said nothing at all about any requirement for a spouse. But when I attempted to board the ship, Considérant declared that as a widowed woman with an infant, my life in the colony would be too difficult, and he forbade my joining the group. He told me that only married couples and bachelor men would be allowed to join La Réunion."

"No single women?" Brazos interrupted. "What kind of a Utopia is that?"

Madeline ignored his question. "I wish desperately to go to Texas, and I heard you say how imperative it was for you to be on this ship. I can only imagine that your reasons are important, considering the intensity of your argument with Considérant. Am I right?"

His expression hardened, and he nodded once. "Lives are at stake."

Probably his own, Madeline surmised. She'd not be surprised if he had a cuckolded husband hot on his trail. She stared him straight in the eyes. "So, we could solve each other's problem, could we not?"

Sinclair watched her for a long, silent moment before asking abruptly, "When did he die?"

"Who?"

"Your husband."

"Oh, umm, well . . . Christmas, yes . . . poor dear . . . umm, François died at Christmastime."

Brazos pinned her with a shrewd, measuring look. "You runnin' from somebody, lady?"

Madeline's heart thumped, and her hands grew clammy. "No," she denied, a little too quickly.

He lifted an eyebrow.

"I'm not. Truly. I . . ." As she fought for a believable explanation, the solution burst across her mind. She beamed up at him. "I'm running *to* someone."

"Who?"

"Rose's father."

"You *do* have a husband?"

Madeline gazed out over the water. "Well, actually no, I don't." She straightened her back and leveled an unapologetic look on the Texan. "I couldn't very well marry you then, could I?"

"Lady, I wouldn't put anything past you at this point." Brazos sat on the bench beside her, leaned back, and crossed his arms and legs. "So your . . . lover is in Texas?"

Madeline nodded. She knew this story by heart, the plot straight from a novel she'd found hidden away at Château St. Germaine. For once her shameful secret of a preference for romantic fiction over more literary works served her well. "Yes, we'd planned to travel together, but there was a little matter that forced him to leave without me, given that I was in a family way."

She clasped her hands to her breast and sighed. "Oh, how he hated to leave me! But he's there, in a town called Galveston, waiting for me even as we speak. So you see, Mr. Sinclair, all you need do is wed me for the voyage, and then as soon as we reach Texas, you can annul the marriage, you go your way, and I to my beloved Emile."

He lifted a skeptical brow. "And what caused this paragon to abandon you, pregnant and unmarried in France, while he hightailed it to Texas?"

Madeline closed her eyes and smiled. This had been a heartbreaking twist in the novel's plot. "A duel—he wounded a powerful man in a duel."

"A powerful man?"

"My fiancé, Denis."

"By God, lady!" Sinclair exclaimed, sitting up straight and shaking his head. "You've got more males after you than a mare in season. I doubt I'd be doin' myself much of a favor by gettin' mixed up with the likes of you."

Her eyes widened with alarm. "No, no, no. That's all over now. You must marry me, Mr. Sinclair. For both our sakes."

Frowning thoughtfully, he slipped his hand into his pocket and withdrew a leather ball. Tossing it repeatedly into the air, he said, "Just for the sake of argument here, why do you think we need to marry? Why don't we just tell ol' Considérant we're sharin' space?"

"That wouldn't get either one of us aboard the

Uriel. Believe me, sir, I've considered all the possibilities. Marriage is the only way."

"Nah, it wouldn't work," Brazos said, shaking his head. "It'd be just my luck to get leg-shackled and still have Considérant refuse to let me aboard that boat."

"He couldn't do that," Madeline stressed, placing her hand on his knee to emphasize her point. "Don't you see, he's testing the bounds of his power as it is. My lack of a husband was his lone justification for denying me my place among the colonists. As long as I provide the husband—along with marriage papers to prove my point—he could not in good faith refuse to allow us to join them."

Sinclair lifted his gaze from where her hand rested on his thigh, and Madeline recognized the gleam in his eye. She snatched her hand back. He said, "Don't you worry about your reputation? What do you think the other colonists will say when you show up with a brand-new husband so soon after burying the old?"

"Mr. Sinclair, La Réunion will be a colony based upon the philosophy of Charles Fourier. The Phalansterians are freethinkers, libertarians. They won't—"

His brows lifted in shock, he interrupted, "Phallus what?"

Madeline sighed disgustedly. "Phalansterians. It's another name for the followers of Fourier. Although this particular colony has voted to retain the institution of marriage, they won't think ill of me for using the tradition to suit my needs. Besides, it will be a simple marriage of convenience. Everyone will accept that."

"No marriage is *ever* convenient," he absently observed as he tossed his ball and considered her argument. "Freethinkers, huh? And these folks are movin' to Texas?" His shoulders shook with a silent chuckle. "Hell, it'd almost be worth gettin' hitched just to be around to watch."

"Well?" she asked.

"What about once we reach Galveston? What's

your lover gonna have to say about you taggin' a husband along from home?"

"Oh," Madeline said, waving a hand, "I'm sure we will work around that when the time comes. We'll obtain an immediate annulment; then you can conveniently disappear."

"Conveniently disappear," he echoed as he studied the woman at his side and attempted to see past the beauty of her face into her mind. All right, so maybe he was a bit disappointed in her story. A virtuous widow was much more appealing than a promiscuous miss, but what else could you expect from these Europeans?

Still, her idea did have merit, and at this point, he'd do damn near anything to get aboard the *Uriel*. Sleeping with a beauty like Madeline Christophe was a helluva lot better way to cross the Atlantic than hiding in the ship's hold. Except she wasn't actually proposing to sleep with him, was she?

"Annulment, huh?" he asked. "Based on what grounds?"

The woman's spine went stiff as a fence post as she replied, "Nonconsummation, of course."

"Of course." It would have to be that way. Brazos recognized that if he agreed to her proposal, procuring an annulment the moment they reached Texas would be a necessity. Not only was he unwilling to get stuck with a light-skirt for a wife, he couldn't afford to waste any time before trying to help Juanita and the kids. Too, there was no telling what Salezan might do were he to learn that Brazos had taken a wife.

That could be dangerous for them all, Madeline Christophe included.

Still, a little company on the voyage home sounded nice. *Who are you trying to fool?* his inner voice scorned. Brazos scowled and dropped his ball. He couldn't spend his nights in the woman's private cabin even if she'd let him.

Brazos couldn't bear to go below a ship's deck.

Madeline cleared her throat nervously before saying, "The staterooms aboard the *Uriel* have but a single bunk. I'm certain we could secure enough bedding, however, to make a comfortable pallet for you on the floor."

Sitting up, he eyed Madeline Christophe, and in a dry tone of voice said, "You are too kind." He returned his leather ball to his pocket and withdrew another peppermint stick. This time he didn't bother to offer one to Madeline. He took a few thoughtful licks and considered her proposition. Then he said, "Your story has more holes in it than Sam Houston's socks, woman. While I can see how this marriage idea might work, I want it clear from the git go that I won't hold to your gettin' any *more* ideas along the way to Texas. You needn't worry about any pallet. I prefer sleepin' on deck when I sail."

He ignored her incredulous look and continued, "If I choose to take you up on your offer, you can damn well be assured that the minute I step off the boat, I'll see to securin' an annulment. In fact, I know of a law firm in Galveston that'd take care of our business as fast as small-town gossip." He chuckled softly and added, "The attorneys at Melbourne P. King and Associates would certainly get a kick out of doin' so, too."

"Mr. Sinclair," Madeline said, her smile stiff and her hands clasped tightly in her lap, "rest assured that I'll not do anything to interfere with the securing of an annulment at first opportunity. You are the last man I'd wish to keep as husband and father to my child."

"And you can feel certain I wouldn't wish a mother like you on any of my children, either." On that note, Brazos finished his candy, licked the stickiness from his fingers, and stood. One corner of his mouth lifting in a wry grin, Brazos Sinclair took Madeline Christophe's hand and placed a honeyed kiss to her palm. In French, the very last time he intended to use that particular language, he said, "Mademoiselle Madeline, I accept your proposal."

He pulled her to her feet. "Come on, Beauty. Let's find us a preacher and get hitched."

MADELINE AND BRAZOS stood at the base of the church steps, each wearing a frown of doubt as they gazed up toward the broad oaken doors.

"Catholic? Are you certain?" Madeline asked.

"Not in the least," he replied. "But this is what the men in the tavern recommended. Supposedly this monsignor fellow, Father Pearson, needs money somethin' fierce. He's buildin' a children's home and is willin' to do just about anything to get some coin. They said of all the preachers in town, he'd be the most likely to do the deed under the circumstances."

Madeline's stomach felt as heavy as one of the gray granite blocks that formed the walls of the church and adjoining rectory. Sacrilege, nothing less. Oh, Lord, forgive me, she thought, and climbed the first step.

Brazos grabbed her elbow, saying, "Wait a minute. Before we go through with this, I need to know something. Are the rules any different here than at home?"

"Rules?"

"Marriage rules. There are no European knots that a Texan couldn't untie, are there?"

She sighed. "Mr. Sinclair, surely the requirements for the granting of an annulment are universal. Besides, I have no doubt there are corrupt officials to be found in Texas just as there are here. And if but one such man exists, certainly you could find him."

"Fair enough," he said, grinning. He took her arm and escorted her to the rectory's front door.

Minutes, and a substantial bribe, later, Madeline and Brazos stood before the altar. The afternoon sun beamed through the windows as stained-glass saints watched over the proceedings, the blues and greens and oranges of their robes casting rainbows upon the priest, the groom, and the bride. Madeline looked down. Her pale pink dress glowed bright red. A hysterical giggle threatened to burst from within her.

How inappropriate, she thought. A scarlet dress as she knelt at her wedding. For though she was known to the man-to-be-her-husband as a fallen woman, she wore the color of the wrong sin. *Is it black, I wonder, falsehood's hue?* A giggle did escape her then. *I come to him virgin but far from pure.*

Brazos watched her, scowling, while the monsignor approached. The effort of finding the church and the not-so-good prelate, Father Pearson, had left him grumpier with each inquiry. As terrible as was his French, his Flemish had been barely recognizable. Madeline's innocent offer of help had led to nothing short of a little boy's frustrated tantrum, during which he'd claimed the ability to read three languages and had proven his mastery of Spanish—a litany of curses and distasteful sexual phrases.

"You may kneel." The priest made the sign of the cross above their heads and said, "*In Domu Dei iniuriam hanc Emendare vinimus.*"

"Hold it a dad-blamed minute," Brazos snapped.

He's changed his mind, Madeline thought. *He won't go through with it. I never should have told Father Pearson that we'd made a child together. I could tell that made Sinclair mad. Mary Smithwick, you're a fool!*

Brazos's slow drawl brimmed with annoyance. "No Latin, Padre. I've had enough foreign words for a lifetime. In fact, I've had all the foreign food and foreign drink and foreign land and foreigners that I can stomach. Make these words to where I can understand 'em. English, this time, if you please."

The priest's expression tightened. He cleared his throat and began again, "In the Lord's house we gather to correct this wrong. Do you, Brazos Sinclair, take this *foreign woman* to wife?"

"Oh, dear Lord!"

CHÂTEAU ST. GERMAINE, FRANCE

Warily, the secretary, William, knocked on the library door. The master had just returned from his afternoon ride. "Enter," a crisp, authoritative voice called.

Julian Desseau stood before the hearth, staring into the crackling fire, one hand holding a snifter of brandy, the other fingering a blue porcelain vase atop the marble mantle. He did not look up. "Well?"

The servant wiped wet palms upon his trousers. "A message has arrived from Paris, Monsieur."

Slowly, Desseau turned his head and pinned the servant with his gaze. The fire in his dark eyes could have been a reflection from the hearth, but it was not. Wings of gray at his temples, an unholy arch of thick, salt-and-pepper eyebrows, and the vermillion flash of his cape's satin lining created a vision of Lucifer himself. "And?" he asked softly.

After a deep breath, William replied, "Nothing. The Bureau of Wet-Nurses shows no record of a woman fitting Mistress Smithwick's description requesting either placement of an infant or hiring of a private nurse."

"Doctors?"

"Investigation of leads on three suspects led nowhere."

The tick of a wall clock echoed through the silence in the room. Desseau returned his gaze to the fire. When he spoke, his voice grated with menace. "And the jewels?"

"None have been offered for sale in any shop in France. Your man continues to investigate the less legitimate methods of disposal for such valuable pieces."

Desseau's jaw hardened, and he shut his eyes. Grasping the vase on the mantle, he lifted it, held it motionless in his hand, then whirled and threw it violently against the opposite wall. "Goddamn the woman!" he shouted. His fingers wrenched at the fastening on his cape, and he threw it from his shoulders. Then he sank into the black leather chair that sat before the hearth and folded his hands, thumping his chin with his fist as he thought.

"You know, I rather liked Mary Smithwick," he said after a time, more to himself than to the servant, who scurried to retrieve the cloak, then retreated to the doorway. "She had a way about her, a wounded air that awakened all my protective instincts. Who would have guessed that beneath that beauty, that vulnerable facade, lurked an evil quite brazen? I wonder how many other men she has duped in her young life."

He sighed and lifted the brass poker from its stand beside the chair. Stirring the fire, he mused, "I shall have to ask her before I kill her."

Chapter 3

The wind blew half a gale, and the seas ran high as Madeline strolled the ship's deck, nodding and greeting other colonists, thankful to rejoin the living. The mal de mer that had plagued her since their departure from Antwerp almost a week ago had finally subsided, and though the *Uriel* continued to roll and pitch, her stomach was steady as she lifted her face into a chilly spray and mused, "Perhaps I shall live after all."

Over the course of her illness, Madeline had discovered a great truth. The moralists and philosophers of the age who claimed that a well-regulated mind was essential to happiness were mistaken. After days of nausea, dizziness, and retching, she could unequivocally swear that state of mind and temper depended almost entirely on the condition of one's digestive organs. For a time there, she'd wished for death.

That's when she'd first realized she'd overlooked a potentially serious problem. People died at sea all the time. Illness and disease abounded. Accidents happened. And what about after the *Uriel* reached America? She'd

read James Fenimore Cooper; she could be scalped by a
marauding Indian, for goodness' sake. These unpleasant
possibilities led to the question she'd never before
thought to ask. If something unfortunate happened to
her, what would happen to Rose?

The worry had become a full-blown fear after the
mishap yesterday afternoon. As accidents go, Madeline's had been minor. It had been foolish of her to leave
her stateroom when the seas were so high, but in her
muddled state she'd thought a bit of fresh air might help
settle her stomach. A high green wave had lunged over
the deck, swept her off her feet, and deposited her in the
Uriel's lee scuppers, half drowned, bruised, and miser-
able. She'd been lucky not to go overboard.

The frigid seawater had shocked Madeline to her
senses, and before she'd climbed to her feet, she'd
realized that making provisions for Rose was imperative. An even more frightful thought had occurred to
her. As far as anyone aboard the *Uriel* knew, after
herself, Rose's next of kin was none other than Brazos
Sinclair.

Madeline believed she shivered from the cold, but
she couldn't be certain. Brazos Sinclair as Rose's father?
Absolutely not! She'd decided then and there to immediately investigate the possibilities of arranging guard-
ianship for the baby.

Over the long night, between bouts of sickness,
Madeline debated her options. Although she did con-
sider one or two of the other La Réunion families, the
Brunets were the obvious choice.

Madeline worried whether it would be fair to ask
Lillibet to accept the responsibility of another child
when her own required so much care. Agreeing to
wet-nurse Rose was different from agreeing to assume
the obligation for the girl for a lifetime. Plus, Madeline
fretted about André. He made no apology for his
obvious preference for boys over girls. What kind of
father would he make little Rose?

Unbidden, the vision of a tall, blue-eyed Texan
flashed through her mind. *Absolutely not!* she told
herself again.

Finally, Madeline slept, and after awakening the next morning feeling almost human again, she ventured on deck. The exercise cleared her mind and helped her to think. At the ship's railing, she paused. Gazing across the water toward the storm building on the western horizon, she made her decision. "I'll talk to Lil," she said aloud. She would suggest a temporary agreement until the colonists reached Texas and Madeline could find a more permanent solution. In the meantime, she'd simply have to do her best to stay out of harm's way.

With that question settled, Madeline focused her attention on the ocean. The power of the sea excited her, and she watched with awe the demonstration of man's attempt to bend nature's will to his own. As the timber strained and wind whistled through the rigging, Madeline marveled that man possessed both the skill and the courage to harness such unstable elements. She turned her face into the breeze.

A tiny fist hit her shoulder, startling Madeline so that she gasped an inadvertent "Oh!" She turned to see Rose's double-toothed grin beaming at her from the comfort of Lillibet's arms. "Rose!" she exclaimed, lifting the child and smothering her face with kisses. "I've missed you so much."

Lillibet folded her arms and smiled. "She's been a sad little bunny without her mama around. I was beginning to wonder if you'd be the first person of my acquaintance who expired from excessive mal de mer."

"The idea crossed my mind," Madeline replied in a rueful tone. She nuzzled the baby's neck, grinning at Rose's giggles, and said, "At times I'd have welcomed anything to put me out of my misery."

"I sympathize with you entirely, my dear. I had similar thoughts while I lay ill; but of course, they passed along with the squeamishness. Although I do confess that if I hadn't had help with the babies, I might very well have succumbed."

Madeline caught hold of Rose's fist and made a mental note to cut the child's sharp fingernails. "I'm so sorry about leaving you to deal with my baby by yourself. I feel terrible about being so useless. Every time I moved I would retch and then—"

Lillibet waved away her apology. "Don't give it another thought. After all, Madeline, it is my job. You are paying me to care for the child. Besides, if anyone should apologize, it is I. Mr. Sinclair minded Rose the entire time."

"What did you say?" Madeline questioned, certain she'd misheard. Brazos Sinclair tended Rose? Her arms tightened around the child. "Oh, my. Is she all right? He didn't hurt her, did he?"

"Mr. Sinclair?" Lillibet replied, displaying a puzzled frown. "Why, of course not. He took wonderful care of the babies."

"Babies!" Madeline wondered if she were still ill and hallucinating. "What do you mean, babies?"

"Rose and Thomas. Both André and I were indisposed, and Mr. Sinclair volunteered to help."

Madeline blinked. Uneasy laughter bubbled up inside her at the image of Brazos Sinclair with a baby in each arm. "Oh, Lil, quit teasing me. I can just imagine that mountain of a Texan changing a soiled diaper. I appreciate your efforts to lessen my guilt, but I'm afraid you'll need to come up with something a little more believable."

"I'm telling the truth, Madeline," Lillibet protested. "I was so grateful for your husband's help. He took both babies for the entire day, and he *did* change diapers." She frowned slightly as she added, "Of course, I'm afraid he threw the soiled ones overboard. He returned the wet ones, though."

Madeline shook her head in amazement. "You really do mean it?" At Lillibet's nod, Madeline held Rose out in front of her and studied the baby. "She doesn't appear any the worse for wear."

Rose began to wiggle, her arms and legs flailing about. She kicked off one of her knitted booties, and Lil bent to retrieve it, saying, "He's a good man, Madeline. You were lucky to find him in Antwerp. You know, it's not every man that would agree to the scheme you concocted to get aboard the *Uriel*."

Madeline bristled at Lil's praises of Brazos Sinclair. "He wished to join the colonists just as badly as I. Victor Considérant's decision to bar me from the colony because I had lost my husband was unfair and arbitrarily made. In fact, I'm convinced it is a betrayal of Fourier's teachings. If women are to be considered equal to men at La Réunion, then how can we allow bachelors to join us and not a widowed woman?"

"I agree with you, dear, and so do a number of others," Lillibet said, attempting to pull the bootie over Rose's wiggling toes. "The majority of the colonists admire how you outsmarted Considérant, what with convincing Mr. Sinclair to marry you and join the Society. Madame Correll informed me that those in steerage have enjoyed a brisk discussion of your situation over the last few days. I'm afraid it bodes ill for the goal of Harmony at La Réunion. Opinion appears to fall along gender lines."

A strong gust of wind snapped the sails above them, and Rose startled at the noise. Lillibet clicked her tongue soothingly as Madeline held Rose's leg still so the Frenchwoman could successfully tie the bootie's ribbon. "I've been studying Fourier's teachings quite closely," Madeline said, resting Rose against her shoulder. She patted the baby's back as she added, "He did admit that as much as two years might be required to complete the abolishment of Civilization and the establishment of total Harmony."

"Two years?" Lillibet repeated, grimacing. "Yes, I can see how some men might be slower in accepting equality for women than others. André must work at that a bit himself. How about your husband, Madeline? What about Mr. Sinclair?"

Madeline laughed. "I imagine it would take years to convert Brazos. Of course, if he did change those diapers, perhaps there is hope for him after all."

"Oh, there's definitely hope for him. I quite admire the man, Madeline. He's knowledgeable and intelligent. He's been tutoring some of our members about farming methods well suited for Texas." She lowered her voice. "He's also handsome enough to swoon over. I have to tell you that a number of wagers have been made on the question of whether this marriage of convenience becomes one of fact."

Madeline laughed aloud. "Oh, Lil, I hope you didn't waste your money. That is one point Brazos and I agree on completely. There will be no consummation of this marriage."

"But he has joined the Society and paid a considerable amount of money to do so. Doesn't he intend to join us at La Réunion?"

The *Uriel* took a long pitch forward, and Madeline closed her eyes against a lingering quiver of seasickness. She groaned, whether as a result of the illness or of the idea of making a home with Brazos Sinclair, she could not say.

Uncertain how to reply to Lillibet's question, Madeline hesitated. With the trip well under way and the next port of call Galveston, Texas, she could afford to make public Brazos's intentions to leave the colonists as soon as the *Uriel* made landfall. After all, Considérant wasn't likely to put her and her temporary husband overboard in a lifeboat once the truth was out. Everyone aboard knew the circumstances of her marriage. Few would be surprised by the announcement of a pending annulment.

But for some strange reason, she wasn't prepared to have the colonists learn that the boorish Texan wanted as little to do with her as she wanted to do with him. Well acquainted with rejection, Madeline knew it shouldn't matter. But it did.

She phrased her reply carefully. "Mr. Sinclair and I have yet to settle all of our plans. In fact, Lil, that brings up a point I wish to discuss with you." She tenderly brushed a finger down Rose's petal-soft cheek and asked, "Could we stroll for a bit and talk? I've something important to discuss with you."

Lillibet frowned. "I don't know that this is a good time, dear. Rose is tired. I've noticed that she always fidgets like that when she needs her sleep. Why don't I bring her to you after she wakes, and we can have a nice chat then."

Madeline sighed as guilt added another dimension to the sick feeling inside her. Of course the baby was tired. She should have recognized it herself. I'm terrible at this mothering business, she thought. Simply awful. Her chin trembled as she pressed a kiss to the baby's forehead and handed her to Lillibet. "Certainly," Madeline agreed, attempting a smile. "We can talk later, after Rose's nap."

Her steps heavier than before, Madeline resumed her walk around the ship's deck. Worry assailed her. Maybe she should ask the Brunets for more than a temporary arrangement. Maybe Rose would be better off without Madeline as a mother altogether. Maybe they all would have been better off if she'd succumbed to mal de mer.

She shuddered at the thought. What an awful way to die, with one's head poised over a chamber pot.

The briny scent of damp wood and wet hemp swirled in the air around her, replacing the odor of sickness in her memory. She stopped at the *Uriel*'s railing and lifted her head to the wind. Tasting salt on the air that buffeted her face, Madeline grabbed at her bonnet as it threatened to sail away on the strong breeze. She imagined a picture of wind filling the hat and lifting her bodily from the ship's deck to sail away on the trade winds. It'd be better than dying over a chamber pot, she decided. Closing her eyes, she said dreamily, "I can almost believe I'm flying."

Beside her a deep voice rumbled, "It's the only thing that makes it bearable."

Madeline turned. Her husband stood leaning out over the railing, staring at the foam bubbling in the ship's wake. He wore his denim pants and a white linen shirt, and he carried a copy of Fourier's disciples' periodical, *La Phalange*, tucked beneath his arm. It was the first time she'd seen him since the voyage began, and she hadn't yet decided whether she was grateful he'd not bothered her during her indisposition or annoyed that he'd abandoned her to her misery with such ease. Maintaining a neutral tone, she asked, "You don't enjoy sailing?"

"Lady, I'd just as soon tussle with a Comanche countin' coup on black-headed Texans as to be aboard this boat. I read somewhere that a ship is like a prison with the contingency of bein' drowned. That pretty well sums it up, as far as I see it."

Madeline didn't know how to reply to that. In fact, she wasn't certain whether she wished to speak to him at all. Heavens, the man could scowl! She pulled her black wool cape tighter and lifted her chin in a perfect aristocrat's snub.

Amusement kindled in his eyes. He rolled the magazine and held it in one hand as he crossed his arms and turned sideways, resting a hip against the rail. "You still feelin' puny, Maddie? I heard you had a right fine case of green gills."

Madeline made her decision; she was definitely annoyed. "Oh, really?" she replied, shoving a stray strand of hair back into her bonnet. "So you *did* inquire after me? And I was under the impression that you'd forgotten I was aboard ship. Well, silly me."

He grinned and said, "How could I forget about you? Everyone aboard ship could hear you moanin' and groanin' all night long. Personally, I was glad to hear that you were sick. I'd hate to think you'd been carryin' on for any other reason—especially on our wedding night."

Of all the nerve, Madeline thought, flexing her fingers as the need to slap him caused her hand to tingle. Has he no sense of propriety whatsoever? She'd met many rough-cut men in her day, but even among the more criminal element, men tended to temper their language around a lady. But then, Brazos Sinclair didn't consider her a lady, did he?

Deflated, she said, "And what has occupied your time this past week, sir?"

"Oh, I've been studyin'."

"Improving your French, I hope?"

"Nope." He held up the magazine. "I've been reading up on this philosopher fella you people set such store in. I've got to tell you, Maddie, I think what he's preachin' is just a bunch of heifer dust."

Heifer dust? What *was* this language Brazos Sinclair spoke? She sniffed with disdain and said, "Charles Fourier was an exceptional man, a great thinker. Someday his name will be mentioned with Plato and Aristotle."

Brazos thumped his chin with the magazine, then said thoughtfully, "Plato and Aristotle, aren't they those two guys who wrestled alligators in the Paris carnival last year?"

Madeline's mouth fell open in disbelief. "Wrestled alligators! Why . . ."

Chuckling, Brazos reached out with a finger and nudged her mouth closed. "I'm just teasin' you, Maddie. About the Greeks, anyway." He lifted his gaze to the men climbing the rigging to furl the sheets. "While you were laid up, I spent some time gettin' to know some of our shipmates. For the most part they're real nice people, and I especially like your friends the Brunets. It sounds like André knows is way around a cornfield, and that'll serve him handy in Texas. Worries me to think what the rest of them will do."

Madeline frowned. "What do you mean?"

"Darlin', I don't know what you've been told about the frontier, but there's simply no demand for an orchestra conductor, or a jeweler's apprentice, or, for that matter, a banker. We only have one chartered bank in Texas, and it's had its business tied up in the courts for years." He crossed his arms and mused, "Yep, people in Texas don't care much for bankers."

Madeline had her own opinion concerning bankers, aware that Julian Desseau counted at least two banks among his vast enterprises. But Brazos's criticisms struck a defensive chord in her, and she challenged him. "Just what is it that you are trying to say, Monsieur Sinclair?"

His expression was serious and sincere as he replied, "La Réunion won't succeed. The reasoning is faulty."

"Oh, really?" Madeline smiled a falsely sweet smile. "And I suppose it is the years you have spent at philosophical study and debate that have guided you toward this conclusion?"

"Hell, no. It's plain ol' common sense. Somethin' that appears to be in short supply with you Fourierists."

He is one to talk, the thickheaded lout. Madeline eyed the way his hip rested against the ship's rail. An unexpected shove would send him overboard. Her fingers itched to hit him, but she soothed them by stealing five bullets from the gunbelt ever present around his hips. Calmed somewhat, she said, "You are quite vociferous with your opinions, sir. However, I've yet to hear any specifics. Pray, tell me just why you think La Réunion is doomed to failure."

"All right." Brazos rubbed his cheek with his palm. "Hmm, where do I start?" He flashed her an arrogant grin and added, "It's hard to pick from so many stupid ideas."

Poison, Madeline thought. Yes, death by poison had a certain allure. Who aboard the *Uriel* would have poison she could appropriate?

"I reckon I could pick on Considérant's agricultural plan, but in all honesty, I can see some benefits in his ideas about cooperative farming. I think he needs some more farmers in this group to make it work, but at least there's a slight chance for success."

He shrugged his shoulders. "Let's see . . . I've plenty to say about the Fourierists' beliefs concerning the destruction of Civilization by the release of man's thirteen passions, but I'm afraid I find the subject matter to embarrassing to discuss." He tilted his chin and looked at her, asking, "I wouldn't mind an invitation to the event, though. Just as an interested observer, a student of philosophy, if you will."

She recognized that Brazos was referring to Fourier's ideas concerning sexual freedom and the Court of Love. While she didn't for one moment believe he'd be embarrassed to discuss the philosophies of *The New Amorous World* or *The Laws of Passionate Attraction*, she was grateful he apparently intended to avoid the subject. Monsieur Bourgin is a veterinarian, she remembered. Perhaps he could provide an appropriate toxin. Something that makes the tongue swell . . .

"So, what do you think, Maddie? Will you invite me to this passion release?"

"Not in this lifetime, Monsieur Sinclair," she said dryly.

He flashed her a boyish grin. Suddenly, Madeline found herself wanting to grin right back. In a strange sort of way, his outrageousness could be appealing. For the first time, she looked at him in a new, different light. Perhaps Brazos Sinclair wasn't as bad as she had imagined. He was a handsome rogue; there was no denying that.

Then he opened his mouth once more. "Back to your question about why I believe La Réunion is doomed to failure. I think a good example is the position they take on a woman's place in society. Come on, now, Maddie, equality for women?"

Madeline sucked on her lower lip. Of the myriad points he could have argued, he had to pick the one nearest to her heart. She put the chill of the North Sea into her voice as she said, "Why is it that I am not surprised by your attitude? I suppose you don't believe that women are as intelligent as men?"

Brazos shook his head. "I'm not sayin' some women aren't clever about some things—I've never known a man who could bake a cake worth a damn—and I'm not claimin' they don't have their uses. But as smart as men? Don't be ridiculous!"

A fencing foil, she thought, right through the heart. Or perhaps the liver, he mightn't have a heart. Monsieur Rejebian was a fencing master, surely he could furnish her a weapon. Lifting her chin, she said, "What about Cleopatra and Catherine the Great? Queen Elizabeth? Now, *there* was an intelligent woman for you. She never married!"

Brazos blew a slow whistle. "Ooh, Maddie. You could slice beef jerky with that tongue of yours. Look, you can't count those women—they're royalty, freaks of nature. They don't have anything to do with a normal female."

Madeline breathed deeply to maintain the tenuous hold on her anger. "Mr. Sinclair, La Réunion *will* succeed, and much of that success will be due to the respect the men of the society have for the female members."

"Yeah, that same respect that caused you to propose marriage to a total stranger, right?" He folded his arms and waited, a victorious grin on his face.

Lightning slashed the sky in the distance. It could just as easily have been coming from her eyes. Her voice was tight as she said, "A woman at La Réunion will have the freedom to choose her occupation. If she has an idea for a piece of machinery or a suggestion on where to build what, she'll be listened to, and *she'll* be the one doing the creating and building."

Ignoring Brazos's snort, she continued, "At La Réunion, a woman can earn and keep her own money, separate from her husband." She flashed her own winning grin right back at him. "And at La Réunion, women will have the vote."

"No!"

"Yes."

"Now, there's a scary thought." Brazos grimaced. "I can see it now, they'd vote to make gingham curtains mandatory on every window in America."

"Pink ones, probably."

"Hell, I'd have to emigrate myself if that happened. Yellow I could abide, maybe blue. Never pink."

Madeline shrugged.

Brazos, with a penitent expression on his face, took her hand and gave it a squeeze. "I'm not sayin' women are dumb, Maddie. I want you to understand that. They just don't think like men."

"Thank heaven for that."

This time Brazos did the ignoring. "Women simply don't think logically," he said. "They lack common sense." Madeline snatched her hand away from his as he continued, "I think it must have something to do with the size of their brains. A man's is bigger, so he's just naturally smarter, and ladies get shorted a bit on horse sense. Instead, they think with their emotions, and I, for one, can't think of a better way to end up in trouble."

Madeline sputtered indignantly. The foolish man actually believed this nonsense! Why was she even listening to him. *Be honest,* a voice inside her whispered. *Isn't that what most men think of women? Isn't that why you are so intrigued by the Fourierist philosophy?* The thought of living in a society that judged women as equal to men was seductive. Listening to Brazos Sinclair made the idea irresistible. "Mr. Sinclair," she said, her voice dripping sarcasm, "your logic leaves me speechless. It must be that emotional part of me, wouldn't you say?"

"I imagine so."

She lifted her gaze to the heavens, and frustration added a sharp edge to her voice as she said, "Let me get this straight. You are claiming that La Réunion will fail because, in part, women will be treated equally to men in both work and responsibility."

"That's right."

"You believe that a woman is incapable of being a man's equal."

Brazos nodded. "Honey, the day a woman becomes my equal, I'll tie on an apron and bake a cake."

Neither a fencing foil nor poison was at hand. Brazos's Colt revolver was, however. He never noticed her hand reach out and spirit it away.

Madeline's emotional intellect convinced her not to kill him where he stood. She tucked the gun into the deep pocket of her skirt and said, "Brazos, about that cake? Make it chocolate."

She pivoted and marched away, muttering about Texans, men in general, and the silly women who found them attractive.

As Brazos watched her leave, a roguish smile played across his face. Damn, but the woman was glorious when she was riled. Her purr turned to a growl; those gorgeous brown eyes snapped like a well-worn whip; and with all the huffin' and puffin' she did, that bountiful bosom of hers liked to spill right out of her dress. 'Twas enough to make a man's mouth water.

Madeline Christophe Sinclair might be round-heeled and fickle, but there was no denying her beauty. He had observed her as Mrs. Brunet approached with the baby. The smile that had lit Madeline's face had damn near blinded him. He'd watched her snuggle little Rose, and he'd been surprised as a puppy with his first prickly pear at the intensity of emotion in the woman's gaze. For all her faults, the woman truly loved her child.

In Brazos's eyes, that went a long way toward making up for some of her failings. He'd always had a thing for kids. But since Perote, well, a child's innocence alone had been able to penetrate that darkness inside him. Being with children, playing with them and basking in their love, had come closer to healing him than anything else. The trip to Europe had been a waste of time. That know-everything doctor hadn't helped at all. Brazos would have been better off staying home and playing with his children.

He'd enjoyed spending time with Madeline's Rose and the Brunet boy. Little babies were special in their own way, although he had to admit he fancied them more once they were up and running around. He'd the notion Rose would walk early; already she played at crawling. She was a feisty little thing—determined. Just like her mama.

Brazos's gaze searched the deck for Madeline. She stood at the center of the bow, and she'd removed her bonnet. Glistening golden tresses blew free in the wind, and Brazos thought she competed well with the *Uriel*'s figurehead. "Get Maddie to bare her breasts, and she'd put the wooden beauty to shame," he observed, visualizing the picture, sighing ruefully when a surge of desire swept through him. He wouldn't mind one bit having a taste of what this Denis and Emile and who knows how many others had enjoyed. Brazos had a bad case of yearning for Madeline Christophe Sinclair.

He didn't doubt he could seduce her. Hell, she had men on two continents. She'd probably be proud to have one in between. But it couldn't happen. The little detail of a pending annulment on grounds of nonconsummation of marriage stood in the way.

No, Brazos wasn't about to risk ending up married to the scheming, wanton beauty. While his acquaintance with the La Réunion colonists had convinced him to be more open-minded and accepting of this libertarian way of living, that didn't mean he was ready to embrace the life-style himself. These ideas of free love went against his raising, and no matter how appealing the idea might be at times, any lovin' with Madeline Sinclair would damn sure give him a peck of trouble. For one thing, it'd make her his wife. Brazos didn't have it in him to bed her, then swear on a legal document it never happened.

His gaze locked on her again, and he cursed his own honor. She smiled serenely as she lifted her head to catch the sea spray on her face. "Holy hell," he muttered, tossing the Fourierist magazine over the side of the ship. Briefly, he considered following it, as he needed a nice cold swim at the moment. Diving into the North Atlantic during February couldn't be any more dangerous than taking a dip in Madeline's bed.

From here on out, he'd stay clear the hell away from the woman. He'd learned his lessons the hard way in the past, but this time would be different. Brazos was determined to stay out of harm's way.

THEY SAILED INTO the storm that evening. Heavy seas tossed the *Uriel* about like flotsam, and a bitter, icy wind buffeted all aboard. Sleet pinged against the single porthole in Madeline's cabin, and she stuffed a towel against it, hoping to contain the chill seeping through the glass.

An hour earlier, the captain had ordered all fires extinguished. Madeline's cabin was pitch-black and gloomy—and lonely. Beneath her flannel nightgown she pulled on extra petticoats and stockings for warmth. Then she crawled into her bed, wrapped a blanket around herself, and waited.

She wanted Rose, she worried about her. She'd had her talk with Lillibet earlier and received assurance that the Brunets would act as guardians if need be. Madeline's relief had been short-lived, however. In the course of the conversation, Lillibet disclosed that she and André were expecting another child. Madeline realized she must see about making permanent arrangements as soon as possible. Caring for two babies of such a young age would be difficult. Three would be overwhelming.

Right now, she wished she had even one to cuddle. "Quit being selfish," she scolded herself. "Rose is better off with Lillibet. If she's scared, Lil can nurse her. Nothing is as comforting as being put to the breast."

Again, an annoyingly recurrent picture of Brazos Sinclair flashed through her mind.

A prolonged yawn of timber scattered her thoughts. She hugged herself tight as the ship creaked violently, and the ghostly howl of the wind warned of souls resting below in a watery grave. She prayed that none of the *Uriel*'s company would join them on this hellish night. Intent upon her petitions, she didn't notice her cabin door open.

"Maddie?" Brazos's voice was a strained whisper.

"Brazos, is that you?"

"Yeah."

A sudden wave of relief washed over her. She was no longer alone. "I'd wondered if you had remained on deck. I'm sure conditions must be awful out there. It's bad enough down here in the cabin. This is my first experience with a storm at sea, and I admit I'm a bit frightened." She was babbling, she knew, but she couldn't seem to stop. "Would you care to join me? I'd appreciate the company, and you are welcome as long as you mind your manners."

"Is Rose here with you?"

She stared into the darkness, trying to make out his form. He sounded strange. "No, she sleeps with the Brunets because she sometimes wakes to nurse in the middle of the night. I wish she were here, I wish I could . . . oh, never mind. Brazos, listen to me. Just because I invited you inside doesn't mean I'm inviting you in any other way. I meant what I said about a marriage in name alone. Brazos? What are you doing? I can't see you."

"Does this cabin have a window?"

"It has a porthole, yes."

"Open it."

"What? Why? It's freezing outside; it's sleeting, Brazos."

"Dammit, I know that. The captain ordered me below. Maddie, just do it." He paused for a moment then added, "Please!"

"But why? I don't understand."

"Please!" he repeated.

Shaking her head, shivering already, Madeline reached up and pulled the towel from the porthole, then twisted the cold brass screw and pulled the glass open. A spray of frigid sea water slapped her face. "Bloody hell," she muttered beneath her breath.

Brazos stepped inside. "Is there a chair or somethin' in here that's not fastened to the floor?"

"No," she answered, wiping her cheeks with an edge of her blanket. "Why? Brazos, what is going on here? This is ridiculous; I'm freezing! It was bad enough before, but with the porthole open . . ."

"Give me the blanket."

"What? Why?" She heard him step toward her. He yanked the cover right off of her. "Brazos!" she cried. Somehow, he used the blanket to prop open the door. A steady stream of wind and ice whipped into and out of the cabin. "What are you doing?" she squealed. "This is stupid, Brazos! I've had enough. Unless you can give me an excellent reason for your requests, I'm shutting this porthole. We'll catch our deaths—if we don't drown first, that is!"

His voice tight, he demanded, "Stay away from the window, Maddie. Just climb under your covers."

"You took my cover."

"You have more. Look, I'm sorry, but I need a bit of accommodation right now."

The rustle of cloth made her hope he was donning extra clothing, as she had. Then she heard something that sounded suspiciously like a belt buckle hit the wooden floor.

"Brazos?" Beside her, the mattress sagged beneath his weight. The unmistakable contour of a taut, masculine muscle—a taut, masculine, *naked* muscle—curled against her. She gasped. "Brazos Sinclair! How dare you! I distinctly told you that . . ." Her sentence trailed off when she realized he'd laid the handle of a knife across her palm. "What in heaven's name is going on?"

Chapter 4

"Keep the knife, Maddie. You might need it," Brazos said. "Sorry about the clothes, but I'm so damned hot." His voice trailed off, "I'm so damned."

Oh, God, don't let me hurt her. Brazos was fighting for all he was worth. Panic poised at the edge of his consciousness, ready to consume him. He trembled, waves of hot terror washing over his body, soaking the sheet beneath him with his sweat. His heart raced, and he gasped for every breath against the terrible weight on his chest, the heavy, suffocating weight.

God, he was scared. He shouldn't have come here. He should have stayed away from her like he'd intended.

But something drew him to her, something strong, Powerful. He sensed a light within Madeline, a brightness that called to the darkness of his soul. "Talk to me, Maddie. Please. Share it with me."

"You're frightening me. What is it Brazos? What's wrong? Why are you doing this?"

It would get worse, he knew it. Like a woman

giving birth, only these were emotional contractions. Now that they'd started, he couldn't stop them. At least, he never had before. Maybe this time though. Maddie was with him. Maddie with that warm, soothing inner light. "Talk, just talk. I need your voice."

"I need some answers. What is the knife for, Brazos? Did something happen on deck? Has there been a mutiny? Are you here to protect me?"

Brazos groaned, "Maddie, just shut up and talk, would you?"

"Shut up and talk. Well, that makes as much sense as everything else. Fine, you want me to talk? Well, I'm cold. I'm very, very cold. I don't understand how you can lie there like . . . uh, well, you know, like you are. I guess you have a reason for opening the porthole in the middle of a sleet storm, and for choosing this particular way to slither into my bed. I imagine you even have a reason for handing me a weapon, although I can't say I say I find it reassuring. Is it some sort of Texan custom?"

When he didn't answer she said in a sugary tone, "But since I'm only an inferior woman, I'll not question your intelligence or any lack thereof. Besides, it appears as if I could question you till dawn and not receive a single answer."

Lost within the hell of his mind, Brazos held on to her voice like a lifeline. He even smiled faintly at her wit. He wrapped his arm around her, and when he spoke, his voice came from far away. "Here, sweet, somebody ought to get some use from all this heat."

"Ow! What's that metal thing around your arm? It's poking me, Brazos, move it." Her hand splayed across his bare chest. "Why, you're burning up! But you're sweating. What is this . . . oh, Brazos, is it . . . is it . . . consumption?"

"I'm not that lucky—or contagious," he forced the words past the lump in his throat. "Keep talking, Maddie."

She looked at him, gazed deeply into his eyes. In his overwhelming need, Brazos buried his pride and allowed her a glimpse of his torment.

"Oh, my," she said softly.

He saw the sheen of tears she did not try to hide as she lay down beside him. And Madeline began to speak.

Curled against him, she recounted happenings during her childhood. She told tales of Mistress Poggi's boarding school, of growing up an orphan among girls who returned to their homes for holidays. Her stories were silly ones, nothing that betrayed her secrets, except, perhaps, the loneliness he sensed was so much a part of her.

Brazos gripped her hand, concentrating on her voice, and on the fresh air streaming through the porthole. It's open, he told himself. The window, the door. He could get out. He wasn't alone. He could get out.

But deep inside him, the beast stirred.

Madeline continued to talk, and Brazos battled to hear her words. Her voice was a rope of life, a rhythm of light. He grasped it, basked in it. And with Madeline's help, he held the terror at bay.

Eventually, amazingly, he slept.

For a time, Madeline lay awake, thinking about the man now sleeping peacefully at her side. The poor man. Tonight's events had proven that Brazos Sinclair was more than the handsome, arrogant lunkhead she'd considered him to be. She wasn't the only person aboard this boat hiding things. And whatever his secrets were, she wondered if they might not be as horrible as her own.

With such ideas floating through her mind, Madeline drifted toward sleep. But before she slumbered, she opened her heart just a bit, and the injured boy living within the man beside her slipped inside.

BRAZOS DREAMED HE was a child again, wrapped in the blessed comfort of his mother's arms. Her gentle fingers stroked his hair, and her perfume took him back to the gardens at Magnolia Bend. Mama always favored the scent of roses.

She cushioned him with her breasts. Brazos burrowed into the softness. Something was different, the pillow was fluffier than he remembered. A rush of heat stirred him, inspiring horror that he'd react this way to his own mother. His eyes flew open wide, and all dreams of childhood disappeared as he encountered the luscious sight of a bountiful bosom within tongue's reach. This was *not* his mother.

He must've died last night, after all.

Slowly, Brazos lifted his head. His stare crawled up the length of patterned blue flannel, pausing at the sight of creamy bare skin left visible by a loosened ribbon, then climbing higher to an elegant stretch of neck and to lips, full and red and slightly parted. Almost against his will, he lifted his gaze to her eyes. Deep and as dark as the velvet sea, they silently offered both plea and promise, and Brazos responded to their siren call.

He lowered his head, and his mouth touched hers.

He drowned in the pleasure of her kiss. Sensations swirled around him, creating an aching need that craved satisfaction. He groaned a low, masculine declaration of desire, and her answering whimper destroyed the few lingering remnants of resistance he'd possessed.

He rolled to his back, pulling her with him so that she lay pressed against his chest. His hands raced down the warm, soft texture of the flannel nightgown, then delved beneath to wander over skin even softer, silky and hot.

He deepened the kiss, his tongue stroking, seeking, and he felt the shudder of desire sweep through the body pressed so close to his. "Oh, Brazos," she whispered when he tore his mouth from hers, his lips trailing downward to taste the bounty that had pillowed his head such a short time ago. Her breathy tone sent frissons of heat along his nerves. He tugged at her gown with his teeth, baring a rosy, pebbled peak to his gaze. "Yeah, Beauty," he answered reverently.

It was as he bent and took her breast into his mouth that he remembered. *Beauty. Maddie. Madeline Christophe. Madeline Sinclair. His wife! He couldn't make love to his wife. Not this wife, not Madeline Sinclair. Not ever.*

He pulled away just as Madeline sighed a throaty moan. He felt like groaning right along with her. Brazos was used to wanting things he couldn't have, but this was the first time he remembered having something he couldn't—or shouldn't, anyway—want.

Then she opened her eyes, and what he saw there had him scrambling off the bed and diving for his pants. Those big, brown, beautiful eyes had gone all misty with desire. "Brazos?" she asked, her voice husky and soft.

He had a helluva time fitting himself inside his denims. Keeping his back to her until he'd managed to get buttoned, he took a deep breath, then turned. She was sitting up in the bunk, and she had that wounded-doe look about her again. The sight of it was like a punch to the gut. "Don't do that," he demanded roughly.

"Do what?"

"Look at me like that."

The sheen of tears sparkled in her eyes. "Like what?"

Brazos raked his fingers through his hair. "Never mind." She'd retied the ribbon at the neck of her nightgown, and above the lace collar, her skin shone a light pink. Brazos shook his head, chasing away the mental image of other rose-color body parts. "Look, Maddie, we can't . . . I don't . . . aw, hell." Leaning against the cabin wall opposite the bed, Brazos slowly slid down to sit on the floor. Propping an elbow on a knee, he held his palm to his forehead and repeated, "Aw, hell."

For a long moment, Madeline stared at him. Then she plopped down onto the mattress and said vehemently, "Bloody hell."

Brazos looked up, shocked.

She darted him a sheepish glance. "Oops."

He felt a grin tug at the corners of his mouth. He saw amusement kindle in her eyes. Their gazes locked, and suddenly, they both began to laugh.

"My word, Maddie, you certainly know how to surprise a fella."

She rolled over to her side and propped her head

on her elbow. "You've a few surprises of your own. I'd never have guessed—" She stopped abruptly, and he saw her gaze focus upon the scar on his chest. "What happened to you, Brazos?"

Automatically, his hand lifted to touch the band around his arm. "It's nothin'."

"You're doing it again," she said. "You kept touching that armband last night." Madeline paused before hesitantly asking, "What was it all about? What happened last night?"

He barely heard her question because the look in her eyes filled him with such . . . shame. He pushed roughly to his feet. *Damn the woman. I won't be pitied.*

"Brazos?"

"What?" he snapped, glaring at her.

She frowned with annoyance and said, "Well, you needn't use that tone. All I did was ask you a question, which, under the circumstances, I believe I have every right to ask."

He ground his teeth together. "Don't fool yourself. If you're thinkin' that what happened in that bunk a few minutes ago gives you any rights at all, you prove the point I was arguin' yesterday."

"What point?"

"That women don't have any more sense than an armadillo."

She sat up. "And what, dare I ask, is an armadillo?"

"An armadillo is one of the dumbest critters the good Lord put on this earth."

Madeline's mouth fell open. "I don't believe you're saying something like that to me." She straightened her spine and lifted her chin, and her fiery beauty rekindled the desire that had continued to smolder inside him.

Shame and desire create a volatile mixture. With the two emotions whipping around inside him, Brazos resorted to a defense he seldom used. He lied. "Honey, you're a perfect example. You fell for my story last night like deadwood in a gale." Shoulders squared, a cocky expression in place, Brazos said, "I thought to get in out of the cold for a bit last night, that's all," he said with a shrug. "I figured I'd best do somethin' peculiar so that you'd leave me the hell alone. That's why I put on that little act of bein' crazy."

He swept her with a contemptuous gaze. "And I was right, wasn't I? Soon as my eyes are shut, you up and bare your breasts, hopin' to catch me unaware."

Her mouth rounded in a silent "Oh." Then she crossed her arms and glared at him. "I did not. When I went to sleep, my gown was securely fastened. You're the one with wandering fingers."

"Yeah, sure." He scooped his shirt from the floor. "You almost pulled off your scheme, didn't you?" Shoving his arms through the shirtsleeves, he added, "Thank God I didn't let my pecker do my thinkin' for me, or you'd have well me and truly leg-shackled this minute. For the last time, Maddie, my dear, I'm *not* gonna be your stud."

She waited a moment, then said softly, "You've a nasty mouth on you, Brazos Sinclair."

Lord, he knew it was true. Never in his life had he talked to a woman the way he'd spoken to Madeline. He lifted his gaze toward heaven and asked, Dear God, what am I becoming?

That's when he noticed the ceiling—the very low ceiling. Against his will, his stare slowly traveled the wooden planks to the wall and then to the floorboards. The room shrank. Anxiety replaced all emotion, and he muttered hoarsely, "I've gotta get out of here."

"Don't you dare leave now, you contemptible cur. I'm not through . . ."

But Brazos fled the cabin, barefoot and embarrassed. He was halfway up the companionway stairs when the door to Madeline's room flew open and his boots came sailing out to thump against the opposite wall.

Inside the cabin, Madeline started to slam the door shut, but then remembered the babies asleep in the next room. So with deliberate movements, she grasped the handle and quietly closed the door. Emotion threatened to choke her, and she blinked her eyes rapidly as her gaze wandered aimlessly around the room. Then she noticed his hat hanging on a hook on the wall.

Madeline's imagination ran wild as she used bare feet to stomp the hat into an unrecognizable form, heedless of the tears that coursed down her cheeks. Then she crawled back into her bunk and curled into a ball beneath the sheets.

Brazos was right, she *was* a fool. How else could she explain allowing him the liberties he'd taken this morning? "Hah," she scoffed. "At least be honest with yourself, Madeline. Liberties you offered."

Madeline was baffled by her own behavior. Never had she acted so free with a man before. It wasn't like her at all! She replayed the morning's events in her mind. Still, answers eluded her. She was thinking of men in general, Brazos specifically, when she murmured, "Why do I allow them to hurt me?"

It wasn't as if Brazos was the man of her dreams. Far from it. The man Madeline fantasized sharing her life with would recognize and respect her intelligence and abilities. He'd understand the reasons behind her more unsavory actions, and if not approve of them, he'd at least forgive her for having committed the deeds.

Most of all, he'd love her.

Never in her life had Madeline known a man's love—not a true, abiding love, anyway. She'd never known her father, and Gentleman Jack, the man who'd taught her how to steal, had rejected her once her developing body proved her a girl, not the boy he'd believed.

Madeline threw back the covers, leaned over the bunk, and yanked open a drawer of the chest built beneath the bed. She fumbled through her clothes for a handkerchief. "I'll find my man," she said, tugging a cloth from the drawer and sitting up. "I will." She blew her nose. "He's out there somewhere, and I simply have to look around a bit to meet him."

Then she'd show Brazos Sinclair. She'd prove to him just how wrong he was. The man of her dreams would propose to her. He'd be drowning in desire to have her in his bed. He wouldn't flee it as if the hounds of hell were nipping at his heels. He'd . . .

She stopped. Lowering the handkerchief to her

lap, Madeline stared through the porthole at the white-capped sea. Faced with the sting of Brazos's rejection, she had forgotten his conduct during the previous night. "The hounds of hell *were* after him," Madeline murmured.

Slowly, she climbed from her bed, thinking past this morning's incident to the events of the previous evening. As she dressed, she made a decision. She'd be magnanimous. She would remember that he, too, had a cross of some sort to bear, and she'd forget the hurtful words he'd spoken to her this morning.

But a lingering ache made her realize she still had some memories to lose. Where Brazos Sinclair was concerned, some things were easier to forget than others.

TWO DAYS LATER, Brazos searched the deck of the *Uriel* with a package in his hand and a notion in his mind. It was time to apologize to his wife. His behavior the other morning had been deplorable. The cruel, dishonest words he had spoken had hurt someone who'd been more than kind to him during his hour of need. Although he'd numerous excuses, he'd allow himself none. He considered himself an honorable man, and he'd acted with dishonor. So, the only option he had was to apologize.

Then he planned to go after what he really wanted.

Sleep. Warm, comfortable, uninterrupted sleep. The type he'd enjoyed before boarding the *Uriel,* the kind he'd known only one night since—the night he'd spent in Madeline Christophe Sinclair's bed.

He'd talked his way right out of that pleasant little heaven, and he felt ashamed as he remembered the words he'd hurled. He'd mean every word of this apology when he offered it. But that didn't suggest he wouldn't use every available resource to move right back into Madeline's bed.

Platonically, of course.

True, he had every right to demand a place in her

cabin. She'd offered him the floor when she first mentioned the idea of this marriage. But Brazos had given the idea careful consideration, and he'd decided that any attempt now to strong-arm his way in would undoubtedly lead to war. A man didn't get much rest when he was fighting battles.

Brazos was tired, exhausted. A bedroll and blanket simply weren't enough protection against North Atlantic nights, and the nightmares he'd suffered since the storm weren't helping the situation. Neither were the memories of how he'd made a fool of himself in Madeline's cabin.

So he pondered a bit and arrived at what he believed to be a foolproof plan for talking his way back into the beauty's bed. At least, he hoped it was a good plan. He had based his ideas on a concept every man with any sense held close to heart. *If you want something from a woman, you tell her what she wants to hear first.*

Brazos had been exposed to the idea at an early age, watching his father with his mother, his uncles with his aunts. He'd employed it for the first time at the age of eleven when he'd been intent on stealing a kiss off of Sarah Jane Davis. Today he planned to tell Madeline what he figured she wanted to hear.

"Let's hope I've got it figured right," he muttered, stepping over a coil of rope.

It was shortly after eight bells, twelve o'clock, when he found her playing with Rose on a blanket spread atop an out-of-the-way section of the deck. The baby lay on her back, arms and legs all in the air as she tugged on a knitted green bootie. "You do have a problem with shoes, don't you Miss Magic," Brazos said, sitting down beside them. "Afternoon, Maddie."

She turned her head, looked at him, and nodded.

The woman can say more with her eyes than anyone I've met before, Brazos acknowledged. Right then, she was telling him to go to hell. "It's kinda nice having the wind fall away for a day, isn't it? The sea looks like a sheet of glass. Funny how it can change. The last couple of days, it was downright angry—roaring surges, the ridges of the waves all roughened and broken into foam. Now, today the mood's gone calm and peaceful. Nice to know things can change, right?"

The look in her eyes clearly proclaimed him a fool, but she deigned not to answer him aloud. Ease into it, man, he told himself. She'd been just as close-mouthed that first day, and everything had worked out all right. Sort of.

"Did you see the whale that swam with us a bit today?" he asked. "Simply fascinating. I've never seen such a magnificent animal. And the porpoises are always fun to watch. A sailor told me they're attracted by the *Uriel*'s copper sheathing. You think that's true?"

She didn't even bother to look at him. Watching as she lifted the baby into her lap, Brazos allowed himself a frustrated sigh. "I swear, Maddie. I've never met a woman so accomplished at ignorin' a man."

Dryly, she replied, "And I've never met a man more deserving of being ignored."

He couldn't stop the grin, rueful though it was. "I've a far piece to travel, don't I."

She lifted an eyebrow.

"I'm here to apologize, Madeline. I didn't mean those things I said to you the other mornin'. They were ugly and mean-spirited. You deserve to be treated better than that."

He paused, gauging her reaction. Well, he'd known it wasn't going to be easy.

"I'm here with my hat in my hand—or I would be if I still had a hat—to beg your forgiveness. I brought a little somethin' for Rose as a way of sayin' I'm sorry." He held out the burlap-wrapped package.

Madeline looked at the gift, then looked at him, then looked at the gift again. Brazos could tell she wanted it. He also figured she wasn't ready to let bygones be. He tried flashing her a winsome smile.

She wrinkled her nose at him, and Brazos laughed. "Ah, Maddie, you're an all-standing tough ol' gal."

"Pardon me?"

"That's high praise for a woman in Texas." He motioned with the gift. "Here, Beauty, open it. Let me have Rose. My arms have been achin' to hold her these last few days."

That one worked, he told himself, observing the softening of Madeline's eyes. Why hadn't he thought of it sooner? And it was nothing more than the truth. Rose, with her smiles and charming little giggles, had wiggled her way right into his heart. "Come here, Miss Magic," he said, trading the package for the child. "Wait till you get a gander at what your Mama's unwrappin'."

While Rose busied herself with pulling at the lobe of his ear, Brazos watched Madeline's suspicious delight as she turned the gift this way and that, sniffing and measuring and guessing. The lady liked presents, he noted, satisfied he'd chosen well in this next step of his strategy.

He'd figured Madeline would cotton to a gift for her baby. The saying went that the way to a man's heart was through his stomach. Personally, Brazos had always felt it was lower than that. Anyway, the counterpart to that adage was, in his theory, that the way to a woman's bed was through kindness to her children.

He'd never put the idea into practice before—in truth he'd thought of it only yesterday. But as Madeline slowly unwrapped the twine from around the gift, he decided he was right on target.

"It's something wooden," Madeline said, nodding with certainty.

"Come on, Maddie. At the rate you're goin', we'll hit Galveston before you get it open." Her answering smile was a burst of sunshine that packed a wallop to his gut. *Think platonic, Sinclair. Only platonic. A warm place to sleep for eight hours straight.*

Madeline finally removed the cloth. "Why, it's a puzzle," she said, her expression beaming with delight as she traced the pieces with her finger. Five rectangles were carved from the wood, their edges smoothed, and each one large enough not to be a danger to Rose. The shapes were painted in bright, eye-catching colors and designs.

"They're flags!" Madeline exclaimed.

"Yep. The five national flags that have flown over

Texas. See?" He lifted one out and displayed it before Rose. "This is the flag of France—the old one with the fleur-de-lis. But listen, Rose, don't get too excited about it. France's claim on Texas was the most doubtful of the lot."

Shaking her head, Madeline laughed, "Really, Brazos, a history lesson for a seven-month-old?"

"Hey, now," he faked a frown. "Texans are proud folks. Miss Magic's got to learn that from the git go."

Madeline sent him a sharp, knowing glance. "Yes, Texans are complicated people, aren't they?" Brazos's false frown became genuine. Damn, but the woman looked right into a man.

Uneasy now, Brazos moved to lay the baby on her back so she could freely wave the flags she held in both hands. Madeline placed a restraining hand on his arm. "Wait," she said. "Let me have her. I want you to see what she has learned."

"Madeline," he began, but he lost the thought. His gaze snagged on the swell of her bosom as she leaned over and set Rose in front of her. Slowly, Madeline removed her hands from around the child's waist. Finally, Rose's birdlike trill distracted Brazos from the delectable display before his eyes. He turned his attention to the baby, and a delighted smile spread across his face. "Why, look at that!" he exclaimed. "She can sit by herself. When did she learn that little trick?"

"She's been trying for a while, but today is the first time she's managed not to fall over after a few minutes," Madeline answered, glowing with pride.

Rose listed to port, and Brazos caught her before she fell. Lifting the baby up, he made faces at her and said, "Aren't you somethin' special, Miss Magic." He looked at Madeline and added, "Just like your mother."

Madeline offered him a hesitant smile. He sat Rose on the blanket and took her mother's hand. "I *am* sorry, Madeline."

She nodded. "Would you tell me about it?"

Brazos considered it. Telling her about Perote would undoubtedly further his cause, but as he released her hand to retrieve a puzzle piece Rose had tossed out of reach, he knew he wouldn't do it. A man could swallow only so much pride before he choked. He'd stick with the scheme he'd concocted. "I made a mistake. Let's leave it at that, all right? Look at Miss Magic, she's having a fine time with her toy."

Madeline allowed the question to drop, glancing over at Rose, whose little hands busily banged rectangular flags against their slots on the board. "The poor child has skin just like mine," she said regretfully. "I must remain on constant guard to ensure that she avoids unattractive spots."

"I think your freckles are cute, Maddie," Brazos said, deciding that a little flattery wouldn't hurt before he launched the next stage of his plan. Besides, he was telling the truth about that, too.

After a few moments of silence, Madeline said, "Thank you for the gift, Brazos. At times, you are a fine man."

He couldn't ask for a more perfect opening. "I'm glad you think so. In fact, I want you to keep that in mind. You see, I've decided to take you up on your offer."

The wooden puzzle piece in Madeline's hand dropped to the ground. In a flat voice, she asked, "What offer?"

Brazos took one look at the hard glint in her eyes and realized her mind was on the other morning. *Bad choice of words, Sinclair.* He hurried to cover his mistake. "I guess it wasn't actually an offer, but I've been thinking' about that conversation we had the other day. The one about La Réunion—remember it?"

"Yes," she answered, frowning suspiciously. Still, he thought she looked a little relieved.

Brazos chose his words carefully. He hoped that the sincerity of his apology would linger over into this second part of his strategy. This was the tricky part. He'd need all his acting ability to get her to believe he meant this next bit of business. "I've rethought my position."

"What position?"

On this stupid idea that appears to mean so much

to you, he wanted to say. "On the idea that men and women are equals. Now, I'm not sayin' I've changed my mind," he cautioned. *That'd be a stupid move. She'd never believe that.* "But I will allow that I can see some merit in your arguments. I'd be willing to listen to more." *And I hope to hell warm, dry nights'll be worth it.*

He tried so hard to look sincere. The way he had it figured, Madeline would find the opportunity to prove to him the error of his ways too hard to pass up. Then she'd have to spend time talking with him—just as she had the night of the storm.

"Just what brought this on?" she asked, pinning him with a shrewd gaze.

"You just got me to thinkin'."

"What a dangerous occupation."

He pretended not to hear her droll reply as he looked around for a distraction. He didn't want Maddie questioning him too closely right yet. His gaze snagged on the sight of a young sailor being tugged in their direction by Madame Benoit, the most irritating colonist aboard the *Uriel.* "Damn, that woman is dangerous with a parasol," he observed.

"Brazos, are you serious about this?"

"Yep, I am. Look at that, Maddie, Mrs. Benoit is all but bangin' that boy over the head with her umbrella." He whistled softly. "He's opening that hatch. I wonder why. Usually a ship's hold stays closed the entire voyage."

Madeline muttered something about "frustrating fools."

A second sailor, older and bewhiskered, noticed the goings-on and spat out a rapid flurry of French Brazos had no chance of following. Both sailors were waving their arms, Madame Benoit was waving her weapon, and they all shouted at one another. Brazos did catch the word *capitaine* just as they all marched off in a cloud of commotion.

"Mrs. Benoit'll be lucky if the old salt doesn't toss her overboard," Brazos observed as the trio disappeared.

Madeline answered his smile with one of her own. *So far, so good, Sinclair.* He was encouraged by her look and pleased she'd had a moment to warm to his idea.

"Brazos," she asked, "have I truly convinced you that women should be treated equally to men?"

"Well, you don't need to give me a cake recipe just yet." He stretched out his legs and wiggled his foot as Rose played with the toe of his boot. "But I figure it won't hurt us to pass some time together and chew on the idea a bit."

"Speaking of chewing on things . . ." Madeline gently tugged the piece of burlap away from Rose. "This child puts everything in her mouth these days," she fussed. Then she asked, "Why do I have the feeling, Brazos Sinclair, that you want something from me?"

Damn. He couldn't forget that for a woman, Madeline was pretty smart. Brazos decided it was time to pursue the third objective in his plan. Madeline needed to be reminded just how badly she'd wanted aboard the *Uriel.* "When we were stumbling around Antwerp trying to find us a preacher, how come you were so set on my not mentioning your name?"

Madeline averted her gaze. "That's a personal question, Mr. Sinclair."

"You've asked me personal questions."

"You wouldn't answer."

"Maybe I will if you will. Besides, I think we've about graduated to personal between us. Don't you, Mrs. Sinclair?"

Pursing her lips, she nodded. "Maybe we have at that. Very well, sir, I'll even gift you with the truth. I was afraid. I don't want anyone to find me."

She watched him closely, as though his reaction were important. "Your fiancé?" he asked, careful to keep his face a blank.

"Who?"

"The one who got wounded in the duel." Her vacant stare frustrated him. Really, the woman needed to do a better job keeping her men straight. "The fella your Emile plugged."

"Oh." She winced. "Yes, yes, him. Or anyone else,

for that matter. I want to start over, Brazos. A new life in a new country. I want to create a secure home and family for Rose."

"Will he do it for you, your Emile?"

She looked at him then, her eyes steady and determined, and shrugged. "I don't know. But if he won't, I shall find a man who will."

"Just like that?"

"Just like that."

Brazos dropped his gaze to his hand and the flag he squeezed in his fist. She's a real piece of work, he told himself. Yet, there was something about her that didn't fit. For all her hard talk, she had an innocence about her that called to a man, made him want to grab a sword and slay her dragons.

Yeah. Like I could battle someone else's demons when I can't even handle my own.

He frowned and offered the puzzle piece to Rose, who gurgled and banged the red-and-gold standard of Imperial Spain against the red, white, and blue of the United States. "Aren't you in love with the man? He is Rose's father after all."

Minutes passed in silence. Her smile was bittersweet when she finally said, "Without Rose's father, I wouldn't have Rose. So I guess there must be something there to love." Her expression tightened. "I was in an impossible situation, Brazos. I did what I had to in order to escape."

Her words knocked the wind from his lungs. He'd known there was more to her story than she let on. Could it be that the beauty left something ugly behind? "I can understand hard circumstances, Maddie," he agreed, studying the proud tilt of her chin. "There are all sorts of prisons in this life, aren't there?"

Gently, her fingers stroked her daughter's dimpled cheek. Such was the look in her eyes, a velvet sadness poignant with love, that he knew a pang of heartbreak at the sight. "I think," Madeline said, accepting the French flag from Rose, "that I may have found the key to unlock the door." She turned toward him with a devastating smile. "I love her, Brazos."

He'd never seen her look more beautiful than she did in that moment. He took her hand, lifted it to his lips, and pressed a kiss against her knuckles. "You're a lucky woman to have her, Maddie. And she's a lucky little lady to have you for a mother."

Madeline shut her eyes, though not quickly enough to hide the wash of tears collected there. Deciding the time was right, Brazos said, "Maddie, about our marriage agreement. There's something I want to ask you. I know we discussed this in the beginning, but . . . well . . . I want you to consider everything we've just talked about. You see, I've changed my mind."

She trembled, almost imperceptibly. "You want a real marriage?"

For just a moment, he considered it. Madeline and Rose at Magnolia Bend, maybe a blue-eyed son with golden hair. Then he remembered Lana, the woman he had once loved and planned to marry. Before Perote. Afterward . . . well . . . she'd still wanted a home and family. Brazos had needed to run.

He was still running, and he would continue to run until he'd dealt with Damasso Salezan.

"Aw, Maddie," he said, and the regret in his voice was honest. "I can't do that. A wife doesn't fit into my life right now. I doubt one ever will. You see, I've got too much tumbleweed in my blood to ever settle down. If I try to hang around any one place for more than a few weeks, my feet get to itchin' somethin' fierce. Besides, I've got my own prisons to deal with."

She looked away. A chill of loss touched him as he added, "I can be your friend, though. I'm good at that. I'd like to be your friend, Maddie."

"I . . . I . . ." she stuttered, smoothing her skirt and staring down at her lap.

"Maddie?"

She lifted her head, and her eyes reflected confusion as she gazed at him, sunlight dancing a red-gold waltz in the coil of her braid. She said, "I'm not making sense of this conversation. Just what is it you are asking me, Brazos?"

He'd intended to do this with finesse. It was the crowning moment of his entire plan. He'd concocted a scheme that would hold up well against one of Maddie's any day. He'd put it into motion, and it had arrived here at fruition. All he needed to do was to sum up what he'd been saying for the last half hour—tell her that he'd told her what she wanted to hear—and he knew he'd be spending that night in Maddie's bed.

Platonically.

Instead, unplanned words just popped out of his mouth. "I want to move into your bed."

"What!"

"Platonically, of course. For those reasons, remember? Equality, friendship, your earlier offer. I helped you, Maddie; you owe me."

"I do not," she snapped. Madeline stood, planted her hands on her hips, and glared down at him.

"Yes, you do," Brazos replied, following her up and mimicking her stance. "*I* got you on this boat."

"I got myself on this boat!"

"Well, I helped."

She leaned forward, speaking through set teeth. "It was my plan."

He leaned, too, and they were but inches apart when he said, "I had a good plan, too. You've got to admit it. It worked like a charm up until the end."

Then Rose began to cry.

"Oh, dear." Madeline pulled away and scrambled over to her daughter. "What's the matter, sweetheart?" she crooned.

Lillibet Brunet's voice cut across the air. "Well, dearling, if you'd not been so distracted, you'd have seen that she tossed her toy into that hole." She pointed toward a square hatch, its lid propped open with a metal bar.

Madeline flushed bright red, and even Brazos shrugged sheepishly. She lifted the wailing baby and rocked her in her arms, patting the child's back and cooing, "Oh, poor Rose. Don't you worry, though. Brazos will get it for you." She raised her eyebrows, watching him expectantly, until he dragged himself over to peer down the hole.

Steep steps descended into darkness.

"That's the hold, Maddie. I'm not goin' down there."

She glared at him.

He braced his hands on his hips and glared back.

"Fine," she said after a long pause. "I'll go get it myself. Lil, please take Rose for me. It's her nap time—I assume that's why you looked for us?"

Lillibet nodded. "I expected you to bring her to me an hour ago, Madeline. You know, you really should be more careful with her out in the sun like this. She could get freckles."

"I know, Lil," Madeline said, handing her the sobbing child. "I'm sorry. I lost track of time."

"Yes, well, no harm done, although it probably will confuse my schedule." Lillibet turned to Brazos. "This is most likely your fault."

"Yes'm. I do apologize." He bent over and kissed Rose's forehead. "Good night, Miss Magic. Have a good nap."

Holding Rose in her arms, Lillibet began to walk away. Then abruptly she stopped and looked over her shoulder. "Mr. Brazos, don't you let Madeline go down into that place."

"I won't," he promised.

Lillibet nodded once before continuing on her way.

"If you're not going, I am," Madeline challenged.

"Don't be stupid, Maddie," Brazos snapped. "It's just a toy. Rose won't even remember it after she sleeps."

Madeline's tone was fierce. "It's hers, Brazos, her very own toy. She doesn't have to share it or give it away; she can keep it forever. I'm going to make sure." Lifting her chin, she straightened her shoulders and began to climb down the steps.

"Madeline!" His voice was urgent now. "Come on, Maddie. I'll make her another to replace it. It's not important. Come on up!"

All he heard was a short scream and then silence. A long silence. "Maddie?"

Nothing.

"Hell's bells." He stood there, staring into the blackness. With a heavy sigh, his hands wet with sweat, he began his descent down the steep stairs. His breathing accelerated, and as the dizziness come over him, he grabbed at the rope hanging free beside the steps for support.

"Maddie?"

Silence. For chrissakes, how did she think she'd find the stupid puzzle piece in this little bit of light anyway? His knees wobbled.

"Brazos? I'm down here," Madeline called. "It's awful. Help me, Brazos. I think he's dead."

Peering below, he could just make out her shape at the base of the steps. She stood atop a crate and stared into a space between two hogsheads. Forcing every step, he descended the stairs and stood beside her.

His arm went rigid as he reached for her hand and his eyes followed her gaze.

The dead man's glassy-eyed stare and leering grin were the last things he saw before the hatch's door slammed shut, casting the hold into total darkness.

"Maddie," he croaked.

And then the hell began.

Chapter 5

The black, endless sea engulfs Sinclair's body, his will, the very core of his spirit. In flows an acid that eats away the shackles of his resolve, freeing me to roam and to ravage. He no longer possesses the power or the desire to control me. He is the Sinclair, the Weak One.

I am the Night, the embodiment of hell's beastly triumphs.

PLUNGED INTO BLINDNESS by the total absence of light, Madeline momentarily panicked, losing her sense of time and place. Frantically, she stretched out her hands, searching for something, anything, to anchor herself in this abyss. Her fingers brushed a surface—rough and wooden—a crate. Then the creaking timbers of a ship at sea completed the picture, and she drew a deep, calming breath and whispered, "Brazos?"

An agonized, inhuman roar answered her.

She turned, fearfully repeating, "Brazos?"

Hands thrust forward and clasped her neck, and for just a moment, she stood frozen in shock. Then the fingers gradually applied pressure, and Madeline began to struggle. She twisted and tugged, hit and clawed, pounding the beast who slowly stole the life from her body. She acted instinctively, not thinking, not able to think. Too afraid.

A rush, a roaring sound filled her ears as brilliant bursts of white light exploded in her mind. Madeline felt herself falling toward the void, and the will to fight deserted her.

Then she remembered Rose. Innocent, vulnerable Rose. Madeline summoned her strength for a single last effort, and she wrenched herself free.

Of Brazos Sinclair's murdering hands.

She backed away, gasping for air, massaging her throat where his fingers had crushed just moments before. Dear Lord, what was happening here?

Fear clawed at her heart as she stared with useless eyes into the darkness. Stretching out a hand, she felt her way along the narrow path between the crates, desperate to flee from the stranger who was her husband. He'd tried to kill her; it was unbelievable!

But—oh, God—it was true.

Madeline tripped on the hem of her skirt, tumbling forward. Her hands slapped the rough wooden decking, and a splinter pierced her palm. She whimpered. But the cry erupted from the pain in her heart—not her hand.

Brazos Sinclair had hurt her.

Behind her, she heard him move. His boots dragged across the planking. She lay frozen in fear. Wood scraped wood as a hogshead shifted, followed by a thud. Then, only ship sounds interrupted the silence. Where was he? What was he doing?

Then she heard a squeak—a rhythmic creak of wood created by continuous rocking. Tentatively, she asked, "Brazos?"

Creak . . . creak . . . creak.

The sound escalated her fear. She climbed to her feet, intending to flee from the noise, but four short steps brought her to the end of the path. She was blocked on three sides.

Creak . . . creak . . . creak.

"Brazos, you're frightening me. Stop it, please!"

The squeaking continued. "Talk to me, Brazos. Please! I don't know what's happening here, but it's all right, no one is hurt."

Creak . . . creak . . . creak.

She steepled her hands in front of her mouth and unconsciously swayed in time with the sound. What now? Why had he tried to hurt her? Would he do it again? He blocked the stairway. She was trapped in the bowels of the ship with a dead man and a mad man.

Brazos groaned, a tortured, inhuman noise that swelled in the darkness, stabbing her with its misery, writhing along her nerves. He was in pain, and her breath caught at the exposure of utter agony. Physically, he sat a few feet from where she stood, but she sensed he'd left her for a place far away—an awful, evil place.

He was a man lost among private demons, and Madeline realized—no, she knew with a faith born of her own bitter trials—that the danger had passed. He would not abuse her again.

She crossed the distance separating them and knelt at his side. Placing her hand on his shoulder, she said softly, soothingly, "I'm here, Brazos, let me help you. Speak to me."

His shirt was wet with sweat, and the muscles beneath her hand were tensed cords of steel. Compassion misted Madeline's eyes, but she forced herself to think. Why had this happened? What triggered this event? He'd been his normal, cocky self while they talked above deck. But he hadn't wanted to come below.

With the hem of her petticoat, she wiped the perspiration from his brow. That may be it, she told herself. He'd refused to descend into the hold, where it was dark. She shook her head. No, that couldn't be it. Brazos Sinclair afraid of the dark? She'd laugh if she weren't already crying.

Still, she couldn't deny that he'd resisted entering her darkened cabin the other night. He'd propped the door ajar, and he'd demanded she open the porthole. She kneaded the knots in his shoulder muscles and asked, "Is it the dark that brings this on, Brazos? It was dark that night in my cabin. But you wanted the porthole open, and the door. Is it the hatch, you need the hatch open again?"

His arms clutched his knees to his chest as he continued to move back and forth, over and over. Madeline lifted her fingers to his forehead and gently brushed back his bangs. His skin was clammy to the touch. "I'll try to open the hatch. Would you like that? Everything's fine, Brazos. I'll be right back." Swiftly, she climbed the ladder. She pushed against the covering, straining with all her might. It would not budge. She banged with her fist and shouted, "Help, please! We're trapped in the hold. Help!" Nothing.

Brazos made a sound—a strangled, tormented moan. Clenching her teeth, she heaved against the hatch one last time and cursed herself. She'd unlocked hundreds of doors in her years as a prowler—why couldn't she manage one simple little hatch? What kind of thief was she, after all?

Thoroughly disgusted with herself, she picked up her skirts and carefully descended the ladder. "You poor man," she murmured, kneeling beside her husband. Wrapping her arms around him, she brought his head to her breast, and they rocked. Together.

CHÂTEAU ST. GERMAINE, FRANCE

Julian Desseau lifted the white eyelet quilt from the crib and brought it to his face. With each passing day, the precious infant fragrance that clung to the blanket faded a little more. He set his teeth as he tenderly returned the quilt to the bed. "Damn Mary Smithwick to the lowest level of hell!"

A nervous cough interrupted his reverie. Turning, he noticed the servant waiting in the doorway. "Yes?"

"Excuse me, monsieur, but the man from Paris has arrived. He is waiting in the library."

Julian nodded abruptly and left the room. As he

made his way from the fourth story in the family wing of the great house to the ground floor, he indulged in his favorite pastime of late: imagining new and varied tortures for Mademoiselle Smithwick.

He yanked open the library's heavy walnut door and strode directly to the liquor cabinet. Without speaking, he poured a measure of brandy into two Baccarat snifters and offered one to his guest. "Well?" he asked as the man accepted the glass. The newcomer sipped his drink appreciatively before stating, "I have learned something."

Desseau stiffened. "You found them?"

"No. I am afraid not. But I have traced her to Antwerp."

"Belgium? Why Belgium?" Desseau gripped the armrest of a black leather chair and sat. The man from Paris, Pierre Corot, was more than an investigator. He was a friend. "Tell me all of it, Pierre, please."

Corot settled back in his own chair and spoke. "It was chance that we found it at all. My operative located a hackman in Brussels who recalled a woman matching Mary Smithwick's description. She used the name Madeline Christophe, and she traveled with a baby she called Rose. The infant developed a fever, and the driver delivered them to a doctor."

"She's sick! My Elise is sick?"

Corot shook his head. "No, teething, I'm told. My investigator asked the doctor specifically. The physician recalled that the woman appeared quite upset over the baby's troubles. Her thinking must have been confused because she tripped up on the names, Julian. My man checked the patient book. She signed it 'Mary Christophe and daughter, Elise'."

"It *is* her."

"I'm certain of it. Anyway, the woman and child left Brussels on a coach bound for Antwerp. However, we could find no evidence of her in the city until we checked with the churches."

His voice flat, Desseau muttered, "She died. My baby died."

"Ah, Julian, have faith! No, Elise is not listed among burial records. But we did find Mary Smithwick."

"*She's* dead?"

"Married. In mid-January in St. Alban's Church in Antwerp, Madeline Christophe married a Mr. Brazos Sinclair."

Dessau's brow furrowed. He stared at Corot and slowly shook his head. He'd never heard of the man before. "Brazos Sinclair. What do you know of this man?"

"He is a Texan."

Julian smiled grimly. "That should make tracing the woman easier. Texans tend to attract attention in Europe, not always favorable, but usually memorable. Was he part of the kidnapping?"

"That I cannot say," Corot answered, shrugging. "We only just discovered the marriage, and we are presently researching Sinclair. I knew you'd want to hear this new information we have concerning Elise's whereabouts as soon as possible."

Rising from his chair, Julian sighed and walked to the hearth. Two polished brass andirons shaped like ravens' heads supported oak and cedar logs that crackled and spat as they burned, filling the room with warmth and a pleasing aroma. He absently stirred the fire with a poker, then thumped a raven's head with a finger as he considered what he'd been told.

Perhaps he'd find his daughter, after all.

"There is something else," Corot commented, standing and stepping to the liquor cabinet to refill his drink.

Julian looked over his shoulder, his eyebrows lifted in question.

"Mary Smithwick is from England, not France, as she led you to believe. Prior to her arrival at Château St. Germaine, she resided in a boarding school for young women of means in Brighton. I followed this lead myself and spoke with the school's headmistress."

Corot returned to his seat and stretched out, crossing his legs at the ankles. "I tell you, Julian, the headmistress is an absolute terror. I do believe I'd have turned criminal myself if I'd been raised by the likes of Mistress Poggi."

Impatiently, Desseau gestured for the investigator to continue.

"The old harridan was only too pleased to talk as long as pound notes continued to paper her hand." Corot grinned, adding, "I'm spending an inordinate amount of money on this case. It's fortunate you have so much of it, my friend."

"Please, Pierre, get on with your story," Julian demanded. He paced to one of the large windows that looked out over the rose garden and fingered the heavy damask drapery as he listened.

"Mary Smithwick's family enrolled her in the school when she was little more than a baby. The child's mother provided sufficient funds to support the girl until she reached eleven years of age. She left the school at that time, returning some seven years later to accept a position as a teacher."

"Where was she in the intervening years?" Julian asked.

Corot shrugged. "That my investigator has yet to discover. But he will. 'Tis only a matter of time."

"Did she come to St. Germaine straight from England?" Julian asked, glancing over his shoulder.

"Yes. According to the blustering Mistress Poggi, Mary Smithwick received a letter from France one day and left the next. The old battle-ax wasn't too happy about it, either. It was right in the middle of a term."

Julian slammed a fist against the wall beside the window and bellowed, "How in the hell did my wife find this woman, this stealer of children? It makes no sense. Celeste knew no one in England; she'd never even traveled there. Why did she send for a stranger and then lie to me about it?"

The investigator absently studied the mural painted above the mantle and sipped his drink. Frowning, he asked, "Explain to me again, Julian, the circumstances under which Mary Smithwick came to Château St. Germaine."

"It was shortly before the baby was due," Julian said, scowling as he straightened the frame of a portrait his blow had jostled. "Celeste said she needed help and that Mistress Smithwick's name had come to her highly recommended." Hesitantly, he added, "My wife and I were experiencing difficulties in our marriage. I believed it was due in part to the coming baby. Celeste was emotional, withdrawn. I thought perhaps with a woman around, Celeste would feel better. I let her have her way."

He heard the bleakness in his voice as he looked at his friend and confessed, "It's my fault that Elise is gone. I allowed Celeste to pressure me into hiring the chit without personally checking her references. I believed Celeste when she told me that Mary Smithwick had served in some of the finest homes in France."

Corot shook his head. "Do not blame yourself, Julian. Celeste was expecting your child. You pampered her wishes, just as many a loving husband has done."

"Ah, but there's the difference," Julian replied, his knuckles whitening around the snifter of brandy, "I was not a loving husband. At least, not at first. I was a man bent upon revenge. I married Celeste because I hated her mother and wanted to hurt Bernadette Compton in the worst possible manner—by stealing away her daughter." He tossed back a drink, and the brandy burned his throat as hatred scorched his heart. "I've had experience with that type of grief."

Scowling, Corot studied his friend. "You've never recovered from your first daughter's disappearance, have you, Julian?"

Desseau stared into his empty glass. "A man never gets over losing a child, even after twenty years have passed. And the fact that there's never been a trace . . . we never found Nicole's body . . . it simply doesn't end. And now, to have the same thing happen with Elise . . ."

"It's not the same," Corot insisted. "We'll find Elise. We know who took her. We know where they went. It's just a matter of time, man. Give me and my men a little more time. Don't give up hope."

The anguish ravaging Julian's soul was reflected in his voice when he looked Pierre and asked, "Why? Why did she do it? What possessed Mary Smithwick to steal an innocent baby?"

Corot set his glass on the table beside his seat. "Julian, what about Celeste's mother? Could Bernadette Compton have something to do with this crime?"

"She's the first person I thought of. I'll always believe that she was behind whatever happened to Nicole. In my grief following the death of Nicole's mother, Anne, I was easy prey for a woman like Bernadette. She hated Nicole, and was a poor stepmother to her. That's something I'll always regret, that my daughter knew so little of a mother's love." He closed his eyes as remorse overcame him. Softly he added, "I waited so many years to remarry, and when Celeste told me we were expecting a child, I swore not to make the same mistakes as I had with Nicole. I wished so much more for Elise; it made my grief over Celeste's death that much more difficult to bear."

Corot stood and straightened his jacket. "I'll begin an investigation of Bernadette Compton immediately."

Julian waved a hand. "Sit back down, Pierre," he said, carrying the two empty glasses toward the cabinet. "There's no need to rush off. Even as I set you and your men upon Mary Smithwick's heels, I sent my own people after Bernadette. They will find her eventually, and I intend to question her quite thoroughly."

Corot eyed Julian, who tipped the brandy decanter and splashed the amber liquid into the snifters. "Don't kill her, Julian," Pierre said.

"Now, how could I possibly kill Bernadette Compton, or should I say, Bernadette Compton Desseau?" An evil smile stretched across Julian's face as he handed Corot his drink, then lifted his own glass in salute. "You know my beloved second wife, Bernadette, drowned at sea over twenty years ago. It would be rather redundant to kill someone who's been legally dead for years?"

MADELINE HAD LOST her perception of time. An hour had passed, maybe two. Enough time that she no longer gagged at the fetid stench permeating the hold. Long enough that she'd developed a craving for water. She was more uncomfortable than worried. Lillibet would look for her after Rose's nap, and when Madeline turned up missing, Lil would certainly suggest a search of the hold.

At first, Madeline hadn't been content to wait. She'd shouted for help until it pained her already hurting throat. Giving up on that, she'd talked to an unresponsive Brazos until her mouth was as dry as—no, she wouldn't think about the corpse. She wouldn't wonder as to its identity or worry over the sinister possibilities its presence suggested.

Instead, she'd continue to talk in gentle, soothing tones to the man who so recently almost choked her to death.

Brazos no longer rocked; he sat with his head buried against his knees. The only movement she noted was the frequent quiver of a muscle beneath her hand as she stroked him, her touch a constant offer of comfort.

"Oh, Brazos," she murmured softly. "You are a tortured man. I sensed you had secrets, but now . . ." Her voice trailed off. Madeline knew that his mysteries were of a different nature than those she kept confidential. The proof sat physically before her, and mentally, he was worlds away.

Yet, as he had shown her the night of the storm, her touch, the sound of her voice, must in some way reach through whatever terrors lived in his mind. She curled her fingers in his silky hair, and with her thumb wiped away a rivulet of sweat that dripped down the whisker-rough surface of his face. During the past hour, she'd given Brazos's situation considerable thought.

"You're not afraid of the dark, Brazos. I've heard you above deck on the blackest of nights talking and laughing with the sailors." Standing behind him, she massaged the tight muscles at his shoulders, gladdening at the slight give she felt beneath the linen as the tendons relaxed.

"I'm certain it has something to do with being inside closed places. You never go below deck, not even at midday, when the sun is shining and the lamps are lit. But you're not really *afraid* of enclosed spaces, are you? Fear isn't the proper word for what holds you in its grasp." Her fingers stilled, and her hands moved across his shoulders to his upper arms. Beneath her left hand, she felt the hard edge of the metal armband.

Madeline wrapped her arms around him, hugging him and saying, "Judging by your actions, I think it's something that goes beyond even terror."

She paused a moment, listening. Oh, how she wished that she'd get through to him, that he'd suddenly speak to her in a clear and rational voice. "I guess I shouldn't complain. At least, you're not choking me. That was the reason for the knife, wasn't it? You were afraid you'd hurt me."

Inside the circle of her arms he shuddered. She paused and listened, thinking for a moment he might have heard her. The air around them throbbed with ship sounds, but it was the silence here with her that sounded thunderous in her ears.

She detested it. She absolutely hated the way the cocky, egotistical, totally charming Texan had lost himself in this silent, wretched man.

"You hate it, too, don't you Brazos? That's what lay behind all that talk earlier. The apology, the gift." She stepped away from him and, in the darkness, crossed her arms and fussed. "You've no intention of changing your opinion about a woman's place in society, do you? It was all a scheme to get me to allow you into my bed!" She sniffed disdainfully, then wished she hadn't. She kept forgetting about the corpse.

Madeline sat beside Brazos. She wrapped an arm around his and said ruefully, "Actually, you presented a fine argument. You exploited my weaknesses. I'm impressed, Sinclair, I didn't think you had that sort of scheming in you. Of course, I undoubtedly have more practice at it than you, and I'd have determined your game in short order—probably when you went glassy-eyed hearing me talk about women's talents."

She chuckled softly, and the more she thought about it, the more intriguing the idea became. Brazos

Sinclair sharing a bunk with her each night. It offered interesting possibilities.

As she sat in the dark, Madeline's heart told her to help this poor man, to offer him the comfort of her bed, and the protection her company appeared to provide him. But Madeline had been a thief too long to listen only to her heart. She put her mind to work.

She knew what such an arrangement would bring Brazos, but what would it offer her? Her goals in life had not changed. She still wanted a real home and a family to love, including a wonderful father for Rose and any other children a marriage might bring.

Brazos Sinclair wasn't part of that dream. It shamed her to admit, but after she'd seen him like this, her opinion in that regard had only been reinforced.

So, in keeping with her long-standing rule of never giving without taking in return, if she allowed Brazos into her bed, what could she expect from him?

Money? Madeline shook her head. She didn't need money. Prestige or power in society might motivate others, but she'd no interest in them. "You tell me, Brazos. What do you have to offer a woman?"

Immediately, the memory of his naked body intertwined with hers flashed brilliant in her mind. "Not that. It's not exactly the sort of thing a woman can take to the bank." Besides, he'd said *platonically*. He'd made quite a point about it. An annoying point, in fact.

"You know, Brazos, you needn't have made such an issue about a physical relationship between us. I have quite specific goals about that also."

She leaned against him, rested her head on his shoulder. The steady rhythm of his heartbeat gave her comfort as she said in a dreamy tone of voice, "When I find my man, he'll love me desperately. It won't matter that I've another man's child I'll be bringing to the marriage. He won't care whether I'm wealthy or poor—of course, I'll be wealthy, but he won't necessarily know that. He'll be a romantic, and he'll woo me, and pursue me, and claim he's in agony with wanting before I finally allow him to marry me and carry me to the marriage bed. Then—"

Madeline stopped abruptly. She sat up straight and stared into the darkness. The idea had never occurred to her before. "At least, not where you're concerned, Brazos." She had always known she'd need to deal with the obstacle sometime. When she married for real, she didn't want her new husband to make any discoveries that would lead to uncomfortable questions. She had to protect Rose at all costs. But to use Brazos? Frowning in concentration, she said, "It is a problem, and it would be a solution." She turned and looked toward him, although she couldn't see him, nor he her. "We wouldn't have to tell anyone about it. Our Texas plans wouldn't have to change."

She lifted her hand to touch his face, brushing that independent lock of hair back off his forehead. If she pursued this plan of action, she wouldn't have to feel bad about giving and not taking.

And, a voice inside her whispered, *you could help him. It's what you really want, the other is an excuse.*

"No, it's not!" Madeline snapped. "This is a real problem, one I must deal with before I can marry the man of my dreams." She took Brazos's hand. "If you can hear me in there, Mr. Sinclair, I want you to know that I accept your offer. If we are ever rescued from this place, you are more than welcome to move into my bed." Because then, no matter what he intended, she'd convince him to make a minor adjustment in this platonic idea.

Madeline planned to use Brazos to rid her of this pesky problem called virginity.

A RATTLING AT the hatch woke Madeline from a light sleep. The door swung back, and sunlight poured through the casement, along with the strident sounds of Lillibet Brunet's voice.

"I tell you man, when I last saw her, Madame Sinclair planned to enter the hold. It's been almost two hours, and no one I can find has seen either her or her husband. She'd never leave her baby with me for that length of time without informing me of her intentions beforehand. You must remove that lock and open the hatch immediately!"

"Thank goodness!" Madeline exclaimed, relief rushing through her body as sunshine warmed her skin. Immediately she looked at Brazos. Light illuminated a ravaged face, and slowly he began to stir.

"What the hell—" he said hoarsely.

Lillibet peered down at them and squealed, "Oh, Madeline, Madeline. I knew it. I just knew you'd been trapped in that dank and dreary old hold. Bless your heart. Are you all right? Thank heavens you had Monsieur Sinclair to take care of you; otherwise, I imagine you'd have been scared to death."

The beam of light was a brilliant sword plunging into Brazos's eyes, burning into his mind and lighting the darkness within. Oh, Lord, it's happened again. Frozen in place at the foot of the stairs, he grimaced against the shame that flushed his body. She'd seen him like that.

A crew member stood beside the hatch, babbling questions and comments as he extended a hand to assist Brazos to the deck. Brazos ignored the man's scolding tone and tried to orient himself. He didn't remember. The steps, he'd gone down the steps. Then the void. That damnable darkness.

Brazos turned and grabbed Madeline's outstretched arm, pulling her up to stand beside him. He wouldn't, couldn't, meet her gaze. His grip on her hand was punishing, he knew. He forced his fingers to relax. What else happened down there? *Please, this time, just this one time, let me remember!*

The ship's captain approached. "Monsieur Sinclair, Madame Sinclair, I am relieved to see you both are well. I am aware that in their carelessness, two of my men left the hatch open. What I do not understand is why you and your wife entered my hold without permission, thereby risking your lives when my men belatedly returned and locked the door."

Brazos stiffened and cleared his throat, praying he'd be able to talk, when Madeline spoke up. "Captain,

I'm afraid it's all my fault. I went to retrieve my daughter's special toy, and Mr. Sinclair only came down when I discovered the . . ."

From the corner of his eye, Brazos noted Madeline's sharp glance. "Captain, I'm afraid we have made a terrible discovery," she said. "There is a man down there. He's dead."

Dead. Holy hell. Confusion, anger, and fear swirled around inside Brazos like a Texas twister as he searched the emptiness of his memory for an explanation. He strained to keep his expression impassive, but inside his mind was screaming, *What did I do?*

"What is this?" the captain demanded, fixing his stare on Brazos.

"Please, sir," Madeline asked, "if I may have a cup of water? Is my daughter all right? I need to see her, this has been such an ordeal. I must sit down." She tugged on Brazos's sleeve until he looked at her. She jerked her head toward a crate to their right, and he took her unsubtle hint, lifting her to sit upon it. His hands trembled.

The captain considered them for a moment then asked, "Where is this body?"

Madeline answered, "Near the foot of the steps. He's between two crates."

"Sailor, take a lantern and see below," the captain ordered the man who had opened the hatch. "Madame Brunet, if you would please bring Madame Sinclair her daughter?" He turned to another crewman, who watched the proceeding with interest. "Wilson, water for the Sinclairs."

As those addressed scrambled to do the captain's bidding, Brazos kept his hold on Madeline's waist. He looked past her shoulder, unwilling to see what knowledge lived in her eyes. Yet he continued to touch her. He feared that Madeline had become his lifeline to sanity.

The sound of the sailor ascending the steps rang a death knell in his ears. He was handed a cup of water just as the lantern held above the man's head broke the plane of the deck. He tossed back his drink as though it were the greenest of home-brewed beer and braced himself.

"Well?" the captain asked.

"Stowaway, sir. Must have run out of water. His tongue is as thick as a halyard."

I didn't kill him, Brazos realized, relief washing through him.

The captain muttered, "Desperate fool." Then, "Take Jenkins here and deal with the body."

The sailor snapped a salute as Lillibet rushed up with Rose in her arms. "Here she is, dearling, all ready for her mama." Madeline scrambled from the crate and enfolded the child in her arms. She raised misty eyes to the captain and asked, "Sir, may we go?"

He frowned. "I trust, Monsieur and Madame Sinclair, that in the future, you will restrict yourselves to the passenger areas of the *Uriel*?" After they nodded, he said, "Good. You may leave."

"Brazos?" Madeline said with surprise when he turned to leave her.

He refused to meet her eyes. "Take Rose to the cabin and get some rest, Madeline. I'll see you later." He took a step, but her hand on his sleeve stopped him. She stared at him with a challenge in her eyes.

"Yes, you will see me later. I agree to your proposition, Brazos Sinclair. Feel free to move your belongings into my cabin whenever you like. I'll be waiting for you tonight."

"Forget it," Brazos said, shaking off her touch. Hell, he was too embarrassed to even look at her. No way in hell could he crawl into bed with her. Not now.

Without looking back, he crossed the *Uriel*'s deck and stood beside the ship's railing. As he stared down at the frothy white splash churning beside the hull, he had the strange thought that perhaps his mind was like the sea: deep, dark, empty of humanity, teeming with a life of its own. Something, someone plagued him. It had been born in the bowels of Perote Prison, and it scared the bejabbers out of him.

YOU ARE RIGHT *to be afraid, Weak One. I live and breathe within you, like a tethered hellhound straining to be loosed upon the protected part of yourself. I am what you are, stripped of everything but the instinctive will to live. I am death and life from death. I know the secret that will be your death.*

Oh, Lucifer, I am hungry.

Chapter 6

The lantern on the wall swayed in its brass gimbal, the rhythmic squeak of comforting sound in the lonely cabin. Madeline lay awake, waiting for Brazos. She knew he'd find it harder to come to her, but she believed in the end he'd find it hard to stay away. Brazos would want company tonight, and she would be here for him.

The bed sheet rustled as she rolled onto her side. She tugged the satin binding of her blanket up to her chin and curled into a ball in an effort to keep warm. The night had grown bitter cold. "Good," she murmured. All the more reason for him to seek her bed. Then she'd offer him the comfort of her voice and of her touch, but she'd wait a few days to ask for something in return.

A good thief understood that preparation was simply part of the job.

It was after midnight when she heard the cabin door creak open. The smoky yellow glow of lantern light failed to soften the hard edges of Brazos's expression as he stood in the doorway, silently waiting.

Madeline reached up, twisted the latch on the porthole, and pushed it open. The dank fragrance of wet wood and the briny scent of the sea swept inside with the cold air.

He appeared almost angry as he took a short rope from his pocket and tied open the door. With jerky movements, he yanked off his boots and shrugged out of his shirt and pants. This time he wore long underwear beneath his clothing.

Madeline hid a smile as he climbed into bed beside her. Did he believe he went to war, did he sense this bed might become a battlefield? She thought of his insistent declaration, *Platonically, of course*. Perhaps a suit of armor made of cotton, dyed red, and soft as Rose's skin made him feel less vulnerable. Silly man.

They lay without touching or speaking until Brazos finally asked gruffly, "You want the light on or off?"

"Whichever you prefer." She heard his teeth grind together as he sat up and turned down the lamp wick. When he lay back down, Madeline snuggled next against him and fired her first salvo, saying, "I'm glad you came tonight. I've been thinking about home, and I'm a bit lonely. I'm really not in the mood to argue moral issues; I hope you don't mind."

Brazos was as stiff as Mistress Poggi's corset. A soft laugh escaped Madeline at the comparison. It must be his nearness; she'd best be careful, or soon she'd say something utterly Texan.

"What are you laughin' at?" he asked in a defensive tone.

"I was thinking about someone from home," she answered. "Well, it wasn't truly a home, just the place where I grew up. I was raised in a boarding school in England. The headmistress was terribly strict, and I was forever running afoul of her." After tugging her braid out from beneath his shoulder, Madeline related a brief story involving her, Lord Carruther's daughter, Regina, and a turkey destined for the dinner table that mysteriously disappeared. As she talked, she felt the stiffness begin to seep from his limbs.

"But the funny thing about it," she finished, "even

as I was misbehaving, I wished so badly to please her."

"Children do that," Brazos said.

"Really?"

"Yeah. And just because someone is an adult, that doesn't mean they're right to be supervisin' young'uns. Your Mistress Piggy sounds to me like she should've had another occupation."

"Mistress Poggi," Madeline repeated. "And she wasn't terrible to live with, just difficult. She meant well. She always tried to protect her charges." Madeline laughed again. "Once every fall and again in the spring, she would summon all the girls over the age of five and warn them about rakes and rogues." Because Brazos seemed to have relaxed, she dared to tease him. "Are you certain you're not acquainted with Beatrice Poggi, Brazos?"

He propped himself up on his elbows. "England? What part?"

"Brighton."

"Hmm, thirtyish, dark brown hair?"

"Sixty if she's a day, and she's been gray as long as I've known her."

"Well . . ." he sank back onto the mattress. "There was one older woman . . ."

Madeline punched him in the side and said, "You, sir, are a scoundrel."

"Yeah," he clasped her hand and held it against his chest. "And I'm proud of it, too."

They fell silent then, and Madeline felt cozy and warm as sleep stole over her. The last thing she heard before drifting off was Brazos's gentle whisper, "Thanks, Beauty."

The next few nights passed in a similar manner, and Madeline believed she was progressing splendidly toward her goal. Each morning she woke to find limbs intertwined, and invariably, his hand cupped either her breast or her buttock. Of course, as soon as he awoke, he was out the door in an instant.

But with each evening that passed, Brazos relaxed and opened up a little more. He even seem to listen to her ideas concerning the issue of women's equality.

Madeline had been surprised to learn that many of the problems women faced in Europe apparently were not issues of controversy in Texas. "On the frontier," Brazos had explained, "there are times when every warm body matters, and nobody checks to see whether that pair of helping hands is wearin' a dress."

She made no headway, however, when she argued that women were disenfranchised. "Women don't need to vote, Maddie," he'd claimed. "As a whole, women simply can't grasp the complex issues involved. Besides, they're free to express their opinions to their men." He'd grabbed the hand ready to hit him. "Now, stop that sputterin'. I said on the whole; I'll admit you have a good-size brain in your head." He'd flashed her a grin, kissed her knuckles, and winked at her. At that point, Madeline shut her mouth, rolled over, and went to sleep.

On the fourth night, the conversation took a surprising turn. He'd been telling her about Texas, describing the land in the section of the state where La Réunion would be built. They discussed the details of the Europeans' plan for building their Utopia, and Madeline mentioned she hoped to live in her own house.

"Where else would you be livin'?" Brazos asked. "Is ol' Emile gonna make you live with his mother or somthin'?"

"No, Brazos." Tonight the lantern inside the cabin remained lit, and his disgusted expression made Madeline smile. "The majority of the colonists will live in a *phalange*. It's like a large dormitory, and families will all live together."

"That's the dumbest thing I've ever heard." He lay with his hands clasped beneath his head, elbows outstretched. He slid her a look from the corner of his eyes and said, "But at least, you've some sense; you want your own house."

He rolled over to his side, facing her. She smelled the faint scent of brandy about him and that musky, masculine scent so uniquely his. His fingers lifted the end of her braid. "What kind of house do you want, Beauty?"

Madeline licked her suddenly dry lips. She

watched his fingers move across the twists in her hair, and she had trouble remembering what he had asked. "What?"

"A cabin made of wood? A mansion made of stone? What's the house of your dreams look like, Maddie?"

Immediately, the picture came to mind. She'd built this house a hundred times in her thoughts. How strange that Brazos would ask about it; he couldn't know how much this dream meant to her. She said, "It'll be comfortable. Not stone, that's too cold. My home will be warm and welcoming with a fireplace in every room. And flowers. Pink roses. I want pink roses planted beneath my windows."

"You're just like my mama. She's planted so many flowers in the gardens around the house that every spring my pa threatens to hunt up a perfumer to come harvest the crop."

Madeline heard the wistfulness in her voice as she asked, "Tell me about your family, Brazos. Are your parents nice people? Do you have any brothers or sisters?"

His eyes sparkled like sunlight on blue water. "I've the best folks in the world. My people are planters, mostly cotton, a little sugarcane, although Pa's real passion is horse racing. Mother's mission in life is to guard all her little chicks from harm, and believe me, with fourteen of us, not to mention all the grandchildren, she has plenty to keep herself busy. And on the rare occasions when all of the immediate family is doin' fine, there are always the cousins to see to. Yep, the rate my family's growin', soon there won't be a town in Texas that doesn't have at least one Sinclair livin' there."

Madeline could hardly speak past the lump in her throat. "You have thirteen siblings?"

He nodded. "Seven brothers, six sisters. We're split ten to four, married to not." He lifted his hand and gently brushed her bangs off of her forehead. "That's countin' me on the bachelor side. Anyway, by the time you add in all the children, there's a regular passel of us."

"How many nieces and nephews do you have?" Madeline asked, wondering if he had any idea just how lucky he was.

"Hmm. That's hard to keep up with." He frowned in concentration. "I'll name 'em. You keep count. John has Charles, Edward, and Mary Ann. Mark has Daniel and Sarah. Ann has Catherine, Michael, Holly, and Christopher. Mary has Joe and Molly." He paused and looked at Madeline. "You should see Molly. That girl's gonna be a beauty when she grows up, but I pity the man who tries to handle her. Hardheaded—I think she might could give you lessons, Maddie. Let's see, who am I forgettin'?" He nodded. "My brother Paul has Stephen, another Michael, and Christina. That's how many?"

"Fourteen."

"That sounds about right. Of course, by now, we could have a couple more. It's hard keepin' track when you're so far away."

"How long were you in Europe, Brazos?"

"Almost two years."

That surprised her. He didn't seem the sort of man to stay away from home for so long. "That's too much time to spend away from your family," she said, disapproval obvious in her tone. She must have struck a sensitive chord, because Brazos abruptly stiffened.

"Don't you think I tried to go home?" he snapped. "I *couldn't*, Madeline! Haven't you figured it out by now? I'm yellow through to the backbone to set foot aboard a goddamned ship."

"I didn't mean—"

"But I found out they're in trouble, big trouble. That's what it took to get me on the *Uriel*. My family needs me, Madeline. That's the reason I married you, why I walked aboard this floatin' hellhole, and how I came to be lyin' here wantin' you so badly that my teeth hurt and not doin' a damned thing about it." He roared as he repeated, "My family's in trouble, and they need me. Now, shut up and go to sleep!"

Her eyes were as round as an owl's at midnight. My heavens, she thought, watching the tick of muscle at his temple. There were depths to this man she had never suspected.

Madeline silently turned away, sensing his immediate relief. She needed to think. He'd said he wanted her. Wanted her so badly that his teeth hurt. For Brazos, that sounded like a lot. Well, her next step was obvious. She closed her eyes and prayed that sleep would come swiftly.

Tomorrow she'd do her utmost to seduce him. She couldn't wait for the morning to arrive.

Brazos lay awake well into the morning hours. Along with the usual nightly problem of convincing his body to ignore the proximity of such a beautiful, desirable woman, tonight he'd even more difficult problems to consider. While his worries concerning the children and Juanita always hovered at the edges of his mind, the conversation tonight had brought them roaring to the forefront of his thoughts.

As he heard the watch strike four bells, he hoped to hell that Salezan hadn't made the connection between him and St. Michael's Children's Home. The orphans had a hard enough lot in life, they didn't need some insane Mexican warlord using them in a plot of revenge.

But Brazos *was* worried. If Salezan discovered the link between Brazos and the children he considered family, the bastard wouldn't hesitate to use the innocents for his own nefarious purposes. Sighing, Brazos reached out to turn down the lamp. With Salezan so heavily on his mind, he could feel the terrors rumbling around inside him more strongly than usual. A slight tremble shook his bones as he settled back into bed.

He pulled Madeline close, hugging her tight, and his lips brushed a kiss at the nape of her neck. Eventually, surrounded by the fragrance of roses and the blanket of silken hair he'd loosened from its braid, Brazos found surcease in sleep.

WIND SWELLING ITS sails, the *Uriel* charged forward like a courser from the spur, meeting and defeating the mountains of waves that challenged her. She tossed from her timbers clouds of spray and foam, a high-mettled horse chomping and shaking the froth from the bit. Hovering above the horizon, clouds colored by the setting sun added to the majesty of the scene. The world was a living, breathing, dream of vermilion, gold, and aquamarine.

Brazos stood at the port bow and gazed at the sunset. Eyeing the palette of colors, he yearned for a bit of brown—the dull, dusty brown of dirt. Texas dirt. Dirt that remained motionless beneath his boots, solid and stable. "Damn, I want off this boat."

Grasping the smooth wooden railing, he stared down at the white foam churning in the ship's wake and gave a short, derisive laugh. After all those months in prison, who'd have figured he'd be pining after dirt? Of course, that had been Mexican dirt—a different thing entirely.

Texas dirt meant freedom for his body and his soul. It was a part of him, something he carried with him wherever he went. But the soil that clung to his heels was growing mighty thin, and it was time for another coat. "Dammit to hell, I want off this boat!"

"I'd suggest waiting until we're closer to land. The swim would be less strenuous."

Brazos looked over his shoulder and saw Madeline standing a few feet behind him. She was dressed in a formfitting gown of shimmering green silk, the décolletage cut lower than anything he'd seen her wear before. Even as his gaze locked on the tempting swell of her breasts, he cursed the sight of her. He should never have admitted to wanting her—somehow speaking the words made the near constant ache even more acute. Even harder to ignore.

As she approached him, he tried to tear his gaze away, but the gentle sway of her rounded hips captured his attention and led to the rise of more than mortification. He wanted her, badly, even though he knew the consequences would be disastrous. The hell of it was, he was just in the mood to go courting disaster.

She walked to his side and gazed out to sea. The

wind wrapped her floral scent around him, and he ruefully acknowledged that for the rest of his life the sight of a rose or the whiff of its fragrance would remind him of Madeline and her child. "Where's the baby?" he asked.

Madeline lifted her shoulders in a nervous shrug. "I took her to Lillibet early this evening. She was tired. She'd played hard today."

He nodded, and silence fell between them. He heard the gurgle of water against the *Uriel*'s bow, a burst of masculine laughter filtering up through the wide mouth of the wooden scoop that provided air to the lower decks, and the slightest, faintest rustle of silk from the woman beside him.

Sea mist billowed up above them, then floated down in an iridescent cloud, surrounding them with an air of isolation in a realm of fantasy. Brazos felt a strong and immediate surge of desire.

Droplets of water clung to the tips of Madeline's impossibly long eyelashes. Brazos caught them with his finger and softly said, "You're like a sea nymph risen from crystalline waters."

She trembled, though she tried to hide it. "Such pretty words. But you needn't make the effort, Brazos. I've known since I was a child just how I measured up with other girls, so you needn't attempt to humor me. At least let's be honest in that."

"Humor you?" he drawled, offended and amused at once. Really, the woman either thought next to nothing of herself or else was big on fishing for compliments. "Fine, darlin', you want honest, I'll give you honest. Watchin' you here on the deck of this ship in that shimmerin' green thing some folks might call a dress, I find myself wantin' to check you for scales. You sure you're not a mermaid, Maddie? A siren sent from the sea to lure me into trouble?"

"Brazos, I have serious doubts that anyone could ever lure you into anything."

Heat spread through the hollow of his chest. In a raspy voice, he replied, "Aw, Maddie, you obviously don't know the first thing about fishin'. When there's a trophy catch out there, a man finds it powerful hard to resist dangerous waters."

Her eyes went round, and she swallowed hard. "Oh."

He brushed her windblown hair away from her face with a gentle touch. "You see, Maddie, fishin' demands a number of a man's skills and fulfills so many of his needs." He brushed a feathery kiss across her lips.

Breathlessly she asked, "Skills?"

"Intelligence, for one. A man must know just how to bait his hook to attract the game he's pursuin'. In my case, I don't waste time fishin' for perch. You won't find a worm in my bag of tackle."

"What would I find?" The words seemed to escape Madeline's mouth.

In the waning daylight, Brazos saw her face wash red as the question hung between them. He knew better than to flirt with dark, dangerous waters, but a primitive need to challenge nature compelled him to continue the game. He chuckled and wrapped her tightly in his arms, pulling her flush against him. "I go after the trophies, like mermaids and sea nymphs, and for those a man has to fish deep. I use a strong pole, a hardy line, and bait that promises pleasure. Of course, many men can hook a prize, it's landing it that requires the stamina."

She pushed at his chest, and he released her. Silence lengthened between them as night stole slowly over the vessel. Finally, in a hesitant voice, she asked, "And you have endurance?"

He wanted to laugh, and he couldn't quite hide the teasing twinkle in his eyes as he gave her a slow smile and said, "Ah, honey, I'm good for hours. It's a fundamental, just like I told you, only some men are better at it than others." He captured her hand and pulled her back into his arms. "It's the battle and the conquest that make victory so sweet. And when you taste the fruits of your labor, well, that satisfies yet another need."

A faint whisper escaped her lips as Brazos bent his head and nibbled at her neck. In that moment, his amusement died. He looked at her and wanted as he'd never wanted before.

Bathed in the milky moonlight, Madeline seemed as mystical as the sea. Her skin glowed like the creamiest of pearls, and her smile had the promise of hidden treasure. But it was the look in her eyes, the mix of innocence and worldliness, that caught him in a tide of sensation so intense, Brazos thought he just might find drowning enjoyable. "Maddie," he said, "do us both a favor. Wiggle off this hook, now."

Madeline stepped away from him, took a deep breath, and smoothed her skirt with trembling hands. "Brazos," she said softly, "I don't want to."

He lifted his gaze to the foresail, billowed and straining, much like himself. Damn, he'd not believed she'd really do it. It gave him a sneaking suspicion that he wasn't the only one danglin' bait here tonight. Only he didn't plan on getting hooked.

His voice hoarse, he said, "No more games, mermaid. We can't do this. The annulment. We've gotta get an annulment. Go below, please."

In answer, she stepped into his embrace. "Divorce me, then, Brazos. But love me now."

He groaned and buried his face in her hair, smelling roses and salty seawater. She put her hand at the back of his neck, her touch a silent siren song.

Brazos slid his fingers down her cheek, tilted her head, and covered her mouth with his in an urgent, demanding kiss. He pressed his tongue through her lips, probing the softness inside, exploring the wine-sweet taste of her. Yanking the ribbon from her hair, he loosened her braid and spread the heavy tresses in a silky fan across her back.

She moaned against him, pressing herself tighter, bringing her hips into intimate contact with him. His hand drifted lower, molding to the curve of her bottom, and he pushed, grinding his aching hardness against the cradle of her femininity.

"Inside, we must go inside," she murmured as his lips left her mouth to trace a wet path down her throat toward the taunting swell of her breasts. She wiggled away and led him to the companionway.

Brazos stood there, his breath heaving as the heat pumped through his body, and he knew that he shouldn't go down those stairs. Madeline descended the first two steps. She reached for his hand and gently tugged. He stared down at her. Lighted by the soft glow of the wall lamp, she smiled at him, and her eyes made promises he wanted desperately to accept.

But he couldn't. They couldn't. Too much was at stake. Divorce? There had never been a divorce in his family before. He rasped, "Maddie, I can't—"

"—make love to me in public," she finished for him. "Please, Brazos. Come below with me. I'm losing my nerve here. You'll have to help me."

Brazos stepped down one stair, feeling the urgent need to bury himself inside her. He watched her float below, aching for her and knowing that he'd been bewitched. A grim smile stretched his lips. The dread of family scandal was no match for Madeline. The woman could charm the hallelujah from a preacher.

In a flash of movement, he was down the stairs, in her cabin, and lying atop her on the bunk. He took control, any doubts or fears locked away in a corner of his mind. Breathing ragged breaths, he quickly divested her of the green silk dress and feasted on the sight of dusky round nipples covered by a thin white film of batiste. "No corset, Madeline?" he murmured, and traced the circles with his tongue, dampening the fabric.

"Mmm," she sighed. "Not the thing for mermaids."

"With a tail like yours, you don't need one." He took the chemise between his teeth and ripped the fragile fabric, baring her breasts to his eyes. My God, she was beautiful. Achingly exquisite. The thought occurred to him to take things slower, but when he stripped away the last of her clothing and exposed her femininity to his view, he felt the little control he knew he had begin to wane.

His hands roamed over her body as he parted her legs with one thigh, and settled himself against her. He gazed into her eyes and felt a catch in his heart as said, "You're a wave weaver, Madeline."

She wriggled beneath him, sending flashes of fierce, intense need throughout his body. He sucked in a breath. He simply couldn't wait anymore. Backing away, he shrugged off his jacket and shirt, then kicked off his boots.

It was as his hands moved to the buttons of his pants that the sound of a voice raised in laughter broke through the whirlpool of his senses. Though the sound quickly died, the damage had been done.

Brazos had realized that the cabin door was closed.

His gaze darted for the porthole. Shut. *Oh, damn.* The walls, all four of them, moved closer. And the ceiling. His fingers froze with but a single button undone as his muscles clenched against the fear. He swallowed hard and grimaced as a wave of terror threatened to drown him. "Oh, God."

"Brazos?"

He yanked off his trousers and reached for her, frantically touching her, tasting her, seeking desperately to find an island of physical pleasure in this ocean of emotional pain. He felt the pressure pounding at the back of his eyes.

He felt pressure between his legs seep away. He grew soft. Useless.

Brazos's agonized voice groaned, "Oh, goddamn!"

Waves of humiliation rocked him as he rolled off of her, not daring to meet her gaze. He couldn't face the scorn he knew he'd see there. Keeping his back to her, he pulled on his pants. Grabbing his shirt and boots, he fled the room—and Madeline—without a word.

HE'D BEEN LIKE like a beast running away to privately lick his wounds. For a few moments, Madeline considered allowing him the opportunity and leaving him—for good. But her body continued to tingle from the touch of Brazos's hands and mouth, and her heart ached at the knowledge of having failed him—and herself.

She'd seen his expression the moment he'd noticed the stateroom's closed door. But what choice had there been? A woman didn't share herself with a man with the door standing wide open. Especially when it was her first time. If only she'd thought to open the porthole, maybe that would have been enough.

But she hadn't exactly been thinking straight at the time.

For that matter, if she'd been better at the entire business, maybe he'd never have noticed. "If I weren't a virgin, I'd have known what to do," she muttered. "I know I could be good at sex with a little practice. I do better at kissing every time." If only she could kiss the hurt and make it go away.

Maybe she could try. After all, what more could he do than send her away? "Wounded beasts are dangerous," she told herself as she dressed. But Brazos Sinclair had been both wounded and dangerous from the day she first met him. Besides, she was a thief. She had experience treading upon dangerous ground.

And she still had this virginity problem to take care of.

As she emerged onto the deck, she paused, listening to the sigh of the wind through the ropes and the rattle of the cross-timbers' metal rings. The ship sounds were different at night, more pronounced, but at the same time more comforting. It felt good. She found she needed some soothing tonight. Probably Brazos did too.

She located him in the stern of the ship this time, standing at the railing. He watched the foamy bubbles of the ship's wake fade toward the horizon, and something in his expression gave Madeline the idea he stared into his past. She wondered what horrors he saw. So she questioned him, "Brazos, I asked you before, but you wouldn't tell me. This time . . . well . . . I'm hurting, too. It doesn't exactly help a woman's ego to be abandoned at such a moment. I think you owe me an explanation."

He whispered a short, succinct curse. "Maddie,

with all of the men in your life, your ego oughta be as strong as a new well rope."

"You'd be surprised."

He shrugged. Minutes passed before he spoke, and when he did, his raspy voice betrayed no emotion.

"I had a friend, a very close friend, who was a priest. He and I were doin' a bit of prospecting down in South Texas not long after the Mexican War. We got ambushed by a bunch of renegade Mexican soldiers who took an interest in some cargo we were carryin'. They decided that their boss would want to question my friend and me, so they marched us to their headquarters, a prison a good ways south of the Rio Grande."

He stared at the scuffed toe of his black leather boots as he continued, "I'll never forget walkin' into that place. It actually had a moat, probably a hundred feet wide. We crossed a drawbridge leading to the only gate in the place.

"These huge carved figures flanked the gate like they were guarding the entrance. Strange-lookin' statues—wore this headdress-type of hat." He smiled ruefully as he glanced at her and said, "I know it sounds ridiculous, but something about them frightened me more than the walls or the guardhouses or the damned cannon."

His laugh sounded like a mean, cold wind. "I spent over two years in Perote. After the first couple of months they kept me in a cell they called The Hole." Briefly, he met Madeline's spellbound gaze. "I don't remember it, Maddie. I spent two years of my life in the dungeon of a Mexican prison, and I don't remember a goddamned minute of the entire time."

Abruptly, he stood. Shoving his hands in his pockets, he lifted his head and focused on the jibs. "You've probably figured this out by now after seeing me go crazy. I get scared, Maddie. I can't stand to be cooped up; the dark only makes it worse. It's not this bad on land, but there's just something about being on a ship surrounded by water that, well, it gets to me. I get lost in my own mind—somewhere awful."

Madeline stood and reached for him. "Brazos, I'm so sorry. I know it must be—"

"I don't want your pity, Madeline," he snapped, shaking off her touch and putting some distance between them. "I could tell you that . . . well . . . what happened to me in your cabin had never happened to me before. But you'd probably think I said that every time, so I won't bother. And as far as tonight goes, just forget it ever occurred. It shouldn't have then, and it's not goin' to again. I don't want a divorce. I want an annulment. They are simple and easy to get, and it can't happen soon enough to suit me."

He looked at her then, his eyes blue ice and his voice just as cold. "Now, I'd really appreciate it if you'd stay the hell away from me. I plan to do you the same favor. The nights are warmer. I'll be sleepin' on deck again from now on."

Madeline swayed as if his words had been a physical blow. Watching her, Brazos felt like a total bastard. An angry, humiliated, total bastard. A part of him—the part that wasn't raw and hurting—approved of the way she stiffened her spine and lifted her chin.

In a regal voice, she said, "Fine. I was quite growing tired of the way you continually stole my covers." She dipped her head in a prideful nod, then turned and walked away.

With his gaze following the gentle sway of her skirts, Brazos was tempted to call her back. He didn't.

And so he was left alone to deal with his demons and desires.

MADELINE ABANDONED the idea of using Brazos to rid her of her virginity and turned her attention to finding a husband, a permanent husband. Once she'd selected the man, she would then make a decision as to the best method of dealing with the problem of her chastity. It occurred to her that a medical solution might be possible, as well, and she decided to investigate the idea upon the *Uriel*'s arrival in Galveston.

As the weeks passed, she accepted that speculation concerning her relationship with Brazos Sinclair undoubtedly ran rampant in the 'tween decks, where most of the colonists made their berths. According to Lillibet, some of the wagers made concerning the status of her marriage of convenience had been collected upon. Everyone aboard ship understood that any relationship between Mr. and Mrs. Sinclair had ended. Her own behavior had clarified that fact.

Seventeen bachelors could be counted among the La Réunion colonists, and Madeline had made it her business to become acquainted with each of them. Having learned from her mistake, Madeline had contrived criteria for the next man in her life. No more reckless marriage proposals for her. Her next husband would share her vision of the future, not be grounded in the past. It wouldn't matter one little bit whether he made her blood race or not. To her dismay, Madeline discovered the need to remind herself repeatedly of that last part.

Every day, while Brazos claimed his playtime with Rose, she had strolled the deck with one bachelor and finagled a dinner invitation from another. Through these efforts, she'd become quite adept at flirting, although she made certain that her speech and actions remained well within the bounds of what was considered proper. Of course, considering that her fellow passengers were Fourierists, overstepping the boundaries of the New Amorous World would have been extremely difficult.

Truly, if she heard one more word about the higher order of erotic pleasure or the Court of Love, she would lock herself and Rose in her cabin for the rest of the voyage.

Madeline had thought that out of seventeen men, she could find at least one who shared her dream of home and family, and who respected the Fourierist principle of equality for women. She'd gone about her search methodically, and out of the field of available gentlemen, she had narrowed her choice to two: Monsieur Loupot, the botanist, and Monsieur Guyot, the mason. In the beginning, she'd had hopes for Monsieur Loupot. He was closer to her age than was Brazos Sinclair and, truth be told, more attractive. He didn't have that hard, angry look her husband possessed, and although his muscles weren't as well developed, the physical work that awaited them in Texas would take care of that.

He was a gentleman, educated and mannerly. He had all his teeth. She'd given him careful consideration until an incident with Rose had removed him from her list of potential husbands. Really, a man who bounces a baby on his knee should expect wet trousers.

Monsieur Guyot, too, had met most of her requirements. By the time she'd worked her way down the list to him, she'd realized she'd been comparing each of the bachelors with Brazos, and she'd sworn not to repeat her mistake. She made a determined effort not to compare a balding pate and a thick mane of overly long black hair.

But after the groping episode, she'd written Monsieur Guyot off also. He'd been such a boiled noodle when Brazos had suddenly appeared with that wicked-looking knife in his hand. Whittling, that's all it was. He'd been making something for Rose. Had Guyot stood up to her husband, she might have settled on the man then and there.

As it was, the *Uriel* was less than a week from Texas, and she had run out of bachelors. What was she to do?

BRAZOS KNEW WHAT he was going to do. As soon as the boat hit Galveston—right after he saw to the annulment—he was gonna find ol' Emile and tell him just what a fickle, unfaithful woman he'd picked to be the mother of his daughter. It had been a gradual decision, made sometime between Madeline's rendezvous with the Italian cobbler on the quarterdeck and the interlude with the French baker with the octopus arms.

Damn the woman for flinging her men in his face. Damn himself for caring.

Brazos prowled the deck of the *Uriel,* dodging the raindrops that dripped from the sails following an early morning squall. The wet pitch used as caulking between the deck planks gave loose an occasional scent of pine, bringing to mind the evergreens of the eastern Texas forests. He couldn't wait to get home. Soon now, just a few days if the winds held, they'd sail past the lighthouse on Bolivar Point and head into Galveston Bay.

Then he'd look up the Frenchman. "Emile," he muttered. "Just what sort of name is that anyway? Sounds like a flower." Brazos had always intended to check up on the man before saying good-bye to Madeline and Rose. He had his doubts about this fella's suitability as a father for Miss Magic. After all, what sort of man would run off to America, leaving a pregnant lover behind? Not one good enough for Rose; he'd bet his last bottle of French brandy on that.

Brazos almost tripped over a sailor scrubbing the deck with a holystone. "Sorry, mate," he said absently, his thoughts growing blacker by the moment. From the looks of things, Maddie didn't put much store in her European lover either. She'd up and said as much that one time—said if Emile didn't give her what she needed, she'd find a man who did.

"Maybe that's what she's doin'," Brazos wondered aloud when he caught a whiff of roasting chicken drifting up through one of the vents he passed by. "Maybe she's checkin' out her options." Surely, though, she could find better prospects than fellas like Loupot and Guyot.

Who, Sinclair? the voice inside him asked. *You?* He stopped short and loudly declared, "Not hardly." It earned him a puzzled look from the sailor cleaning the deck. "My days as a married man are near over—just a quick legal document, a couple of signatures, and a brief appearance before Cousin Judge Miram P. Tate, and Madeline Christophe Sinclair can shorten her name by two full syllables!"

Why, then, he wondered as the sailor picked up his

holystone and scuttled away, throwing an anxious look over his shoulder, did he feel like he had a clod of mud in his churn?

CHÂTEAU ST. GERMAINE

The vulgarity of the woman's speech, a varied spattering of English, French, and Italian, alerted Julian that his visitor had arrived, kicking and cursing, as he had anticipated. Bernadette Compton likely feared for her life, because the terms of their twenty-odd year pact had been quite specific.

The illegality of divorce in France had left Julian with few options for ending his marriage to the betraying bitch. The quickest and simplest way had been for Bernadette to die. He'd considered killing her outright; in truth, he'd come quite close to doing so. But after a bit of soul-searching, he'd chosen to fake her death instead. In return for her compliance with the plan, Bernadette received both a large sum of money and the promise that were she ever to set foot on St. Germaine again, Julian would, in fact, kill her.

"I never envisioned that I'd be the one to bring her back," Julian murmured, stirring the fire in his library. He remembered the emotions as though it had all happened yesterday—the rage, the anguish, and the love.

Yes, once he had loved Bernadette above all else. And in his heart, he knew that his daughter Nicole had suffered for it—died because of it. Which meant *he* was ultimately responsible.

Julian twirled the brass poker in his hand. Was that the reason he'd never taken Bernadette's life despite his longing to do so? Was it his own guilt holding him back? Or had he always harbored the hope that she'd come to him with news of Nicole?

Had Elise now paid for that futile wish?

"It is time I found out." Julian returned the poker to its stand. If he chose to end Bernadette's life this night, he'd not use a weapon like a fireplace tool. He'd use his hands.

Julian was smiling as he left the library.

Upon her arrival, as per his instructions, Bernadette had been escorted directly to his bedroom suite. Conducting this interview under such circumstances implied a threat he hoped might put her off balance. He stood outside the door for a moment, drew a deep breath, and straightened his lapels. Exhaling in a rush, he twisted the key in the lock and opened the door.

She was as beautiful as ever. More than twenty years had passed since he last had seen this woman, but time had worn few wrinkles upon her face. Her ivory skin glowed with a false youth, and her hair remained a golden halo around her head. He gazed into her eyes, recognized the wickedness, and wondered how he ever had been so blind.

He'd taken one look at this dazzling woman and forgotten his grief for two-year-old Nicole's mother, his beloved first wife, Anne, who'd died giving birth to a stillborn son. For an entire year, he'd allowed Bernadette to push Nicole from his life, and after his daughter disappeared, he'd clung to this woman in his pain. Only when he witnessed her betrayal firsthand did he recognize her for the deceiver that she was.

Hatred stimulated the syrupy tone of his voice as he walked into the room and said, "Ah, Mère, I am so pleased you could join me."

"I am not your mother."

"That is true, you were never my mother," Julian replied, nodding. "You were my wife. You realize, don't you, Bernadette, that I have had three wives in my lifetime? Two of them are dead, and because they died in childbirth, it could well be argued that I killed them. That is something you should probably remember during your visit to St. Germaine."

Bernadette tossed her head and straightened, lifting her chest in silent invitation. "Is that why you brought me here? Is it a child that you want? Are you telling me you plan to rape me until I swell with your child?"

Thoughtfully, he studied her, his gaze making a slow perusal of her assets. Then he sighed and said, "My dear mother-in-law. I wouldn't touch you with the stable dog's cock. Besides, you're too old to bear children." Ignoring her gasp of rage, he continued, "I'm telling you to take care. I'm closer than I've ever been before to wrapping my fingers around your neck and choking the life from you."

"What do you want, Julian?" Bernadette demanded, struggling against the ropes tying her wrists and ankles.

He turned abruptly and walked to the armoire, where he deliberately removed his jacket and stock. Putting them away he said casually, "Family matters, one might say. We do have such close ties. You were Celeste's mother. You are her daughter's—my daughter's—grandmother." The chill of the Alpine winter seeped into his voice as he looked over his shoulder and demanded, "Tell me, Bernadette, what have you done with my child?"

Suddenly, she stilled. A wary expression entered her eyes as she asked, "What do you mean?"

"Where is Elise?"

"Elise! Celeste's daughter? What has happened to her?" She laughed spitefully and said, "Don't tell me you've misplaced another of your daughters, Julian."

He whirled and was upon her in an instant. Grabbing her chin in a cruel grip, he forced her to meet the rage of his gaze. "So help me God, I'll kill you here and now, bitch."

Bernadette read the honesty of his words in his gaze and knew she must convince him of her innocence. Her lies must be well told. So she began with the truth. "I don't know where she is. I know nothing of what has happened here since my Celeste died."

He put his hands on the arms of the chair and loomed over her. "What about before? The nursemaid, Mary Smithwick. Did she work for you? Did you instruct her to kidnap my child?"

"No! I never cared about that baby!" That, too, was true. Though Bernadette had worked to destroy

Julian's marriage from the day she had learned he'd wed her daughter, her plans never included the child. The Smithwick chit must have thought that one up all on her own. Or Celeste may have helped. By the time Celeste died, Bernadette had managed to destroy the love her daughter had felt for Julian Desseau. Celeste might well have enlisted Mary Smithwick's help in wresting the baby away from its father. How delicious, really. She held his gaze and spoke with utter sincerity. "Believe me, Julian, I have no idea where your daughter is."

He pushed away from the chair and walked to the window, where he stared out across the rose garden. Fingering the heavy damask drapery, he asked softly, "Either of them, Bernadette?"

"Bah, Julian, give it up. It's Nicole again, isn't it? It always has been Nicole. You did it all because you suspected me, didn't you?" Venom dripped from her voice as she said, "It was revenge."

Julian turned and offered her an evil smile. "You figured that out, did you? And it worked quite well. Celeste loved me, more than she loved you."

Had Bernadette been free, she'd have spat in his face. Rage made her careless. "Just for a time, Julian. I won in the end. Celeste didn't love you when she died, did she? She hated you, and she was afraid of you."

"It *was* you!" Three strides brought him to her. He grabbed at her hair, pulled her braid free of its pins, and wrapped the coil around his fist. Tears stung Bernadette's eyes as he yanked and demanded, "What did you do, bitch?"

"Celeste! I wanted Celeste back. That's why I told her—" She snapped her mouth shut. She'd said entirely too much as it was. She couldn't tell him about the Smithwick chit.

He truly would kill her then.

Julian loosened her chin and with a finger, traced a line across her throat, the edge of his nail mimicking a knife slash. In a frigid voice, he quietly asked, "Told her what?"

A heady sense of power came over Bernadette. This was it, what she had planned for. Let him hurt her;

she didn't care. The moment was at hand for Julian Desseau to learn the price of vengeance. "Celeste was the one person in my life whom I loved, who loved me in return."

"What did you tell her!"

"Then you spoiled it for me." Tears spilled from her eyes and rolled down her face. "You took her from me. Well, I showed you, didn't I? I stole Celeste back from you."

Eyes blazing, Julian grabbed Bernadette by the shoulders and shook her. "God damn you, bitch! Talk to me."

She cackled like the wickedest of witches. "I told her your secret, Julian. I told her the truth."

"What truth?" he demanded.

"I told her that you and I were married. I told her that you banished me from St. Germaine while I was carrying your heir, and that you told all of France that I had died."

He slapped her, hard.

Blood seeped from the corner of her mouth as she smiled crookedly and said, "I told Celeste, Julian, that you were her father."

Chapter 7

Ripples of anticipation rolled across the *Uriel*'s main deck as the La Réunion colonists awaited landfall at Galveston, Texas. Passengers crowded shoulder to shoulder and chattered in a mix of English and French, sharing their excitement, their trepidations, and their thankfulness for having safely reached the end of this leg of their journey.

From her position toward the ship's bow, Madeline watched as large flocks of diving white gulls fed on jumping shrimp, the occasional splash and roll on the surface confirming the feast was being shared both above and below the waters of the bay. As the city's buildings came into view, she snuggled Rose close and murmured into her ear, "Well, darling, here we are. A new land, a new life. I promise you I'll do my best to see you safe and happy. I swore as much to your mother, and I swear it to you now."

Tears stung her eyes at the memory of Celeste, so weak and pale as she lay dying. So afraid, but not of death. Celeste Desseau had feared her husband, her emotions a confused collection of love and hate. She'd confessed to Madeline her greatest shame, that despite having learned the awful truth, she couldn't kill the tenderness she felt in her heart for Julian Desseau.

Then, she'd confessed her greatest fear, that Julian would someday use Elise in the same evil, wicked way he had used Celeste.

Madeline had wanted to confront him, to bring all the secrets into the light of day. Celeste had flatly refused. She claimed to fear what Julian would do when challenged with the dreadful facts. Madeline believed the dying woman clung to the faint hope that the story was all a lie, and that Celeste desperately needed to take that hope to the grave. She'd done exactly that, after extracting from Madeline the promise to protect at all costs the daughter she was leaving behind.

Rose's delighted laughter broke through Madeline's reverie, and through watery eyes, Madeline watched the nervous winging of waterfowl whose antics entertained the child. The thoughts of her past and the impending arrival of her future made Madeline more than a little nervous herself. As a result, her palms itched. Before she quite knew what had happened, she'd slid up to Monsieur Thevenet, slipped her hand into his pocket, and relieved him of his purse.

Almost immediately, she returned it. Madeline had promised herself never to take from her fellow colonists—it was a matter of honor. But old habits brought comfort in times of need, and the familiar action had succeeded in calming Madeline's overwrought nerves. Until she suddenly realized that, for the first time in her life, she had returned something she had stolen.

The idea made her shiver. What in the world was wrong with her? Next thing she knew, she'd be returning the penknife she'd snatched from Brazos Sinclair's bedroll a week ago.

The uneasy sensation in her stomach grew. She looked over her shoulder and almost moaned aloud. Speak of the devil. Brazos Sinclair was watching her. He began to thread his way toward her through the swarm of people. Had he noticed her sleight of hand?

"Wonderful," Madeline muttered. He doesn't pay her a bit of attention for days on end, but let her do something a tiny bit questionable, and there he was. If he had noticed the theft, would he put it together with the loss of his knife? His gun? That crystal swan he'd stored in that gift box, or any of the other items she'd acquired from him over the last few weeks? "I'll bribe him with his pocket watch if I must," she quietly told Rose, who was happily chewing on a teething ring Brazos had fashioned for her out of wood and leather.

That's right, Madeline, she scolded herself. Why don't you just return everything while you're about it. At that rate, you'll soon be taking Rose back to Julian.

A hollow roar blasted her ears and shook her bones. She started, and Rose began to cry. Dazedly, Madeline realized that a steamboat's whistle was announcing its presence off the *Uriel*'s starboard bow.

Brazos arrived and calmly took Rose from Madeline's arms, laid her against his shoulder, and began patting her back. "Listen, sweetheart," he said when the baby had quieted. "Hear the calliope?" Turning to Madeline, he added, "Makes me feel like a kid myself to hear a calliope play."

Madeline flicked an imaginary bit of dust from the sleeve of her brown velvet traveling cape. During the past few weeks conversation between her and Brazos had been both minimal and uncomfortable. While he never referred to either his last visit to her cabin or the harsh words he'd spoken later, both incidents hovered in the air between them like a swarm of mosquitoes lighting every so often to bite. "Life makes you feel like a child, Brazos," she finally replied. "Do you think you'll ever grow up?"

"Not if I can help it." Brazos waved the baby's arm in time with the music drifting across the water. He had donned gentleman's attire, a black frock coat over a ruffled shirtfront and red brocade vest. Madeline was surprised he owned such clothing.

Beneath the wide brim of his hat, his eyes gleamed

like sapphires, and her nervousness returned in a rush. Surely, had he noticed her pick that pocket, he'd have mentioned it right away. Or maybe he toyed with her. Brazos Sinclair was one to play games; it'd be just like him. But he didn't appear playful today, and that made her extra nervous. Brazos looked downright dangerous.

She surreptitiously stole a handkerchief from his jacket pocket as she said, "I wish I could adopt a perspective like yours. I'm nervous, Brazos. This is quite an occasion for me and Rose. Our first glimpse of America."

One corner of his mouth lifted in a rueful grin. "Officially, this land might be America, Maddie," Brazos said, obliging as Rose indicated she wished to return to Madeline's arms. "But to those of us born here, it'll always be Texas first. Wait till you see my home, Beauty. It's wild and free, with an endless sky—and unlike the folks where you come from, Texans care more about the character of a man than what his surname is or what he has named his house."

Madeline thought of the boarding school where society daughters had little tolerance for an orphan girl with no family title. She said, "Texas sounds like a nice place."

"It's home," Brazos said simply. Home. Family. Country. Texas. The single word held a wealth of meaning. He'd been a boy when Texas had declared its independence from Mexico. He'd become a man a few short months later, when he first killed in defense of the struggling republic. After a decade of independence, his country had embraced statehood and joined the Union, and Brazos had supported the move. But those ten years of sovereignty had left their mark on the people of Texas, himself included, and he believed that for years to come, Texans would be turned a little different than other Americans.

He glanced at Madeline, who stood at his side, her daughter in her arms. She'd been his wife for seven weeks, slept with him, laughed with him, and seen him at his worst. She was a light-skirt, a conniving bit of fluff with ridiculous beliefs—women's equality, really—but he had to admit he'd miss having her around. He reached out a finger to tickle Rose beneath the chin. And Miss Magic . . . well . . . she'd forever hold a special place within his heart.

How would life on the Texas frontier treat Madeline and Rose and his European friends? From what they had said during the voyage, few of them realized the enormity of the challenge they faced. Brazos had his doubts that La Réunion would ever become a reality.

And what of good old Emile? Would he be a good husband and father? Brazos's plans hadn't changed; he still intended to investigate the man. Just what he'd do if he didn't like what he discovered, Brazos hadn't quite figured out. It'd be better for everyone if the Frenchman turned out to be a man who sat tall in the saddle.

Knowing that, he was surprised at the surge of jealousy that prompted him to say, "The newspaper will carry word that our quarantine is over and that we'll arrive today. He'll most likely be there to meet the boat."

"Who?" Madeline asked, busy with wrestling a bootie back onto Rose's foot.

He stared at her, one corner of his mouth lifted in a disgusted smile. "I swear, woman," he answered, shaking his head. "It must take some real work on your part to be so good at forgettin' a man. I almost pity your Emile. I'm sure I wouldn't be too happy if my wife had spent her time steppin' out with other men all the way from Antwerp to Galveston."

Madeline said drolly, "Your wife did spend her time with other men, Brazos."

He chuckled. "Yeah, I guess you're right. If I thought about it, I probably wouldn't be too happy, either. You're a fickle woman, Madeline. It's a good thing we're not in this marriage for the long haul—I'd end up killin' some poor fool for takin' a shine to you."

Her answering smile wavered a bit, and Brazos realized he'd brought up the subject he'd been dancing around all morning. He scowled as he watched her lift her chin and ask, "How shall we tend to the arrangements, Brazos? The annulment will, or course, be the first order of business when we disembark."

"Of course." Brazos looked out over the water toward the rooftops of Galveston's business district. His hands gripped the railing as he said, "While you have your reunion with your Emile, I figure to head on over to King and Associates and look up a lawyer. He can draw up the papers, and we can meet later this afternoon to sign them. I've a connection with a judge, and most likely you'll be free to marry Rose's father this very evenin' if it suits you."

Madeline shuddered at the thought. *If he only knew.* Hesitantly, she began, "Brazos, I want to thank you for all—"

He cut her off. "Never mind, Maddie. It worked out fine for both of us. We'll be dockin' in a few moments, so why don't we get in line. I'm gonna be first man off this boat if I have to jump the sides to do it."

He ended up being the twenty-second passenger in line to disembark, and he grumbled the entire length of the wait. Madeline ignored his grousing as she watched roustabouts secure the hawsers as the *Uriel* docked at the Port of Galveston.

Brazos heaved a grateful sigh when the gangplank was lowered to form a bridge to the land. He shut his eyes and exclaimed, "Thank God!"

The line began to move, slowly, and frustration radiated from Brazos in waves. His muttering grew louder and more demanding. Madeline laid a restraining hand on his arm and in a wry tone said, "Really, Moses, this is not the Red Sea."

He showed her a snarl, but amusement sparkled in his eyes. "Your mother is such a wit, Miss Magic," he said, flicking the strings of Rose's bonnet with his finger. Then he lifted Madeline's hand and tucked it around his arm. "Come on. Help me encourage these folks into movin' before their shadows fall asleep."

Somehow, they made it to the gangplank without inciting a riot, and after seven weeks at sea, Madeline crossed onto dry land. She promptly stumbled into her husband's arms.

"Whoa there, girl. Don't drop the baby!" Brazos steadied her, saying, "Hold on a minute, Maddie. You'll get your land legs back right quick."

Cautiously, she stepped away from him. The ground swayed a bit, but she managed to remain standing. She noticed Brazos was having a little trouble of his own. "Does grinding your feet into the dirt help?"

Grinning, he shook his head. "Nope. I'm just doin' somethin' I promised myself I'd do. Gettin' a good coat of Texas on my boots. Brings me luck, Maddie."

Madeline stared at him a moment. Then she nodded and lowered Rose to the ground, allowing the child's kicking feet to stir up the sandy soil. Next, she scuffed her own shoes.

Brazos's eyes filled with a bittersweet tenderness as he looked at her and said, "That's the way, Beauty. Welcome to Texas. I wish you and Miss Magic all the luck in the world." Then he leaned over and kissed her.

Her knees threatened to buckle as his lips moved like a gentle breeze over hers. He pulled back for just a moment; then she heard him mutter, "Oh, hell."

His mouth crushed hers. He lifted Rose from her arms and held the child securely in one arm as he pulled Madeline close with the other. Vaguely, she heard the exclamations in French, the cheers in English, and the catcalls that were the same in any language.

He kissed her soundly, thoroughly, with a hint of desperation and the taste of good-bye. Madeline lost herself in the pleasure, meeting his stroking tongue with her own, answering him with an honesty her words never allowed.

Until a particularly grating shriek pierced the haze of her desire. "Brazos!" a woman's voice exclaimed. "Sin . . . Sin is that you?"

He broke off the kiss. Madeline stepped away just as a woman with bright red hair and a bosom you could set bottles on launched herself at Brazos, squealing, "Oh, my Lord, Sin has finally returned to Galveston!"

"Trixie," he answered, laughing as he handed Rose back to Madeline. "That old joke is gettin' down-right moldy."

Madeline's spine snapped straight as he bent his head and kissed the woman just as he'd kissed her only a moment before. Madeline muttered, "Welcome to Texas, my . . ." She closed her mouth before Rose heard a word she shouldn't be learning.

TRIXIE WALLACE SIMPLY loved men. She loved the rumbling timber of a male voice. She loved the scratch of whiskers on her skin. She loved the earthy, musky scent of a man and the salty taste of his skin when covered with a fine sheen of sweat during physical exertion. Trixie especially loved the raw power of male muscle flexing beneath her touch.

That was why she continued to work, selectively and enthusiastically, long after basic survival required she do so. She enjoyed being a whore because she loved men, and the one man she loved above all others was Brazos "Sin" Sinclair. And although the love they shared was strictly platonic, that didn't stop her from enjoying a kiss or two now and then.

Wrapped in his very public embrace, she sensed the disapproval of the crowd milling along the wharf and dismissed it. She never had, and never would, seek approval from a society that denounced her by day and sought her company by night. Brazos Sinclair had never condemned her for anything.

"Damn you, woman, you get prettier every day," Brazos said, drawing back and looking her over from head to toe.

"Sin, I *do* like the way you kiss," she answered. Smiling, Trixie held Brazos's face between her hands and studied him. The tiny scar over his left eyebrow was new. His skin showed evidence of exposure to sun and sea. The twinkling blue eyes hadn't changed, however. He loved her still. "I was beginning to think you'd never come home, honey."

"Don't tell me things have gotten so bad, you've taken to workin' the waterfront, Trix," Brazos said wryly. "Is business at the Club that bad?"

Trixie's laugh rang out above the sounds of vendors hawking their wares and cotton planters arguing the latest news from points east. "If I'd known there were men like you hangin' around these docks, I'd have tried them long before now." She tucked her arm through his and pulled him toward a waiting barouche, saying, "One of our girls is due to arrive on the New Orleans steamer today. I brought the buggy down to give her a lift home. But I'd rather give you a ride, Sin. Where were you headed?"

He stopped short. "Madeline!"

"Madeline?"

Brazos pounded his forehead with his palm, then slowly looked over his shoulder and searched the thinning crowed with a wincing gaze. "She's gone." His gaze darted back and forth, hunting. "Aw, dammit all, she's gone!"

"Who's gone, darlin? That woman you were with?"

He nodded, and the sense of loss seemed to kick him in the gut. "He must have been here to meet her. I missed it. Damn, I wanted to see how he acted when he saw them. I wanted to see how he greeted Rose!"

"Rose?"

"My Miss Magic," Brazos answered, hurrying toward the line of carriages for hire. He found the Santerres, the Reverchons, and the Lanottis. He asked the Frichots, the Coirets, and the Brunets if they'd seen where Madeline had gone. "Go on, Mr. Sinclair," Lillibet replied, wrinkling her nose in disgust. "After that public display you indulged in, you've no right at all to question my dear Madeline." She looked pointedly at Trixie, sniffed, and said, "I'm sure that right now, Madeline can do without the dubious pleasure of your company."

She moved to snap shut the carriage's window curtain, but Trixie extended a hand to hold it open.

"Don't get your bloomers in a bind, deary. You needn't worry. Sin and I are family."

"That's right, Lillibet," Brazos hastened to agree. "I'd like you to meet my cousin, Trixie Wallace."

Trixie gave him a questioning look. "What is the connection, Sin? I never can quite remember."

He shrugged, frowning. "I forget. I'll have to ask my mother when I see her. I think it's kissin' cousins on Pa's side, three times removed."

"What does that mean?" Lillibet asked.

Trixie patted Lillibet's hand, saying, "Honey, let me give you some advice. Half the folks in Texas are related to the Sinclairs one way or another. Now, why don't you help out my poor cousin, and tell him what he wants to know."

Lillibet remained stubbornly silent, but André leaned forward and said, "Madeline spoke with my tight-lipped wife, here, Brazos, then got into a carriage and left."

"Was a man with her?"

Brunet shrugged. "I'm sorry, I didn't notice. I was helping Lillibet with Thomas."

"Who is tired and needs to be settled down for his nap," Lillibet interjected. "Please excuse us, Mr. Sinclair." She leaned forward and instructed the driver to take them to the Powhattan Hotel.

As the carriage creaked away toward the center of town, Brazos realized he knew where to find Madeline—if not right now, then later. Even if Emile planned to house his family wherever he was living, Madeline would still need to take Rose to Lillibet. "Thank God, the child's not totally weaned," he muttered. Then he thought about Maddie and her Emile together and alone, and his mood darkened like a bushel of wet coal. "Come on, Trixie. Buy me a drink. I reckon I'm in no rush, as Tyler's probably at lunch already. Anything but French brandy, all right?"

She took his arm, and her expression wrinkled with concern. "Sin, honey, what's wrong? Who is that woman?"

"We didn't even discuss where and when to meet to sign the papers. Now that I think about it, she'd a helluva nerve runnin' off like that." Brazos glanced around the wharves one last time, then followed Trixie to her carriage. Stepping up into it, he nodded at the driver and finally answered her question. "Her name is Madeline, Trix. And until I get over to Tyler's and take care of a bit of business, she's my wife."

"Your wife!"

"Yeah. And she's probably tippin' her fiancé even as we speak."

"Her fiancé?" Trixie shook her head. "Oh, Sin, it sounds to me as if you've quite a story to tell."

Brazos grimaced. The last thing he wanted to do was to tell this tale. Some parts of it he would never share with another soul—although if he were to tell anyone about the difficulties he'd experienced in Madeline's cabin, it would probably be Trixie.

Simple arithmetic meant that Trix might well have run across a similar thing once or twice. "Maybe you'd have some advice for me," he murmured.

"Hmm?" she asked, turning her head to smile at him. "Advice about what?"

Advice. Advice. The word echoed in his mind. There was another person to whom he could risk relating this particular story. Dr. Louis Castillon. Brazos would have to go see him while he was in Galveston. Although he'd written a doctor a letter detailing some of the Swiss physician's recommendations, Brazos had promised to provide the old family friend a full report upon his return to Texas.

As Trixie's carriage drove down Market Street, Brazos caught from the corner of his eye a glimpse of a golden-haired woman on the arm of a tall, dark-haired man. Brazos twisted around for a better look.

No, it wasn't Maddie and her flowery Emile. But the sight brought back to the forefront of his thoughts a vision of Madeline saying hello to her Frenchman in an extremely personal manner. Brazos made his decision. "I've changed my mind, Trixie. Drop me off at Louis Castillon's office, would you? I'll be by for that drink later on."

Trixie offered him a compassionate look. She patted his knee. "Of course, darlin'. I know that Louis has been waiting anxiously to speak with you."

Hell, Brazos thought. Does everyone in this dad-blamed town know why I went to Europe?

No, that voice within him answered, but everyone in your family has been worried sick about you since you returned from Mexico.

The carriage rolled to a stop at the Castillon home. Semiretired, Louis treated his patients in an office on the first floor, and as Brazos made his way along the familiar stone path leading to the front porch, the futility of the trip to Europe, the fact of two wasted years, rolled over him like a black tide. As he knocked on the doctor's door, he softly cursed, "God damn the bastard. God damn Damasso Salezan."

MADELINE BOUNCED ROSE on her knees as she sat waiting in a carved mahogany ladies' chair in the office of Melbourne P. King, attorney-at-law. Since Brazos was otherwise occupied, she'd decided to take care of this little matter of an annulment herself. She'd thought it best to leave before he decided to wait around to meet her phantom fiancé.

Then, too she'd found she couldn't stomach witnessing for another moment the public display he'd put on with that—woman.

The lawyer entered his office and sat behind his desk. After short introductions, Madeline stated her business. He pulled at the tip of his neatly trimmed mustache, looked over the rims of his wire spectacles at his prospective client, and said, "Mrs. Sinclair, I'm afraid I can't possibly draw up this type of agreement without your husband's consent."

Madeline wanted to hit him. The sooner I get to La Réunion, the better, she told herself. Pasting a false smile upon her face, she took a leather ball from her reticule and handed it to a squirming Rose as she said, "He'll be here shortly. I'm afraid he was unavoidably detained. While I understand that you cannot possibly accept a mere woman's word for the need for this document, I'd like to provide the information for the drafting of the paper. It will speed things up when my husband arrives, don't you see?"

"This is quite irregular, but very well. I shall need some particulars." King pulled a sheet of paper from a desk drawer, inked his pen, and began, "Your full name, madam?"

"Madeline Christophe Sinclair."

"Your husband's?"

"Brazos Sinclair."

The lawyer lifted his gaze from the paper. Madeline shifted Rose from one knee to the other as she noted puzzlement written upon his face. "May I inquire, Mrs. Sinclair, how it is you chose this particular office for your legal needs?"

She leaned forward in her chair and asked, "Is something wrong, sir?"

He thrummed his fingers on the polished top of his desk and said, "Did your husband request my services, or those of my partner?"

Rose dropped the ball and began to cry. Madeline considered joining in. "What does it matter? Mr. King, we need a document drawn up. My husband mentioned your firm; therefore, I assumed you'd be the one to do the work." King stood and retrieved the toy. He handed it to Rose as Madeline continued, "Personally, I don't care if the governor himself drafts the paper. I simply want my annulment!"

King pushed his glasses up the bridge of his nose. "If you don't mind, ma'am," he said, "I'd like to bring my partner in on your case. I suspect we'll need his help."

"Is this necessary?"

He nodded. "I suspect that in this case it is."

As King excused himself and left the office, Madeline allowed Rose down to crawl around. Casually, Madeline inspected the framed documents hanging on the wall. One was signed by Senator Sam Houston; another by Sam Houston, president of the Republic of Texas; and a third by General Sam Houston. "Mr. Houston has been a busy man," she murmured.

The sound of a male voice raised in disbelief

snagged her attention. She clutched her reticule with straining fingers and stared intently at the dust particles floating in the sunlight that beamed through the window and listened. "Such rough language," she observed, shaking her head.

King returned to his office, followed by a tall, spare man who looked to be in his late twenties, wearing a well-tailored business suit and a frown. "Mrs. Sinclair," King said, "this is my partner, Tyler. I apologize for the delay." He took his seat.

Mr. Tyler nodded toward her and refused a chair, preferring to stand against the wall, his arms crossed, his countenance skeptical. His gaze kept wandering to Rose.

Beneath her skirt, Madeline's foot began an agitated tap. She grabbed up her daughter and held her close. Something about Mr. Tyler bothered her.

"Now, where were we?" King asked, stroking his beard. "Ah, yes, your husband's name."

"Brazos Sinclair."

Tyler's gray-eyed gaze bore into her. She returned Rose's ball to her reticule, yanking the strings to pull the bag closed.

King continued, "I need to know where the wedding took place and the circumstances surrounding it."

Do it all at once, Madeline, she told herself. It'll be easier that way. Be done with it. "Mr. Sinclair and I met in Antwerp, Belgium, this past January. Both of us desired to sail upon a ship leaving Antwerp for America the following day, and we each had difficulties securing passage. We concluded that marriage would solve both our problems, so we did the deed, with the intention of obtaining an annulment once we reached Texas." She lifted her shoulders, silently saying, Here I am.

Tyler spoke for the first time. "And you will claim what reason for the annulment of this marriage?"

Madeline took a deep breath, then said in a rush, "It has not been consummated."

Tyler made a choking sound and turned away. He tapped his fingers against the windowpane and gazed out toward the street. King cleared his throat. "Mrs.

Sinclair, please pardon my indelicacy, but as I understand what you are saying, you and Brazos Sinclair lived as man and wife for a period of time as was required to sail the Atlantic—"

"Seven weeks," Madeline interrupted. "We were delayed by ill winds."

"You lived as wife to Brazos Sinclair for seven weeks in the intimate confines of a ship, and you are claiming nonconsummation?" King shook his head slowly. "I know Brazos Sinclair, madam. Do you truly expect us to believe this story?"

Madeline took great pleasure in allowing Rose to lean forward and tip the inkwell she'd been reaching for. "Oh, dear," Madeline exclaimed sweetly as King scrambled to contain the slowly spreading indigo stain with his pristine handkerchief. "I am *so* sorry."

Tyler stepped forward, his shoulders quaking with suppressed mirth. "I'll draw up the document, Melbourne. Please, Mrs. Sinclair, let's adjourn to my office. I've a puzzle board in there that your daughter might enjoy."

Only too glad to flee Mr. King's personal questions, Madeline followed Mr. Tyler, determined to ignore the uneasy feeling he created within her. "I should have waited and let Brazos do this, after all," she grumbled beneath her breath. Leave it to him to make something sound easy when in truth, it wasn't easy at all.

In his office, Tyler gestured for Madeline to take a chair, then walked to a cabinet. He pulled both a puzzle and a rag doll from its interior, saying, "My nieces and nephews regularly come to visit. I keep a few things around for them." He shrugged and handed the toys to Rose.

Madeline felt it again. Something about how he holds himself, she thought, studying him. He was quite handsome, with a patrician nose and square jaw. A single curl of coarse black hair tumbled across his brow, but it was the gleam in his bluish gray eyes that she suddenly recognized. "Mr. Tyler?"

He grinned, and then she knew for sure.

"Sinclair. Tyler Sinclair at your service. Brazos is my older brother."

LOUIS CASTILLON HIMSELF answered Brazos's knock. "Sin!" the physician exclaimed. "Heaven be praised, Sin has finally returned to Galveston."

"That's an old joke, Louis, and it still isn't funny." Brazos grinned as he grasped the elderly gentleman's outstretched hand and clapped him on the shoulder. "However, it tells me I'm home, and that's a right fine feelin'. How've you been, sir?"

"Fine, fine. Busy of course, but then, that's what keeps me young." He stepped back for Brazos to enter his home. "I was in the kitchen shelling shrimp for tonight's dinner. Come on back," he paused and gave Brazos a serious look. "Unless this is a professional call?"

Brazos shook his head. "No, although if that's gumbo I'm smellin', I could be persuaded to stay for supper."

A pleased smile wreathed Louis's face. "You always did like my cooking, didn't you. Over the years, I've found but a few people who have the stomach for my special spices."

Thinking of the peppery blend favored by this longtime friend, Brazos grinned. "I always liked the ale you'd let me drink to cool off my tongue."

"Medicinal purposes," Louis said cheerfully, grabbing his apron as he walked through the kitchen door. Watching the doctor tie the cloth around his waist, Brazos recalled the argument with Madeline. "You know how to bake chocolate cake, Doc?" he asked.

"What?"

"Never mind." Liquid in a cast-iron pot bubbled on the stove, and Brazos walked over to check the contents. He sniffed. Tomato, onion, garlic. He drew a deep breath, and immediately, his eyes began to water. "What's in this stuff?"

"Just experimenting with some peppers out of South America," the doctor explained. "I believe this gumbo may be my best yet."

Brazos decided to find somewhere else to eat his supper. He washed his hands, then sat at the table to peel shrimp with the doctor. After a few moments of conversation catching up on family and friends, Brazos got down to business. "I need your advice, Louis."

The physician paused and looked up. "You continue to suffer the blackouts?"

Brazos nodded. He tossed a peeled shrimp into the wooden bowl between them and said, "For a long time, I had none; then a letter arrived from Juanita. I was in Paris in a coffee shop—I'd been there many times, the owner was a friend of mine. I opened the letter and began to read." Abruptly, he stood and pushed away from the table. Walking to the stove, he picked up a long-handled spoon and began stirring the gumbo. "I woke up three days later in Spain. My shirt was splattered with blood."

Castillon wiped his hands on his apron. "What did you learn?"

"Nothing. No missing persons, no unaccounted for bodies, no wounds of my own." Brazos shrugged. "I couldn't eat for three days afterward. It scares the hell out of me, Louis."

Louis leaned back in his chair. "Traveling as you were, it is quite possible you hunted food, Brazos. That would account for the blood." The Creole's brow furrowed thoughtfully as he asked, "And the Swiss doctor, the one I sent you to see. You left so much out of your letter, my friend. What did he say?"

Brazos's laugh sounded like death itself. "I traveled thousands of miles to see your 'expert,' Louis, on board ship—which, by the way, is the greatest torture known to man—and the one solution the good doctor had to offer is the one thing Christ Himself couldn't convince me to do."

"Which was?"

"He told me to return to Perote and face my demon."

"Salezan."

"No, he meant the demon inside of me. The one who protects whatever truth is hidden within my memory."

Louis nodded and drummed his fingers on the table as he looked at Brazos and said, "It makes sense, son. I've always believed that physically, nothing is wrong with you."

"I know. You've always thought I was crazy." Brazos slapped the spoon down onto the work counter next to the stove. He turned his head toward the kitchen's open window and gazed across the bay, where a line of the Texas mainland was barely visible.

A salty breeze brushed his face as he heard Louis Castillon say, "No, Brazos, that is not what I have thought. But I do believe that the Swiss is right. Something has a hold on you, and until you face it, you will always be troubled. Quit running, son; one cannot flee from oneself. How old are you, thirty-two, thirty-three? It's time you settled and had a family."

"I'm thirty-four." Brazos crossed his arms and leaned against the wall facing Louis. "And I've got another problem that's givin' me some grief." He took a deep breath, then said, "The sting's missin' from my stinger."

Castillon looked at him blankly.

"There's no lead in my pencil," Brazos said through set teeth.

Still the doctor failed to react.

"Hell, Doc. Do I gotta say it out loud?" Scowling, he said succinctly, "I'm impotent."

"Oh." Castillon's eyes widened, and he leaned back in his chair. "This is a little detail you neglected to mention before in our discussions?"

"No, it's a recent, singular development," Brazos replied, and briefly went on to explain the particulars. He finished with a question. "So, Louis, please, as a physician, tell me. Could this trouble reoccur?"

Castillon frowned and began to shell another shrimp. He asked a few pointed and personal questions of his own before answering Brazos by saying, "I believe this to be a physical manifestation of a mental problem. Until that is dealt with, you will always risk a return of your difficulty."

Brazos slumped into his chair as Castillon held up his hand and shook his head. "No, no, don't jump ahead of me. I don't anticipate it happening again unless you re-create the circumstances."

Glumly, Brazos replied, "Well, that damn sure isn't goin' to happen. Not the exact same circumstances anyway. I'm never sailin' on a ship again for as long as I live." And he'd never be with Madeline Christophe Sinclair again, either.

"Then don't borrow trouble, son. From what you've told me, you've little to worry about. Now, we've still fifty shrimp here to deal with. Get to work, boy. Earn your supper."

A short time later, Dr. Castillon stood on his front porch and watched his young friend saunter down the street toward the city. "I fear my Swiss colleague is right," he murmured.

Brazos Sinclair would know no peace until he faced and defeated his fears. He would continue to run from himself and from those he loved, those who loved him. Louis pitied the boy, but he agreed that Brazos must return to Perote. But what would it take to get him there? What force could be greater than the terror he held inside himself?

A carriage pulled up in front of the house, and he heard the sound of his wife's gentle laughter and his grandchild's giggles. Then Louis knew the answer to his question. His gaze followed the direction in which Brazos had disappeared. "Yes, it might just be your salvation. Look for it, son. Find it."

Brazos Sinclair needed the greatest force on earth to defeat his beast. He needed love.

Chapter 8

CHÂTEAU ST. GERMAINE

Puffs of gravel dust trailed the horse and rider as they thundered up the drive toward the château. Reaching the courtyard, Pierre Corot lifted his voice above the clatter of hooves against stone and shouted, "Julian!"

A young servant boy came running as the sound echoed off the stone walls surrounding the U-shape courtyard. Sliding from his horse, Corot tossed the boy the reins and ran toward the east wing. Without pausing to knock, he pushed open the doors and rushed inside. "Julian," he called again, going directly to the first-floor office. Empty.

His boots clacked against the floor as he crossed to the staircase and took the steps two at a time. "Julian, it's Pierre," he called from the first landing. "Where are you?"

Julian Desseau's rumbling voice answered from the second-floor hallway. "Here, Pierre. What is it?"

At the top of the stairs, Corot paused just a

moment to catch his breath, then said, "I've found them, Julian. I've found Elise and the woman."

Julian froze. Sunshine beaming through one of the tall windows that lined the hallway illuminated the sudden, exultant expression on his face. Slowly, he leaned a hand against the wall for support and asked, "She's safe?"

Corot knew that Julian spoke of his daughter, and because his information was weeks old, he hesitated before answering, "Yes."

Julian's jaw hardened, and a winter's chill dripped from the single word he uttered, "But?"

"They have left Europe, Julian. In January. My investigators found them listed on a ship's manifest. They joined a group of immigrants and sailed for America."

"America!" Julian exclaimed.

Pierre nodded. "Texas. The Sinclairs sailed with members of an organization called the Colonization Society of Texas. A roster of their membership includes one Madeline Sinclair and daughter, Rose."

"So you've no knowledge of my daughter's safety since they sailed?"

"I'm afraid not. But barring any problems, the ship should have reached American shores by now."

"Should have reached," Julian repeated bleakly. "The ship, what kind of ship? Was it sound?"

"Yes, Julian. These colonists were for the most part wealthy people. They chartered a Liverpool-built packet whose captain makes the run routinely. I'm sure they reached America just fine." In response to the hard gaze Desseau fixed upon him, Pierre added softly, "Don't doubt it, my friend."

Julian shut his eyes, threw back his head, and sighed. "You are right. I cannot believe any differently, or my sanity would be lost."

After a moment, he shrugged and said, "Come to my rooms, Pierre. I'll fix you a drink. You look as though you made the trip from Paris in an hour."

"Not much more than that," Corot replied, dragging a weary hand through his hair as he followed Desseau down the long hallway.

As they walked, Desseau mused, "The Colonization Society of Texas. I've heard of them. They solicited money and sold shares in their company. Fellow named Condé or something—"

"Considérant. They follow the philosophical teachings of Charles Fourier."

Julian stopped and snapped his fingers. "That's it. Fourierists. They're the fools who plan to allow women to vote. I remembering hearing the Smithwick woman pattering on about it with Celeste."

Corot halted in front of a window. He stared out at the green, rolling farmland that surrounded Château St. Germaine as he thought aloud. "Madeline Christophe purchased membership in the colony. Not Mary Smithwick. I doubt she planned the trip until after Celeste died. Julian"—he looked over at his friend—"have you ever deduced why Mary Smithwick chose to steal your daughter?"

Julian's expression grew as cold and as hard as the stone walls of St. Germaine. "I may have. I have spoken with Bernadette." Saying no more, he marched down the hall toward his rooms, the sound of his footsteps echoing from the walls.

"And?" Corot called, following him.

"Suffice to say that she found a way to interfere in my marriage," Julian answered.

"You proved she planned the kidnapping?"

"No." Julian stopped abruptly and looked over his shoulder. He wore a mocking smile as he added, "If I had, she would be dead, and Bernadette is still alive, Pierre."

Pierre waited for Julian to elaborate, and when he didn't, the investigator sighed in frustration. Leave it to Desseau to hire a man and provide only half the facts needed to do the job properly. "Julian," he said, "it's bad enough that you didn't share with me your suspicions about Bernadette in the beginning of this investigation. But for my men to successfully return Elise to your arms, they need every bit of information I can give them. Please, tell me what you know!"

A ghost of a smile flickered in Julian's eyes. "Pierre, you have my most profound thanks for your superior work. If it will ease your mind, I'll tell you that Bernadette is now confined to St. Anne's convent. A lifetime of prayer is just what the woman needs. And as far as Mary Smithwick is concerned, I care not what her motives might have been. The fact remains that she stole my child. For that, she will pay."

"But, Julian, it will help my men trace her if they understand—"

"They don't need to understand, Pierre. Now that you've told me where my daughter is, I shall see to bringing her home. I wish to deal personally with Mary Smithwick. I am going to Texas."

His eyebrows lifted as he looked at Corot and asked, "I trust you brought sailing information with you?"

Pierre nodded. "A ship sails for Galveston in three days."

"Good." Entering his bedroom suite, Julian stepped straight to the liquor decanters as he called to his valet, "Henri, pack my bags."

GALVESTON, TEXAS

Tyler Sinclair spotted his brother as he rode his horse into the stable at his home south of the city. Brazos stood on the captain's walk at the top of the house, peering through the telescope Tyler used to watch ships at sea. Brazos, however, had the telescope pointed toward town. "Probably peeking through windows," Tyler muttered aloud.

He wondered just what was going on with his brother. Brazos never had come by the office, although Trixie had stopped by with the message that Brazos would see Tyler that evening at his brother's home. Until then, Madeline had waited in his office for her husband to arrive and sign the papers ending their marriage. As time passed, she'd grown agitated, and eventually Tyler had questioned Brazos's commitment to seeking an annulment. Madeline had smiled stiffly and said, "Your bother has insisted on a daily basis that his first order of business upon arrival in Galveston would be to contact an attorney at King and Associates." The following sentence she had whispered to herself in French, and Tyler carefully masked both his comprehension and his astonishment. The woman certainly possessed a broad, if not necessarily polite, vocabulary.

They'd gone on to discuss a wide range of topics, and he had begun to wonder if Brazos wasn't making a big mistake. Madeline Christophe Sinclair seemed like just the sort of woman to whom his brother should be married.

With his horse cared for, Tyler entered his home through the back door, waving a greeting to his house-keeper, an Irish widow named Bridget Callahan, and ruffling the hair of her young son, Sean. "Supper will be ready in half an hour, Mr. Sinclair," Bridget called.

Not for the first time, he noted the way the calico stretched across her bosom. One of these days, he'd do something about that. Not today, however. This after-noon he had his brother to deal with. "Why don't you head on home, Bridget. Brazos and I will manage all right by ourselves tonight."

She looked doubtful. "Are you certain?"

"Yeah." He pulled a coin out of his pocket and gave it to Sean. "Here, scamp. Make your mama take you by Cooper's Mercantile and buy you a rope of licorice."

The boy beamed at him, and Tyler ruffled the child's hair once more before climbing the stairs to meet his brother.

Brazos heard Tyler thumping up the stairs. Not lifting his eye from the telescope, he said, "I congratu-late you on your taste in housekeepers, Ty. I imagine Mrs. Callahan is a right fine cook."

In the manner of brothers, Tyler suggested Brazos do something anatomically impossible. Brazos grinned and shifted the scope toward the left, seeking a clearer picture of the garden party taking place at one of the mansions on The Strand.

Tyler asked, "Do you want a drink?"

"No, thanks," Brazos replied. "I had one—or was it twenty-one—earlier with Trix." He'd been on his way to get unmarried at King and Associates when he stopped by The Gentleman's Club long enough to get a little loop-legged. Then he'd stumbled his way over to Powhattan Hotel in time to discover that Madeline had come and gone. All Lillibet would say was that Rose had been nursed for the final time that day and that a man who drank too much didn't deserve to know where his wife spent the night.

He'd not been at all happy to return to the Club and the news that his soon-to-be-former wife had been waiting on him at his brother's offices. Especially when Trixie couldn't tell him a thing about Emile.

Brazos considered asking first about The Flower, but he realized other matters came first. "So, how's the family?"

Tyler folded his arms and looked toward the harbor and the collection of masts and sails reaching toward the sky. He said, "The folks delayed this trip to Georgia for a year while waiting for you to come home. Pa finally convinced Mama they could put off visiting his family no longer. I'd hate to be Pa when she learns you managed to drag yourself home only two weeks after they left."

"She'll be spittin' knittin' needles," Brazos replied, wincing at the thought as he stepped away from the telescope.

"Or worse."

"I was sorely disappointed when I learned they'd left Magnolia Bend. But I'll be around for a while, at least until they return. It'll take me that long to finish my business."

"And what business is that?" Tyler asked as the wind picked up and sent a loose shutter banging against the side of the house one floor below them. "Something to do with your wife, I imagine?"

Brazos followed Tyler inside, saying, "Listen, Ty, I'll tell you the entire, ugly story, but first I want to hear about Juanita and the children."

Tyler paused on the stairway's landing. He lifted an eyebrow. "You swear?"

"My word on it," Brazos said, following his brother. He stood in the doorway of the upstairs room that Tyler used as an office and watched as Tyler secured the shutter. "Tell me about Nita, Ty."

"She's safe, but not very happy. I have her stashed in Brazoria with Cousin Jeffrey."

Brazos frowned. "Jeffrey . . . Jeffrey . . . hmm. I don't rightly place him."

"Jeffrey Henderson." Tyler sat at his desk and laced his fingers behind his head, elbows outstretched, as he added, "Mama's second cousin Lucy's third husband's stepbrother. Runs the dry goods on Commerce Street."

"Oh, yeah. Wasn't he the one who got drunk at Sam Houston's inaugural ball?"

"And yanked off that bald woman's wig." Tyler nodded. "That's him."

Brazos sprawled on the horsehair sofa. "Well, hell. No wonder Nita isn't happy. You know how proud she is of her hair. Ol' Jeffrey best not be touchin' it."

Tyler scowled. "He was the best I could do on short notice. Salezan's men had nabbed her in Marshall, and it was just dumb luck that Cousin Linda's oldest boy managed to foil their plan."

"I'm not criticizin', Tyler. I'm thankful you were able to help. I thought for sure she was safe in East Texas. I'd like to know just how the hell they found her."

Disgust laced Tyler's voice as he replied, "She took to singin' during mass on Sundays. As if that voice of hers wasn't enough, the padre at St. Mary's brought her down from the choir loft and stuck her at the front of the church for people to gawk at. I asked him why, and he claimed that she was the closest thing to an angel his parishioners would see on earth. Truth was, according to one of the nuns, collections tripled with Juanita singing hymns up near the altar. Word got around, and Salezan's men obviously listened."

"Damn," Brazos cursed, cracking his knuckles and scowling. "If I'd known she'd pull a stunt like that, I'd have sent the padre a load of silver and told him to keep the woman's mouth shut. I swear, that Juanita is as stubborn as a two-headed mule. She promised she'd behave herself. Damn me for a fool for believin' her."

"Well, she's behaving now," Tyler said drolly, opening a desk drawer and taking out a bottle. "The thirty minutes she spent with Salezan's henchman managed to put the fear of God back into her."

Brazos shook his head as his brother offered up the bottle. "Not the fear of God, Ty. The fear of Damasso Salezan. What news do you have of him?"

"He never leaves that castle of his. But his men are all over Texas looking for you—even after all this time." Tyler poured himself a drink, sipped it, grimaced, and said, "In fact, brother, I hate to mention this, but it wouldn't surprise me one bit if one of his people watched you leave the boat this morning."

"No one would have recognized me; I was just another European traveler. Besides, my looks have changed in the past couple of years." He flashed a wide smile. "I've gotten prettier."

"Hell," Tyler responded, "I'd forgotten how obnoxious you are. If I were you, I wouldn't stake my life—which is exactly what you'd be doing—on your arrival going unnoticed. After all, one of his men noticed Juanita, right?"

"Yeah, but then a man would have to be blind, deaf, and half dead not to notice Nita."

Tyler nodded and sipped his drink. "I almost swallowed my tongue the first time I saw her. I thought you'd won the grand prize when you brought her home. Come on downstairs," he continued, standing up. "Bridget left us supper, and I'm getting hungry." As he led the way from the room, he glanced casually at Brazos and added, "This time, I figure you got second or third place."

"Madeline is beautiful," Brazos defended automatically, following his brother down the circular staircase. "Maybe not as beautiful as Nita, but I think—" He broke off abruptly and scowled. "Stop it, Tyler. I told you I'd explain it all later."

The younger Sinclair brother shrugged as he reached the ground floor and entered the dining room. Brazos stopped on the second-floor landing. Fishing in his pocket for a marble, he called out, "What makes you think Salezan's henchman would recognize me?"

Tyler reappeared a few moments later, carrying a single sheet of paper. He held it up for his brother to see. "This."

The broadside bearing Brazos's likeness had been sketched in pen and ink. "Who did that?"

"Uncle Philbert. They told him it was for a newspaper story of your travels in Europe. Salezan wants you bad, Brazos."

"Damn." Brazos balanced a shiny green marble in a groove on the banister, then sent it rolling. The brothers watched silently as the marble gyrated down the handrail and clattered against the yellow pine floor. "He doesn't want me," Brazos said flatly. "He wants the silver. And I've been toyin' with the idea of givin' it to him."

Tyler's gaze followed the marble until it rolled to a stop against the carved mahogany hat tree. He nodded his head slowly and said, "That might be the answer. Even after building the children's home and funding the other charities as you instructed, you still have a substantial amount."

Brazos started down the stairs. "I'm anxious to visit the home and see the children. Mother kept me apprised of their progress through her letters. She told me we've gained a few since I've been gone." Glancing back at his brother, he asked, "How are the children, Ty? Has Salezan made any move against them? Do you think he's made the link between St. Michael's Children's Home and me?"

"No," Tyler said without hesitation. "I've buried the connection so deep, he'd have to be in hell to find it."

Brazos gave a mirthless laugh. "If that's the case, Tyler, you've put the information right in his hands. Salezan is the prince of Perote Castle. If that place isn't hell, I don't know what is." Instinctively, he touched his sleeve and the armband that lay beneath it. "When I mentioned offering Salezan the mine, I didn't mean I thought to give him our cache of silver bars. I know where the mine is, Ty. I figured it out almost a year ago."

"What?" Tyler asked. "You mean the mine itself? I don't understand. I thought the only information Miguel found was where the priests had buried their silver bars when the Indians attacked."

Brazos nodded. "Those old church documents pinpointed the location of the cache, but Miguel found something else—a map of sorts that leads the way to the El Regalo de Dios mine. My idea is to—" he paused, noting the sharp look his brother sent his way. "What?"

Tyler appeared to choose his words carefully. "You said a year ago. Just when did Miguel tell you about this map?"

A yawning sickness spread through Brazos's gut as he remembered those moments he and Miguel shared in the dungeons of Perote. He didn't know which bothered him more, that he recalled the atrocities committed against them, or that he couldn't recall much else. Whatever it was he'd forgotten must've been really bad. "Miguel had it all the time. Remember that armband he wore?"

Tyler nodded. "I always thought it a strange thing for a priest to wear jewelry like that."

"Not jewelry so much as a puzzle. You put all the pieces together, and it gives you El Regalo."

"Let me get this straight," Tyler said, holding up his hand. "You know the location of the mother lode of all that silver, and you're going to give it to your worst enemy?"

Brazos scoffed, "Of course not. I'm going to use the secret to lure Salezan from his lair." He bent and scooped up his marble. Tossing it from one hand to the other, he added, "And then I'm going to kill him."

Tyler's gaze followed the green sphere of glass. "It just might work," he agreed.

"I believe it's got a decent chance. First, though, I have to make sure that Nita is safe and that the children won't be endangered." Brazos tucked the toy into his pocket as he said, "Salezan wants more than the silver, Ty. He wants the woman I stole from him."

"Yeah, he wants Juanita." Tyler rubbed the back of his neck as he asked, "Who is she, Brazos? Trying to figure out the relationship between you and that Mexican beauty has given the family a collective headache. Why have you married a European and not your Mexican lover? Why did you bring her home with you?"

"My relationship with Juanita is complicated, Ty, and private."

"Is she somehow connected to Miguel? Is that why you won't explain what's between the two of you?" Tyler Sinclair's softly spoken words hit Brazos like grapeshot to the gut.

"Be quiet, brother," Brazos warned, lifting his hat from the rack and opening the front door. "Go ahead and eat your supper. I'm not hungry anymore." He stood on the porch creasing the felt brim with brisk, angry movements.

But Tyler, having broached the subject, was obviously unwilling to let it go. He followed his brother outside, saying, "Every time anyone mentions Miguel Alcortez, you run. Why, Brazos? From the time you were boys, you were best of friends. You were the one who pleaded his case to his folks when Miguel decided to become a priest. You were the one he came to when he stumbled across church records that referred to the silver. By God, Brazos, you were his friend!"

Tyler's voice rang with passionate appeal as he asked, "Why do you pretend as though he never existed? What happened to him, to Juanita, to you? Are you guilty of something, brother?"

Brazos whirled around, swinging. His fist caught Tyler square on the jaw and sent him sprawling against the whitewashed porch planks. "I told you to shut the hell up," he said through set teeth. "It's not like that at all. You don't know, Tyler."

Tyler sat up, rubbing his jaw, his gaze reflecting the anguish Brazos knew lived in his own eyes. "You're right," he said slowly. "I *don't* know. When you returned from Mexico, all you ever said was that Miguel was dead. You offered nothing more, even to Miguel's family." Climbing to his feet, he dusted himself off and fastened a compassionate gaze upon his brother. "What happened, Brazos? It's eating you alive, I can tell."

Eating him alive. Brazos inhaled deep breaths, gasping for air as though he'd run for miles. In truth, he'd been running for years. The terror clawed at him, even here on his brother's front porch, beneath the wide open Texas sky. He shut his eyes, fighting a silent battle against the monster lurking within him.

In his mind, a scream echoed, *Oh, God. Miguel.*

He shivered violently, his hands fisting repeatedly at his sides. Then, as if from far away, he felt a touch on his shoulder. Brazos lay his hand atop his brother's, and the warmth Tyler Sinclair shared spread through him, replacing the icy, evil cold. When he could speak, he said, "Please, let it go, Ty. I can't talk about it."

"I want to help you."

Brazos sighed explosively. "I wish you could, brother, but I'm handling this the only way I know how. C'mon, I'm hungry again. Let's go see what your Miss Bridget left us for supper."

They were halfway through the meal when Brazos buttered a roll and said, "You offered your help. I reckon you know by now that I could use it regardin' another matter. I gather you've met my wife?"

"Feisty little thing. Pretty, though." Tyler gave his brother a hard look. "I've the papers she asked for in my jacket pocket. She's already signed them; all we need is your henscratch to make it legal. But as your attorney, brother, and since an annulment is a legal document, I have to ask you one thing. Did you truly not bed the woman during seven weeks at sea?"

Brazos bent his attention to the roasted pork on his plate and asked gruffly, "She give you any details?"

"No."

"I didn't bed the woman during seven weeks at sea."

"Pull the other one, brother."

"Pass the gravy, would ya?"

Tyler gave him both the sauce and a dubious look. Brazos pretended not to notice and waited until they'd both finished their meals to ask, "So, what'd you think of her fiancé?"

Tyler's brows lifted in surprise. "What are you talking about?"

"Madeline. Didn't she bring Emile with her?"

"No. She was alone, except for the baby, that is. The little girl is awfully cute, but I wish she hadn't chewed an arm off the doll I keep in my office."

"Buy a new one," Brazos said, laying his napkin on the table and standing. "So, she didn't bring Emile with her."

"You want to sign the annulment now? I know that Cousin Judge is home tonight. You could ride the papers over and be done with it." He led the way into the hallway, where he'd left his jacket draped across the back of a chair. Pulling the document from his pocket, he handed the paper to Brazos, saying, "I'll ride with you, if you'd like. In fact, it might be a good idea to check on your lady friend while we're out."

Brazos carried the papers to Tyler's desk and glanced at them briefly. At the bottom, he noted the signature: Madeline Christophe Sinclair. "What lady friend?" he replied, inking his name above Madeline's.

Tyler pointed toward the annulment papers. "Her. Madeline's out at the beach house. She said she'd like some time to herself, so I offered her the family cottage. No one's using it now, so . . . Brazos?" He followed his brother out the door. "Brazos, what's going on?"

"You take the papers over for me, all right, Ty? I've some unfinished business to take care of." Brazos paused at the bottom of the front steps and looked back. "Oh, and Ty? Thanks. Maddie and I needed that annulment somethin' fierce."

Tyler watched his brother saddle a horse and

gallop out of the drive, heading south. Walking back inside, he shook his head bewilderedly as he slipped into his jacket and picked up the annulment papers from his desk.

He'd tucked the documents in his pocket and had lifted his hat from the rack when he stopped. For a full moment he stood thinking. Then, very carefully, Tyler returned his hat to the hook. Walking into the parlor, he poured himself a tall glass of bourbon.

He stared at a boot scuff on the polished pine floor until a slow grin spread across his face. Tyler turned down the wicks on all the downstairs lamps and, with drink in hand, climbed the stairs to his bedroom.

Tyler Sinclair went to sleep that night with a smile on his face.

A LONE ROSEBUSH grew beside the steps leading up to the Sinclair cottage. Built on stilts, as were most of the homes on Galveston Island, the house was painted white but for the wide slatted shutters covering all windows and both doors. Those were painted pink. "To match the roses," Madeline murmured, inhaling the exquisite perfume as she sat in a porch rocker, listening to the rumbling sounds of the surf and the whistle of sea breeze through the tall prairie grass growing near the cottage.

Except for the baby sleeping peacefully in one of the two bedrooms inside, Madeline was alone. How pleasant she found it after weeks of constant companionship aboard ship and in public carriages and inns. She'd be surrounded with people once again tomorrow, when the colonists boarded a steamer to begin the next stage of their journey, up Buffalo Bayou to the city of Houston.

Tyler's offer of the cottage had been both unexpected and exactly what she'd needed. Madeline had wanted some time to herself, craved it to deal with this strange sense of loss she experienced at the finish of her time with Brazos Sinclair. Somehow, spending the night in his family home just seemed right.

Inside, she'd found a box of toys—soldiers, balls, marbles, and the makings for a kite. She could picture him here as a boy out on the dunes sailing a creation of paper, glue, and string. "As a man, for that matter," she said, envisioning a laughing Brazos running barefoot and shirtless across the stretch of sand, a paper-fancy trailing behind him, catching air and soaring.

Madeline shook herself. It was time to put all thoughts of him behind her. The rocking chair creaked as she stood and stepped to the porch railing. Looping an arm around a support post, she leaned out and down and brushed the velvet softness of a rose past full blossom. As the flower broke apart and individual petals fell to the ground, Madeline smiled sadly and reached for a rosebud just ready to burst into bloom. "Reach for your dreams, Madeline Christophe," she told herself. "Bury the past, and look toward your future." Snapping the stem, she brought the bud to her nose and sniffed the spicy fragrance. Then she sucked at the tip of her finger and added, "But watch out for thorns."

His voice floated on the wings of the night. "Thorns from your past or those you've yet to discover, Beauty?"

Brazos stood at the base of the steps, the eddy of a light ground fog swirling around his boots. The glow from a three-quarter moon shone blue-black upon his hair. His eyes were glittering jewels. Madeline closed her eyes as a wave of longing crashed over her like surf upon the sand in the face of a violent storm. "Are you really here, or have my dreams conjured you up?"

His laugh was mocking as he replied, "I don't know, Maddie. Maybe it was your nightmares."

She died a little at that. "Never, Brazos," she said, shaking her head. "Never that. I know what true nightmares are. I've lived them. You are nothing of them." After a moment's pause, she asked, "Why are you here?"

"Are you alone?" he countered.

"Rose is asleep."

"Anyone else?"

"No." Her brow wrinkled. "Who would be here?"

He lifted a foot to the first step. "Hell's bells, Maddie. You can damn well tear a man's ego to shreds. I hope you never forget me that way. I'm talkin' about Emile. Didn't he meet you?"

In a voice as soft as the moonlight, Madeline swore, "Brazos Sinclair, I'll never forget you." Then she added the lie, "Emile decided to wait at La Réunion."

Brazos's eyebrows lifted. "He did? Why?"

"Umm . . . planting. Spring planting," Madeline answered. Was that disgust flashing through his eyes? Maybe disapproval? Whatever the emotion, it was gone in an instant, replaced by a pleased, almost predatory light.

"I reckon a man does have to see to life's necessities. I know I do." He took a second step up.

Madeline asked again, the answer terribly important. "Why are you here, Brazos?"

"You didn't say good-bye."

She tossed her head. "You were otherwise occupied."

"I wished you'd stayed around to meet my cousin. Trixie was curious about you. She and I have always been close; she's like a sister to me."

"You didn't kiss her like a sister."

He grinned, and she felt it to her toes. "We're kissin' cousins," he said, taking a third step.

"I met your brother." Madeline tried to ignore the pounding of her pulse.

"He told me. We're not married anymore."

"Oh."

Moving like a wraith, he stood beside her. His hand lifted, and his fingers brushed her cheek. Their gazes met, his burning and hungry. Ravenous. Madeline's filled with yearning.

It was a night out of time. Between yesterday, the past and all its trials, and tomorrow, the future and its promises. It was a moment in and of itself, when she could put aside responsibilities and schemes and dreams. Madeline could live for this instant, because somewhere deep in her heart, she knew that this time, this intensity, this emotion, might never be repeated.

So she kissed him, the touch of her lips as soft as the rose petals in her hand, the whisper of her breath as it mingled with his as gentle as the breeze off the ocean.

Madeline's kiss sparked the flame that had been burning inside Brazos all across the Atlantic. She wasn't his to take, not any longer, but he didn't give a damn. Emile should never have left this woman in Europe. He sure as hell should have been here to meet the boat. In Brazos's eyes, the bastard was getting what he deserved.

Because Brazos was taking what he'd wanted for so long. He surrendered to his need, his hands cupping her buttocks and pulling her against him. His tongue explored her, tasted her, and he groaned in satisfaction as she began to imitate his motions.

Good Lord, she was sweet. Tearing his mouth from hers, he lifted her into his arms and carried her inside. A quick glance around revealed one bedroom door open and one closed, indicating where Madeline had put Rose to sleep. Swiftly, he carried her to the empty bed. She gave a soft sigh of pleasure as he lowered her to the mattress, and the hot throbbing in his loins intensified. "Ah, Beauty," he whispered raggedly before bending to steal her breath once again. His tongue stroked hers in a steady, erotic rhythm, stoking the fire inside him and stirring the heat within her.

The room smelled of sea and sand and flowers. It smelled of home. And as Brazos's fingers worked the buttons on her dress, revealing a chemise made of near-transparent lawn and a corset trimmed in delicate white lace, he breathed of her fragrance and smiled. Forever after, this bed, this room, this cottage would remind him of Madeline. Of his Beauty.

He stripped off his linen shirt. Bracing his weight on his elbows, Brazos covered her body with his own, cradling himself to her, pressing, seeking that which man had sought from woman since the beginning of time. Desire pounded through him hard and wild, the ache to claim her overwhelming.

But he drew a deep breath, forcing himself to slow down. After all the weeks of waiting, he wanted the moment to last. As elemental as was his need for her was his desire to create a memory Madeline could not forget. He'd make damn sure that she'd never have trouble remembering *his* name.

Though his body strained at the barrier of clothing between them, he continued to kiss her. Softly, slowly, deeply—lifting his head every so often for them to catch their breaths, and then he'd gaze into her eyes, speaking to her silently, telling her of his need and of his desire.

His lips trailed scattered kisses across her cheeks, her eyes, her brow. "Can you feel what you do to me, Maddie mine?" he asked, grinding himself against her softness as he smothered her reply with questing lips. He burned at the touch of her fingers on the bare skin of his back.

He kissed her until his control tested its limits. "Enough." He stood up and pulled off his boots.

Madeline's breath came in gasps. She whimpered and shut her eyes when his fingers moved to the buttons on his pants.

Brazos chuckled softly. "I'd not have guessed you for a shy one." He was naked now and straining with need. In a husky voice, he demanded, "Look at me, Madeline. Look at me, and see what you do to me."

Slowly, she did just that. "Oh, my."

Brazos tangibly felt her gaze, and his body surged in response.

"Oh, my," she repeated.

He reached out and pulled her to her feet, then pushed her gown from her shoulders and her petticoats from her hips. Finally, his fingers touched her corset's metal hooks, and one by one, he unfastened them. Madeline shivered as the corset fell to the ground and his hands stroked her hips, grasping the hem of her chemise and pulling it up and off in a single, fluid motion.

She was bare above the waist, and Brazos could wait no longer to taste her. He sank to his knees, trailing his tongue through the deep valley between her breasts before circling the spots where palest white met dusky rose. Finally, he took a nipple into his mouth to suckle.

Madeline moaned and arched her back. Brazos's heart pounded as he fought the raging heat that threatened his control. He yanked the tie of her pantalets, and his palms slid the soft linen over her hips, down her legs, and to the floor. His hands slipped between her inner thighs and eased them slightly apart.

She was soft and hot to his touch. And wet. Slippery velvet heat ready to welcome him. He kissed the flat plain of her stomach and wanted more. He wanted to taste her, to drink of her desire until she trembled in his arms and screamed for him to take her.

He wanted to make her forget every other man she'd ever had.

He dipped his head and kissed the shield of golden curls at the juncture of her thighs.

She pulled away. "What . . . Brazos?"

"Shh, Beauty, let me love you." He grasped her buttocks and pulled her back to him. And his mouth covered her sex.

Madeline had never imagined this sort of intimacy, and somewhere in the midst of the consuming storm of sensation came the feeling that she should be embarrassed. But she couldn't think straight enough to be embarrassed. Her legs parted, opening like a blossom beneath the onslaught of his tongue.

He eased her back onto the bed and spread her thighs wider. Madeline clutched the bed sheets in her fists and instinctively lifted her hips. Tension built inside her, an exhilarating, frustrating, frightening coil that had a scream hovering at the back of her throat.

Brazos lifted his head just long enough to say, "*L'extase, ma Belle, l'extase.*"

Climax, my Beauty, Madeline translated his words as the tremors began. Lightning sizzled along her nerves, and a great burst of pleasure exploded inside her. She cried aloud as wave after wave of supreme sensation swept through her, and her last coherent thought was, *His accent was perfect.*

As he felt her release, the last shred of Brazos's

control shattered. Never before had he wanted a woman as much as he wanted Madeline, never. He could wait no longer. "Look at me, Maddie. Say my name. Say it now."

He knelt on the bed above her, his body poised to claim her, as Madeline breathed, "Brazos, oh, Brazos."

With a swift, deep stroke he entered her.

He heard her cry of pain. Belatedly, he sensed the barrier that had given way before him. For a few moments, none of it made sense to him. Powerless over the demands of his body, he quickly spent himself inside her. He rolled off of her and onto his back. With his forearm flung over his eyes, he fought for breath. What the hell, he thought.

Apparently, he had just bedded a virgin mother.

Chapter 9

In a voice as cold as a West Texas norther, he asked, "Who the hell are you?"

Madeline's bed of roses had turned downright thorny. Her heart plummeted, all the wondrous, heavenly feelings Brazos had awakened within her vanishing at the prick of his tone. And if that wasn't enough, he turned his head and looked at her, and the barb of fury in his eyes stabbed deep. Madeline caught her breath against the pain of a wound in an area of her body she normally kept well protected.

She seldom indulged in heartache.

"You are obviously not that poor baby's mother—unless you somehow figured a way to give birth and still leave your chastity intact. I doubt even the Virgin Mother managed that little trick, but then, she wasn't a lying, conniving, scheming—"

"That's blasphemous," Madeline interrupted.

"Yeah?" Brazos shot back. "Well, so is your claimin' to be that sweet little girl's mother. Rose. Let's talk about Rose, shall we?" He sat up and pushed off the bed. Heedless of his nudity, he braced his hands on his hips and glared down at her. "Who is she, Madeline? Where's her real mother? Who the hell are you?"

Instinctively clutching the sheet to her chest, Madeline considered telling him the truth. She could calmly explain how an anonymous letter had arrived at the boarding school addressed to her and containing the offer of a position, travel money, and impeccable—though spurious—references in her name. Madeline could inform Brazos that although the missive had appealed to the larcenous part of herself, it had been the dream it had dangled before her that resulted in Madeline's departure on a ship bound for France that very day. The message had claimed that at Château St. Germaine, Mary Smithwick would find family.

Madeline could reveal to Brazos that she had found family, all right—a pathetic, diseased, nightmare of a household that eventually set her on a course that had led her here tonight. Here to Brazos Sinclair's bed.

But to tell Brazos would involve trusting him with Rose's secret. Dare she? Were it only herself at risk, she'd tell him the entire ugly story immediately. After all, she'd entrusted him with the taking of her virginity, and a woman simply didn't do that unless she'd some bit of faith in the man.

"You'd best start talkin', Madeline. My patience is wearin' mighty thin."

Madeline noted the muscle working in his jaw, and she grimaced at the fierceness of his gaze. He could certainly be a dangerous man; there was no debating that. And what about that dark side of this man? He fought it now, but what if in years to come evil defeated the goodness in Brazos Sinclair? Madeline dared not ignore the possibility that someday, a different Brazos might use Rose's secret for his own gain. "Brazos, it's a long and involved story," she said as a way of delay.

"Get on with it then. I'm all ears."

Her gaze swept his naked body, and a giggle that bordered on hysterics escaped her. "No, actually, you're not."

Pinning her with an expression both glacial and

unwavering, Brazos reached for his denims. The look in his eyes was bad enough. The way he donned his pants in a such a casual manner—as if, she imagined, it were a whore's bed he'd arisen from, rather than her own—didn't help matters at all. Neither did the disgust she read in his face when his gaze lit on the section of sheet stained with her virgin's blood. But Madeline could have handled all of those. It was the muttered comment she overheard when he sat on the edge of the bed to don his boots that drove her to recklessness.

"Dad-fool woman is as dumb as a box of rocks," he said beneath his breath. "Doesn't she know that females pretend to be virgins and not the other way around? What did she think, I wasn't gonna notice?" Standing, he grabbed up his shirt from the floor and slipped it on. As he worked the buttons, he snidely asked, "What's ol' Emile gonna think about all this, Madeline? I just took his bride-to-be's virginity. Will he be comin' after me with a gun? I know that's what I'd do. Of course, aimin' at the guilty party might be a bit confusin' for the man in this instance." Accusation narrowed his icy blue eyes as he said, "I want answers, Madeline, and I want them now."

Guilty party. Wasn't that just like a man? He's the one who came here looking for . . . for . . .

Sitting up, she snapped, "I don't give a bloody hell what you want."

He froze, his eyes growing wide with disbelief. "What did you say?"

"I said, Mr. Sinclair, that it matters little what questions you ask, because I'm not providing any answers. I don't see that I owe you any at all. You're a fake, Brazos Sinclair." The longer she spoke, the more shrill her voice became. "You pretend to care, feign affection, when it is but your own needs you wish to serve. You wanted a hand to hold to ward off your demons, so you come to me, appealing to my dearly held beliefs. You alleviate your boredom by taking advantage of my Rose, plying her with toys and buying her affections, unmindful of how she'll hurt and yearn for you once you are gone from her life."

Madeline rose to her knees, a Valkyrie proud and sure, as she said, "You want a woman on whom to slake your lust, so you choose the one who has seen you less than a man. Are you proud you demonstrated your manhood on me, Brazos Sinclair? Are you reassured that you are no longer impotent?"

His mouth was a tight, angry slash across his face. At his sides, his fists clenched, then released, then clenched again. "You know, Madeline," he said, his voice so full of studied indifference that she felt a slice of cold fear. "I don't know whether to hit you or throw you back down on that mattress and show you just how unimpotent I am."

Bravely, she lifted her chin. "Leave here, Brazos. It's over. The marriage, the lies, the game."

His granite gaze raked her nakedness. "Yeah, you're right about that much."

From the other bedroom came the sound of a child's tearful cry. Brazos and Madeline both hurried to Rose. He reached the baby first, lifting her from the crib and laying her against his shoulder. He patted her back and crooned comfortingly as Madeline tucked the trailing end of the bed sheet securely around herself like a toga.

"Give her to me, Brazos," she said, lifting her arms and trying vainly to disguise the trembling. "She needs me." Brazos ignored her, and as Rose continued to whimper, he pressed a gentle kiss to her golden curls, then said, "Too bad she doesn't have a mother to comfort her."

"*I* am her mother."

He looked her directly in the eye and whispered, "Bullshit."

Madeline blinked back the tears that had suddenly pooled in her eyes. "Her mother died. I'm her mother now. That's all you need to know. The rest of it doesn't matter."

"It damn sure does. I love the little squirt; I figure that gives me all the rights I need. Who is she, Madeline? *Who are you?*"

"She's my daughter. Give her to me."

She could see in his expression that a new thought had occurred. He watched her closely as he asked, "What about her father? Is this missin' Emile her father?"

Madeline flinched. This was a subject she wished desperately to avoid. "Rose's father is dead, too," she snapped too loudly. The baby let out a wail.

Brazos swayed slowly back and forth, clicking his tongue and saying, "Shh, Miss Magic. It's all right." His gaze, however, never left Madeline. When Rose had quieted again, he softly said, "I remember that day on the quay in Antwerp. You were desperate. You were runnin' from him, weren't you? That's what the hurry to get out of Europe was all about."

Memories rushed back, and she shook her head, denying both them and his words. In a harsh, angry whisper, he said, "My God, woman, did you kidnap this poor child?"

"Think what you want," she hissed through gritted teeth. "It matters not. I love Rose, Brazos. You know that, and you know I'd never do anything to hurt her. *Never.*" She held out her hands, steady this time. "Now, giver her to me. Sometimes she has nightmares, and she'll need me close by."

"Nightmares, huh. Well, I guess it's a night for 'em." Gently, he returned the sleeping baby to her bed. Straightening, he looked at Madeline. Her heart plummeted as she witnessed the iron determination reflected in his eyes. "I guess she's safe enough for now. I know that in your own way, you love her. Guard her well, Madeline, while you still can. I suspect your nightmares are only just beginning."

At the door, he paused and promised. "I'll find my answers. I'll discover who you stole her from. Rose deserves better than a mother who's a thief."

Softly, the door closed behind him.

STEAM ROSE FROM the horses' nostrils like a cloud of cigar smoke with every blow. The air was wet with early morning fog that could chill a man to the marrow were the flames of anger not burning inside him. Mounted on a sturdy buckskin, Brazos ran no risk of being cold.

The tide lapped at hard-packed sand as Brazos and Tyler followed the edge of the surf toward the sparsely populated southern end of the island. Brazos rode hard, the exercise providing an outlet for the emotions he'd locked within himself during the endless, sleepless night just past. He'd spent long hours thinking and making decisions, and when he'd banged on his brother's front door just after dawn, he'd known what course his actions must take.

And he hated it like hell.

Tyler reined in his horse and dismounted. An unbroken sand dollar lay at the edge of the surf, and he bent to pick it up. "A lady friend of mine collects these," he explained apologetically when Brazos lifted a brow in inquiry.

Leather creaked softly as Brazos swung from the saddle. "Better than collectin' diamonds, I suppose."

As the sun climbed higher in the sky, burning off the fog and toasting the air, the two men walked their horses in companionable silence. Then Tyler ruined the peace by saying, "I've been amazingly patient up till now, little brother, but I think it's time you told me a bit about this marriage of yours."

"Yeah, I know. I've been workin' up to it." He grimaced and said, "My dear, former wife, Madeline." Her name tasted bitter on his tongue. "Tyler, I discovered last night that my sweet little bride stole that baby from its father. I want to hire someone to investigate Madeline Christophe, and I'm gonna need your help."

Tyler dug his boots into the sand. "A kidnapper! I don't believe it." A slow, anxious look dawned across his face. "Tell me it isn't true, brother. She seemed like such a nice young woman."

"Yeah, she's nice, all right," Brazos drawled. "Kinda like the oleander bushes bloomin' here around town. Nice, pretty, soft blossoms—makes you want to pick 'em. Smell 'em." He sneered as he added, "Give the oleander a taste, though, and its poison will kill you deader'n hell."

His brow wrinkled in worry, Tyler quizzed, "Brazos, are you certain of this? I spent some time with her in my office. She was so very congenial, under difficult circumstances, I might add. Ladylike, sincere, and she certainly seemed to dote on that baby." He shook his head. "No, it can't be. Besides, the girl looks just like your Madeline."

"She's not my Madeline!"

Tyler took off his hat, scratched his head, and winced as he said, "Well, actually . . ."

Brazos shot him a sharp glance. "Actually what?"

Shoving his hat back onto his head, Tyler resumed walking. Briskly. Brazos frowned as he caught up with his brother. "Ty, is there some sort of problem here? I'm dead set on hirin' a man to look into this, so there's no sense tryin' to talk me out of it, if that's what you're thinkin'."

"I can hire someone for you," Tyler said, waving his hand. "That's nothing."

"Well, what is it? I can tell you've somethin' stuck in your craw."

Both brothers stared at Tyler's horse when he snorted. Tyler stroked the roan gelding's nose, then asked, "How do you know Madeline kidnapped that child? What did she do, come right out and tell you?"

"In a manner of speakin', yeah."

"What did she say?"

"Actually, she kinda yelped." He noted his brother's confusion, but decided enough had been said on the subject. After all, a fella shared only so much about his personal life, and Brazos had already confessed to having been married to a kidnapper. Tyler didn't need to know any more.

Brazos tossed Tyler his horse's reins and strode back up the beach, where a slender piece of driftwood lay. He lifted the tree branch and shook it, testing its weight. Then he reached into his jacket pocket and withdrew a small leather ball. Setting the ball upon the sand, he eyed a long scrub some fifty yards up the beach. "Listen, Tyler, I'm wantin' this information as fast as I can get it. What kind of time would you expect we'd be lookin' at, sendin' to Europe for it and all?" He took a swing at the ball. When it hooked right of the bush, he grimaced and started walking. "It purely worries me to think of a father somewhere grievin' over his lost baby."

Tyler followed him. "It'll take some time, Brazos. I'd say five, six months at the earliest. But I'll get started on it first thing. Well, second thing. I've something important to see to first."

Brazos stood over the ball, preparing to roll it toward his target, and shook his head. "Nothin's more important than this, Tyler."

Tyler opened his mouth, started to speak, then abruptly shut it.

"Ty?"

He replied in a rush. "What are you doing with that stick?"

"This is great, Tyler. I've discovered the best game." Brazos lifted the ball from the sand and handed it to his brother, saying, "You're gonna have to play it with me. I met an old Scot who spoke of nothing else. He taught me the game on a course on the west coast of France, a place called Pau. In my trunks, I have a set of the sticks you use to play the game with—those and three dozen of these balls. Spent a pretty penny on the balls, too."

Tyler studied the smooth leather sphere. "I've never known another man so obsessed with toys," he mused.

Brazos glanced up at a pair of screeching gulls. "This isn't a toy. It's a sport. Like fox hunting in England, only nothin' dies." He grabbed the ball, set it on the sand, and took a wide swing at it with his stick. It sailed up and over the top of a dune. He started after it.

"Brazos, about the woman," Tyler said, climbing the dunes behind his brother. "Do you remember when we were kids and went to visit Cousin Reece out in Pine Bluff?" Brazos nodded. Tyler kicked at a tuft of grass, helping to search for the ball, and continued, "You recall the church social, when you were suppose to take

Mama's pecan pie down and enter it in the contest, only you made it about halfway to church before deciding to eat it instead?"

"There's my ball." Brazos pointed toward a bare spot some twenty yards away. As they walked, he said, "I ate the whole thing—made me sicker than a big dog. Can't stomach pecan pie to this day." He sighed with disgust. "Damn, she curved to the right again. I wonder why."

They reached the ball, and Tyler laid his hand on Brazos's arm. "Do you remember what you told Pa when he asked you why you did it?"

"Before or after the woodshed?"

"Before."

Brazos frowned thoughtfully as he drew lines in the sand with his stick. "I remember now. He gave me an extra set of lickin's because I told him I'd done it just to stir up trouble." A slow smile of remembrance inched across his face. "Couldn't sit down for three days."

Tyler took the stick from Brazos's hand and gave a whack at the ball. It missed a pelican by inches, then landed in the gulf. Tyler tossed down the stick. "Stupid game, chasing after a ball with a stick. What do you call it."

"Golf," Brazos replied.

"I guess all the other four letter words were taken." Tyler watched the ruined ball wash ashore and confessed, "Brazos, I'm afraid that last night I indulged a craving for pecan pie."

Brazos gave him a sidelong look. "What did you say?"

"No harm done, really," Tyler hastened to say, pasting a sickly grin on his face. "I can take care of the matter just as soon as we get back to town." He ran nervous fingers through his hair. "I thought she was a nice woman, you see. Didn't know she was a kidnapper. Thought to pay you back for that mess you caused me with Lilah May McPherson." Nothing his brother's granite expression, Tyler added prayerfully, "Please, Brazos, tell me you didn't bed her last night."

Brazos shut his eyes. *Tyler didn't file the god-*

damned papers. Nightmares, hell. Looks as if one of his own just reached up and bit him square on the . . . "I'm goin' swimmin'." He began to peel of his shirt.

"Brazos, you can't go swimming. It can't be more than sixty-five degrees out here. You'll freeze."

"Better that than deckin' you again, dear brother. That's what I'd really like to do." Stripped naked, Brazos made a running dive into the surf. He swam with long, even strokes until the water's chill melted the hot rush of anger from his body and his mind went back to work.

Standing waist-deep, he stared out to sea as he wiped water away from his salt-numbed lips and considered his predicament. He was still married to Madeline Christophe. "Hell," he muttered, "I'm even more married to her than I was yesterday." Memories of their passionate lovemaking flickered across his brain. Determinedly, he buried them, just as he had a hundred times over the long night recently ended.

Vaguely aware that Tyler called his name, Brazos watched the white, foamy breakers and repeated aloud, "I'm still married to Madeline Christophe."

Then he realized that, under the circumstances, it wasn't necessarily a bad thing.

Brazos smiled grimly as he left the water. Tyler met him at surf's edge with his clothes, saying, "You did it, didn't you? You bedded her. And because of my interference, the Sinclair family will have its first divorce. Oh, hell, Brazos, I'm so damned sorry."

Brazos took one look at his brother's hangdog face and laughed. Tyler looked at him as if he'd lost his mind. "Buck up, brother," Brazos said, grabbing his garments. "It's not as bad as you think. In fact, you've actually done me a good turn."

"Excuse me?" Tyler blinked. "I'm afraid you've lost me. What is it you are saying, that you're happy being married to a kidnapper?"

"Yep." Having used his shirt as a towel, Brazos slung it over his shoulder and pulled on his pants. "You see, Tyler, though you managed it quite by accident, you've offered me a solution to one of the problems that might have upset my plan."

"What plan?"

Brazos explained as they headed back toward the horses. "I came home to take care of Salezan. Before I can do that, though, I need to rescue Juanita from Cousin Jeffrey and hide her in a place no one would think to look."

"What's that have to do with your being married?"

Brazos gave the buckskin a pat on the neck, then swung into the saddle. "Mr. and Mrs. Brazos Sinclair are members of the Colonization Society of Texas. La Réunion has a lot of strange rules, but I've never seen or heard anything that would prevent a family member from comin' along for a visit."

As Tyler mounted his horse, a glimmer of understanding stole across his face. "You mean—"

Brazos nodded. "I'm goin' to need your help, Ty. Any reason you couldn't leave Galveston for a bit?"

"Well, no. What do you want me to do?"

"Our sister mentioned in her last letter that St. Michael's money cache is runnin' light. Since I'm headed in that direction, I figure to take a wagonload with me. While I'm fetchin' the silver, I'd like you to go to Cousin Jeffrey's and gather up—" He paused and rubbed his hand across his chin. "Let's see, shall we call her a cousin? Yes, that sounds good. You carry Cousin Juanita along to Anderson, and I'll meet you there."

"Anderson. That's just on the far side of the forest region north of Houston, isn't it?"

Brazos nodded and continued, "The colonists will pass that way on the trail to La Réunion. I intend for us to join the wagon train at that point."

"Hell, Brazos, I don't know if that's such a good idea after all." Tyler took off his hat and twirled it on a finger, frowning at it. "If Salezan's men have spotted you here in Galveston, we could end up leading them right to the silver *and* Juanita."

Brazos reached out and grabbed Tyler's hat. Tossing it at him, Brazos said, "Leave it on your head, brother; you're lettin' the sun bake your brain. I *want* Salezan to know I'm back. In fact, before we leave Anderson, I plan to send him a letter—a personal invitation to leave his lair and meet me here in Texas."

"Letter?" Tyler asked. Then realization dawned in his expression. "The location of the silver mine."

"Yep."

"I don't know, Brazos." Tyler shook his head. "Wouldn't it be better for Juanita to remain with Cousin Jeffrey until you've killed Salezan?"

"Probably. But knowin' Nita, since she doesn't like livin' where she's at, she's liable to up and do somethin' dumb. I think she'll enjoy being with the Europeans. They're cultured folk, and Nita loves to talk music and art and that sort of business." The buckskin snorted as Brazos nudged her into a walk.

"Well, you know her better than I," Tyler answered, following his brother. "But what about Salezan's men? Don't underestimate them, Brazos. They might be following us this very moment."

"Good. See, Tyler, later this morning, you and I will make a quite public departure from Galveston as we head home to visit with the family. I figure we can spend a week or so at Magnolia Bend, and that'll give the colonists time to get a good start north. Then, the family can create some sort of diversion, and you and I can sneak away from the plantation and go about our separate tasks."

"It might work," Tyler said, slowly nodding. "Family resemblance the way it is, strangers have a hard time telling us apart. If we work it right, Salezan's men might think we're still at Magnolia Bend long after we've left."

"We'll time it so we'll be a day or two ahead of the Europeans," Brazos continued. "While I really don't think there'll be any trouble, having your gun along the trail will make the plan just that much safer."

Tyler pulled a piece of straw from his horse's mane as he asked, "What about the colonists? Aren't you afraid Salezan's men might follow them?"

"Why would they? There'd be no reason to. Before

we leave Galveston, I'll make a public break with the Réunionists by telling a few of the island's busybodies that the marriage between Madeline Christophe and Brazos Sinclair has been annulled. I'll make sure they know I only used the woman to gain passage home from Europe. If Salezan has men here, they'll be bound to hear that kind of gossip. They won't follow the Phalansterians from Galveston."

"Phallus what?" Tyler asked.

Brazos grinned, recalling his own similar reaction. "Phalansterians. Followers of Charles Fourier. Builders of a Texas Utopia. Tell me, Tyler, can you think of a better place to hide the most beautiful woman on earth than in Utopia?"

"It does seem appropriate. Juanita will fit right in. I only hope Salezan's men won't realize it too." He hesitated a moment before asking, "But what about Madeline? She's liable to put up a fuss over this."

"I know how to keep her mouth shut." At Tyler's questioning look, Brazos smiled meanly and said, "I'll simply follow my bride's example. I don't figure blackmail is near as bad a crime as kidnappin'. I'll make certain she does as we want." As he gigged his horse into a canter, he called back over his shoulder. "Don't worry, Tyler. Salezan's men will follow you and me to Magnolia Bend. They'll leave the colonists completely alone. I'm certain of it."

Watching the puffs of sand kicked up by his brother's horse, Tyler considered Brazos's plan and thought of a saying their father often repeated. *Nerve succeeds.* "I hope to hell Pa's right," he said, kicking his horse into a run and trailing Brazos.

But he couldn't shake the worry that this time, nerve wouldn't be enough.

Chapter 10

While making travel arrangements for the next leg of
their journey, Victor Considérant learned that a local
merchant expected the arrival of a shipment of farm
implements from New Orleans within the week. After
consulting with his assistants, he made the decision to
delay the colonists' departure from Galveston until the
valuable supplies could be purchased.

Madeline took a room at the Powhattan Hotel
along with the other colonists, and what had begun as a
way of spending idle hours developed into a frenzy of
shopping that left the islanders awestruck. All around
town, Galvestonians shook their heads in Madeline's
wake. It simply wasn't done that way. Texans traveled *to*
Europe to shop. The fool woman had it backward.

In truth, she had discovered that by burying herself
in the island shops, few that they were, she was able to
forget—at least for a little while—the ache she'd carried
in her chest since Brazos Sinclair had left her at the
cottage.

She'd also determined that paying for items from

baby bonnets to cheese using Julian Desseau's money had a certain charm of its own. She'd actually found it more satisfying than stealing. It'd been quite a revelation for a woman who'd never before had money to spend as she pleased. Madeline spent three full days in the shops of Galveston without snatching a thing.

Well, almost three days. She had indulged the itch yesterday when she encountered Brazos's cousin Trixie at a milliner's. The handkerchief in the woman's pocket had fluttered temptingly, catching Rose's eye before disappearing into Madeline's hand. The child waved it about even now, as the colonists gathered at the harbor to board a steamboat for the trip up Buffalo Bayou to Houston.

Lillibet Brunet took one look at the vessel and said, "Oh, my heavens, we'll not live to see the sunset. Listen to that engine. It's roaring and boiling as though it's alive and in a rage."

"Actually, it reminds me of Brazos," Madeline observed, foolishly breaking her silence on the subject of her former husband.

It was all the opening Lillibet required. As the steamer, *Christy Ann,* chugged its way across Galveston Bay and into the mouth of Buffalo Bayou, she plied Madeline with questions concerning the missing Mr. Sinclair. "Lillibet, please," Madeline finally said as she fed Rose tiny bites of a banana. "I told you when I returned to the Powhattan that Brazos had left me. Neither you nor anyone else should have been surprised by it. After all, we never made any secret of the reasons behind our marriage."

"I know," Lillibet said with a sigh. "It's just that I had great hopes for the two of you. You were such a beautiful pair, and I truly believed we'd convinced Mr. Brazos to embrace the Phalansterian way of life."

Madeline stifled an inelegant snort. "Really, Lil. Brazos only paid attention to the Fourierist doctrines concerning Free Love. Once he discovered the La Réunion colony wouldn't put those ideas into practice, he lost all interest." She punctuated her point by taking a bite from the banana.

"Well, I suppose you're right. Still, I shall miss him. You have to admit, the man was wonderful with the children."

Madeline felt a tingle of unease at her friend's words. Brazos had developed an undeniable affection for Rose, and the words he'd spoken that difficult night continued to haunt her. *Your nightmares are only just beginning.*

What had he meant? What did he intend to do? For two days, she'd expected a visit from him, half afraid he'd appear with the authorities in tow. Yesterday, when Trixie's offhand comment revealed that Brazos had departed Galveston Island two days earlier, Madeline had reeled in shock. He'd not only left her following their night together, he'd left the entire island.

That was when Madeline had picked Trixie's pocket.

Buffalo Bayou was little more than a narrow creek, and twice during the trip, passengers were pressed into service to pole the boat upstream. By early afternoon, the colonists cheered the sight of the three-story warehouses lining the shore that announced the steamer's arrival in Houston.

Named after the hero of San Jacinto and the president of the Republic of Texas, Houston was a rowdy town where saloons outnumbered churches six to one. The steamer's captain assured the Europeans that a number of hotels in town offered safe, comfortable lodging for travelers, but one of the Fourierists suggested they establish a campsite instead. Victor Considérant called for a vote, and Madeline waved her hand high along with the majority as the immigrants chose to begin camp life on their first night in Houston.

Locating an appropriate spot on the prairie west of town, the colonists circled their chests and trunks and established cooking and sleeping arrangements to be observed during the three-week overland trek to Central Texas. Anxious to begin the final leg of their journey to La Réunion, they made quick work of buying wagons and oxen and hiring teamsters to lead them to their final destination.

Madeline used Julian Desseau's money to purchase a wagon and the livestock required to pull it. She hired a tall, wiry man, Mr. Cole Johnston, to act as her driver. Mr. Johnston handled the team well, and Madeline found his anecdotes about Texas both informative and amusing. In many ways, he reminded her of Brazos.

On a bright spring morning four days following their arrival in Houston, and accompanied by the serenade of a raucous mob of robins, the wagon train headed north toward a section of land just across the Trinity River from the small village called Dallas. There they would build Utopia.

At first, their trail took them over prairie, making good time at ten to twelve miles a day. But on the fourth day, the wisps of clouds drifting high on a bleached sky disappeared from sight as the line of wagons entered a region of towering forests.

In places, the road was no more than a trail, and the colonists took axes and hoes to clear a path through the underbrush and ravines. Twice Madeline hopped down from the wagon to help, although in the second instance, the sight of an ugly green snake with black markings had her scrambling back into her seat. Through it all, the teamsters preached sermons to their oxen, urging them forward with language that at times had Madeline covering little Rose's ears.

Though travel through the forests was slower, the end of each day afforded the colonists a sense of accomplishment, and by the close of the first week, they'd established a smooth routine for setting up camp. Once a site had been chosen, a handful of colonists cut brush and piled it into a heap for a fire. Others put up the tents and dug trenches around them to keep out the snakes. Still others got out the pots and kettles and began cooking the meal.

Madeline enjoyed the camp-making most of all. She found it quite in keeping with Fourier's philosophies that she was able to choose trench digging over cooking for her part of the work.

Not that she ever was allowed to do much work. It quickly became obvious that when Victor Considérant had argued back in Antwerp that a woman alone on the frontier would face insurmountable difficulties, he had failed to take into account the economies of supply and demand. Single men, from wealthy Phalansterians to impoverished wagon drivers, all but came to blows over the opportunity to haul water, move trunks, build fires, or any other job Madeline might wish done. As her wagon driver, Mr. Johnston, took to saying, "Goldurn, Miz Madeline, you've done got the pick of whatever litter you want."

And she'd been working at picking. Madeline's top priority was finding a husband. Only this time, she intended to be more selective. If she searched for blue eyes or wavy black hair or a toe-tingling smile in every man she met, well, that didn't mean anything.

All right, so maybe it meant a little something. But she was trying her very best to stop it.

Brazos Sinclair had touched her deeply, in a way she could not define. Was it because she'd given herself to him physically? Would she know this same sense of . . . depth with any man?

Whatever it was, it had caused great pain. Madeline hoped she'd never again experience the ache she had known the night he left her.

One week into the overland trip, Madeline rode in the bed of her wagon, cuddling Rose, who sniffled and snored her way through her afternoon nap. As she had so often since that night out of time in Galveston, she thought back over her weeks spent with Brazos and sighed. As badly as this had hurt, it could have been much worse. Imagine what it would have felt like if she had been in love with him.

It probably would have killed her.

Madeline didn't know exactly what it was she felt for Brazos Sinclair, but it wasn't love. She knew what love was. Love was the joy she knew in her heart when she'd watched Rose learn to crawl. Love was that warm feeling that filled her when she heard Rose's laughter. Love was the tears that swam in her eyes whenever Rose lifted her chin for a kiss.

Madeline loved Rose. True, she'd never experienced the emotion before, but she recognized it in what she felt for her daughter. She prayed she would find the same sort of sentiments with a man—those feelings of warmth, safety, security. Not that dangerous, reckless, blood-pounding nonsense she experienced around Brazos Sinclair.

The wagon lurched to a stop, and Madeline sat up. After opening her eyes and staring up at her mother, Rose blinked, stuck her thumb in her mouth, and went back to sleep. Madeline smoothed the blanket over the baby's back, pressed a kiss to her cheek, then left the wagon.

The wagon train had exited the great forest. She stared around her, and a delighted smile spread across her face. How wonderful to see so much sky once again! Before her stretched miles of rolling hills dotted with hardwood trees and covered with prairie grass and wildflowers of every hue. Upon checking with Lillibet, Madeline learned that Considérant had called an early halt to the day's travel. In recognition of having traversed one-third of the distance between Houston and La Réunion, the colonists would hold a fete that evening. Lillibet had a gleam in her eye as she said, "Dearling, you must wear that blue rosebud-patterned silk. Mr. Litty will be blinded by your beauty in that dress."

Madeline looked at her friend sharply. "Mr. Litty?"

"Now, Madeline, I am not a stupid woman. I know you want a man—as right you should. It's the way of the world. Rose needs a father, and you need a man to keep you warm at night. While I hate to give up on Mr. Brazos, I fear we've seen the last of him."

"I certainly hope so," Madeline said softly.

Lillibet tilted her head, giving Madeline a knowing glance. "After watching you aboard the *Uriel*, I know that none of our Frenchmen have caught your fancy. Am I wrong?"

Watching a hawk sail circles against an azure sky, Madeline shook her head and sighed. "You wouldn't be speaking this way if I were a bachelor, Lil. It's not fair—*not equal*—that an unmarried woman should be treated as though she wishes for nothing more in life than to have a man on her arm."

Lillibet laughed and rested her hands on her stomach, now well rounded in pregnancy. "You are absolutely right, Madeline. If you were a man, I would never suggest the blue silk as an appropriate dress." Madeline rolled her eyes as Lillibet continued, "Now, Madeline, I understand what you are saying, but I've also seen the wistful looks you send our way when André and I discuss the home we plan to make with Thomas and the new baby. You can't deny that."

"You're right, Lil. I want to make a home and family for Rose. That is very important to me."

"Well, then. You wear that blue silk this evening. I'm loath to admit it, but I've done a bit of snooping where our wagon master is concerned."

Madeline refused to ask outright, but she would listen. Benjamin Litty was the nicest and most gentlemanly man among the Texans who had been hired by the colonists to lead the wagon train north. Without being a pest like some of the single men—and a few of the married ones, truth be told—Mr. Litty had managed to convey his interest in her through an occasional smile or significant look. They'd shared a number of pleasant, casual conversations over the past week. He was definitely the best prospect for a husband Madeline had met so far.

"He's a widower, Madeline," Lillibet allowed, a gleam of anticipation in her eyes. "He owns a ranch near Dallas, and he has two young children, both boys. He's looking for a mother for them. Considérant was able to hire him to lead us because he had traveled to South Texas to meet a Yankee woman with whom he'd been corresponding. She was to have sailed to Galveston where they planned to marry. Only she sent a letter of regret instead."

"He doesn't seem the type of man who'd have told you all this," Madeline commented suspiciously.

Lillibet nodded. "I received the information directly from Marie Deauville, who heard it from Michelle

Louis, who learned it from Charley, the man driving their wagon. Charley was disgruntled because Mr. Litty wanted nothing to do with the wagoner's sister, a horse-faced woman I myself met in the Houston mercantile. One cannot get information much more reliable, dearling."

Madeline glanced across the camp to see Ben Litty assist the Deauvilles' driver in fettering the oxen. He was a quite handsome man. With brilliant green eyes and sun-bleached hair, he was even more handsome than Brazos Sinclair. "You know, Lillibet," she said, "I believe that blue dress is in the smaller of my trunks."

THE BALLROOM'S WALLS were cedar trees, its ceiling the vast expanse of heaven. The luminous, full moon hung as chandelier, and the thousands of stars dangled, glittering crystals reflecting the light. The carpet was a rug of natural green, soft and sweet-scented and new. A lone violin accompanied an orchestra of trilling toads, chirping crickets, twittering birds, and the haunting whisper of wind through the forest at the colonists' backs. The setting was as fine a salon as any ever visited in Europe.

The colonists and their Texan friends ate and drank and debated the politics of the time, from the Know-Nothing Party's gaining strength across the country to the benefits of communal agriculture.

Madeline danced. She twirled and whirled almost exclusively on the arms of the handsome and attentive wagon master. A tall, rugged-looking man, Ben Litty had entertained her throughout supper with stories about a pet pig he'd owned while growing up on a farm in East Texas. She'd found herself laughing, really laughing, for the first time since Brazos had left her.

It felt wonderful.

Desiring a break from the dancing, Madeline allowed Ben to lead her away from the campsite. They walked in the meadow along the edge of the forest, watching the stars and talking. "I certainly enjoyed the stew you fixed, Miz Madeline," he said, holding her elbow for support as she stepped over a fallen log.

Madeline shrugged. "The stew was edible, but I am sorry about those biscuits."

"Not to worry, ma'am, the oxen'll eat 'em. You'll find very little goes to waste on the frontier."

The air rippled with the sweet, clean scent of pine, and Madeline found it a pleasing change from days of travel downwind of oxen. Mr. Litty took her hand.

Suddenly and without any outward change in the surroundings, Madeline sensed a sinister presence around her. Uneasy, she slowed her step. "Perhaps we should return to camp, Ben. Mr. Johnston has told me stories about the panthers that stalk the woods and prairies, and I'll admit I've the strangest feeling that I'm being watched."

Ben Litty turned to her, a half-teasing, half-serious look in his eyes. "Are you afraid I can't protect you, Miz Madeline? That's a hard blow to a Texan, ma'am. We're terribly protective of our womenfolk, you know."

"It's not you," Madeline hastened to say. "I'll admit that after traveling through the forest day after day, I came to see things in the trees—things that weren't there."

Litty smiled in understanding. "It can be a little spooky, I know. But there's nothing to worry about. I've got a gun, and the animals are truly more afraid of us than we are of them. I reckon, though, we ought to turn back. We have been gone a bit. I enjoy your company, Madeline. I wouldn't want to hurt your reputation in any way."

"Oh, Ben." Madeline couldn't help laughing. "Believe me, the colonists won't think a thing of my spending time with you. I can see you're not overly familiar with Phalansterian beliefs."

From somewhere deep in the trees came a crashing sound, and instinctively, Madeline stepped closer to Litty. Chuckling, he rested a hand on her shoulder. "Come on, Madeline, I don't want you to be afraid."

She looked up at him and recognized the flash of desire in his gaze. Well, Madeline, she said to herself, if you're serious about replacing Brazos Sinclair, you'd best be about it.

And Mr. Litty did have such a nice smile. And pretty eyes, such a deep green with little flecks of amber. As it turned out, his kiss wasn't half bad, either. He brushed her lips with his, gentle and questioning at first, and when she offered no protest, he drew her closer and fit his mouth firmly against hers.

It was nice, Madeline thought, relaxing in his arms. Warm and comforting, peaceful. Not like that roaring, raging storm she'd felt with Brazos Sinclair.

Litty's hands slipped to her waist, and Madeline knew it was time to call a halt to this experiment. She tugged her head away from his just as a feral scream sliced through the forest behind them.

"Eeek!" Madeline clutched at Litty's shirt. In the blink of an eye his hand held a gun pointed in the direction of the noise. "What was that?" her voice quaked as tremors of fear slithered up her spine.

For a long moment, Litty stood totally still, and she could see his concentration as he listened. Then his features eased, and he said, "Well, Madeline, as best I can tell, it was a cougar with terrible timing." He squeezed her hand reassuringly and added, "Funniest sounding cat I've ever heard, though."

Walking back, Madeline heard the violin's song drifting across the night. The cougar's cry had long since died, but the sensation of malice that had disturbed her earlier remained even stronger. The tiny hairs at the back of her neck bristled.

As she and Ben joined the others back at the campsite, she looked over her shoulder and again searched for the source of her unease. She'd have been better off looking where she was going. As it was, she almost ran right into the new addition to the train.

A female figure garbed totally in black sat on the seat of a buckboard that carried a coffin in its bed. Madeline's gaze drifted over the strange sight and stopped. The man standing beside the wagon bore the familiar face of Tyler Sinclair.

The crowd hushed. Madeline felt a distinctive chill sweep over her. Turning, she saw a form standing before the fire, a dark-haired devil with fire in his eyes, who said in a voice as cold as ice, "Hello, Madeline. I'm back."

Chapter 11

He should have known she'd have a man with her. Brazos tried to tell himself he didn't care, but the sick sensation in his gut suggested differently. As he watched Madeline's face drain of color, some of the fury inside him eased. At least he wasn't the only one affected by this scene. His wife wasn't happy to see him. Not happy at all. In fact, she looked scared half to death. Good.

"What are you doing here?" she asked in a trembling voice.

The fellow Madeline was with scowled and stepped protectively toward her. André Brunet, bless his soul, laid a restraining hand on the man's arm and mumbled something in his ear.

Brazos smiled a slow, predatory grin and advanced a step toward her. "Oh, I've got a number of reasons for showin' up. If you think real hard, you can probably come up with one or two of them. I brought my lawyer with me, Madeline."

She swayed on her feet, and Brazos almost felt sorry for her. Almost. A good, decent woman would have nothing to fear from an attorney. He said, "We have a bit of a problem, and it's one reason Tyler's here with me. You see, a lawyer is good for gettin' a man out of the trouble he'd never have gotten into in the first place if it weren't for a lawyer."

"Watch it there, brother," Tyler warned.

Juanita, her features concealed by the widow's veil, laughed huskily. In a Spanish-accented voice, she said, "Sin, how many times you resurrect this old argument! You must be nicer to Tyler."

"That's right, Brazos. You'd best not make me angry now; you need me." He fixed his gaze on Madeline and added, "Badly."

Madeline managed to appear hurt as Tyler stared at her, his expression totally devoid of sympathy. A twinge of compassion snuck right by Brazos's best intentions, and that riled him all over again.

Why was he letting her get to him? She was a lying, thieving, child stealer! In a harsh voice, he said, "I'm afraid your new beau is gonna have to put his plans on the back shelf for a bit. It seems you and I are still married, Mrs. Sinclair."

"What!" Madeline's eyes went wide with shock.

"When I first heard the news, it took me down with the miseries, too," he observed. "But once I got to thinkin' about it, I decided it might not be so terrible after all." Shrugging, he stated, "Our marriage was not annulled."

Madeline lost what little color she'd regained. "That can't be! I signed the papers. You told me you signed them. We *can't* still be married."

Around them, the crowd began to buzz, and a corner of Brazos's mouth lifted in a crooked smile. There were times when it mattered not at all what nationality a person might be. Folks all over the world were alike when it came to enjoying a right juicy bit of gossip. "It seems that my brother neglected to file the papers, Madeline. By the time I found out about it . . ."

He saw from her expression that she'd made the connection. It would serve her right if he announced right here in front of God and everybody that by then, the grounds for an annulment no longer existed. But Brazos resisted the temptation. These Free Love Europeans wouldn't give a damn, and it went against the grain to air all of his private life in public.

Madeline stared at him, wide-eyed and silent. The color flooded back into her face as she puffed up like a spitting hen. "Well, why didn't he simply file the bloody things anyway?" she snapped.

He quirked a brow and said in a disapproving tone, "Cursing in public? Really, wife." And when he smiled at her, the light didn't reach his eyes. "Why, Tyler couldn't do that. It would be illegal. You wouldn't want to participate in any activity on the hot side of the law, would you, Madeline?"

Closing her eyes, she swallowed hard. Softly, she asked, "What do you want, Brazos?"

"Well, I've come to talk with you about our marriage. But first, I think, I'd like a dance."

"D . . . d . . . dance?"

The crowd of colonists shuffled as Lillibet waved them back from the riveting scene. Brazos pulled Madeline into his arms and waited for the music to begin again. He held her gaze, and they stood without speaking until the lilting strains of a harmonica began to play "The Lost Child" waltz. Damn that Tyler, Brazos thought as he stepped into the song. He has a wicked sense of humor.

With the show apparently over, the Europeans' fiddler—or violinist, as the man was too new to Texas to be a real fiddler—took control of the music making. Brazos waltzed his wife beneath the bower of cedar and the sparkling Texas sky, and to his shame, he enjoyed the experience.

For the first time ever, he acquired an understanding of why the evangelists preached about the evils of dancing. Resting at her waist, his hand developed an itch to drift lower. The fragrance of roses teased his nostrils, and against his own good judgment, he pulled her closer and felt the brush of her bosom against his chest. Damn, but it made him want to sin.

Madeline wasn't thinking about sin. She couldn't think. She was too afraid to think. But she had to think. What was Brazos up to? She doubted she really wanted to know.

So she danced with him, her mind whirling as fast as her feet. It must have something to do with the coffin and the widow, she told herself. She prayed it was so. Otherwise, he might be here on account of his threat. His words echoed in her mind, *Your nightmares are only just beginning.* "Brazos, why have you followed me?"

"Don't flatter yourself. If I came after anybody, it's the poor little baby you kidnapped."

Madeline tripped. His hold on her tightened, preventing her from falling. "You tired, wife? All that dancin' and flirtin' can plumb wear a woman out, huh? Come on, let's rest a spell. Maybe you know a nice place in the woods where we could stretch out? Bet your pretty-boy wagon master showed you one." Stopping only to grab a lantern, he all but yanked her into the cover of the forest.

Inside the woods, the night was black, the only light the small flame Brazos carried and a few stray moonbeams that pierced the canopy of leaves and branches above them. Unerringly, he led her to a spot beside a narrow creek where a dead campfire, trampled grass, and wagon ruts in the earth gave proof of recent habitation. The cane pole, its line left dangling in the water, made her guess the camper had been Brazos.

Setting the lamp atop a flat rock, he hunkered down beside the stream and checked the line. "Damn. Stole my bait. You know, I do detest stealin', I truly do."

Some people tolerate anxiety better than others. Normally, Madeline managed to deal with stress better than most. But everyone has limits, and Brazos's snide remark pushed her over the edge. She tugged the pole from Brazos's hand, slung it over the creek, and cried, "That's enough. Why are you here, Brazos? Tell me what you want. I demand answers."

He stared after the fishing pole, frowning. "Well, Madeline," he drawled. "What makes you think I'd even consider answering your questions? You certainly didn't reply to mine last time we spoke. I don't think I owe you anything when it comes to answers."

He was right. Madeline realized she'd taken the wrong tack. "I apologize." She sank to the ground, knowing he'd get around to his business in his own good time.

Which turned out to be after he'd retrieved his pole, dug for worms, baited his hook, and dropped it into the water. "I'd like to hook a big ol' catfish tonight. You could fry it up for us for breakfast in the mornin'."

"I could?"

"Yep. Nita really likes catfish, but she hates like hell to clean them. It'll be nice for her to have you around to do that sort of stuff for her."

"It will?" Beneath her fear of his intentions, an ember of anger sparked to life. The nerve of the man, she thought. Her tone dripped sugar when she asked, "The widow? Is she another cousin?"

He'd a gleam in his eye as he answered, "I'll let you in on a secret, here, wife. Juanita is *not* my cousin."

She wanted to push him into the stream. "Is she even a widow?"

Like a chameleon, Brazos changed. If earlier she'd thought him cold, now he was a block of ice. She shivered when he bit out, "No." He laid his pole down. "I've introduced Juanita as my widowed cousin. We are taking the dearly departed to his home north of here a ways for burial. Being as we're all family, you are going to offer her a place in your home at La Réunion."

"I'm what!" Madeline exclaimed.

"Listen, my blushin' bride, Juanita is a very dear friend of mine. In fact, she's the reason I was so anxious to get aboard the *Uriel* that I married a lyin', thievin' witch like you. Now, she needs a place to hide until I have taken care of a certain situation, and you are going to provide it. *And* you're gonna be as sweet as a watermelon's heart while you're about it."

The unspoken threat hung between them like a fog. Rose. They both knew she'd do whatever he wanted. "It's blackmail," she mumbled beneath her breath.

Brazos heard her. "Not near as bad a crime as kidnappin'. I said as much to Tyler."

She ignored that, asking instead about the marriage. "Your announcement back at camp. It was a lie, wasn't it? Our marriage has been annulled. It was only an excuse to rejoin the colonists."

"'Fraid not, Madeline. That much was true." Brazos lunged for the pole as something yanked the line, nearly dragging it into the water. He pulled a large, scaly fish out of the stream. "Damn crappie. Too bony to mess with." Without looking at her, he said, "I know that your Emile is waiting for you at La Réunion, but I figure since he's waited for you this long, a little extra time won't matter. You see, there's a part of this plan I simply haven't been able to work another way. As distasteful as the idea is, you and I are gonna pretend to reconcile." After removing the hook from the fish's mouth, Brazos tossed the crappie back into the water, where it landed with a *kuthunk*.

The fish sounded the way Madeline's stomach felt. "What do you mean, 'pretend to reconcile'?"

Brazos grimaced. "I know. Gives me the willies to think about it, too. Look, I need a good reason to rejoin the colonists, and I figure you're the best I have to work with. You and I are going to make believe that our recent separation has proven how much we grew to care about one another on the trip over from Europe. Now that we've seen the error of our ways, we've decided that 'for better or for worse' means for good."

"No one in their right minds would believe that tale," she scoffed, staring at the spot where the fish had disappeared.

"They believe you are Rose's mother. You've pulled off one bald-faced lie, Madeline; I'm sure you can manage another. You dance with the facts well enough to put 'em to music."

"Brazos." Madeline rubbed her temples with her fingertips. "We don't need to do this. You are a member of the Society, if you want to take a guest to La Réunion, no one will stop you. There's no reason for you and me to be involved any further."

Brazos baited his fish hook and said dryly, "I realize this may interfere with your romance with the wagon master, but in all honesty, I don't give a damn. I've thought this through, Madeline. The colonists will demand an explanation for my return, especially since I made such a to-do over our separation in Galveston. For my plan to work, we need to blend with the Europeans like butter on hot cornbread."

He ignored her broken moan, saying, "Most of them wanted us to stay together, and I figure we'll be less conspicuous as lovers than we would be as estranged mates. You and I are gonna be so happy and boring that any gossip that gets started and works its way across the Trinity River to Dallas won't have a thing to do with us. I can't have outsiders knowin' that Brazos Sinclair and a couple of his women are travelin' with the Colonization Society of Texas. Got it?"

Couple of his women! Madeline's gaze snagged on the new Colt revolver holstered at his thigh, and her fingers itched to steal it. "Brazos, this simply will not work."

"Sure it will. If you're concerned about that poor fool waiting for you at La Réunion, you needn't worry." Brazos rinsed his hands at the edge of the stream, then lobbed the hook into the water. "That's another one of the reasons I brought Tyler along. Once we get close to Dallas, I'm going to send him on ahead to find your fiancé and warn him we're coming. Tyler can take care of any trouble Emile might try to give us."

Madeline's fingers rubbed her forehead. He was sending Tyler to find Emile? Whatever else could go wrong? "You have, I assume, begun divorce proceedings?" she asked, feeling sicker by the minute.

"Not yet. A divorce is a bit harder to get in Texas than is an annulment, but as long as you cooperate, I figure Tyler can work it out by the time I come back for Nita."

"What do you mean, 'come back for Nita'? I thought you were going to La Réunion."

"I'm goin', I'm just not stayin'. I'll be there long

enough to see Nita settled, and then I'll be about business."

Madeline shut her eyes and tried to think. This would probably ruin her chance of marrying Ben Litty. Rose would still be without a guardian, and . . . Madeline groaned silently as a new thought occurred. *Rose does have a guardian. She has Brazos.*

A divorce must be Madeline's main priority.

"I want it first—the divorce, I mean. I won't cooperate unless your brother sees to the divorce immediately."

His features could have been carved from the rock beneath them. "We'll get the divorce when I see fit to do it. And you might like to know, Madeline, that kidnappin' is a hangin' offense in Texas."

With false bravado, she said, "You've no proof."

"I've hired an investigator to find Rose's father. I'll have my proof before long."

"You've what?" For the first time in her life, Madeline almost swooned.

"I told you I'd have my answers. Remember, Madeline? Nightmares? I've a feelin' that whatever my man discovers is gonna cause you plenty of bad dreams."

Biting the inside of her lip, Madeline thought hard. He must call off his spy! She couldn't risk Julian's learning anything about Rose. *Tell him the truth, here and now,* a voice within her urged. She considered it, even opened her mouth to speak, but hesitated. She couldn't forget the dark side of Brazos. Grabbing his shirtsleeve, she begged, "Please, Brazos, call this man off."

"Why should I?"

"He could endanger Rose."

"How? What's he going to discover, Madeline— maybe Rose's true identity? Perhaps it's not Rose he'd imperil, but you. Is that nearer the truth?"

Shaking her head furiously, Madeline said, "No, Brazos, you don't understand!"

"Then tell me, damn it! Who *is* Rose? Who are her true parents?"

She hesitated, and the memory of a beastly Brazos Sinclair choking her in the *Uriel*'s hold rose in her mind. She couldn't give that Brazos the truth. "Madeline?"

"Gypsies."

"What!"

Her mind swept back to another novel she'd found hidden in Celeste Desseau's bedroom at Château St. Germaine. "Gypsies stole Rose from a manor house near my boarding school in England. I'd tended the nursery, and the authorities suspected me, but I knew it was the gypsies, and no one believed me. I escaped right before they came to arrest me. I tracked her down, Brazos, and found her. When I took her home, I learned that her parents had grieved themselves to death. There was no other family, so I took her with me. If your investigator tracks Rose back to England, they'll arrest me and throw me in jail and take her away from me. She'll live in a workhouse, Brazos. Have you ever seen an English workhouse?"

"Madeline, that tale is as shy of the truth as a pig is of feathers." For a long moment, he was silent. Then he said, "Look, obviously this is important to you. It's just as clear that you'd rather not tell me why. Because my needs as far as Nita is concerned are immediate, and because it would make my life easier if you'd simply cooperate without a fuss, I'm willin' to do a bit of dealin'. The man I hired is only collecting information at this point. He's not to contact anyone until I give him the nod."

She looked at him, her gaze filled with hope, as he continued, "Now, if you do as I say and help settle Nita among the colonists, I'll give you my word to pay you a visit once I receive the truth about Rose. I'll give you a chance to explain yourself, Madeline, and if you ask me, I think that's bein' pretty damn generous."

He folded his arms across his chest as he added, "You'll get a little somethin' out of this deal, too. I can't leave Nita stranded at La Réunion without a place to live. Seein' how she's not actually a colonist, I can't in good conscience allow the Europeans to provide for her. Before I leave La Réunion, I'll build her a house. You can have it for yourself once this business is over. You've always talked about wantin' your own house. Now you'll have it."

He'd build a house for that woman, then give it to her by default. Brazos was giving Juanita something Madeline had always dreamed of having. Only he was doing it for another woman. Who was this Juanita? What peril did she face that she needed a place to hide? Madeline voiced the thought the instant it arrived, "Will this Juanita's presence in any way be a threat to Rose?"

Rising to his feet, Brazos said, "Madeline, I'm watchin' out for Rose." In the light from the lantern, his eyes glowed with promise. "You can rest assured of that. Nothing or no one is gonna hurt that little girl in any shape, form, or fashion. I'm making sure of it. Now, have we reached an agreement?"

Madeline realized that it was the best she could do. "All right," she said softly. "I'll be your loving wife."

Brazos grimaced and said ruefully, "I'm thrilled." He pulled the fishing line from the water and rested the pole against a tree. "Come on. Let's get back and start the show."

They'd almost reached camp when Madeline realized Brazos had not identified the body occupying the coffin in his wagon. "By the way," she asked, "who died?"

His soft chuckle floated through the night. "That's no corpse; it's my golf clubs. Good place to store 'em. Those and a few other items I want to keep private. People won't often go to snoopin' in a coffin."

Golf clubs in a coffin. Madeline shook her head. Somehow, with Brazos, it fit. "Why are you doing this? You've gone to so much trouble—why?"

The firelight flickered just up ahead. Brazos took Madeline's hand and said, "Because of her."

The ill sensation in Madeline's stomach intensified. "Rose?"

"Well, her, too. I have made my plans with Miss Magic in mind. Actually, though, I was thinking about Nita. You see, Madeline, there's something special between me and Juanita. You ought to know by now that I'd do just about anything for the woman."

TWO HOURS LATER, Brazos was strung tight as a fiddle at a San Jacinto Day Ball. He'd known when he'd proposed this idea that he'd be forced to spend a portion of his nights with Madeline Christophe. The colonists would never believe he and Madeline had reconciled if he didn't join his wife in the semiprivacy of her wagon for at least a little while. Lillibet had even insisted Rose spend the night in the Brunets' wagon, totally ignoring Brazos's objections that he'd missed his Miss Magic and wanted to spend time with her. Everyone in camp assumed his protest had been feigned.

"Everyone in camp is damn sure sawin' the wrong limb," he grumbled beneath his breath. Lying in the darkness as far from his wife as he could get in the confines of the heavily loaded wagon, Brazos replayed the evening's events in his mind. He tried to ignore both the subtle scent of roses hanging in the air and the electric awareness that sizzled between him and his wife.

She wasn't asleep, either. Every so often, he heard a snivel from her direction. Probably still crying over the emotional scene she'd had with ol' pretty-boy Litty, he said to himself. After their return to camp and Brazos's announcement of pending wedded bliss, she had asked for privacy to speak with her insulted former beau. Brazos had allowed it to a point. He knew Litty had been aware of his eavesdropping, but Madeline had been oblivious. She was too busy being devious.

The story that woman had told the wagon master was almost as dumb as the gypsy tale she'd run by him. What was it she'd said, something about forgiving Brazos for his other women and the thefts he repeatedly committed? The woman had a nerve.

Nerve succeeds. The words echoed in Brazos's mind. Well, he guessed Pa had it right. Madeline Christophe Sinclair was certainly one successful, nervy witch. She managed to make men fall all over her. Litty had dared to offer the sobbing woman both the comfort of a shoulder to weep wet and a promise of eternal help should it ever be needed, aware all the while that Brazos observed the entire sappy scene. "Nervy bastard himself," Brazos muttered.

At least, Lillibet had been glad to see him. She'd taken the news right well, hugging him and clapping her hands. When Lillibet started crying with delight, Madeline's complexion had taken on a greenish hue. It reminded Brazos of the early days aboard the *Uriel*, and he thought it appropriate that someone wicked enough to kidnap a baby would walk around feeling nauseated.

Scowling into the darkness as a particularly loud cricket chirped beneath the wagon, Brazos told himself to be on guard against the ugliness hidden within one so beautiful as Madeline. At times tonight, when he'd seen the firelight glimmering in her hair, or watched her cuddling Rose, or heard her singing a lullaby as she put the child to sleep, he found himself forgetting just how sinful a person she had turned out to be.

The murmured voices coming from outside the wagon stilled as the colonists settled into their beds for the night. Brazos decided to wait a few more minutes before escaping to the bedroll lying on the ground between Madeline's wagon and the buckboard fixed up with a bed for Juanita. But when the regular breaths of the woman beside him indicated she'd fallen asleep, he relaxed. He stayed where he was and eventually drifted off to sleep. Curled like a spoon against his wife, Brazos suffered no nightmares that night.

Chapter 12

A gusty breeze whished through the treetops as Brazos chopped a thick branch of an elm into chunks for a fire and waited for the women to awaken and the show to begin. He was feeling mean as eight acres of snakes, the result of waking up entangled with a beautiful, black-hearted woman. It shamed him that his body continued to want her so fiercely when his mind knew what an evil woman she was. He wanted to strike out at her, make her feel just as rotten as he felt. So he waited with gloating anticipation for Madeline to get a good look at Juanita in the daylight.

She'd be as green as the pine trees touching the sky, greener than her face when she'd hung over the railing of the *Uriel*. He wasn't setting out to make her jealous—only women resorted to those infantile games—but Madeline would react like any other woman when she caught sight of Nita. And he *had* noticed the way her expression had taken on that sour lemon look when he'd told her how he felt about the Mexican beauty.

He tossed the wood onto the crackling fire and

grinned. After he'd watched Madeline flirt her way across the Atlantic, he figured she deserved to be on the receiving end for a change. Besides, he'd told the truth last night. He cared deeply for Juanita, and she felt the same way about him. She was a kind, beautiful, exceptionally brave woman. A survivor. He liked that about her. Nita had taken some of the worst life had to offer and turned it plumb around.

Madeline would misunderstand the relationship between them. Hell, his own family couldn't figure it out. But how did a man explain the bond that developed between two people who had shared a nightmare together?

Brazos didn't even try. Actually, he'd come closer to explaining to Madeline last night than he had to anyone in quite some time, and a blind man couldn't have missed her reaction. The woman was jealous. Brazos tossed a handful of wood cuttings into the fire and said softly, "Isn't it a hoot?"

Truth be told, he'd never felt much of a hankering for Juanita. Considering that general consensus held her to be the most stunning woman ever to walk the face of the earth, no one would have believed him had he attempted to claim a lack of lust. Even Tyler believed them to be lovers.

Nita understood, though, because she felt the same way he did. Oh, she might try to tell herself she wanted him as a lover, but it wouldn't be the truth. Their feelings for one another were all tied up with Perote. Even had they wanted to, neither could ever get beyond that. She'd been the one to secure his escape. She'd seen him at his very worst. He, in turn, knew her secret shame.

He loved Juanita as the dearest of friends, but not as a lover, a distinction he failed to mention to his wife. Perhaps he could have been a little more forthcoming, but then he wouldn't have enjoyed the anticipation of watching Madeline get her comeuppance. A minor victory, true. But under the circumstances, every little bit helped.

After filling a pot with creek water, he tossed in a

handful of coffee and set it over the fire to boil. Morning coughs and yawns signaled the stirring of others around the campsite as he crossed the small space between Madeline's wagon and the buckboard he'd brought along.

Brazos spied his brother's form lying between the bois d'arc wagon wheel and the coffin made of pine, which they hauled out of the buckboard every night to make room for Juanita to sleep. He nudged his brother with his foot. "I swear, Ty, you could sleep through a stampede. See if you can't pry your eyelids open. Coffee's about done, and the day's a-wastin'."

A mockingbird sang a subdued morning song as he walked back to the fire and splayed his fingers wide above it to absorb the warmth. Tyler stood, yawned loudly, and twisted his back, stretching the kinks from his muscles. Brazos ignored his brother, his gaze darting between the pair of wagons where the two women slept.

Madeline poked her head out first. Her braid had loosened during the night, and a pair of feathers had escaped her pillow to tangle in her yellow tresses. She resembled a scruffy barn cat, right down to the angry hiss. Brazos nodded a hello, but didn't bother to speak.

Juanita emerged looking as if she'd stepped off an artist's canvas. The blue-black hair that was her one true vanity remained neatly in its braid, and as she smiled sleepily at Brazos, her jade green eyes softened with love. "Good morning, my Sin," her husky voice rolled.

Brazos smiled tenderly and bent to kiss her cheek. "Good morning, love. I trust you slept well?" From the corner of his eye, he witnessed the widening of Madeline's eyes and the paling of her complexion. Yep, he thought, some days it's just pure pleasure to be alive.

"Hmm, I slept fine," Juanita replied, loosening her braid and finger-combing the luxurious lengths of hair that tumbled to her knees.

Brazos clicked his tongue. "I tell you what, Nita, a man looks at you and can't help imagining that hair of yours spread across his pillow. I can see why you're so particular about it." He turned to his wife and said without a trace of emotion. "Good morning, Madeline."

He filled a tin cup with cold water and poured it into the coffee, settling the grounds. Then, filling the cup from the pot, he handed it to Juanita with a smile. As she sipped her drink, Brazos looked at Madeline and said, "With our arrival creating such a stir last night, I never found the opportunity to introduce you to the people traveling with me. I believe you have met my brother?"

Madeline nodded and said a subdued, "Hello, Tyler."

"And also," Brazos continued, "I must introduce you to my . . . special friend. Madeline, this is Juanita, who, besides being an exquisitely beautiful woman, has a voice pretty enough to make an angel cry."

Juanita nodded, accepting his praise as though it were her due. When Brazos opened his mouth to carry on, she held up her hand, looked Madeline in the eyes and said, "And you are the one who has so foolishly attempted to trap my Sin into marriage."

"No," Madeline snapped. "You have it backward."

"Hmm." Juanita folded her arms and walked around Madeline, studying her from head to toe. She blurted a rapid sentence in Spanish.

"No," Brazos answered. Then, because he found he didn't much like the peaked look on Madeline's face, he added, "A little extra on the hips, maybe."

That put the whalebone right back in her corset. She sputtered. She huffed. She lifted her chin regally and sniffed with disdain. The rest of the morning she spoke only with Tyler and the other colonists.

The exchange set the tone for the next week. Brazos learned real quick to keep Juanita and Madeline separated as much as possible. They spat and hissed at one another like a pair of whampus cats—part wildcat, part badger, and a little wolf thrown in for good measure. At times he doubted the wisdom of forcing Juanita and Madeline to share a house at La Réunion, but he didn't want to spare the time to build more than one house.

To make matters worse, Madeline had taken it into her head to play the loving wife to absurd extremes. The woman touched him all the time. Anytime he got within reach, those fingers whipped out to stroke his arm, brush his chest, or rest against his thigh. The one that really got to him was when she'd play with the ends of his hair at the bottom of his neck.

And through it all, Brazos had to smile and act loving, when what he wanted to do was to push her away. Or pull her to him and give her what she asked for.

A couple of times, he attempted to turn the tables on her and match her stroke for stroke, brush for brush. But the frustration wasn't worth it. The streams they crossed were just too damned cold to be swimming in this time of year.

The wagon train had stopped to make camp a little over an hour ago. Brazos sat alone atop a cottonwood stump, firewood stacked at his feet, his axe blade buried into the ground beside him. He watched a big red-brown butterfly light on the topmost log, pump its wings, then take flight in a drunken, illogical path. Brazos found himself wanting to follow.

Thank goodness, he'd be getting a couple of days' break from this sensual siege when he left the wagon train tomorrow. They were less than a day's ride from St. Michael's, and he was leaving Madeline behind when he took the load of silver to the orphans' home. He lifted the logs one by one into his arms and headed back to camp, grumbling as he walked, "Maybe at the children's home, I can get a decent night's sleep for a change."

DAWN PAINTED A palette of pink and bronze across the eastern horizon as Madeline peered over her shoulder toward a copse of trees off to her right. She couldn't shake the feeling that someone was watching her.

The sensation had lessened to a degree after the colonists left the forest region and traveled across prairie, but still, sometimes at night the eeriest sensation would creep up her spine. She never mentioned the problem to Brazos, but she found his presence inside her wagon every night reassuring.

Over the past week of travel, the lay of the land had changed from the flat coastal plains to the gently rolling hills of the cross-timbers region. Groves of hardwood trees gave way to sprawling swaths of meadow, and the sight of spring green grass sprinkled with rainbows of wildflowers strummed a previously unplayed chord in Madeline. Land such as this would make a fine home.

If Brazos's descriptions proved true, the area in which the colonists would settle was not as appealing as the land they now traveled. "Dallas is the end of the East, Madeline," he had told her. "The other side of the Trinity River is basically where the West begins. You're talking plains there—wild horses, cactus, scorpions, and Indians, of course."

Personally, Madeline would just as soon do without the Indians. And the cactus. And the scorpions. Horses were all right. The colonists had made camp the previous night in a meadow at the base of a rolling hill and awakened to peaceful coo of a mourning dove perched in a nearby pecan tree. Brazos had mumbled something about repairing a part on the other wagon, while Tyler and Juanita had walked off in search of wild blackberries to eat with the morning meal. Madeline was helping Lillibet fix breakfast when Rose let out a fearful cry.

Whirling around, Madeline saw the child hanging from the side of the wagon, her tiny fingers clutching at a rough wooden slat, her feet dangling.

"Rose," Madeline gasped, dropping the pan of spoon bread and rushing to the wagon to gather the child into her arms. "I swear, darling, if you don't stop this climbing, you are going to seriously injure yourself one day."

Lillibet approached, wiping her hands on her apron. "Is she all right, dearling?"

Madeline sighed heavily. "I don't know what to do with her, Lil. She climbs everything she can reach. I'm really frightened she'll hurt herself."

Lillibet patted the hiccuping child's back. "It is a problem, I'll agree. Why, I've never known a baby quite so daring at such a tender age. She's just about to walk, though, Madeline. Maybe she'll stop acting like a little monkey once she can get around on her feet."

"Yes, then instead of climbing like a monkey, she'll run like a deer, and I'll have to go hunting for her around salt licks," Madeline replied glumly. As she pressed a kiss to Rose's head, the nagging worry caused her to ask, "Lil, do you think this is normal? I mean, could this climbing problem be a sign that something is wrong with Rose? Something mentally?"

Lillibet looked at Madeline as if she had the mental problem. "Now, why would you ask such a foolish thing like that?"

Madeline thought of Julian and replied, "I'm just worried, that's all."

"Well, heaven knows I understand a mother's concern," Lillibet said huffily, "but I never want to hear you speak such foolishness again. There's nothing at all wrong with Rose. In fact, I believe high-spiritedness is a sign of intelligence."

Madeline smiled wanly, and silently swore to set aside that particular worry. Rose's cries had settled to occasional sobs when Ben Litty walked up beside them a few moments later. Frowning with concern, he asked, "Is the little one all right, Madeline?"

"Yes, she's fine. We had a bit of a scare, that's all."

Litty extended his hand to tickle Rose beneath the chin. "Aw, darlin', don't be doing that," he said, smiling gently at the sniffling child. "It'll give your mama gray hairs, and she's too young and pretty to be having those."

"Now, Ben," Madeline scolded, although she couldn't hide her pleasure. How nice to be complimented by a man, especially one as handsome as the wagon master. She certainly wasn't hearing anything of a similar nature from her husband.

Who, she noticed, had stuck his head from beneath the buckboard and was glaring at her. She reacted by smiling sweetly up at Ben, whose temples sported streaks of white, and said in a voice that carried, "I think gray hair on a man is quite attractive."

"Why, thank you, ma'am," he answered. Then he lowered his voice and grinned as he added, "I've decided I'm lucky you're in love with your husband, Madeline Sinclair. You can be a right ornery woman."

Madeline felt a touch of chagrin. Perhaps she shouldn't attempt to stir up jealousy in Brazos. But hadn't he done the same thing just last night when he'd fussed so over Juanita? Self-defense, that's all her devilishness was. She'd learned early in her life never to give up the fight, and living in close concert with Brazos Sinclair had become nothing less than all-out war. Today's battle had only begun. "Ben," she asked, smiling sweetly, "I dread the thought of riding in the wagon today. Do I have time for a bit of a ride before the train heads out? I'm in the mood to go for a gallop."

Litty chuckled. "Like I said, you're as ornery as a mule colt. Get your horse, Madeline. I'll take you." Then he said in a voice only she could hear, "But I'll expect that introduction to the Reverchons' eldest daughter you promised me at dinner tonight."

"It's a deal, Mr. Litty." Then Madeline, Ben, and Lillibet all looked toward the wagon as Brazos yelped a curse and rubbed at a bump on his head.

Madeline and Ben rode for only twenty minutes before he indicated they should return to the train. Being less than a week from La Réunion land, the colonists anticipated the end of their long journey and tended to ready themselves for the day's trip quicker than they had before.

The riders were discussing the merits of different methods of child discipline when they cantered into the bustling camp. Madeline's gaze snagged at the sight of Juanita, waving her hand and calling directions as Brazos toted one of her trunks from his wagon into

Madeline's. The Mexican woman looked up at Madeline and frowned. "Tell him, girl, that we women need many changes of clothing. He listens to you, *si?* Explain I must have everything with me."

"Brazos, what are you doing—" Madeline began, halting abruptly when she saw him open one of her trunks and riffle through its contents.

He was about to find her stash. The one that included his watch, his gun, three of his toys, and a few other insignificant items to which he could lay claim. She made quick excuses to Ben and galloped over to her wagon. "What is going on?" she demanded.

"My Lord, woman. You've got more junk. What are you plannin' to do, open a mercantile at La Réunion?" He withdrew a pair of white silk pantalets. Holding them up in front of him, he whistled and said, "Maybe I ought to go through these chests of yours a bit more carefully."

Madeline vaulted from the saddle and grabbed the underwear from his hands. Stuffing it into a corner, she demanded, "Brazos, why are you going through my things?"

He peered into the trunk with considerably more interest than he'd previously shown. "I'm lookin' for some things for you and Rose to wear. After switchin' Nita's things from the buckboard to your wagon, I don't have the gumption to haul another trunk. You and me and Rose are gonna be leavin' the train. Get the things you'll need for a few days—only the necessities, mind you—and put them in the back of my wagon."

"What? Why?"

"You're my wife. I don't need a reason."

Madeline simply glared at him.

Brazos looked toward the wagon master and drawled, "Maybe I'm lookin' to get you out of here before you present me with a pair of cuckold's horns."

Her mouth gaped open, and she blinked hard. "Before I—" She put her hands on her hips, stiffened her spine, and questioned, "You dare say that to me? You, who can't keep your eyes off wanton Juanita?" From the corner of her eye, she noticed the Mexican woman's smug smile.

Brazos's expression hardened. "Watch your mouth, Madeline. You're fixin' to flap that tongue of yours into a heap of trouble."

Fuming, she sucked on her lower lip and folded her arms. When Brazos turned to the trunkful of stolen items, she moved quickly and sat on the lid. "Rose and I are not going anywhere with you. Thank you, though, for asking."

"I'm not asking," Brazos replied flatly. And he meant it. He was determined that Madeline—and the baby—make the trip to St. Michael's with him. He wanted her with him just as much as he'd wanted to leave her behind only the day before.

Good Lord, he'd gone plumb crazy.

Still, he wasn't leaving Madeline here with pretty-boy Litty. He'd made that decision the moment he'd watched her smile vapidly up into the wagon master's eyes. "Fool," he muttered.

"I am not a fool!" She glared at him mutinously, looking so beautiful, it made him ache.

"I wasn't referrin' to you, wife," he said, sighing. "Look, Rose will get a kick out of bein' where we're goin'. And I've an idea that you might just like it, too."

"And where is it you think to take us?"

"I'm taking you to meet my children."

Her mouth gaped, and she blinked her eyes. "Your what?"

"My children." Observing her face bleed white, he added maliciously, "All twenty-three of them."

Chapter 13

St. Michael's Children's Home had officially been named for St. Michael the archangel, the one who will battle the antichrist and cast the beast into the abyss of darkness for all eternity. Brazos had thought the name appropriate when he chose it in honor of another Michael, one who had lived and died carrying the standard of Christ, but who never would be canonized.

The devil responsible for his death would pay for his sins, however. Brazos had sworn it.

Madeline hardly spoke to him during the trip, and he was too busy worrying about the upcoming reunion to battle with her. After hours of travel along a bumpy, rutted trail, the wagon pulled to a stop in front of a three-story clapboard house. A wide, gingerbread porch stretched around the house on three sides, and at its center, a sign squeaked as it rocked in the westerly breeze. Madeline read aloud, "St. Michael's Children's Home." She gave Brazos a curious glance, "What a charming house."

"Yeah," Brazos replied, a surge of satisfaction

sweeping through him as he studied the home from chimney to pier. The place was looking good, real good. He took a quick count of the rosebushes lining the walkway to the front steps. "Twenty-four. There's twenty-four. We've added another one."

"Twenty-four. Children. An orphanage." Madeline slapped her forehead with a palm. "They aren't *your* children, they're orphans!"

Brazos glared at her. "Listen, I may not have fathered these kids, but I care for them as though they were my own. My money supports them, my family helps run St. Michael's, all of them have permission to take the Sinclair name as their own. Any insult you give them, you give me. So I don't want to hear any snide remarks out of you, woman, about these children who've been unlucky enough to have lost their parents."

Madeline stammered, "I'd never . . . I didn't. Oh, Brazos, I thought . . ."

"You thought what?"

For a long moment, Madeline held his gaze, then she reached over and squeezed his hand. "Brazos Sinclair, you'd make a wonderful father."

"Well, hell," he gruffly cursed. Hopping down from the wagon, he extended his arms for Rose. "Come here, Miss Magic. You're gonna have a merry time here at St. Michael's." He assisted Madeline to the ground, then led the way up the path to the house.

He didn't bother to knock. A fierce anticipation gripped him as the sound of children's laughter floated from one of the back rooms. "They must be havin' a late lunch or an early supper," he told Madeline as he shifted Rose into her arms. He took off his hat and hung it on the top rung of a tall hat tree already holding caps and bonnets of all shapes and sizes. Wiping his suddenly damp hands on his denims, he finger-combed his hair and asked, "Do I look all right?"

She stared at him in amazement. "Why, yes, Brazos, you look very nice."

He nodded, then took a deep breath and tried to quell the nervousness that had sprung to life in his belly.

"What are you doin' just standin' there, Madeline? Come on."

Shaking her head, Madeline walked at his side toward the dining room. Of course, he *was* dragging her along. "You're about to pinch off my elbow, Mr. Sinclair," she hissed.

He dropped her arm. The children's voices grew louder. He heard his sister Melissa's firm but gentle voice chide them to quiet down. Melissa, or Cecilia as she now was known, always had been good with the kids. He'd been grateful when she'd decided to dedicate her life to helping the young residents of St. Michael's, thankful that the name change allowed her to do so without alerting Salezan of her connection to the Sinclair family. Even though Lana and Mason Kennard ran the daily operations of the home, the children needed a teacher. No one was better at teaching than Melissa.

Then he was there, in the doorway, gazing at those whose very existence had saved his sanity. The orphans, Miguel's orphans—healthy, happy, in their home.

Melissa sat at the head of the table with her back to Brazos. She was saying, "Billy, if you don't eat your peas, you'll not be given a slice of vinegar pie for dessert."

"Are you still arguin' about eatin' your peas, Billy Justice?"

For just a moment, it grew so quiet that he could have heard Billy's peas plop against the floor. Then the room exploded with noise. Chair legs scraped, children squealed, and Melissa screamed. Brazos went down beneath a flurry of hugs, kisses, and shouts of joyous welcome.

Never before in her entire life had Madeline felt so alone.

HE HAD INTRODUCED her as Madeline Christophe to his sister. His sister, Melissa. His sister, Melissa, the Catholic nun, who had changed her name to Sister Cecilia Mary Catherine when she took her vows.

Madeline could accept the idea of carrying golf clubs in a coffin better than she could the fact that Brazos Sinclair had a sister who was a nun.

Brazos had made no mention of the marriage or, for that matter, of why Madeline was visiting St. Michael's with him. At the time, Sister Cecilia had been so wrapped up in welcoming her brother home that she'd not bothered to pursue the topic.

That ended quite abruptly when she joined Madeline on the front porch, carrying a pitcher of lemonade, two glasses, and a burning curiosity in her eyes.

Madeline sat in a white wicker chair, rocking Rose to sleep for her afternoon nap. She eyed the look on the nun's face and stifled a groan. The interrogation was about to begin.

At thirty-seven, Sister Cecilia was an attractive woman with eyes the same brilliant blue as her brother's. She lived at the children's home, serving God by teaching the orphaned children, and in no way fit Madeline's perception of a nun.

Except for the determined stare intent on gaining information. Madeline, however, was no slouch herself in a battle of polite conversation. Within ten minutes, Madeline had learned how a young girl growing up in a family of staunch Methodists managed to hear the calling to become a Catholic nun. Despite Sister Cecilia's best efforts, Madeline gave away nothing more than insignificant information about herself.

Talk turned to Brazos, who, having declared a holiday from school, played in the yard with the children. Madeline watched him scurry up a rope to inspect a treehouse, settle onto a swing with a little girl named Sarah who squealed with delight as he swung them high, and run two footraces, winning against the boys and losing against the girls. "I don't believe I've ever seen a grown man play the way Brazos does," she commented.

Sister Cecilia sipped her lemonade and sighed. "You think he's difficult now, you should have seen him as a boy. He wore the rest of us ragged—always begging us to play some silly game, more often than not, one he made up on the spot." She sniffed disdainfully and grumbled, "And his rules were never fair. They always gave the advantage to the boys. Unless I was on his team, I never won anything playing with Brazos."

Madeline smiled wryly. She had yet to win against Brazos Sinclair herself. His rumbling laughter captured her attention as he sat on one end of a seesaw, sending the five children straddling the other side high into the air. "He does seem to thrive on challenges," she commented, thinking of how he was determined to solve the mystery of Rose's birth.

"He loves challenges of all kinds," Brazos's sister confirmed. "And he forces them on other people. You should have seen what he'd planned for his wedding. He'd arranged horse races for the men, and he'd purchased puzzle boards for the women. For his wedding reception! Lana was quite put out, I tell you."

Madeline almost dropped her lemonade. "Wedding?"

"I don't suppose you know about Lana," Sister Cecilia reflected, a frown marring the serenity of her expression. "Oh, dear. Maybe I shouldn't have mentioned it. Of course, I have no way of knowing for sure, since I don't know what is between you and my brother."

"That makes two of us," Madeline said beneath her breath. A wife. He'd been married before. And he'd never told her. Anger flared red-hot inside her as she thought, Why, who does he think he is, going on about my lies? He's been doing the same thing the entire time.

Sister Cecilia encouraged her with a smile. "Please tell me, Madeline. Are you and Brazos more than friends?"

"I think it best if Brazos explained our situation," Madeline replied stiffly, trying to picture the mysterious Lana. She imagined sea green eyes, red hair, and a bosom to put Madame Trixie's to shame.

"Well, if you think it best," Sister Cecilia said. "But if my brother has done wrong by you, it's best the family knows. We'll make sure he accepts his responsibilities." The nun leaned forward and whispered, "Is he little Rose's father?"

"No." Madeline replied, unwilling to stir that particular pot of trouble. "Pardon me if I speak out of turn here, but for a religious woman, you appear awfully prone to gossip."

Sister Cecilia nodded sadly. "I do so fight it, but it is such a struggle. And where family is concerned, my tendency to indulge in idle chatter is especially difficult to resist. I love them all so very much, you see. I will allow some justification of my actions in that it is impossible for me to pray that they be delivered from their trials if I know not what those trials entail."

"You are good," Madeline said, admiring Sister Cecilia's strategy. She liked this woman.

Brazos's sister smiled and sipped her drink. "In the interest of effective prayers, would you tell me what is between you and my younger brother? Then I'll know whether I should share with you the details of Brazos's relationship with Lana." Offhandedly, she added, "Lana will be here within the hour, most likely."

"Here? At St. Michael's?" Madeline asked. Sister Cecilia's devilish grin looked exactly like Brazos's. Madeline bit her lip. It was tempting. He really should have told her about his first wife. Sister Cecilia's eyes glowed like sapphires as she waited for Madeline's reply. "Why is this Lana woman coming here?"

"She lives here."

Madeline made her decision. "You go first."

The nun nodded, then heaved a wistful sigh. "It was going to be the social event of the season—despite the fact that Brazos was involved. I had returned home from St. Ignatius Convent, and—well, you're probably not interested in my travels, I daresay."

Madeline repeated dryly, "I daresay."

"Anyway, the wedding was to—" Sister Cecilia broke off and frowned as realization dawned in her eyes. "Oh, dear. I should probably begin in another spot. Brazos didn't tell you about Lana, so you must be worried. You want to know about her."

She patted Madeline's knee. "Not to worry, Madeline. I wouldn't tell Lana this, but I never did believe Brazos truly loved her. I thought then and I do today that he was in love with the idea of love. More than anything else, he wanted to have his own home and family. He'd purchased a plantation—"

"This is your brother *Brazos* we are talking about?" Madeline asked incredulously.

Sister Cecilia nodded her head. "Out of all my brothers and sisters—there are fourteen of us, by the by, in case he hasn't told you that, either—Brazos was the one who always played with the babies. He told my twin brother, Stephen, who told me, that one thing that had helped him settle on Lana was her wide hips. He wanted someone big enough to birth his babies, what with him being so large and all."

"Large." Madeline repeated, a flush stealing up her neck.

"He's well over six feet you know, biggest of all my brothers."

"Oh, large."

Sister Cecilia eyed her cautiously. Madeline plunged ahead. "So, Brazos bought a plantation?"

"Yes. In fact, the land is not far from here. It's pretty, a mixture of meadow and wooded area. It backs up right alongside the Brazos River."

"The Brazos River. He's mentioned that to me."

Sister Cecilia smiled. "He gives Mama such a hard time about his name. Papa did her no favor when he allowed it to become known that the baby had been conceived on a sandbar in the middle of the Brazos. Anyway, my brother was all set to marry Lana and build this fine plantation house when Father Miguel asked him to make a trip south to search for the silver."

"Silver?"

"From El Regalo de Dios. It's a silver mine once worked by Franciscan friars." Sister Cecilia reared back. "Don't tell me he hasn't told you about the silver, either!"

"Uh, actually, he hasn't."

Sister Cecilia's brow crinkled in confusion.

"Maybe I should be more discreet then. But in all honesty, I don't see why. None of it is secret, except for the mine's location, and even Brazos doesn't know that. I wouldn't tell secrets, Madeline. I'm quite firm about it."

Madeline lost all patience. She held up her hand and, when Sister Cecilia paused, asked, "Has Brazos been divorced?"

"Divorced! Oh, perish the thought. That would never do, never do. No, no, no. Brazos would never do something like that." Madeline smiled grimly as Sister Cecilia explained, "Brazos is not divorced. He's never been married."

"So, he didn't marry this Lana?"

"No. He went with Miguel—Father Miguel, I mean. I confess, at times it's difficult to remember that the ornery little boy who put a live frog in the milk crock grew up to become a priest."

Madeline couldn't help smiling. She'd done the same thing at Mistress Poggi's.

"Anyway," Sister Cecilia continued, "they needed one more load because Father Miguel had decided to build an orphanage and they needed the funds. That's when they got captured."

"Captured?"

Sister Cecilia nodded. "Some of this part of the story is secret. I don't even know it. If my twin does, he's not telling. That always annoys me, too. Twins are supposed to share everything, but just because he's a boy and I'm a girl—"

"Sister Cecilia!" Madeline exclaimed. "Please go on with your tale."

"Oh, I'm sorry. Actually, the story's just about over. Brazos was held in this awful prison in Mexico for years. When he came home, he was different. Very different. Oh, on the outside he was the same, except for being so thin, but inside . . ." Her voice trailed off, and she shuddered. "I don't know what happened. Brazos came home. Father Miguel never did."

She was silent for a moment, her face slack with grief. Then she said, "Lana had waited for him, but by the time Brazos returned, Mason had the sweets for her. Brazos brought that Juanita woman home with him, and he and Lana called off the wedding. She married Mason a month later. They're the ones who actually oversee the orphanage. You'll get to meet them later. They went into town for supplies this morning, but will be back before dark."

Wonderful, Madeline thought, I get to meet another of Brazos's women. "They all remained friends?"

"Yes. Brazos really liked Mason, and Lana's so kind, she even was friendly to that Spanish woman."

"Juanita." Madeline voiced another question that had nagged her for some time. "Brazos never married her?"

Sister Cecilia shook her head. "He told our brother Tyler—they're closest, you know—that he'd never marry." She gave Madeline a speculative glance. "Has he changed his mind?"

Madeline wasn't about to go into that. Softly she asked, "How did he end up in Europe?"

Sister Cecilia shrugged. "I don't know. For months, he worked on this orphanage, designing it, getting the supplies, and finally starting to build. But every few weeks, he'd take off. Just disappear. No one knew where he went. He told Tyler he needed to wander, that he couldn't bear the thought of remaining in one place. He said he'd never build a home."

She sighed and sipped her lemonade. Sadness filled her voice as she continued, "Then one time, he never came back. Tyler and my parents finally received letters from him. From Italy! We couldn't believe it." Her smile was filled with tenderness as she gazed at her brother and added, "I'm so glad he's come home. We've all been terribly worried."

Madeline's chest ached. *He had wanted a home and a family, just like me.* "My God," she mused, eyeing her husband, "whatever did they do to him in that place called Perote?"

PEROTE PRISON, MEXICO

Rats terrified the woman who knelt between Damasso Salezan's thighs. The prison commander had recognized her fear a week ago when he'd had her brought to the guard house to service him while he gazed out over his kingdom—the fortress, outbuildings, and surrounding battlements that fashioned the Castle of San Carlos, better known as the hellhole, Perote. A rodent had scurried across the floor, eliciting a scream she'd previously denied him, even beneath his whip.

Since terror always heightened his pleasure, Salezan had arranged for today's rendezvous to take place here, in the gloom of a sparsely lit dungeon. The rats grew larger in the pits of Perote, and more bold.

Torchlight flickered along cold stone walls, and Salezan watched the shadows as the woman took his sex into her mouth, whimpering in fear even as she stroked him with her tongue. Lust heated his blood, and his gaze unerringly found the pair of iron shackles hanging against the wall.

Sinclair and his priest. Nothing since them had brought near the delight.

Salezan's hips pumped, and he used his whip on the woman's back. Her screams echoed off the walls as he took his pleasure, his eyes shut tight, remembering another time, another woman, another prisoner. "Ah, *bestia*," he said, sighing, "always you were the best."

Later that afternoon, summoned by a call from the guard tower, Salezan watched the movement along the rocky road that wound its way toward the castle. A cloud of white dust billowed from the heels of a galloping horse, and as it drew closer, he recognized the messenger, Winston Poteet.

Salezan's lips twitched in a faint smile when wood groaned and chains rattled with the lowering of the drawbridge. He watched as Poteet spoke with a guard and then looked up toward the tower. Their gazes met and held, and the newcomer's slow nod answered the question that sizzled like lightning through the air between them.

Pleasure flooded him, a warm, heavy wave that stirred his loins in a manner that surpassed the sexual. It was power—food for his body and drink for a soul long claimed by the devil.

Poteet's boots scuffed against the steps. Salezan turned toward the door and waited.

A plain man with sandy hair and light gray eyes, Winston Poteet was wanted for murder in Tennessee, Kansas, and Georgia, and for lesser crimes in a dozen other states. Salezan bought his allegiance with gold and by providing victims for his other, darker activities. For the past year, Poteet had supervised the search for Juanita and Brazos Sinclair.

"You have found her?" Salezan asked as Poteet's shadow darkened the doorway.

The newcomer moved into the room. "Better than that, Captain. Sinclair has returned to Texas."

Salezan's eyes narrowed. "He is yours?"

"Not yet, but soon," Poteet replied, sitting at a desk in the center of the room. He searched through drawers as he continued, "He and the brother who practices law in Galveston traveled together to their parent's plantation. My men watched the house closely, but somehow the two brothers eluded them. We will find their trail, Governor. It is only a matter of time."

"What incompetents do I employ!" Salezan railed. "How could they have lost Brazos Sinclair?"

"He's smart, Governor," Poteet replied with a shrug. He pulled a glass and a bottle from the desk drawer and said, "Sinclair sent brothers in all directions, and their features were so similar to his that each time, our men thought it was he leaving the plantation."

"Fools! If that is so, how are you certain that it was Brazos Sinclair you followed in Galveston?"

"Because our man spotted it when Sinclair went swimming."

"Saw what?" Salezan questioned impatiently.

"The armband." Poteet grinned at the sudden fire lighting Salezan's eyes. "Brazos Sinclair wore a band that flashed silver in the moonlight."

"The bastard dares to wear it!" Salezan exclaimed, slapping the table and rattling the bottle and glass.

Poteet poured himself a drink of tequila as Salezan paced the room, musing, "He's taking his brother to Juanita."

"I don't doubt it. But we'll find him, Governor. We'll find them both. I have men searching every conceivable place."

Salezan nodded. "He is to be brought here." The governor of Perote Prison lifted his arm and rubbed the spot once circled by a band of silver. "You will leave immediately—take the fastest ship. I want you to personally oversee this operation. Bring me Juanita and Brazos Sinclair. Unharmed." His thoughts returned to the dungeon cell. "I've many plans for my runaways."

MADELINE WAS SITTING in a chair by the dining room window playing pat-a-cake with Rose when Lana and Mason Kennard returned to the orphanage. While observing the enthusiastic reunion of the auburn-haired beauty and her former fiancé, Madeline furtively reached out and swiped a spoon from the table. Before dinner was over, she'd stolen two spoons, a teacup, and a potato masher. It was her largest haul since arriving in Texas, and that in itself had her worried. She was a thief. She stole money and gold and jewels—not kitchen tools. What was wrong with her?

Lana Kennard did not appear to suffer from her ill-fated romance with Brazos Sinclair. In fact, she bloomed with love for her husband, Mason, who obviously returned the affection. Neither seemed uncomfortable with Brazos.

Madeline found the entire situation quite odd.

While the children busied themselves cleaning up after dinner, the adults—Brazos included—sat on the front porch, drinking coffee.

Brazos was saying, "I found it to be quite a challenge, and my host was simply obsessed with the game. Every morning, just after sunup, he'd rap on my door and order me to meet him on the course. Mac-Garey was twice my age, and he could whack the feathers right out of the ball." He grinned in remembrance. "I never did win. Bothered the hell out of me."

Lana Kennard looked at Madeline and said, "The only thing Brazos hates worse than losing is not playing the game in the first place."

Mason Kennard chuckled. "You say you brought a set of these clubs back with you?"

"Sure did. In fact, I have them with me now. You want to see them?"

Madeline was reminded of an eager puppy. At Mason's nod, Brazos pushed off the porch rail and sauntered over toward the wagon. "You know, we might as well unload these bars while we're at it. Y'all come help. It'd take me an hour to do it myself."

Mason and the women followed Brazos, who proceeded to pry the lid off the coffin. Madeline looked around her. None of these people seemed surprised at his action. Curious, Madeline leaned over to peer into the casket. In the center, laid out like a corpse on a blanket, were six wooden sticks, one of which was topped by a metal head.

But the clubs weren't what captured Madeline's attention. A murmured, "Oh, my," escaped her lips at the sight. Stacked inside the coffin, one on top of the other, around and underneath Brazos's sticks, lay a fortune in gleaming silver bars. "Isn't it beautiful?" Brazos asked.

He was holding up and referring to the metal-headed stick. The one he called a rut iron.

LYING IN BED that night, Madeline couldn't make up her mind. She straddled the horns of a dilemma that would make a pair of longhorn cattle proud. She was a thief. She'd been stealing her entire life, providing herself with basic necessities and an occasional luxury or two. She took pride in her professional abilities. Once she'd even lifted something from a duke.

But as of late, she'd stolen spoons and kitchen utensils. She yanked her covers over her head and wailed, "What kind of thief steals potato mashers, for heaven's sake?" None she'd claim as a friend, that's for certain.

Then, as though it weren't enough that she suffer from this crisis of self-identity, she had to go and discover that her soon-to-be-former husband carried around a fortune in silver bars. In a coffin. With his golf clubs. She blew a frustrated puff of breath, making a hill in the sheet above her head.

She sat upright and glared at her reflection in the mirror opposite the bed. As a professional, wasn't she duty-bound to steal the silver from him? After all, no self-respecting thief would allow a bonanza like that to slip through his fingers. "I couldn't hold my head up in a tavern full of good, lawbreaking highwaymen again."

Admittedly, she didn't know whether any place similar to the Harried Hound Tavern even existed in Texas. She'd learned many things there—how to pick pockets, how to shoot a pistol, how to throw a man twice her size. What would Gentleman Jack think if he saw her now, contemplating passing up a coffinload of silver bars. He'd be appalled, that's what.

Gentleman Jack, or GJ as she called him, had been the closest thing to a father Madeline had ever had—until her breasts began to sprout, that is. GJ had been devastated to discover that she wasn't a boy after all. He'd sent her back to the boarding house in search of a position, and although they'd kept in touch—he'd wanted the information she provided concerning the doings of society—things between them had irreparably changed. Still, he'd cried when she'd returned to the Harried Hound that final time. He'd claimed he would worry about her while she visited France.

If he were here now and saw how she was acting, he'd really be worried. She shuddered at the thought of the words GJ would use to blister the air.

Madeline plumped up her pillows and lay back down. The problem here was that she simply didn't want to steal the silver. That treasure was for the orphans. So what if Brazos *did* have plenty more silver where that coffinload had come from? It didn't change the fact that he'd toted this load all the way from wherever to leave it at St. Michael's Children's Home.

But if she passed up this opportunity, did that mean she'd condemned herself to snatching potato mashers for the rest of her life? Was this some self-destructive trend?

She couldn't steal from orphans. Just as she couldn't take from her fellow La Réunion colonists. Unless a treasure worth more than a coffinload of silver came her way and soon, one she could heist with a clear conscience, she would be forced to admit that she wasn't who she'd always thought herself to be.

"And if I'm not a thief," Madeline said to the quiet room, "then who am I?"

She wasn't Rose's mother. She wasn't really Brazos's wife. She was no one's daughter, no one's sister, she wasn't even Rose's aunt—she couldn't be under the circumstances. She was no one's lover.

Well, except in her dreams.

BRAZOS WAS DOWNSTAIRS polishing off a glass of buttermilk when Lana entered the kitchen. She took one look at him and shook her head. "You have crumbs on your face, Brazos. If you're going to steal the cookies, you should at least wipe away the evidence."

"Caught me again, didn't you, Lana," he replied, adopting a fake guilty expression as he brushed away the specks of sugar.

The smile melted from her face, and in a serious tone, she said, "No, Brazos, I never caught you at all." She crossed the kitchen and withdrew a cup from the cabinet. Holding it out, she nodded toward the buttermilk.

He filled the cup, saying, "You're lucky you didn't. I'd have made a horrible husband. You know that, don't you, Lana?"

"I wouldn't say horrible, just not right for me. Not after . . ." Her voice trailed off, and she lifted her shoulders in a shrug. Sitting at the table, she sipped her milk. "I'm happy. Mason and I are happy. We have a good life here at St. Michael's."

Brazos straddled a chair opposite her. "I'm glad for you, honey. You deserve it." She swirled the buttermilk around in her cup, and Brazos felt a tenderness swell inside him. Lana Kennard was a good woman. He'd made the right decision by not holding her to her promise. "You look as if somethin' is on your mind. What is it?"

Her tongue circled her lip, a habit he recognized as nervousness. Then she said, "Mason and I are expecting a baby."

The smile hovering on his lips froze. Pain plucked at his heart like a scavenger's talons. He closed his eyes and fought it, seeking and finding the empty place inside himself. Yet, emotion enough lingered to add a rasp to his voice as he said, "Congratulations."

A sheen of tears floated in Lana's eyes. "Brazos, I remember our dreams. I know how much you wanted children and the house—we spent all that time planning. It breaks my heart to know you've suffered so much, and I feel guilty that Mason and I are so happy while you—"

"Shh, honey." Brazos reached across the table and clasped her hand. "I'm fine, and you don't have a damn thing to feel guilty about. Hell, Lana, you waited for me all that time, even though Mason was silly in love with you. And it was *my* decision to end our engagement. You would have tied yourself to a crazy man if I had let you."

The tears had spilled from her eyes and now trailed down her face. "Brazos, you're not crazy. You are a wonderful man. Look at what you've done for the children, for me and Mason. You gave us St. Michael's."

An icy chill stole through him. He stood abruptly, saying, "No, Lana, Miguel is responsible for St. Michael's. I don't want you or Mason or anyone to ever forget that."

"But, Brazos, you—"

"Don't." He couldn't bear to discuss it. First Lana and her baby, then Miguel. They were middle-of-the-night memories that all but laid him low. "Don't," he repeated softly.

She wiped at her tears and nodded.

Brazos raked his fingers through his hair and scowled. "Now, quit cryin'. It's bound to be bad for the baby."

"Yes, Brazos."

Hell, she looks pitiful sitting there crying, Brazos thought. He strode across the room and lifted the lid of the earthen jar containing the molasses cookies. Pulling out two, he returned to the table and offered one to Lana along with his handkerchief. "Here, honey, make use of these. We've got to cheer you up, or Mason'll be down those stairs lookin' for somethin' to punch. I may be bigger than he is, but he always did fight dirty."

Lana smiled. "I'll never forget the day he knocked you flat. It took a good three weeks for your black eye to heal."

"I was only eight years old," Brazos replied defensively. "Boys heal more slowly than men."

She gave him a searching look. "Have you healed, then, Brazos? Is that why you brought Miss Christophe and her daughter to visit us? Are you finally able to settle down and build that life you once wanted so badly?"

"My Lord, woman!" Brazos exclaimed, forcing a smile. "You always were a nosy one. I think it's time for you to take your questions back upstairs and tuck 'em into Mason's bed."

Lana shook her head sadly and stood. She walked to him and stood on her tiptoes to press a kiss against his cheek. "If I were always nosy, you were always full of secrets, Brazos Sinclair. I'll not pester you, but I want you to know you have friends here. You'll always have friends here, no matter what."

"Good night, honey." Brazos squeezed her hand, then pushed her toward the doorway. As she exited the kitchen, he added softly, "And, Lana, I am happy for you and Mason. About the baby, I mean."

He tried so hard to mean it.

SHORTLY BEFORE DAWN, Brazos awoke to the irritating sound of a barn cat whining right outside his window. He rolled over in his bed and tugged his pillow over his head in a futile attempt to muffle the noise. Damn, he'd have to do something, or the blasted cat would wake the children. Sighing heavily, he sat up and wrenched open his eyes. He scratched his chest, yawned, and stumbled out of bed. Halfway to the window, he stopped.

The noise wasn't a barn cat, and it wasn't coming from outside but from across the hall. "Rose," he murmured. The child continued to cry, and Brazos scowled. Madeline should pick that baby up, not let her scream, he thought. Pulling on his denims, he opened the door and padded barefoot and shirtless to the room across from his. He didn't bother to knock, just walked on in.

Rose was in the process of climbing out of her crib. Madeline was sitting up in bed, looking half asleep and so beautiful, it liked to make his teeth ache. Her flannel nightgown gaped at the neck, and he caught a glimpse of a coral nipple. Resolutely, he turned away. "Lie back down, Madeline. I'll handle her."

While he gently tugged one of Rose's feet from the bars of the crib where it had caught, Madeline said sleepily, "Thank you. She was up a couple of times during the night. Teething, I imagine." She curled into the mattress and fell back asleep before Brazos had changed Rose's diaper.

After a quick breakfast of leftover cornbread and fried bacon, both Brazos and Rose felt ready to take on the world. The child was in fine spirits, babbling and toddling around the kitchen. "You're learnin' to walk right well, Miss Magic," Brazos said, taking a tin pan out of her hands. "But you're bein' a bit loud for so early in the mornin'. What you say we go outside and hit a few balls. You can help me pick them up."

Twenty minutes later, as the sun broke over the tops of the trees and lit the clearing, Brazos stood rolling balls toward a round, shallow hole he'd dug in the yard. Rose busied herself by toddling after the balls, stooping to retrieve them from the hole, and often losing her balance and plopping down on her behind.

After a bit, Brazos backed up and with a different club, began sailing the balls toward the hole. Rose lost interest in the game and chose to chase a yellow butterfly that flitted about the wildflowers. A warmth of emotion filled Brazos as he watched the child at play. Her bright eyes, shining with happiness and innocence, her giggles, hell, even the way she teared up and boo-hooed got to him. The truth of it was, Rose had captured his heart.

"Damn that Madeline." He took a careless swing at his ball, and it sailed into the trees. Glancing over his shoulder to check on Miss Magic, who was intently picking the petals from a black-eyed Susan, Brazos headed into the woods after his ball.

"I'm not lookin' forward to the leave-takin'," he grumbled. Madeline would undoubtedly pitch a fit to wake the dead. She wouldn't be at all happy about leaving Rose behind. But that was exactly what she was going to do.

"There it is." He lifted his ball from a patch of green clover and turned back toward the clearing. Immediately, his gaze returned to the spot where he had left Rose.

She wasn't there.

Chapter 14

"Rose?" Brazos called, his stomach clenching as he rushed forward. She couldn't have gotten far; he'd been gone only a minute. He twisted his head, looking in all directions, searching.

Then he heard Rose's happy laugh, and he began to breathe again. The sound had come from around the side of the barn. With a scolding smile upon his face, Brazos rounded the corner of the barn and froze. "Oh, God."

Rose had climbed up the side of the water well. She was standing on the wide stone rim, reaching toward the bucket. "No, baby," Brazos said gently, walking steadily toward her, careful not to startle her. "Stay still, sweetheart. Brazos'll get the bucket for you."

Rose turned toward him and grinned. "Ba Ba," she said, her word for Brazos. "Ba Ba."

Giggling, she reached for the pail. Each second stretched in slow motion. She leaned, her arm extended, her hand grabbing. Then the toddler lost her balance. Her arm slipped between the bucket and its rope handle, the pail lodging between her arm and her body. And Rose, entangled with the bucket, tumbled out of sight.

"No!" Brazos shouted, dashing the final steps to the well. He grabbed the rope, halting its descent, and rejoiced at the extra weight on its end. The pulley creaked as he carefully worked the rope, bringing Rose back to the surface.

Then, the extra weight disappeared.

He heard her cry, a frightened, fading echo. It seemed forever before he heard the splash.

He stood frozen in terror at the edge of the dark hole, staring into hell. *Go after her. Now. Don't delay. She'll die. Rose will die.* His entire body shook. His hands dripped sweat, and bile rose in his throat. *Go, you goddamned coward. She'll die. That little baby will die.*

"No!" He yanked the pail back to the surface and out of his way. Kicking off his boots—bare feet would better provide purchase on the stone that lined the well—he lowered himself into the blackness. With arms and legs outstretched, he climbed down. Rough stone edges cut his hand and scraped his feet, but he barely felt them. He was listening. So hard.

And he was hearing nothing.

Quickly, he descended the shaft, terror following every step. It nipped at his heels, sniped at his fingers. But his fear for Rose held the animal at bay.

His foot plunged into icy water, and he jumped, arms and legs moving, searching, feeling. His feet touched bottom. The water reached to just below his breast. "Please, God," he prayed, drawing a deep breath and submerging himself. He searched in patterns, intent not to miss a spot. His foot brushed something. Skin. Oh, Lord. He pushed his hand through the water. A leg. Her leg. Even as he gathered her into his arms, he bent his knees and shot to the surface.

Rose lay limp in his hands. He shook her. "Rose? Rose, baby?" She may as well have been a rag doll. "Rose, come on, baby." Water. She had water in her lungs. He pushed her belly. Nothing. He held her above him by the feet and shook her. Silence. He cradled her in his arms. "Oh, God, please." He turned her over and pounded her back. "What do I do? Please, God, tell me, what do I do?"

He floated her flat on her back, his arm supporting her underneath, and pushed hard on her chest. Remembering how his mother used to lift his youngest sister's arms when she had trouble breathing, Brazos did the same to Rose and then pushed on her chest once more.

He felt water spill from her mouth across his arm. "That's it, baby." He pushed again. And again. and again. "Breathe, baby." Nothing. "Dammit, I'll make you breathe." He covered her mouth with his and offered her his breath. "Please, Rose."

She coughed. Water spurted from her mouth. She coughed and coughed, then gasped a breath. Oh, God, she took a breath! Her entire body convulsed as it expelled the life-stealing water. She gasped for more precious air. And she cried, a pitiful, soulful cry.

Brazos had never heard a more beautiful sound in his life.

The entire episode couldn't have taken more than a few minutes, but Brazos felt as though he had aged ten years. Rose was working up a full-bodied caterwaul, and her little fist pounded his chest. After one particularly high shriek that echoed off the surrounding stone walls, she took a deep breath and cried, "Ma-ma-ma-ma-ma-ma."

Brazos laughed with giddy relief. She was breathing. She was moving. She was crying. She was talking.

Miss Magic was safe.

And in the depths of the black, wet, cold well, the terror riding his shoulder reintroduced itself.

THE TETHERS SNAP. I am free.

Breathe deeply of the heady fragrance of dank, moldy darkness. Touch the stone, so smooth and cold. My blind eyes see the world around me. I rule the darkness; I am king. My chest expands as power pulses, erupting from the hollow place of the soul. I move. No!

Something binds me yet. A weight in my arms. Warm and gentle.

Love.

Kill it. Throw it away. Drop it.

I cannot. The warm weight is strong, a shackle wrapping my arm. But only one arm. I will rest and gather my strength. It is but one fetter, and I can defeat it.

I will destroy the heat. I will kill, and I will feed. I am the Night. And I live once more.

MADELINE SAT STRAIGHT up in bed. She clutched the sheet to her breast as her heart thumped a turbulent pulse. Immediately, her gaze swept to the empty crib. Something was wrong, very wrong.

She was not prone to sixth-sense types of feelings. In fact, as she threw on a dress and shoved her feet into her slippers, she tried to convince herself she was being silly. But the raised hairs on the nape of her neck argued otherwise.

She flew downstairs to the kitchen. Sister Cecilia, Lana, and those children with mealtime duties busied themselves with breakfast preparations. Madeline stood in the doorway, her hand grasping the frame as she asked in a breathless voice, "Is Rose with you?"

Both women looked over their shoulders. "No," Lana said, her brow wrinkling. Sister Cecilia scraped biscuit dough off her hands and said matter-of-factly, "Brazos had her outside when I woke up. She was chasing balls for him."

"Oh, good," Madeline said, laying her hand against her chest and breathing deeply. "I woke up, and she wasn't in her crib. I was frightened." As she gave them a little smile, she realized her fear had yet to be relieved. "Let me check on them, and I'll come back and help with breakfast."

Lana waved a hand. "Don't bother. You're our guest. Besides, the children have their assigned chores, and they manage just fine. Go on, now. We'll ring the bell when the food is on the table."

A lazy cock crowed as the front door banged behind Madeline. The sun beamed bright and yellow in a cloudless sky and chased away the morning chill hanging in the spring air. Nevertheless, a shudder washed over her. She stood on the porch, a hand resting against a whitewashed support post, and surveyed the empty yard. "Blast it, Brazos, where have you taken her?"

She spied his clubs tossed haphazardly on the ground, and her tension increased. Brazos never left his toys lying around. "Brazos," she called, a hint of panic in her tone. Like an animal sensing danger, she stood stiff and still, absorbing her surroundings.

Madeline heard the thin, reedy cry.

She swallowed hard, turning her head this way and that, trying desperately to pinpoint the direction of the sound. "Mason," she called, her eyes closed, as she concentrated on Rose's cry. She began to walk toward the barn. "Sister Cecilia. Lana. Help, please. It's Rose."

She broke into a run. The blare of the cry grew stronger with her every step. Madeline rounded the corner of the barn and was confronted with the haunting echo of a young child's fear.

The well.

Oh, Lord, no. "Brazos!" Madeline screamed. Then she saw his boots beside the round wall of stone, and she breathed a sigh of relief. Brazos was with Rose. The baby was crying. He'd saved her. "Thank you, God."

Mason came pounding around the barn followed immediately by Lana and Sister Cecilia. "What's going—" He jerked his head as the sound of Rose's cry exploded from the shaft. "Shit."

"Brazos is with her," Madeline said, her voice high-pitched and shaky. "See, there're his boots."

Mason Kennard leaned over the well and called down, "Brazos?"

He didn't answer. Rose continued to cry. "Brazos!" Mason hollered again.

From the depths of the well came a tormented cry.

Mason's head snapped back. He stared at Madeline, his eyes wide with shock. Sister Cecilia gasped and covered her mouth with her fists as Lana said, "What was that?"

Tears stung Madeline's eyes as she leaned forward and peered into the inky blackness of the well. She remembered the ship—that night in her cabin and then those awful hours trapped in the hold. "Oh, Brazos," she said softly. "You've saved my baby. Such a brave, brave man."

PRESSURE BUILDS IN my head. Pain grows like a cancer. Voices from far away swirl an eddy of heat that does battle with the cold that is my strength. One sound slashes through the darkness, a fiery sword that turns molten at my feet.

"BRAZOS, IT'S MADDIE. I know how hard it must have been for you to go down the well. But you've saved Rose. You're a hero. Look above you, Brazos. See the light? The weather is beautiful this morning—there's not a cloud in the sky. The sun is shining so brightly."

THE PRESSURE SWELLS, my head tilts back. Light, above me. No, I silently scream. The Weak One grows stronger. I try to fight. I try to resist the warmth in my arms. Drop it, I urge. Let go.

"MADDIE?" BRAZOS CROAKED.

"Brazos!" Madeline exclaimed, her voice weak with relief. "Are you all right?"

"Rose . . ."

"I heard her crying. I'll bet you can't wait to get out of there and give your poor ears a rest."

It wasn't his ears giving Brazos problems. Panic had a stranglehold around his neck, constricting his throat so that breathing required enormous effort. Even then, his breaths came in gasps. Sweat rolled in rivulets down his spine, and his heart raced like wildfire across the prairie. "Maddie, I need . . ."

"Is it like before, Brazos? You need me to talk? Well, I'm here, and you know me well enough by now to know that I'm always ready to talk. Mason is with me and he's going to lower the rope. Can you climb up? Do you think you can manage with Rose, or do you want to send her up first?"

As if straining to speak in his sleep, Brazos struggled to force words past his lips. "Got to help Rose. Cold. Wet." He flinched when the thick length of rope brushed against his cheek.

Madeline spoke continuously, and that was the lifeline Brazos grasped as he threaded the rope between Rose's legs, wrapped it around her chest, and knotted it securely against her back. He yanked twice on the line and shouted, "Pull."

Rose, her noisy wail drowning out the soothing sound of Madeline's voice, was tugged from his arms and lifted toward the light.

THE WARM WEIGHT is gone. My strength returns, though the Weak One fights me yet.

Should I allow him to remember?

I am caressed by the velvet chill of the water. I am comforted by the wall's moldy fragrance. Soon, my hunger shall drive me to feed, and I shall glory in the achievement of my freedom. Yes, the moment is arrived. I shall take him back to the beginnings, to my birth, and I will show him the Truth.

Then, Brazos Sinclair will die.

Come, Weak One. Return with me to the Pits of

Perote. You are there, with Miguel, and Damasso Salezan. You are so very hungry.

"BRAZOS, WE HAVE Rose. She's fine, just fine. A little bedraggled is all. Your sister is taking her up to the house for a warm bath and dry clothes. Oh, Brazos, if I could reach you, I'd hug you so hard. If you'd allow it, I'd even kiss you. Come on up, Brazos. Let me hold you and thank you for saving my Rose's life."

THE WARM VOICE slings fire-tipped arrows that pierce my frigid form, seeking the heart of the Weak One. I dive beneath the soundproof water and extinguish the danger. But I must breathe, and I surface, and she continues to hurl her weapons of words.

"ROSE LOVES YOU, you know," Madeline was saying. "And I am certain that you love her in return. It's a funny thing—love—isn't it? It sneaks up on us when we are not looking, and once we have it, there's really no getting rid of it."

Brazos focused on the light above him and concentrated on Madeline's voice.

"We've lowered the rope again. Do you have it, Brazos? Mason thinks you could climb out better than we could pull you. Is that right, are you climbing up, Brazos?"

"Maddie," he whispered, grabbing the rope. Hand over hand, with feet braced against the well's wall, Brazos began to climb toward Madeline and the light.

NO, I SCREAM, freezing his fingers in a stationary death grip. Advance no farther. I am stronger than you, stronger than she. I'll not allow you to bind me in tethers again.

HANGING HALFWAY UP the rope, suspended between heaven and hell, Brazos grimaced and gave a violent shake of his head in a vain attempt to rid himself of the panic. "Ma . . . Ma . . . Maddie!"

"Yes, Brazos. I'm still here. You're climbing out, aren't you? I can tell by the way the rope moves and your voice sounds closer. Hurry, though, Brazos. I know you must be cold. We've a warm bath waiting for you. And Rose—of course, you'll want to hold Rose. She's saying your name quite well now. Ba Ba. That's what she says. She loves you so much."

He moved. His toes grabbed for purchase against a rough-edged stone, feeling mortar crumble beneath his maneuvering. But the constant sound of Madeline's voice pulled him upward. The pressure in his head swelled, and pain pounded behind his eyes as he looked above into the soul-sustaining light. He heard the demon inside him yell, *Halt. Come back. You are the Weak One. I can defeat the woman, and I can defeat you.*

"Maybe so," Brazos panted. "Alone. But not together. You can't beat Maddie and me when we're workin' together." He felt the kiss of sunshine on his fists, and then strong hands gripped him and pulled him up and out. His feet touched dry ground, and suddenly Madeline was in his arms, heedless of his soggy, dripping state, hugging him fiercely and raining sweet kisses across his chest, his neck, his face.

"Oh, darling," she cried. "Thank you. Thank God you were there to save her." She gazed up at him, her eyes swimming and shining with emotion. She pushed a wet lock of hair away from his forehead and said, "Oh, Brazos, what can I say? I know how difficult it must have been for you to go down into that well."

Brazos swallowed hard. Stepping back, he stared at Madeline—at the picture she made in a formfitting dress the color of the Texas sky. Her plaited hair fell in a golden rope over one shoulder while her teeth tugged uncertainly at lips the color of strawberries. She watched him with warm, glowing eyes, and he knew a bitter burning deep in his belly.

Shame. God, he wanted to vomit, he was so ashamed.

So he left her. He sought the cover of the woods and the anonymity they offered, fleeing at a dead run.

BY THE TIME she had finished bathing Rose, Madeline was as wet as the child. Between wrestling with a girl who'd had enough of water that day, and the tears Madeline couldn't seem to prevent from running down her cheeks, she was forced to change clothes before joining the search. Mason and some of the older boys had scoured the forest around St. Michael's looking for Brazos before Sister Cecilia convinced them to allow her brother his privacy. She claimed he needed time alone and would return when he felt ready.

Madeline disagreed. No one but she had seen his pain; no one but she had seemed to affect it. Brazos needed her, perhaps as never before.

After she offered a convincing argument, Mason suggested she check the bluff a half mile south of Rocky Point, because in the past the hill had proven to be a favorite spot of Brazos's. While Mason saddled a horse for her, Lana filled a bag with bread, cheese, and a bottle of Mason's elderberry wine. Sister Cecilia gathered a blanket and a change of clothing for her brother.

"Head west, toward town," Mason directed, "until you come to Antelope Creek. Follow the creek south for a bit, and you'll see the bluff. There's a cropping of flat rock. That's my best guess as to where he might be."

Saddle leather creaked as Mason gave Madeline a hand in mounting the roan mare one of the orphans had named Bunny. "Are you certain you don't want me to tag along, Madeline?" he asked. "I hate to say it, but I'm worried about you going after him alone. He looked downright dangerous when he came up out of that well."

She shook her head. "He's not dangerous, Mason, just in pain. I believe I can help him. I have before, you see." With that, Madeline waved at Sister Cecilia and Lana and rode off.

Bunny traveled at a slow canter, no matter what Madeline did in an attempt to increase her pace. "You remind me of the horse I rode that time I robbed Lord Greeley's carriage," Madeline grumbled. That little fiasco had nearly landed her in jail, and she'd sworn never again to commit a theft while riding an inferior horse. Of course, she wasn't planning to steal anything today.

The idea hit her like a slap in the face. Maybe there was something she could steal. Yanking back on the reins, she jerked Bunny to a stop. She nervously licked her lips and stared straight ahead, seeing nothing as she rolled the notion over in her head. Could she do it?

It would be her greatest challenge. It would require the use of all of her talents—those she'd spent years developing and those she'd only recently acquired. If she could pull off this heist, it would be one for the history books.

Dare she try? Doing so would put her at terrible risk. Failure would likely destroy her. Though she'd never say it aloud and she had yet to accept the idea as fact, she suspected that she already harbored deep feelings for the man. Was she being a fool by even entertaining the idea? Did she stand any chance at all of success?

She remembered her words to Mason just a short time ago. *I believe I can help him. I have before.* It was true, she had given Brazos Sinclair something he'd desperately needed, and she believed she'd identified just what that something was.

Brazos needed someone to hold him, someone to offer him comfort when besieged by whatever demons haunted him. He needed the proverbial port in a storm. Madeline could offer him that port.

Oh, he'd resist. He'd give her that spiel about having tumbleweed in his blood, he'd tell her he'd never be able to provide her and Rose with the home they required. But Madeline knew Brazos well enough to know that if she could pull off this theft, the tumbleweed would blow right out of him. He'd quit running, and he'd want nothing more than to stay with her and Rose and build the home and family she dreamed of. Madeline leaned forward and absently patted Bunny's neck. She pursed her lips and said, "I'll do it."

Madeline was a thief. A very good thief. It was that belief in herself that allowed her to gig Bunny's sides and ride in pursuit of her prey. A smile tugged at her lips as she rode beneath a bower of live oak trees to the music of a robin's song. It would be her greatest theft. Plus, she could redeem herself from her recent descent into stealing objects like potato mashers.

Forget the silver; she'd decided to go for the gold. Madeline planned to steal Brazos Sinclair's heart.

Chapter 15

Madeline found Brazos lying naked on a wide, flat rock. He rested on his stomach, sunning himself like one of the alligators she'd seen on the trip up Buffalo Bayou. Only Brazos Sinclair was no reptile.

True, he may act like one at times, and she had witnessed moments when the man had acted downright cold-blooded, but as she gazed at the bronzed expanse of sinew and muscle stretched out before her, Madeline saw no sign at all of scales.

He was beautiful. An Adonis worthy of Michelangelo's talents. Sunlight glistened off the band of silver around his arm, and as he cocked open one eye to pin her with a furious glare, Madeline corrected herself. He was an Adonis with a fearsome disposition.

After securing Bunny to a nearby pine and grabbing the bag containing her husband's shirt and pants and the pouch of food, Madeline picked her way across the outcropping of rocks. Stepping over the pile of soggy clothing, she spread out the blanket and sat down beside him. She smoothed her skirt, then folded her hands in her lap and stared out over the tree-dotted landscape that extended to the western horizon.

Neither she nor Brazos spoke, and as often happens, that silence in itself became a speech. Eventually, she reached for the food bag and dug around in it for an apple. He opened his eye again at the crunching sound when she took a bite. Madeline knew he must be hungry; it was well past noon. Without a word, she found another apple and extended her hand with the shiny red offering.

He took it. Then, heedless of his nudity, he rolled over and sat up. Casually, he took a bite from the apple, swallowed, and said, "Well, Eve, come to tame the serpent?"

"I was thinking along the lines of an alligator," she responded, trying desperately to keep her gaze away from his lap. She reached into the second bag, then tossed him the clothes his sister had provided.

"Beware. A gator's bite will kill ya." He held the apple with his teeth as he stood and pulled on his pants.

Madeline shrugged, wishing he would use the blue chambray shirt for more than a pillow as he assumed a prone position. It was hard enough to force her tongue to tell her story; she didn't need to deal with fingers that itched to follow the line of hair trailing downward from his navel.

But tell her story she would. Otherwise, her scheme had not a prayer of succeeding. Madeline recognized that for Brazos's heart to soften toward her, she must tell him why she'd kidnapped Rose. Then, if he reacted as she suspected he would, she could put the rest of her recently devised plan into motion. With the moment of disclosure upon her, Madeline smoothed her skirts and distractedly wondered how Catholics managed. Confession might be good for the soul, but it played hell on one's digestive organs. Her stomach had that mal de mer feeling again. Drawing a deep breath, she forced herself to say, "I want to explain about Rose, Brazos."

His hand trembled a fraction as he lowered the apple from his mouth. Flatly, he asked, "Is she dead?"

"No," Madeline hastened to say. "She's fine. You saved her, Brazos, I can't tell you how much—"

"I don't want to talk about it. Go on back, Madeline. Leave me alone."

She nibbled at her lower lip before saying, "You called me Maddie earlier." He all but snarled at her, and she quickly continued, "I want to tell you how Rose ended up with me. Why I took her from her home."

His look was both cold and questioning. Am I doing the right thing? Madeline wondered. This was a risk, probably the biggest risk of her life. Yet, she stood to gain more than she'd ever dreamed possible, and besides, she wasn't going to tell him everything.

Taking a deep breath, she began, "I was teaching at an English boarding school when I received a letter. I was instructed to go to a French estate, Château St. Germaine, where I would accept the position of companion to a woman named Celeste Desseau, who was expecting a child. The letter said that Madame Desseau was in possession of certain secrets that would lead me to my family."

Brazos lifted an eyebrow, but remained silent.

Gazing out at the rolling hills of forest and meadow below, Madeline continued, "I couldn't resist. All my life, I'd dreamed of finding my family. I left England that very day." A wistful note entered her voice. "I loved Château St. Germaine. Upon my first view of the house from my carriage, a sense of peace overcame me. It was almost as if it were *my* home I returned to."

She turned to him, her gaze imploring, because this part he simply must understand. "Celeste Desseau greeted me as if I were an old and dear friend. We got along famously from the moment we met. She was so beautiful, so kind—" Madeline paused, and her lips trembled. "I showed her the letter, and she said she was sorry, that she knew nothing about any secrets."

Brazos cleared his throat as though to speak, but she hurried on. "I asked Celeste who could have sent the letter. She said it must have been her mother, Bernadette, because she'd been the one who had told Celeste to expect my arrival. She'd looked so sad when she added that her mother was privy to many secrets. I, of course, immediately wanted to speak to Bernadette, but Celeste said it wouldn't be possible. Bad blood existed between Celeste's husband, Julian, and her mother. Bernadette was forbidden to come to St. Germaine. I couldn't leave Celeste; she needed me. It was less than two months before the child was due. Celeste promised that as soon as she had the baby, she'd take me to see her mother. Then she cautioned me not to mention it to Julian."

Madeline scooped up a handful of pebbles from the ground and began tossing them down the hill as she spoke. "I honestly liked Julian. He was older than Celeste, but quite handsome. He seemed so devoted to her and concerned for her health." Her gaze lifted to espy a hawk circling against a backdrop of brilliant blue sky and puffy white clouds. She envied him his freedom.

"Listen, Madeline," Brazos began.

She continued, "I'd been there only a short time when I began to realize that Celeste was playing Julian false. She'd smile at him, but when he turned away, she'd shudder. Shortly before the birth of the baby, she confided in me that she planned to leave Julian as soon as the baby was born. The visit she'd planned to her mother would be permanent. She and I both believed we'd learn the secrets I'd been promised from Bernadette."

Brazos tugged a handkerchief from his pants pocket and offered it to her. Madeline smiled her thanks and dabbed at watery eyes. "The birth was difficult, and Celeste did not recover. She suffered childbed fever and grew weaker every day. Julian was frantic. He sent for physicians from Paris, but . . ." Madeline shrugged. "She was dying, and she knew it. I half believe in my heart that she wanted to die. A part of her still loved Julian, and she couldn't live with the truth about him."

Madeline grew silent, pausing to gather her strength for the telling of the rest of the tale.

Brazos wanted to shake her and tell her to get on with her story, but instead, he took her hand in his and gave it a comforting squeeze. Though his stomach still churned as a result of his own ordeal, he forgot all about his troubles in the face of Madeline's obvious distress. And the knowledge that *finally* he was going to learn why she'd kidnapped Rose.

Watching the myriad emotions flicker across her face—anguish and condemnation paramount among them—Brazos realized for the first time the weight of the burden she carried. All of a sudden, he lost interest in hearing the details of her story. He damn near told her to keep her mouth shut.

Madeline smiled a bittersweet smile as she said, "Upon learning that Celeste expected a child, her mother, Bernadette, confessed a vile truth. Years earlier, Bernadette had also been married to Julian Desseau."

"What?" Brazos exclaimed.

Madeline nodded. "They'd been married two years when he accused her of betraying her marriage vows with another man. It was a lie, but Bernadette could not convince him otherwise. He sent Bernadette away and told all of France that his wife had accidentally drowned. She had no choice but to cooperate. He'd threatened her with horrible consequences should she resist or interfere with his scheme, so Bernadette assumed a false identity and eventually, married an Italian count."

Brazos was beginning to frown. Madeline spoke swiftly, providing him pieces of the puzzle faster than he could fit them together. Still, he didn't like the way the board was taking shape.

Madeline said, "Bernadette and her count traveled frequently, making trips all over the world. Their daughter, Celeste, went to school in Switzerland, and there she met Julian Desseau. He courted her, wooing her with riches and pretty words. He treated her like a queen. When he proposed they elope, she agreed. They'd been married almost a year when Bernadette returned to Europe and discovered her daughter had married. By then, Celeste was expecting Rose.

"Bernadette traveled to a village near St. Germaine and secretly sent for Celeste. That's when she told Celeste the truth."

"What truth?" Brazos asked, confusion plowing

furrows in his brow. "You've got me purely confounded."

Madeline rubbed her arms as though she were cold. In a flat tone of voice, she stated, "The truth about Julian Desseau. He knew that Bernadette was expecting his child when he banished her from Château St. Germaine. He knew the truth of which Celeste was unaware—that the Italian count was not her father." She looked at Brazos with tortured, angry eyes and said, "Julian was."

Brazos went as still as the stone beneath them. "The hell you say. Damn, Maddie, that's—"

"Incest," she snapped. "Julian Desseau knowingly fathered Rose with his own daughter."

A foul curse exploded from Brazos's mouth, and he pushed to his feet. He stood with his feet spread wide and his hands braced on his hips as he listened to Madeline tell the rest of her story in a flat tone of voice. She said, "Bernadette confessed to Celeste that Julian had left a letter at her villa in Florence for her to read when she returned from her travels. In it, he told Bernadette that the entire scheme had been an act of revenge upon Bernadette for having supposedly cheated on him. Celeste told me the story as she lay dying, and begged me to save her Rose from Julian's depravity. I considered killing the man, but I'm afraid I couldn't bring myself to do it. So I stole her. I knew I couldn't go to Bernadette; Julian would have looked for me there first. So I gave up on the idea of ever learning about my family as promised in my letter, and Rose and I traveled to Antwerp. You know the rest."

A muscle tweaked in Brazos's cheek as rage toward a man thousands of miles away coursed through his veins. He spoke through set teeth. "That's the most disgusting, degenerate, despicable story I've ever heard. Hell, Maddie, you'd have been doin' the world a favor by killin' the bastard. Too bad he's so far away, or I'd see to the deed myself." Then a slow, thoughtful smile spread across his face. "Although I'll bet my investigator could find us someone to do it."

Madeline stood and touched his arm. "So, now do

you see why I lied?" she implored. "I won't apologize for taking Rose. I'd do the very same thing again."

He shrugged. "You could have told me sooner. What did you think I'd do, turn you over to the bastard?"

"No, I never thought you'd turn us over to Julian. But you're not a permanent fixture in our lives, Brazos. I thought it safest for Rose if I alone knew the truth."

"Then why now? Why did you follow me up this hill and tell me your tale—this day of all days?"

Something flickered in her eyes, making him suspicious of her words, as she said, "You saved her life. You went down in that well—something I know must have been terrifying for you—and rescued your 'Miss Magic.' I thought you deserved to know the truth after such a sacrifice."

"It was no goddamned sacrifice," he raged, glaring up toward the sky. "I love Rose. You think I'd have just stood there and let her drown?"

"No, Brazos. I think you're the bravest, most courageous man I've ever met." She trailed her fingers down his chest and said, "I think you're wonderful. You're a hero, Brazos—my hero. I want you to make love with me."

"Hold it right there," Brazos said, grabbing her wrist to prevent her hand from traveling down to his waistband. "I may be insane, but I'm not stupid. What are you tryin' to do here, Madeline? Why do I get the feelin' somethin's different? What is this, some sort of reward? Or maybe some sympathy sex because I went crazy down there? Well, thanks, but no. I've more pride than . . ." His voice trailed off as Madeline tugged her hand from his and moved her fingers to the bodice of her dress.

Slowly, she worked the buttons. "You always enjoy games, Brazos." She laughed, low and seductively. "Now, I know of one even more fun than golf. And we have all the equipment we need to play right here and right now."

Damn, the woman was persistent. And smart. She'd caught him at a low point, then capitalized on it with an ugly story that garnered his sympathy. But his situation hadn't changed just because he understood Madeline's reasons for lying to him. He still needed out of this marriage.

Madeline and Rose deserved roots that stretched deep into the soil and grabbed hold for life. Brazos's roots had dried up and disintegrated in the bowels of Perote Prison. Tumbleweeds simply had no roots to plant.

No matter how much they wished they did.

He scowled and shut his eyes when she bared her breasts before him. "Put your clothes back on, woman."

She ignored him. "And the rules of this game are simple. All we need is to see, and taste, and touch—a lot of touching. Don't you remember, Brazos? We've played this game before." His groan was a deep rumble that served only to encourage her.

"You told me before how soft my skin was, how sweet I tasted," she said. "We did enjoy this game before."

Brazos took a deep breath and consciously relaxed his clenched fists. He looked at her, and his gaze slipped below her neck only twice as he said, "Listen, Madeline, I appreciate the effort. A woman like you bent on seduction is mighty hard to resist. And I'm proud that you shared your story with me. I know it wasn't an easy thing to do. But it hasn't changed anything between us. I'm leaving you at La Réunion, and I'm gettin' that divorce."

Reaching for her, Brazos intended to fasten her buttons. But somehow his fingers got all tangled up with her breasts, and then she was leaning toward him and moaning deep in her throat, and his tongue sort of darted out to taste that hollow where the noise was coming from.

Still, he'd have been all right had she not gone for the buttons on his britches. She touched him then, molded her fingers around him, and all his good intentions disappeared faster than a plate of cookies in St. Michael's kitchen.

"Hell, Maddie," he groaned, lowering her to her

back and kneeling above her. "You've no more conscience than a cow in a stampede. Didn't they teach you the meaning of the word *no* in that boarding school of yours?"

She laughed, a seductive, triumphant song that delved into his heart and invaded that empty, guarded place, filling it with heat. "Actually, my years in England taught me that if the answer is no, I haven't properly asked the question." Her arms curled around his waist, and she pulled him toward her. Rubbing her naked bosom against his bare chest, she asked, "Am I asking properly now?"

"Hussy." His tongue slid between her lips as he took her mouth in a possessive kiss. He tasted the apple's sweetness on her breath and knew he'd been right in the comparison to Eve. A rocky hill in Central Texas wasn't exactly the Garden of Eden, but then, this entire scenario was backward. He was Sin, the devil—not poor, old Adam, who lost it all because he succumbed to a temptress's charms.

He didn't help her when she shimmied out of her petticoats and drawers, but he didn't hinder her, either. Stroking the unbound silk of her long, glistening tresses and gazing down at her mouth, gleaming red and swollen from his kiss, Brazos admitted that he'd never stopped wanting her. Even when he'd tried to convince himself she was nothing short of evil, he'd desired her with an intensity he'd known for no other woman. There was something about Madeline that called to him, a light that battled his inner darkness.

The Beauty clashed with the Beast.

"Aw, to hell with fig leaves," he said, stripping off his denims and positioning himself between her thighs. "Take me to paradise, Beauty." He entered her slowly, reining in the urge to bury himself inside her with one fast thrust. For all her success as a seductress, he knew in his heart she'd practiced her wiles upon him alone.

Brazos braced himself on his elbows and fought his natural hunger. "Relax, darlin'. Last time we took turns. This time I want us to go off together. It's gonna be so fine, Maddie mine." He lowered his head and nuzzled her breast. "First, I'm gonna suck you like a baby and taste that sweetness you promised me." He caught her pebbled nipple between his teeth and gently tugged.

A whimper escaped her throat, and he lowered himself a little more. "I'm gonna work you with my hands till the musk of your arousal surrounds us in a cloud of perfume. And then I'm gonna listen as you scream your release, and our voices will blend as I spill my seed inside you. We'll have a grand time, Maddie mine." He pressed down on her, his breath catching in his throat as she moved beneath him, tilting her hips and taking him completely.

And Brazos proceeded to make good on his promises.

It was more than sex and technique, it was an exquisite blending of need and desire, of gifts freely offered and joyfully received. Brazos made love with Madeline.

Feeling her climax, bathing himself in the hot, dancing flames that made her writhe and quake and cry out his name, he exploded inside her and lost himself in the paradise of her body pulsing around him. Her contractions pulled him deep into a place he'd never known before—a warm, golden Eden, where the hollow in his soul was filled to overflowing with a brilliant, gentle peace.

He sagged against her, desperate to hold on to this new and wondrous sensation. He pressed butterfly kisses against her throat, her cheek, her eyes. "Oh, Brazos," Madeline sighed, "I could love you so easily."

For just a moment, the colors of paradise sparkled brilliantly and beckoned. But the darkness inside him flared in rage as she made her declaration. He rolled off of her and lay on his back with his forearm flung over his eyes. "Please don't, Maddie. I don't want to hurt you. And I will. God help me, but I will."

"I don't believe you, Brazos." She rested her head on his chest, her fingers drawing lazily across his belly. He didn't have either the heart or the strength to push her away. The hurt was inevitable and would undoubtedly come sooner rather than later. But for now, this stolen moment in time, he was content to lie here with this woman he—

Brazos refused to complete the thought. But the word hung in his mind, churning his gut, and piercing his heart. Madeline may have dealt with her demons by telling him her story, but his certainly hadn't gone anywhere. Seeing as what had happened in the bottom of that well, Brazos's personal demon had grown even stronger. He realized that until he dealt with the monster inside him, he'd never be at peace.

To deal with the demon inside meant dealing with the devil outside. Brazos could make no commitments until he'd dealt with Damasso Salezan.

THEY GOT A LATE start away from St. Michael's Children's Home the following morning, what with over twenty teary-eyed children to soothe. At first, Madeline questioned the advisability of passing out gifts to children from an open coffin, but judging from the anticipation and delight present in their faces, she'd worried over nothing. Apparently, they had experience in dealing with Brazos Sinclair's peculiarities.

Madeline watched with detached interest as Brazos and Mason finished unloading the silver from the casket and stored it in an underground chamber disguised as a privy. "I trust all of those in residence understand not to avail themselves of this particular facility?" she asked Sister Cecilia.

The nun smiled. "Mason has threatened each of us with dire consequences should we forget."

Brazos then fussed for almost twenty minutes, rearranging Madeline's trunks in the buckboard to create a safe carrying place for his golf clubs. "You sure you couldn't repack your things in the coffin, Maddie? With the silver gone, I could use a little more weight in the box. Besides, your clothes would help cushion my golf clubs. I don't want them gettin' busted."

"Brazos," Madeline said with a sigh, "I'm sure your toys will be just fine where they are."

Following a final round of good-byes, Brazos and Madeline and Rose headed out. "I can't believe I'm actually bringing Miss Magic back with us," he grumbled as the wagon turned on the road leading toward Rocky Point.

"I can't believe you actually thought to take her away from me," Madeline replied, still bristling at the idea.

On the way back to St. Michael's yesterday, Brazos had confessed a secret of his own. He'd told Madeline how he had planned to leave Rose at St. Micaehl's. After a few tense moments, Madeline admitted she understood his motives. "You were trying to protect her," she'd said. "While I can be angry that you believed so little of me, I can't fault you for watching out for my daughter."

The morning air was cool, and as the wagon creaked its way along the trail, Madeline dug an extra sweater from Rose's bag and worked the squirming youngster's arms into the sleeves. "I don't know, Maddie," Brazos said, a pensive look on his face. "Maybe I'm making a mistake taking you back to the wagon train. What if Salezan's men find you? It could be dangerous."

Madeline shook her head. "I thought we settled this argument yesterday. Let me see if I have this right." She held up her hand and ticked off each point with a finger. "First, you hid Juanita with the colonists because you thought it was the safest place for her. That hasn't changed. Second, there's been no sign of this Salezan or his men. Third, even if the worst happened and this monster you speak of traced Juanita to La Réunion, he certainly wouldn't go after me and Rose. Fourth, even if he did, La Réunion is a closed community. We don't allow strangers among us. The colonists will protect us."

"All right, Maddie," Brazos said. "You don't have to wear out my ears again. You've convinced me; otherwise, I'd have left St. Michael's without you."

Madeline sent him a sidelong look. "Brazos, you

should know by now that no one keeps me anywhere I don't want to be. Had you left me at the children's home, I wouldn't have stayed."

He scowled, but he didn't argue with the truth. A cardinal sang *whoit whoit* to its mate as the buckboard rattled down the road. As they passed a farm, the scent of freshly turned dirt carried on the air. Madeline and Brazos passed the time in idle conversation or comfortable silence. Madeline used those quiet times to ponder the status of her marriage.

Brazos never mentioned the possibility of a future between them beyond the next few weeks. He had told her little of this Salezan, other than the man was a threat to Juanita and to anyone Brazos loved.

That pricked at her a bit. The Mexican beauty was one part of the equation she'd yet to solve. True, Brazos had been open in declaring his love for Juanita. But for all the cooing and touching between the two of them, she'd yet to see signs of a connection beyond that of dear friends. Of course, it could be she saw only what she wanted to see, but she didn't really believe that. Brazos didn't look at Juanita with the same light in his eyes that glowed when he looked at her.

Maybe her plan was working, after all.

Could it be that she was succeeding? Had she made inroads toward this theft she intended? Had she stolen even a piece of his heart?

Perhaps. Only time would tell. Time and Brazos's actions upon their reunion with the colonists. Somehow, she needed to convince him that they had the makings of a perfect family. She could do it, surely she could. She simply had to devise the proper plan.

Madeline was not about to abandon her quest. Difficulties regularly arose in one's designs, and things required a bit of rearranging. That's all she faced now. Confidently, she put her mind to work. She was after his heart; she wouldn't be settling for potato mashers.

They reached the wagon train's trail late that afternoon. Madeline was driving the wagon while Brazos rode her mare when he spotted his brother's horse riding back toward them. Brazos drew a line of brown dust clouds as he raced his horse across the prairie toward Tyler. Her curiosity aroused by the length of the discussion, Madeline absently sang a song for Rose as the wagon finally drew up beside them.

For the first time since Galveston, Tyler looked at her with a smile on his face. "Hello, Madeline," he said.

"Tyler."

Then he turned to Brazos and said, "The wagons are only a day's ride from Dallas. Now that you're back, why don't I ride on ahead and take care of that business we discussed."

"Business?" Brazos asked, his brow wrinkling.

"Yes, Brazos. That detail awaiting your arrival. Remember? Don't you want it taken care of before the colonists arrive?"

A slow light dawned across Brazos's face. Then he scowled. "Damn, I forgot all about him. Yeah, go on, Tyler, and see if you can't escort the—" Brazos stopped suddenly. He twisted in the saddle to look at Madeline. Then he folded his arms, tilted his chin, and stared at her.

She looked up at him blankly.

Slowly, softly at first, Brazos began to laugh. Pretty soon, he was laughing so hard, he was leaning in his saddle. "Brazos, have you lost all your sense?" Madeline asked, grimacing in aggravation.

"He never existed, did he, Maddie mine?"

"What are you talking about?"

"Not what. Who. It's no wonder you never remembered the fella's name. You'd made it all up."

Madeline was growing vexed. Brazos twirled his hat on a finger and chortled. "Mr. Sinclair," she said in a tight voice, "who are you talking about?"

"See. She still can't remember. *Emile*. The phantom fiancé waiting at La Réunion. There's never been an Emile in your life, has there, Maddie?"

Madeline hated to be laughed at. "As a matter of fact, I'm quite close to a male named Emile." She lifted her chin and added, "He broke down and cried when I left him in France."

Brazos sobered abruptly. "Well, who the hell is *he?*"

"He lives at Château St. Germaine, and I'm telling you, Brazos, we were very close." She whipped the reins and started the wagon forward. Grinning at his sour look, she added, "He's the cook's pet collie."

Chapter 16

Brazos took one look at the land along the rocky, white limestone bluffs Victor Considérant had purchased for the La Réunion colony and said, "My God, does nothin' at all happen north of that man's neck? He picked out the worst-lookin' section of land this side of the Louisiana border." He shook his head in amazement and added, "Must've been either a banker or a lawyer who sold him these acres."

"Brazos! Your brother is a lawyer," Madeline replied, gazing around at the site.

"So?"

"I'm going to tell him you said that."

He laughed. "Tyler knows what I think of his profession."

Madeline almost mentioned that Brazos didn't hesitate to use Tyler's professional skills, but she thought it best not to bring up the subject of divorce. "I think this land is quite pretty," she said. "It reminds me of the vineyard country of France."

"Maddie, y'all aren't gonna be needin' wine to see

you through the winter," Brazos said with disgust. "You're gonna need corn—lots of it—and vegetables. Hell, a still and a couple of bushels of grain will take care of a man's drinkin' needs. You folks are gonna have to concentrate on food."

Madeline shrugged, unwilling to think so far ahead. This was springtime in Texas—the sun bright and warm, the air velvety soft and sweetened from the bounty of wildflowers growing in splashes of red, yellow, and blue throughout the surrounding country-side. And Brazos wasn't leaving until he'd built her a house. "Don't be such a spoilsport. I think I shall love my new home."

As a result of the efforts of a small assembly of Fourierists who had previously made the journey from Europe, building of the La Réunion colony was well under way. The president's office, a structure for the making of soap and candles, a laundry, a forge, and a chicken house had been completed. The newest arrivals also found a cottage for the executive agent and two dormitories of eight apartments, each to be allotted to two households, ready for occupancy.

Brazos scoffed at that notion. "Ain't a tepee yet been built that can peaceably house two families," he observed. Immediately, he sought out the agent and offered a substantial amount of money for two weeks' rent on the fellow's cozy cottage. Privacy was a priority for both him and Madeline.

Juanita had accepted the change in Brazos and Madeline's relationship with surprising grace. She'd chosen to sleep in the dormitory until the house was finished, a move that helped her to make friends among the colonists. As she had explained the day they'd taken the empty coffin out for burial during a private family ceremony, more than anything, she wanted her Sin to be happy.

After weeks with the colonists, it was obvious Brazos had been correct in assuming that Juanita would fit right in with the Europeans. While he'd given up on the idea of keeping her extraordinary beauty veiled on a daily basis, she had promised never to leave the colony compound—and to wear the veil when she broke the first promise and left La Réunion anyway.

With the trip from Houston successfully completed, Tyler prepared to return to Galveston. Madeline listened attentively as he and Brazos discussed the letter they'd posted in Anderson some two weeks ago—an invitation to Damasso Salezan to attend the reopening of a silver mine. She smiled with relief when Brazos instructed Tyler to see to the cancellation of the investigation into Rose's background. The other topic of interest to Madeline was the subject of divorce. Neither man mentioned it.

The morning Tyler left La Réunion, as she listened to the two men tease one another like ornery little boys, Madeline felt a pang in her heart that was slow to disappear. They were family. They loved and laughed and bickered and fought. They had tears in their eyes as they took leave of each other.

She wanted to share that. She needed desperately to be part of a family like the Sinclairs. It had been her lifelong dream. Madeline prayed she was a good enough thief to steal it for herself.

Brazos watched Tyler's dust until the red cloud settled back to the ground. When he turned to her, his voice was gruff, "Well, I reckon we'd best get to work on that house I promised you. Where are you supposed to work today?"

Madeline offered him a sunshine smile. "I'm to work in the co-op store this morning, but I think I'll exercise my right as a Phalansterian and change my assignment. I'm of a mind to build houses today."

Brazos looked up toward the sky and groaned. "But, Madeline, building is a man's job. Don't you think you ought to stick to serving up rabbit stew or somethin'?" When she followed him, complaining continuously, he led her back to the cottage, where she found his horse saddled, ready to ride, and her mare saddled right beside it. "I'm ridin' after family to help work on the house. I thought you might like to come along."

"Oh, Brazos," she said, sighing. "At times, you are such a tease."

Locating four cousins, two uncles, and one brother-in-law within a day's ride of the colony, Brazos and his family, and some days Madeline, went to work. Because he defined his relationship with Madeline in a vague manner, each day he suffered numerous sly remarks and innuendos from the men assisting him.

Madeline made it worth his while every night. She cooked and cleaned and mended, and then took him into her arms and proved just how talented a wife she could be. He seemed content, more at peace than at any time since they had met, and Madeline harbored great hopes for the future.

As the days passed, she found herself torn between worry over Brazos's intention to leave and thrill at the prospects of a owning a house of her own—even if she did have to share it with Brazos's Juanita. Each day as she finished her assigned chores, she'd collect Rose from the cooperative nursery and head directly for the lot owned, at least in the colonists' eyes, by Mr. and Mrs. Sinclair.

Madeline's long dreamed of home differed substantially from the mortared rock houses being erected by the Europeans. Brazos was building the home Texas-style. Fashioned from rough-hewn logs, the cabin took shape as two large rooms separated by an open porch or dog run. Rock fireplaces stood at each end of the house, and when it was finished, a tall cedar shake roof would slope to form a long porch or veranda along the front. The room on the west end of the cabin served as a kitchen and living area, while the eastern room would function as Madeline's bedroom. Narrow stairs led to the attic loft, where the majority of her Galveston purchases would be stored. Rose would sleep in the loft when she grew older, but for now, the pine baby's crib Brazos had borrowed from his brother-in-law was placed against a wall in kitchen.

Ten days after the colonists' arrival at La Réunion, Madeline paused to pick a handful of the orange and yellow Indian paintbrushes growing wild in an empty field between the communal dining room and the nursery, where she'd spent the morning with Rose. Madeline was feeling especially happy today. Although she'd never confess the truth to Brazos, she'd discovered her favorite work here at La Réunion was caring for the children. The hours spent at the nursery were much more fulfilling than those spent behind a plow. Of course, if Brazos were to learn it, her crusade for women's equality would be set back weeks, probably even months. He'd never let her hear the end of it.

Madeline laughed to herself. Brazos was another reason for her delight in the beautiful spring day. In his lovemaking last night, Brazos had displayed a tenderness, a sense of connection, he'd not shared with her before. She was beginning to suspect that her scheme was working. Now, if only she didn't run out of time.

Bending over to add some yellow buttercups to her bouquet, Madeline hesitated. The hair on the back of her neck lifted as she sensed someone staring at her. Fear gripped her, similar to what she'd felt at times on the trip from Houston. Slowly, she straightened, and forced herself to look around.

It was Brazos. Bare-chested and covered in a sheen of sweat, he leaned on the handle of his ax beside a stack of split logs. His heated gaze bore into her, and she stood transfixed by its intensity. Then, suddenly, he dropped the ax, picked up his shirt, and left.

Madeline spent the rest of the afternoon being peeved. "He could at least have said hello," she groused. Especially after last night. Her entire day was spoiled as she worked in the dining room preparing supper. He didn't arrive for the evening meal, which made her all the more annoyed. She was fuming and muttering to herself when she walked past her new house that night.

Then she noticed the rosebushes. Pink rosebushes formed a line along the front of her half-finished front porch. She remembered Brazos's asking what her dream house would look like. She'd told him roses, pink roses.

It took Brazos a good half hour to get her to stop crying that night. In the days that followed, her tears came more and more frequently.

• • •

"THE JOURNEY FROM Perote Prison to
Dallas, Texas, had been long and tedious. Winston
Poteet sat in a chair with his boots propped on the
windowsill of a second story room at the Crutchfield
House hotel. He sipped scotch whiskey from a glass,
stared down into the dusty Dallas street, and murmured,
"Working for Salezan has its moments, but this ain't one
of 'em." He wouldn't even get a good rest before he'd hit
the road again.

A knock sounded on the door. "Yeah?" he called.

"Cuellar," a Spanish accented voice replied.

Poteet looked at his pocket watch lying on a table
beside the bed and scowled. The man was early. Probably wanted to get business out of the way so he could
spend the night chasing the ladies.

I'll have to remind him to keep his britches buttoned this trip, Poteet thought. The governor wouldn't
hold for any of his men messing around with his
woman.

He answered the door and crooked his finger for
the younger man to enter. "Well?" he asked, shutting the
door after checking the hallway to confirm that no
curious ears might be listening.

"The men of Governor Salezan's army are gathered and awaiting your orders, Captain."

"Good. We'll go at first light."

Cuellar flashed a smile that he claimed could
convince a woman to strip to her skin in less than a
minute. "Ah, an entire night ahead of us. I invite you to
accompany me, Captain Poteet. There are three women
awaiting me. In truth, I can use your help."

Poteet changed the subject with a wave of his
hand. "I've not time for that, and you don't, either.
You'd best be spending this night sleeping. We'll have to
make the trip south at a record pace, and it ain't gonna
be easy dragging two women along with us. That's why
it's so important for the men to make this raid look as
real as possible."

"They will do well." Cuellar reached into his vest pocket and pulled out a cheroot. "I have distributed the face paint and breechclouts. Willie Norriss has been practicing his Comanche yell. For a Kentuckian, he sounds quite realistic. The only man I had trouble with was Oates. The fellow's skin is too fair. He'd never pass for Indian, so I sent him to spy on the Europeans."

Poteet frowned as he absently watched Cuellar light his smoke and take three deep draws. The acrid scent of tobacco swirled in the room, and Poteet frowned. He couldn't abide tobacco, made him sneeze. "I hope to hell we're going about this the right way," he said. "It's a gamble, taking the women and hoping he'll follow. But since the governor wants Sinclair delivered uninjured, I think it's the only way. It'd take every man Salezan has in Texas to drag Sinclair to Mexico, and even then, I'm not certain we wouldn't end up killing him before we arrived. Still, the governor won't be at all pleased with us if things don't work out as planned."

"It will work, *amigo*," Cuellar insisted. "Believe me. I followed that wagon train for three weeks, and I saw how Sinclair watched his woman. Always his eyes were hungry. And since their mysterious side trip, he has been after her night and day."

"That side trip," Poteet repeated, "still worries me. If you'd been on the job like you were suppose to be, we would know where they went and whether it in any way puts our plan at risk. I promise you, Cuellar, if you allow that pecker of yours to distract you one more time, I'll kill you myself."

The Mexican shrugged and held out his hands, palms up. "But, Captain, I cannot help myself. The women simply won't leave me alone."

"Yeah, well you'll wish they had when I get through with you," Poteet said dryly. "Tell you what. You do your job right, and once we board the ship, you can do whatever you want with Sinclair's woman." A speculative light dawned in Cuellar's eyes as the Texan continued, "As long as the men carry out their job successfully, we should have at least a couple of days' head start on Sinclair. With the women along, we'll need every minute of it."

Cuellar dropped his cheroot on the floor, then ground it out beneath his boot. "Promised such a reward, I'll see that we're given a week, Captain Poteet."

In the yard outside the hotel, the large bell that hung from a post began to ring, signaling time for supper. Poteet grabbed his hat and said, "Let's go downstairs. I'm hungry."

As Cuellar waited for Poteet to lock his door, he asked, "I am curious. When was the last time the Comanche attacked here in Dallas?"

"Years ago," Poteet answered. "But these crazy Frenchmen don't know that, do they?"

THE DAYS HAD rushed past from the time Brazos and his relations felled the first tree until they nailed the last shingle into place. As Brazos waved good-bye to those members of his family who'd offered their help, the Europeans marveled at the speed with which the Americans had worked.

Inside the brand-new house, Lillibet attempted to prod a subdued Madeline into discussing the arrangement of the small amount of furniture she had acquired in Galveston. Brazos, as quiet as his wife, walked into the kitchen and overheard André Brunet say to his Lillibet, "we are still rolling rocks into place while Sinclair has finished his home. Do you think Americans do all things so quickly?"

"Frontier livin' necessitates that some things be done fast," Brazos answered. "We've learned to raise a shelter and put in our crops as fast as a tonic peddler can spot a phony coin." Attempting to liven the atmosphere, he added, "But we know when to slow down, too. Isn't that right, Maddie mine?" He offered her a wicked wink.

Madeline didn't take his bait. She simply said, "Whatever you say, Brazos."

Damn, she was taking his leaving hard. But then, it wasn't a pickle barrel full of fun for him, either. The past two weeks—hell, the past two months, for that matter—had proven just how lonely a life he'd lassoed himself into. Truth be told, leaving the warmth and happiness he'd found with the runaway beauty and her little Miss Magic would be one of the hardest things he'd ever done.

Brazos realized that these short weeks spent with Madeline and Rose might well be all they'd ever have together. Although he'd do his damnedest at it, he couldn't swear he'd be alive when the business with Salezan was over.

He had to go. He'd no choice. The demons inside him wouldn't rest. Juanita would never be safe as long as Salezan lived. The children at St. Michael's—hell, maybe even Madeline and Rose—none would be safe until he'd dealt with the monster of Perote. "Besides," he muttered beneath his breath, "I've already sent the letter."

The Brunets took their leave shortly after Lillibet helped Madeline unload a crate of pots and pans and hang them on the hooks mortared into the chimney. Brazos, having put in a full day's work roofing the cabin, lay sprawled across the puncheon floor while Rose used his back as a hill to climb. "I've heard that in the Orient, there are women who walk on men's backs as a prelude to lovemaking," he said, heaving a grunt as Rose plopped down hard. "Can't say that I rightly understand how it works."

Watching the sun sink below the treetops from her kitchen window, Madeline said, "I imagine you could ask your Juanita about it. She's right outside, walking hand in hand with Allyre Bureau. I don't doubt that she is expert in such matters."

"Meow," Brazos mimicked. "What's the matter, Maddie? Are you jealous because she's managed to snare that orchestra conductor? You didn't have much luck with him aboard the *Uriel* from what I remember."

"Monsieur Bureau is the former musical director of the Odeon in Paris, and I never set my sights on him,"

Madeline replied, turning away from the window with a disdainful sniff. "He's a pompous fool, and I noticed just the other day he's beginning to lose his hair."

Brazos's hand checked the top of his head. Still thick as ever, thank God. "Nita likes him because he's a musician and he brought a piano with him. She's always had the dream of singin' for an audience. Sort of like a Spanish Jenny Lind."

Madeline wrinkled her nose. "I'm sorry I brought up her name." Her somber expression made a lie of her words when she added, "I refuse to feel anything but joy on the first night in my beautiful new home."

She fussed about, lighting the lamps, and Brazos never took his gaze from her. She's more beautiful than ever, he thought. Here in her own house, with Rose, and surrounded by bits and pieces of everyday life, Madeline had come home. And he'd not be here to share it with her. A vicious wrench of emotion caused him to murmur a groan.

Madeline started at the sound, and their gazes met before sliding hastily away. The house was completed. He would leave. Tonight would be the last night he would spend in her bed.

"Nighty-night time, Miss Magic," Brazos said suddenly, rolling over and sitting up. Madeline, who chewed on her lower lip as she pretended to study the two prints of calico she'd tacked beside the window, looked over her shoulder and frowned. "It's only half past six, Brazos. She doesn't go to sleep this early."

"Today she will. It's been a hard day." He gave Madeline a bold yet beseeching stare. "Gettin' harder by the minute. Go to bed, Maddie. I'll be there directly."

She shut her eyes, and for a moment, her shoulders slumped. Then she straightened and smiled a beautiful, bittersweet smile, and it warmed him like a shot of Uncle Barney's day-old corn liquor. "Make sure you cover her well, Brazos," Madeline said, her hands lifting to the pins in her hair. "The nights are cooler here than they were in southern Texas." She was loosening her braid as she exited the room, and as Brazos readied Rose for bed, he pictured that golden wave spread across the feather pillows in the room just a few short steps away.

"Sleep well, Miss Magic," he said, pressing a kiss to the child's brow. "And see if you can't manage to drift off tonight without raisin' a ruckus. I've a little of my own magic I'd like to be makin' with your mother."

HER DREAM WAS done. The time had come to give it up. Madeline sat on the edge of her bed, gazing into her mirror as she brushed the tangles from her hair. For the first time in her life, she saw only her own reflection in the looking glass. Gone were the imaginary home, the imaginary husband, and the imaginary child. For two short weeks, the fantasy had become reality, but now the image had shattered. Brazos would leave her tomorrow.

"Will I find cracks in the glass when I look at you in the morning?" she asked the mirror. She lay the brush beside her and gently touched the swirls of gold and sparkling gems that framed the looking glass. "If I do discover fractures, will it be the fantasy destroyed or myself?" Staring at her reflection, she pleaded, "Work your magic, mirror. Don't take Brazos back, not after giving him to me for this short amount of time. Share your enchantment with me. Show me how to keep him."

The scuff of wood against wood heralded the opening of her bedroom door. Brazos stepped into the room and shut the door behind him. He stood bathed in light from the wall lamp, his eyes dark with passion and hungry with need. For a long moment, they stared at one another.

"Will you have me tonight, Maddie mine?" he asked in a smoky voice. "Knowin' that I'm leavin', that I couldn't stay even if I wanted to, will you take me to your bed and bid me good-bye?"

Madeline's magical mirror had answered her; she knew what she must do. She had to set him free.

"*Non, mon couer*," Madeline said, standing. The green satin wrapper she wore hugged her like a second skin, and she felt his heated gaze rake her as she stepped toward him. "I'll not tell you good-bye, Brazos Sinclair," she said, threading her arms around his neck. "Never. I'll simply say *au revoir*." She kissed him, and they traveled together to the magical place where dreams pale beside reality.

Madeline slept little that night. Time and again Brazos would turn to her and take her into his arms and love her. Sometimes slow and gentle, sometimes fast and fierce, he showed her with his body what his lips could not speak. She was lying with her head pillowed on his chest and blinking back tears when sunlight forced its way through the cracks in the shutters and plunged into her heart.

Determined not to be caught abed as the last time he left her, Madeline got up and exited the room. She'd make breakfast and send him on his way with a brilliant, if false, smile. Careful to work quietly so as not to wake Rose, she mixed biscuits and put bacon on to fry. She jumped, burning her finger on the side of the pan, when a knock sounded on her front door.

It was Lillibet. "I'm sorry to bother you so early, dear, but I noticed the light was on. Thomas has been up for hours, and I was hoping I could bring little Rose over to distract him. I've hotcakes made for breakfast, and those are her favorites."

"Well, she's not up yet. She's been stirring, but I really hate to wake her."

Lillibet frowned. She wandered around the room, three times opening her mouth to speak before snapping it shut.

"Lil?" Madeline inquired as she rolled out her biscuit dough. "What is wrong?"

"Oh, all right," Lillibet huffed, folding her arms. "You've forced the truth from me. André told me a few moments ago that Mr. Brazos is leaving. He said that yesterday your husband asked him to watch over the two of you. Is it true, Madeline? Is he really leaving?"

Madeline wiped her hands on her apron and nodded.

Lillibet sighed. "That scoundrel. Well, I've no intention of making it easy for him. Let me take Rose. I know he won't leave without saying good-bye to her, and I want the opportunity to say a few words of my own."

Madeline didn't have the heart to argue. In fact, she found she didn't have the heart for much of anything. By now, Rose was standing up in her crib, watching the women and chewing on the rail, and Madeline stood silently as Lillibet gathered up the baby and took her home.

It wasn't long afterward that she heard sounds of stirring from the room across the hallway. Brazos wore only denim pants when he entered the room moments later. He wrapped his arms around her and pressed a kiss to the back of her neck. "I wish you'd been with me when I woke up, Beauty. I missed you."

"I guess you'll have to get used to it, won't you," she waspishly replied. Immediately, she regretted her words. His hands dropped away, and tension all but crackled between them. "Brazos," she began, "I'm sorry, I—"

"Forget it. You're right. There's no sense tryin' to pretend. That's done with. The house is finished."

Madeline stiffened her spine and buried her crumbling emotions beneath the hard shell she'd developed as a child. "If you want to gather your things, I'll call you as soon as breakfast is ready. I know you're anxious to be on your way."

She thought she heard him sigh, but he said nothing until he paused in the doorway. "Where's Rose?"

"Lil came by to get her."

"Why'd you let her do that? You know I want to tell her good-bye."

Madeline shrugged and answered, "You can do it at the Brunets'. It'll be easier on Rose if she has Thomas there to distract her."

Brazos opened his mouth to argue, but then abruptly snapped it shut and left the room. Her knees wobbling, Madeline took a seat at the kitchen table and stared, unseeing, toward the hearth.

A few minutes later, Brazos poked his head around

the door and asked, "Do you know where my wool coat is? I haven't seen it since we left the *Uriel*."

Desperate for him to leave before she began to cry, Madeline said without thinking, "It's up in the attic in the trunk with the red leather straps."

She was setting a honey pot on the table when the angry roar exploded from above her. Immediately, she realized her mistake. The crock slipped out of her hand and cracked against the floor, the golden liquid spreading out into a sticky pool. Madeline stood staring at the mess at her feet as she heard Brazos's boots pound down the stairs. He burst through the doorway, her blue velvet pouch crushed in his white-knuckled grip.

"Bloody hell," Madeline cursed softly.

In a voice as sharply edged as the bowie knife sheathed at his hip, Brazos demanded, "I want an explanation."

She remained calm as she answered, "When you shouted, the jar slipped out of my hand and shattered. It's dribbling between the cracks in the floor. Do you think I'll have ants?"

"Crawlin' across your naked body staked out beneath the sun if you don't start talkin'."

For an intelligent woman, Madeline was thinking distressingly slowly. She pushed past him and retreated to her bedroom. Obviously, she needed to dress. She felt entirely too vulnerable wearing only a silk wrapper.

He allowed her to don underwear and a dress before he reached out and grabbed her wrist. "Madeline." He spoke through gritted teeth. "Enough. Talk."

"But my shoes." She pulled away from him and sat on the edge of the bed. "It's dangerous to walk around barefoot, you know. Just the day before yesterday, Jean Charpeau was stung by a scorpion."

"Lady, you've no idea the danger you are in this very moment. Now, enough stallin'. Talk."

"You want to know about my bag," she said, tugging on a stocking.

"I don't give a good goddamn about your bag. I want to know about the stuff that's inside it." Holding the pouch at the bottom, he dumped the contents out onto the bed. "My Colt revolver," he said, lifting it from the jumble of articles. "I thought one of those slimy seamen aboard the ship took it." He tossed the gun aside and lifted a delicate mosaic bracelet, dangling it from one accusing finger. "This I purchased in Italy—it's a gift for my mother. My *mother*, Madeline." Gently, he set the jewelry on the bed; then, raking his fingers through his hair, he began to pace the room.

"That gold watch chain is Tyler's," Brazos declared. "He's been grousin' about losin' it for weeks. Now, Madeline, those are all valuable items. Perhaps you have a rational reason for stealing them. I'm willing to give you the benefit of the doubt in that regard. After all, you managed to explain away stealin' a baby, for God's sake. But the other things?"

He halted, braced his hands on his hips, and demanded, "What possible explanation could you have for stealing them?" He pinned her with a frustrated, yet curious stare. "Buttons from my shirt? Three checkers? The trey and eight of clubs from my favorite card deck?" He pointed toward the bed and said through gritted teeth, "And my *golf ball*! The one I was usin' in France when I holed it with *one shot*. I was savin' that ball, Madeline! It's special." He loomed over her and shouted, "Why?"

She shrugged. "I didn't know it was special. As far as I could tell, it was just like any other old ball."

His eyes glittered like the burning fuse of a firecracker. She offered him a tentative smile, hoping to douse the flame. "There's no harm done, Brazos. Everything is there. You have it all back now."

He blew up at that, but it was a different sort of explosion than she had anticipated. At first, he seemed at a loss for words, but when he finally spoke, she wished he hadn't. He talked much too softly, for one thing, in a voice as cold as the North Sea in January. "My grandfather's watch. You knew how much it meant to me. I told you."

For the first time, Madeline was afraid. She licked her suddenly dry lips. "I'm sorry, Brazos. I considered returning it, but I didn't know how to do it without having you catch on to me. It was quite a dilemma, don't you see? I would have found a way to give it back. I know I would have. It simply had to be done properly."

He narrowed his eyes and spoke roughly, "Don't waste your breath lyin'. I know better. I'm leavin' today, remember? We'll probably never see each other again, thank God. You couldn't give me back my watch even if you had intended to."

In a small voice, she said, "I would have found a way, Brazos. I always work things out."

He arched one brow. "You do, don't you?" Brazos grabbed a ladder-back chair from beside the wall and straddled it. "Why don't you tell me about it, Madeline."

"But, Brazos—"

He interrupted. "Let's see, you've stolen everything from a baby to a potato masher. Quite an interesting string of thefts when one looks at them."

Maddie turned away from the accusation in his eyes, walking to the fireplace to grab a dirty pan and stick it in the wash water.

Brazos wasn't through. "I must admit that you are very good at what you do, Madeline. The majority of those items are mine, and I never once suspected you of being the robber. Tell me how it is you chose for yourself such a lucrative profession as thievery."

She mocked him silently. *Lucrative profession as thievery*—why, he was one to talk, carrying around a casket filled with silver bars.

"Well, Madeline? I'm waiting. Why did you become a thief?"

Into the silence that fell came the unmistakable sound of a pistol being cocked. Before Brazos could react, a knife point bit into his back. A heavily accented voice spoke from behind him, "Yes, this something I've wondered about also. Perhaps, Mistress Smithwick, we'll have time to discuss it before you die. But first you shall answer a more immediate question." The intruder sharply enunciated each word as he asked, "Where is my daughter?"

Brazos didn't need to hear the name Madeline

gasped. The man holding a knife to his back as he threatened Brazos's wife was none other than Rose's father and grandfather.

The bastard, Julian Desseau, had found them.

Chapter 17

"Welcome to Texas, Desseau," Brazos drawled, wincing as the knife bit deeper into his back. "Mistress Smithwick? I reckon that's my wife you're talkin' about, huh? Call her Mrs. Sinclair."

Julian Desseau demanded roughly, "My Elise. What have you done with her?"

"Hold on a minute," Brazos said, lifting his hands from the chair back. Julian stuck him good, and Brazos felt the warmth of his own blood dribbling down his back. "Watch the kidneys there, would ya?"

"You will remain quiet, Monsieur Sinclair."

Madeline trembled visibly as she said, "Don't hurt him, Julian. He has nothing to do with this. I lied to him, I told him Rose was mine."

"Rose?"

"It's what Celeste called her. *Le petit rose.*"

Brazos slapped his hands upon the chair. "Dammit to hell, Maddie. The names are a lie, too? Who the hell—" And he whirled like a Texas twister and knocked first the gun and then the knife from Julian's hands.

The Frenchman landed a punch to Brazos's chin that knocked the Texan to the floor. "I've traveled thousands of miles in search of my stolen daughter, Sinclair. You may be younger and stronger than I, but I've hatred enough in my heart to defeat you and your slut."

"Bull," Brazos replied, catching Julian's leg and yanking his feet out from under him. They rolled and grabbed and grappled across the floor, knocking over chairs and banging into trunks.

Madeline dove across the bed for Brazos's Colt revolver. Chambering a bullet, she pointed the weapon toward the ceiling and squeezed the trigger. "Damn," Brazos said, breathing heavily, his forearm shoved against Julian's throat. "She's got a gun. Probably be best if we ended this scramble here and now, Desseau. The thought of Maddie with a gun scares the bejesus out of me." With that, he grabbed the older man's shirt-front, lifted his head off the floor, and with a right hook to the temple, knocked the Frenchman cold.

Madeline opened one of her trunks and threw her husband a length of rope before uprighting the chair. Brazos hauled Desseau into the seat and tied his hands to the ladder-back slats. His eyes on the slumped figure, Brazos held out his hand and said to Madeline, "Give me the gun—both guns, in fact—and the knife."

Pursing her lips, Madeline hesitated. While she trusted Brazos with her very life, she wasn't absolutely certain that he envisioned an outcome to this confrontation similar to the one she foresaw. So she gathered up the weapons and retreated to sit cross-legged in the middle of the bed. She kept the derringer Desseau had carried pointed in her husband's general direction.

He glowered at her. "Madeline, quit bein' cute. This isn't the time."

"Brazos, you acted in a threatening manner toward me just a few moments ago, and I think it best I watch after my own interests at this particular time. Now, hush and let me think."

Desseau came around as Brazos stood cracking his knuckles, with fury burning in his blue eyes. "Woman, I can take those weapons away from you faster than a six-legged jackrabbit, and I'd hate for one of them to hurt you in the scuffle. I'd rather save that pleasure for my bare hands."

Madeline's anger got the best of her, and she fired a shot that split the distance between Brazos and Julian. "The same man who taught me to steal taught me to shoot, Sinclair. Now, sit down and keep your mouth shut."

"Damn!" Brazos exclaimed, looking over his shoulder at the bullet hole in the wall. His astonished gaze met Desseau's wide-eyed gape. "You know, I think she means it."

Julian whipped his head around and said grimly, "At least, tell me if my daughter is safe, please! I've been frantic."

"Frantic?" Madeline scoffed. "Now, that brings to mind an interesting question. Tell me, Julian—from personal experience, of course—who does more worrying about a child, a father or a grandfather?"

"What nonsense do you speak? Please, Mary Smithwick, I beg you. Tell me of Elise."

Madeline straightened her spine, lifted her chin, and allowed all of the loathing she felt for this man to drip from her voice. "You are a cruel, despicable, filthy excuse for a man. You deserve to die for what you did, and I'm certain Lucifer is waiting anxiously to welcome you to hell. Rose is fine, Julian, happy and healthy and free of your evil influence."

"I don't care about this Rose person! I want to know about my daughter, my Elise."

Madeline raised her voice to be heard over the thud of horses galloping past her house. Ordinarily, such noise would have brought her outside, but the drama taking place within the confines of her bedroom was all the excitement she could stand. "I have renamed Elise, Rose, as Celeste requested," she said loudly. "Rose is safe, and she'll remain so, far away from you."

Desseau shut his eyes and bowed his head. Madeline was shocked when she heard him repeat the heartfelt words of a prayer of thanksgiving. Lifting his head, he pleaded, "Tell me about her."

Madeline shifted uncomfortably. If she didn't know better, she'd take him to be a concerned and loving father, not the monster that he was. She forced herself to remember Celeste, and how he'd pretended such grief upon her death. "You don't deserve to know anything about Rose."

Julian bucked in his chair, straining at his bonds, and rumbling at her. She lifted the gun. "Maddie," Brazos's soft voice held a warning. "Give it some time, honey. We can always kill him, but I get the sense there's more to this story than either one of you knows. Let's hear the explanation of why he did it."

"I don't care why he did it."

"I thought the same way about you, remember? I didn't think anything explained away kidnapping, but you managed to convince me. I'm even willin' to listen as to why you stole my watch—and my golf ball. Ask him, Maddie. Let's hear his story."

"Why I did what?" demanded Julian.

Madeline opened her mouth but she couldn't force the word *incest* past her lips. Instead, she said, "Why you married Celeste."

"It's no business of yours."

Madeline said in a soft, cold voice, "I've made it my business."

"Why?"

"For Rose. Now, Celeste told me you married her for revenge. Can you deny it?"

Desseau's mouth curved downward with disgust. Then he asked, "Who are you, Mary Smithwick? Why did you come to St. Germaine? Why did you steal my daughter?"

Brazos's tone held a warning as he said, "Careful there, Desseau. Maddie's the one askin' questions. I think it's about time you tried an answer. Did you marry Celeste as a way of seeking revenge on a woman called . . . what was her name, Maddie?"

"Bernadette Compton."

Desseau spat on the floor, then answered, "Yes, I did."

Holding the gun, Madeline's hand trembled with her rage. "How could you!"

Julian strained against his ropes, his face flushing red with both the effort and his own fury. "How could I? You want to know why I thought to take Bernadette's precious daughter from her? Because in my heart, I'm certain she stole a daughter from me over twenty years ago, that's why."

His voice broke, but he continued, "In her insane jealousy, she took my Nicole—only four years old, mind you—and did God knows what with her. Yes, I used Celeste to punish Bernadette."

Madeline screamed at him, "You evil, sick, depraved wretch. You married your own daughter! You made a baby with your own baby!"

"No." He spoke quietly, his voice cold and hard as he stared her straight in the eyes and declared, "It is a lie."

Madeline's hand shook with her fury. Brazos took a step forward and said, "Give me the gun, sweetheart, before someone gets hurt."

"I want to kill him, Brazos."

"I know, Maddie."

"I almost wish you would," Julian added, his tone reflecting a deep inner pain. "Celeste believed this, didn't she? She told you this story." Julian's brown eyes glazed, and his voice cracked with emotion as he looked past Madeline and asked, "She died thinking this?"

Madeline lowered the gun. "Julian?"

"Somehow, Bernadette must have contacted her," he mused aloud. "I noticed a change, but I thought it was due to the pregnancy. My first wife, Anne, had often acted strange while she carried our Nicole." His lips curved in a half smile as he said, "You are right about one thing, Mary Smithwick. I married Celeste to gain revenge upon her mother. The joke, however, was on me. I never intended to fall in love with the minx, but I did. And we were happy, for many months we were so very happy. She was a special woman, a good woman; nothing like Bernadette."

"You were married to Bernadette when she became pregnant with Celeste?" Brazos asked.

Julian nodded, "I was in England on business. Actually, her efforts to pass the child off as mine made me more angry than her betrayal. My daughter, Nicole, had disappeared a year earlier. That Bernadette would attempt to deceive me about another child . . . well, it was more than I could tolerate." Then he shrugged and continued, "I allowed Bernadette to remain at Château St. Germaine until she delivered Celeste. It was only after I'd banished her from St. Germaine and fabricated her death I began to suspect that Bernadette had something to do with Nicole's disappearance and—"

"Hold on a minute," Brazos interrupted. "What's this about another daughter?"

Grief carved crevasses in Julian's face. "Twice I have suffered through this," he said, "and I'd just as soon die here and now than have it continue. Please, if you don't believe me, if you will not allow me to see Elise, go on and pull the trigger of your gun."

"You never found the girl, your Nicole?" Brazos asked, rubbing his chin thoughtfully.

Julian shook his head. "Not my daughter, not her body."

"And you think Bernadette did it?"

"I'd bet my life on it."

Brazos scowled. "Well, why did you marry her daughter? Why not just kill the bitch?"

Julian sighed and for a long moment remained silent. Then he said, "I always hoped that someday she'd confess the truth. I couldn't kill Bernadette without destroying the possibility of ever learning what had happened to Nicole. I knew she loved Celeste. It seemed a fitting revenge."

Brazos looked from Julian to Madeline, and back to Julian again. "This Bernadette. Was she a schemer? Could she have orchestrated an elaborate ploy to get back at you?"

"Look at what she told Celeste. She didn't mind

hurting her daughter with her lies. That should give you your answer."

"Nicole," Brazos said thoughtfully. "How old would she be?"

"Mid-twenties."

Being the game player that he was, Brazos had always been adept at solving puzzles. As the pieces of this particular game fell naturally into place, he folded his arms, slowly shook his head, and said, "Well, roll me on the beach and call me Sandy."

Desseau looked at him as though he were crazy. Madeline rolled her eyes and made an inelegant noise. Brazos began to laugh. "This is great," he said, tugging the rocking chair over next to Julian. He approached the bed and grabbed Madeline's hand mirror from its surface. "It's sort of like lookin' through lace curtains at first, but if you study it, it's plain to see. Sit down, Maddie, and look at this."

Obviously, Madeline believed he'd lost his mind. "Brazos," she protested, "there are reasons I am holding a gun on the man. He had threatened to kill me, you remember?"

Warmth stole through Brazos that left him feeling kind of fuzzy. Tenderly, he said, "Trust me on this one. Come here, Beauty. Come gaze into you magical mirror, and see all your dreams come true."

"*Mon Dieu*," Julian exclaimed, his wide-eyed gaze locked on the mirror in Brazos's hand. If possible, his face looked even whiter than before. "Where did you get that?"

Brazos was concentrating on Madeline. He held out his hand for her, and when she took it, he led her to the rocker. Her eyes were dark honey as she gazed up at him, and he smiled gently, held up the mirror, and said, "Look, Beauty, who do you see?"

Tears gathered in Julian Desseau's eyes, and he whispered ever so softly, "Nicole?"

"Brazos?" she said fearfully.

"Look, Maddie, a younger, feminine version of the same face. The letter promised you family, didn't it? This man isn't Celeste's father. He's yours."

Ever so slowly, Madeline's hand stretched out to touch the face of the mirror, the reflection of the man whose eyes streamed tears. His lips moved, and as if from far away, she heard his words. "I commissioned the mirror for my first wife, Anne, upon the birth of our daughter, Nicole. I brought the diamonds back from Africa during Anne's confinement. I purchased the emeralds in Italy on our wedding trip. Bernadette found it among Anne's things when she moved into Château St. Germaine. I didn't like giving it to her, I thought it should be kept for Nicole. But Bernadette fancied it."

"The stones matched her eyes," Madeline said in a small voice. "She used to say that. Her eyes were emerald green, and mine are only brown."

"Like mine," Julian whispered. Two pairs of watery dark eyes met and held in the looking glass.

A hesitant smile was forming on Madeline's face when a pounding sounded on the door and a man's voice cried, "Help me. Sinclair, help! Indians have taken Lillibet and Thomas."

Brazos wrenched open the door, and a bloodied André Brunet stumbled into the room. A bright red stain seeped across the white linen of his shirt as he clutched at Brazos's sleeve and panted, "Snuck into our shelter. Whisked them away. Others, too. Juanita. And . . ." His eyes sought Madeline's, apologetic and fearful. "And Rose. The Indians took Rose."

JULIAN DESSEAU PINNED both his gaze and his hopes upon the broad-shouldered Texan riding ahead of him. He was exhausted, both physically and emotionally, from the events of a day that had dangled his greatest dream before his eyes before whisking it away in a cloud of red Texas dust.

Indians. He had heard the stories of Comanches and Kiowas who arrived with the full moon, hooting and stealing and scalping. Killing. He grimaced with despair.

Why had the savages attacked now and in this

manner, stealthily and in broad daylight? Confusion had been the order of the day as witnesses described savages, painted and feathered, to the men of La Réunion who attempted to organize a rescue mission. But while the Europeans discussed their options, Sinclair had quietly studied the tracks leading from the village, his countenance hard and unyielding.

He'd offered quiet reassurance to his wife—Madeline or Mary or Nicole, Julian would have to figure out what to call her—as he informed her that the doctor was on his way. He instructed her to remain in the cabin until he returned. "Somethin' about this smells like an acre of onions, Maddie," he'd said. "Those weren't Indian ponies they were ridin'. Every last one of those horses was shod."

"You'll find her?" Madeline had asked, her gaze searching Sinclair's as she held a bloodied rag to Brunet's wound.

"My word on it."

Julian and Brazos had left the village before the colonists had made a decision as to who should lead the posse. They followed the tracks west, seldom speaking, each man occupied with his own thoughts. Hoofprints and bruised bushes told the story of rapid retreat by a dozen or so men. Brazos yanked his horse to a halt and muttered a vile curse. Julian patted the sleek, sweaty neck of his mount and inquired, "What?"

"They've split. I was afraid of this." For the first time, Julian noticed a light of hesitation in Brazos's eyes. "Are you anything of a tracker, Desseau?" the Texan asked.

"My experience is limited to hunting game; I don't hunt men."

"You did a pretty good job with my wife," Brazos muttered, walking his horse in a widening circle around the fork in the trail. He cursed again when he spotted a tatter of pink satin snagged on the tall stem of a sunflower.

Julian said, "My daughter—are you able to tell anything, anything at all?"

Brazos shrugged. "Twelve horses rode away from

La Réunion, taking four of our women and two children with them. They're ridin' double on four horses, but Rose and Thomas don't weigh enough to show. Up till now, it figures that six of the twelve carried one of our people with them. But see this?" Brazos pointed to the ground. "That's a man's footprint. They got off their horses here and rearranged folks before splittin' up. Two of 'em cut away toward the northeast. The rest are headed straight out west toward Comancheria."

"Why would they divide themselves? Is this the way of Indians?"

Brazos clutched his reins and stared out toward the horizon. "No. That isn't their way a'tall. That's why I'm fair to middlin' certain that we aren't dealin' with Indians here today."

Julian's eyes went wide and hopeful. "No?"

"A host of folks don't know it, Desseau," Brazos replied with deceptive calm, "but there are worse things roamin' the Texas plains than Indians."

Only the hard edge to his eyes betrayed the rage that was seething inside him. Somehow, despite all of his plans and precautions, Salezan's men had found Juanita. He had failed her and in doing so had placed three other women and two innocent little babies in jeopardy. He deserved to be horsewhipped.

And he had a decision to make. The scrap of satin indicated that Juanita rode one of the horses that had split off the trail. She was alone with one of Salezan's men and in terrible danger.

So, which trail did he follow? He owed Juanita his life. He'd crossed an ocean to help her. But the Europeans were as innocent as newborn lambs out here on the prairie; he could not in good conscience abandon them. He pictured Rose in the arms of one of Salezan's sadistic goons.

"Time's a-wastin'," he said, spurring his horse and following the set of tracks headed west. "Waitin' to climb a hill won't make it any smaller." His only choice was to make quick work of rescuing the colonists. He could sent them back to La Réunion with Desseau—

surely, Considérant's bunch would find their way out here eventually—and then head out after Juanita.

God only help him if he didn't get it all done in time. As he rode, he said a short prayer of thanks involving his one comfort in this entire disaster. At least, Madeline wasn't in danger.

MADELINE HEARD THE cawing of crows from the pecan tree outside her window as she wiped André Brunet's brow and smiled into eyes glassy with pain and worry. "You'll be all right, André," she said in a soothing voice. "The doctor said the bullet passed right through the fleshy part of your shoulder. You'll be sore for a few days, but your recovery will be total."

"Not me," he replied weakly. "Lillibet and Thomas. Your Rose."

This time, Madeline's smile was forced. "They'll be fine, too. Brazos promised me he'd find them and bring them home. He's never lied to me, André, not once. He has help, also. Did you notice the other man here? That's my father. He tracked me all the way from France. Now, if he managed to find me from that far away, you know that he's not going to allow a few Indians to stand in the way of finding his . . . of finding Rose."

Her father. She'd yet to adjust to the idea; she wondered if she ever would. For so long now, she'd thought of him as an evil demon, but instead, it appeared as if the wicked one had been her stepmother, Bernadette. Why was it she accepted that idea with little effort? Perhaps because she'd never forgotten the beautiful woman whose words had been so cruel. Madeline's gaze drifted toward the bed where the mirror—her mother's mirror—lay face down.

She'd been right. The looking glass was enchanted. A gift given and received in love naturally possessed powers beyond the norm. Anne—such a simple, beautiful name. Had she loved Julian to such a great extent that the emotion transcended time and space? Was it a mother's love that called to her daughter, compelling the child to clasp a symbol of that love to her heart?

Madeline liked the idea that her mother had found a way to reach beyond death and offer comfort during difficult times. It was nice to imagine that Anne Desseau had been with her in spirit all these years. And I need you with me now, Mama, Madeline thought.

What could be more difficult than knowing Rose was in danger?

"Indians." André's voice trembled as he restlessly stirred. "The savages do horrible things, though, Madeline. My Lillibet, she could not survive such treatment. And she's carrying our baby. What if . . ."

The stifling heat inside the cabin seemed to intensify. Madeline licked her dry lips and said, "Don't think that way, André. Lillibet is strong, and she can survive anything she faces. I know that for a certainty."

He clutched her hand and pleaded, "Do you truly think so?"

"Yes, André, I mean it. Now, why don't you rest for a while." She leaned down and kissed his cheek.

The cabin door banged open. Madeline's startled gaze darted between the stranger's brutal eyes and the gun he held in his hand. "Well, well, well, isn't that sweet," the man said in a cruelly amused voice. "I must say, Miz Sinclair, that after the promises I've made, I'm proud to see you being free with your kisses. It'll make things easier in the long run." Pushing back the brim of his hat with his index finger, the man sauntered into the room, saying, "I'll give you five minutes to gather a bag of clothing—only clothing, you understand. I will be watching."

"What is going on? Who are you?" She stood up, her spine as stiff as the hardwood logs that formed the walls of her house. Inside, however, she was quaking. "This is my home. I'm not leaving here."

"Four minutes, Miz Sinclair. I suggest you hurry up about it if you don't want to live in that dress for the next few months."

"Months!"

"It's a right far piece to Vera Cruz."

"Vera Cruz?"

The man's gaze roamed around the room, and he spied her carpetbag lying in a corner. He kept his gun trained on her as he walked over and lifted the bag. Tossing it to her, he said, "Mexico. You've three minutes left, Miz Sinclair. I suggest you include something warm. The mountains are cold even in the summer."

"Mountains," Madeline repeated. "Vera Cruz." She stuffed clothes into her case. Filled with dread, she anticipated the answer to the question she was about to ask. "Just where in Mexico do you think to take me?"

It came as no surprise when the stranger replied, "The Castle of San Carlos. Otherwise known as Perote Prison."

JULIAN DESSEAU COULDN'T seem to quit crying. He didn't remember ever having cried before, not when Nicole disappeared or even at the time of Elise's kidnapping. But now, as he carried his sleeping daughter in his arms on the return trip to La Réunion, tears flowed incessantly down his face.

Less than an hour after their brief stop at the fork in the trail, he and Sinclair had topped a hill and spotted Lillibet Brunet, holding her son, Thomas, in her arms and leading a ragtag group of women east. Julian had listened absently as Sinclair exclaimed over the missing "Indians," his gaze locked on the golden curls and sunny expression of the child toddling happily in front of the four women.

With a gleeful shout of "Ba Ba," Rose had run to Sinclair, and he'd scooped her into his arms and they'd exchanged kisses. Turning to Madame Brunet, the Texan had made quick work of ascertaining the ladies' story, demonstrating little surprise when told they'd been literally dumped from the horses some half a mile west.

Then came the moment Julian had dreamed of for months. "Miss Magic, there's someone you must meet,"

Sinclair had said, a strange light entering his eyes. "This here's your papa."

The child had smiled brilliantly at Brazos, then gone without hesitation into Julian's waiting arms. "Call her Rose, please, Desseau," Sinclair had said. "Let's not confuse matters for either her or Maddie at this point." Then he'd turned to an obviously curious Lillibet Brunet and introduced Julian as Madeline's father.

That's when the lump first formed in Julian's throat. He'd held the heavenly weight in his arms and listened intently to Sinclair's instructions for returning to the colony. After giving Rose another kiss, the Texan had ridden off as though the hounds of hell nipped at his horse's hooves. As it turned out, the Europeans had walked for little more than an hour before the colonists' search party found them. Little Rose fell asleep in his arms as soon as they'd climbed into the search party's wagon.

The band was less than a mile from La Réunion when the tears began to overflow. Julian sent a silent prayer of thanksgiving heavenward. No man on earth was as blessed as he. In but a single day he'd had restored to him God's most precious gifts—gifts he'd feared had been lost to him forever. Many questions had yet to be asked, and he felt a burning need for answers. But even stronger within him was the desire to sit quietly and hold his daughters in his arms. Both of them.

As the roofs of the village came into sight, he smiled and wiped the tears from his cheeks. Soon now, he'd be able to do just that.

HAVING SPENT FOUR long days in the saddle and three nights struggling to sleep on the cold, hard ground, Juanita should have appreciated the corn shuck mattress beneath her. But circumstances allowed her little comfort. She needed to keep her wits about her, because she had absolutely no intention of allowing her life to come to an end in a dismal room in a whorehouse outside Corsicanna, Texas—especially not at the hands of a sadistic, leering Latin. She refused to play the victim again. She'd ended that part of her life when she'd fled Perote Prison along with Brazos Sinclair.

She held her breath against the stink of urine, sex, and stale perfume emanating from the mattress. Honesty forced her to admit her part in this disaster. It was her own fault she'd been found by Salezan's lackeys. She'd acted the fool by walking into Dallas with Monsieur Bureau, particularly without wearing that cursed mantilla her Sin forced her to don in public.

Turning her head toward the window, where moonlight beamed a silver ray through the darkness, Juanita smiled sadly. He wasn't really her Sin, was he? He was Madeline's Brazos. Watching the two of them together had been proof enough. Despite all her hopes, Juanita had recognized that Brazos Sinclair would never return the love she offered him. Brazos was her friend, nothing more. Accepting that, she'd decided to leave Texas for good.

So she'd set her sights on the musical director, confident he had the connections to provide her with her second most treasured dream—to sing before an adoring audience in the great halls of Europe. Unhappy at La Réunion, Monsieur Bureau contemplated a return to Paris. Juanita had decided to secure an invitation to accompany him. Hence, the ill-fated trip into Dallas.

She'd known the minute she'd been identified. Oh, she'd never seen the man, but the sense of evil crawling up her spine had been undeniable. More the fool she for not confessing her imprudence to Brazos that very day. If she had, she felt certain, she'd not be tied to a whore's bed awaiting what threatened to be a particularly violent rape.

Juanita knew she could survive such an experience. After all, she'd suffered a similar fate countless times at her husband's hands. But she didn't relish dying, and if she attempted yet another escape, the look in her captor's eyes told her that death would be a distinct possibility.

The obvious option was to do all within her power

to delay any further travel until Brazos found her. Because Brazos would arrive—of that she had no doubt. In the meantime, she'd play the whore and do it so well that Salezan's slimy little man would find it impossible to hurry about his business. He'd never realize that the roles of victim and offender had been transposed.

As she watched the descent of the studded leather strap, Juanita retreated to that place within herself insulated from pain—that space so very similar to the one possessed by her dearly beloved friend. And she waited patiently for Brazos Sinclair.

THE ROOM REEKED of sex and sweat. Joaquin Cuellar rolled off Juanita's supine figure and lay on his back, his forearm covering his eyes as he fought to catch his breath. He was exhausted. The woman had wrung from him the last vestiges of his energy.

At that moment, he wanted nothing more than sleep, and with the woman securely tied, he was free to drift off. But now that his lust had finally been sated, the niggling worry that had bothered him occasionally during the past six or seven hours returned as a major concern.

He'd missed the rendezvous with Poteet, something the Texan would not take too kindly.

It'd been a mistake to stop here with the woman. Had he followed the plan, they'd have camped for the night some three miles north of here. But after spending days in the company of such a beautiful woman, one who challenged him repeatedly by attempting to escape, he'd found his need to master her overwhelming. So he'd pushed on toward this brothel, where he knew a mattress and total privacy would be assured.

But he never intended to stay here so long. A little sex; a little sleep. That's what he'd anticipated. But the woman had been insatiable, and he—well, it had been the sexual zenith of his life. *Madre de Dios*. No wonder Governor Salezan had gone to such lengths to secure the return of this woman. No wonder he planned such a frightening reception for Brazos Sinclair.

Cuellar bolted upright as a new thought occurred to him. He'd been worrying over Poteet's reaction to their delay. Maybe the one he should be concerned about was the governor himself. What would Salezan do if he ever learned that his lieutenant had sampled this woman?

Cuellar shuddered as he rubbed his bristled chin with his hand. He turned his head and looked at Juanita. She watched him with steady black eyes, a hint of amusement warming their depths. *Pinche cabrón,* he cursed. He should have listened to Poteet. Rising from the bed, he searched through his saddlebags for a cheroot. Smoking always helped him think, and Cuellar had the uneasy suspicion that his life might depend on just how well he thought.

Poteet had warned him to keep away from the woman. He'd known she'd be a temptation. He'd known—Cuellar froze. *Poteet must have known that I would find the dark-eyed Juanita irresistible, and still he assigned me the task of escorting the woman to Mexico.* Cuellar tossed away the smoke he'd yet to light, staring as it rolled beneath the bed. He lifted his gaze to the naked beauty lying atop the dirty sheets. Had he been duped? Perhaps Poteet was threatened by his rise in power in the governor's army. Possibly he worried that the second in command might replace him.

"Poteet seeks a hold on me. A threat. He intends to use you, *puta.* Well, I'll not allow it to happen." He lifted his knife from the table by the door and tested its point against the pad of his thumb. Killing her would be an answer. He could kill her and somehow place the blame on Poteet. The Texan would not be expecting that. His hard gaze raked Juanita, and he felt a stab of regret. He didn't enjoy the idea of removing one of such talent and beauty from this world.

"Maybe I could release you," he murmured. "If I had something to offer as proof of your death, something that implicated Poteet. . . . No, it would be too dangerous. I've seen how he pursues you, Señora Juanita. I dare not risk being discovered in a lie."

Knife in hand, he straddled her. "My apologies, but I find I must kill you." He drew the knife slowly across her throat, and a thin red line appeared in its wake. She fought her bindings, biting at the kerchief gagging her mouth, terror flashing in her eyes. Cuellar's loins stirred at the sight. Maybe he wouldn't kill her quite yet. Holding the blade against her throat, he entered her with one hard thrust.

Then the door burst open, and Brazos Sinclair tore into the room. Taken completely by surprise, Cuellar was slow to react. Lifting the knife, he twisted to face the intruder. Sinclair was there, backhanding him across the face with a gun and wrenching the blade from his grip. Sparing Juanita a single quick glance, Brazos knocked Cuellar to the floor with a hard punch to the gut, then threw a vicious kick to the groin. Through a haze of pain, Cuellar heard Sinclair ask, "Nita, you all right?"

Brazos grabbed Cuellar's knife and cut Juanita's ropes. The Mexican rolled to his hands and knees, and Sinclair kicked him down again.

Juanita rubbed her wrists as Brazos gently removed the gag from around her head, then poured her a cup of water from a pitcher by the bed. "I was beginning to worry you'd not arrive in time," she said after quenching her thirst. "He planned to kill me, Sin." She scrambled from the bed and pulled on her dress as Brazos, his expression icy, hauled Cuellar onto the bed and put his gun against his temple.

"Wait," Cuellar breathed, fear turning his bowels watery. "I've information. Spare me, and I'll tell you."

"Information?" Brazos replied. "I don't know. I'd just as soon kill you as look at you any longer." He paused, cocking his head to one side. "Your call, Nita. It was you he hurt."

"I'd rather you not kill on my account, Sin. See what he has to say."

"All right," Brazos agreed. "I guess a few minutes won't hurt anything. What do you know?"

"You will spare my life?"

"I'll make it worth your while, that's all I promise."

Staring up at his enemy, Cuellar realized that any mention of Sinclair's wife would mean an instant death. He'd shadowed the Sinclairs long enough to know that the Texan wouldn't hesitate to kill anyone involved in the abduction of his woman. Instead, he said, "Salezan wants more than Juanita's return. He wants you and the band you wear around your arm."

Brazos's shirtsleeve moved as his muscle flexed. "The band?"

"Yes." Cuellar nodded. "The governor has learned that it holds the secret to El Regalo de Dios."

Juanita looked at Brazos. "The silver mine? But you have all of it, Brazos. Why would Damasso want to know where the mine is?"

"Actually," Brazos answered, his gaze never leaving Cuellar's face, "it wasn't the mine itself that Miguel and I found. That's all beside the point. What I want to know is how Salezan learned this information about my armband."

Referring to the priest imprisoned in an isolated cell in Perote Castle would be only slightly less dangerous than speaking about Sinclair's wife, Cuellar decided. He'd heard whispered tales of the *bestia* and his partner. He said, "I don't know. I only learned about the band because I overheard the governor speaking to my boss, Winston Poteet."

Brazos lifted his eyebrows. "Poteet? Win Poteet? Isn't he a Texas ranger?"

"He is Salezan's right-hand-man."

"Well, son of a bitch. You never can tell about some men, can you." He shrugged, then nudged Cuellar with the gun. "Tell me, son, if Salezan wants my armband so bad, then why didn't one of you folks just shoot me and steal it? Since you got close enough to get Nita, I'm sure you had the opportunity to get me, too."

"He wanted you alive."

"Alive? Y'all thought to take me back to that hellhole alive?" Sinclair's laugh was harsh. "You folks are dumb as dirt if you think you could get me back to Perote still breathin'. I'd just as soon shake hands with the devil before sunset as set foot inside Damasso Salezan's little house of horrors."

Juanita bent to don her shoes and moaned as her injuries pained her. The sound distracted Brazos just long enough for Cuellar to make the move he'd been waiting for. He made a swipe at the water pitcher beside the bed and swung it at Brazos's head. Sinclair ducked, and Cuellar grabbed for the gun.

It proved to be a fatal mistake. The shot reverberated through the room, and the last sound Joaquin Cuellar lived to hear was Brazos Sinclair saying with disgust, "Yep, dumb as a cottonwood stump."

BRAZOS AND JUANITA rode hard to make the return trip to La Réunion in the shortest possible time. Throughout the long hours in the saddle, Brazos felt his mind racing from one worry to another. He fretted about Juanita and how she was making out after her ordeal. He wondered about Salezan and how he had learned the secret of the armband. He troubled over Lillibet and Thomas, and how the fake Indian raid would affect them over the long haul. But most of all, he brooded about Madeline and Rose and how the appearance of Julian Desseau would change their lives. His own included. Because somewhere between Corsicanna and Little Brush Creek, the idea that Desseau might take his daughters back to France had slapped Brazos in the face.

All this time he'd figured he'd be the one doing the leaving. Also, though he hated to admit it, he'd harbored the faint hope that if things with Salezan worked his way, he could return to Madeline and Rose. But now that their daddy had showed up, it looked like any returning would involve a trip to France. Lord knows he couldn't face another boat trip if his life depended on it.

The midafternoon sun beat down upon the riders hot enough to pop corn in the shuck. Perspiration beaded on Brazos's brow and plastered his blue chambray shirt to his back. He licked dry lips and tasted salt and thought of the sea and Maddie. An ocean voyage during the summer would be tough on her, what with the seasickness and all. A person always felt worse when he was ill during the heat of summertime than he did when he was laid up in the cold season. Maddie would be much better off if Desseau would wait a few months to take her back to France. "I'll have to be sure and mention it to the man when we get back," he said, taking the kerchief from around his neck and wiping his face.

"What did you say, Sin?" Juanita called.

He glanced over his shoulder and smiled at his friend. "I asked how you're doin'. Do you want to stop and rest for a bit?" They'd traveled steadily since noon, and she must be getting tired. He certainly was.

"No. We are too close to stop now. I would prefer to reach La Réunion before dark."

He flashed her a grin and spurred his horse. Juanita was nothing short of remarkable. It never ceased to amaze him that so many people fell for her beautiful, empty-headed woman performance. True, few, if any, others had witnessed her in action under circumstances like the ones he and she had shared. As far as he knew, he was the only man she'd ever broken out of jail.

Take now, for instance. Some women would have swooned at the prospect of sneaking out of a whorehouse and leaving a dead man behind. Certainly, few would ever have ridden hellbent for leather back home with little rest. All she'd asked was that he allow her time to fix her hair proper—her one, true vanity—and keep the facts of her abduction between the two of them. She'd every intention of convincing Monsieur Bureau to take her with him to Paris. "Bet Desseau could be of some help to her in France," he mused. Bet Maddie would help her.

Damn. He had to quit thinking about Madeline and France. Gave him a funny hitch in his chest. Brazos grimaced when he realized that even Damasso Salezan was a more palatable topic of thought than the subject of his wife's returning to France.

Salezan. The bastard had come close this time, closer than ever before. It'd be a good thing for Juanita to go to Europe. Brazos felt comfortable that even Salezan's long arms couldn't reach that far. After all, *he'd* been safe enough over there, and if what Nita's captor said was true, Salezan wanted him as much as he wanted Juanita.

The Mexican wanted the armband, and he wanted Brazos alive. Why? An answer hovered at the back of Brazos's mind, but he refused to confront it. He couldn't stop the shudder that racked his body, however. "I wish Cuellar had waited a bit before jumpin' for my gun," he grumbled beneath his breath. "I'd have liked to ask just how they planned to get me to Mexico."

Why had they taken Juanita and not made a play for him? Had they wanted to take them separately, or had he thwarted an attack without realizing it? Of course, nothing they could have tried would have succeeded. He'd have either escaped or died trying.

He'd rather rope a cloud in the great beyond than set a foot within a hundred miles of Perote Prison.

As they forded a shallow creek less than a mile from La Réunion, Juanita called, "Sin, I'd like to stop for just a few moments if you will. We are close, and I'd like to freshen up a bit, brush my hair."

"Sure, darlin'," he replied. "That's a right fine idea." Brazos dismounted and tied his horse to one of the towering cottonwood trees lining the creekbank. Kneeling down, he cupped water in his hands and drank thirstily before splashing his face.

The brisk temperature of the water served to wash some of the cobwebs from his mind, and he was beset by a new and totally disconcerting thought. Maybe Salezan and his men had thought he'd follow Juanita to Mexico and attempt a rescue.

He rocked back on his heels and slowly stood, his gaze turning toward Juanita, who sat atop a fallen cottonwood stump taking the pins from her hair. What would I have done if I hadn't caught up with them in time? he asked himself. Would he have gone after her? Could he have gone after her? He'd like to say yes, but . . .

Brazos expelled a harsh breath. These were questions a man faced late at night, when the teeth of honesty chomped down and took a bite out of all the shields daylight erected. Well, the sun was high in the sky, and he had enough walls built to withstand a siege of self-examination. Thank God.

They were less than a mile from Le Réunion. Less than a mile from Maddie. He wanted—no, he needed—to see her. "Hurry up, would you, Nita? Your hair looks fine, you don't need to mess with it any longer. That music man will be beside himself with lust at first look. If we hope to make it home before dark, we'd best hurry. It'll be dusk before we get there as it is."

Home. As he climbed into the saddle, Brazos was shocked at himself for using that particular word. Home and Rose and Maddie. Funny how the three went together so well, sort of like beans and cornbread and buttermilk.

But for how long? How long would they remain at La Réunion in the log house he'd built. When would Desseau try to take them back to France? He swallowed hard as he wondered, Surely, she'll still be there. She wouldn't leave without telling me good-bye, would she?

Hell, they hadn't even finished the fight they'd started, what with Desseau's showing up and then the raid. If he knew Maddie at all, she wouldn't want to leave with a battle brewing. That'd be too much like surrender, and Madeline Sinclair surrendered to no one.

Still, he heaved a relieved sigh when he saw light shining through the window of their house and recognized the horse tied out front as the one Desseau had been riding. Juanita was right behind him as he pulled his mount to a stop, yelling, "Maddie? Maddie, we're back." He bounded onto the porch and pushed open the door.

Julian sat in a rocking chair before the fireplace, holding Rose, who slept peacefully in his arms. His face was drawn and his eyes tormented as he looked up at

Brazos and said, "Thank the Lord you are back. She's gone, Sinclair. Someone took her while we were gone. To a place called Perote Castle."

Brazos shut his eyes and swayed beneath the assault of wrenching emotion. "Oh, God, Maddie," he groaned. "What have I done to you?"

Chapter 18

A hard wind blew across the barren hills surrounding Perote as Winston Poteet called for the lowering of the drawbridge and led his weary prisoner across the moat. The journey from La Réunion had faded to a single long blur in Madeline's mind. Her captor had set an arduous pace as they raced southward on horseback to Galveston, the trip that had taken the colonists twenty-six days reduced to eight spent mostly tied into the saddle. Immediately upon reaching the coast, they'd boarded a steamer for Vera Cruz, and Madeline had eagerly embraced the misery of seasickness. It was a welcome distraction from saddle sores and concern over her immediate future.

Contrary to his near constant threats, Poteet had refrained from touching her any more than was necessary. She'd found comfort in the fact until he'd explained that he was saving her for his boss, the governor of Perote, Damasso Salezan. That's when the fear that had plagued her since Poteet burst into her home had blossomed into full-blown panic. She remembered the name. Brazos had spoken it in his nightmares—in a tortured voice that had sent shivers up her spine. Damasso Salezan. Who was he? What was he? What evil acts had he committed to have left Brazos so deeply damaged?

And what did he have planned for her?

Madeline stared up at the huge stone effigies flanking the single entrance to Perote and felt a cold chill invade her bones. She recalled Brazos's mentioning the statues and agreed with his assessment. These monstrosities intimidated a person more than did the cannon lining the walls.

"Pretty, aren't they?" Poteet said, a mocking grin on his face. "I understand they are suppose to be a pair of colonial soldiers who feel asleep during guard duty. I'm surprised they were carved with their heads on, though, considering they weren't wearing them when their bodies were tossed into the moat."

Madeline shut her eyes, but the vision of the strangely garbed men made of stone was slow to fade. Poteet led her past masonry walls a good six feet thick to the main parade grounds, where the clink of chains reverberated in her ears.

A second wall rimmed by the black mouths of cannon was met at each corner by a circular lookout tower. The main building housing prisoners occupied the very center of the fortress. After a short discussion with one of the guards, Poteet led Madeline to the far end of the enclosure, where she was startled to see a building reminiscent of an English country house. With a fierce grip on her forearm, Poteet lifted the brass knocker and rapped on the wooden door.

"A butler?" Madeline murmured when a portly, bewhiskered servant opened the door and peered over the top of his silver-framed spectacles.

Poteet wore a smug grin when he said, "Hello, Joseph. Tell the boss I've brought him a present."

"The governor is aware of your arrival, Mr. Poteet," the servant replied formally, straightening the lapels of his jacket. "He will see you in his study." Turning to Madeline, he continued, "A room has been prepared for you, Señora Sinclair, if you would care to refresh yourself before joining the governor in the dining room in one hour."

This wasn't what she had expected. Madeline followed the man called Joseph up the circular staircase, her brows lifting at the sight of a Gainsborough landscape decorating the first landing. By the time she was shown to her room, Madeline was baffled and more than a little uneasy. This place was not exactly Newgate. Eyeing the slipper tub full of steaming, lavender-scented water and the beautiful silk gown lying on the bed, she commented, "Sir, I don't understand. This is not how they build a prison in my country."

Bushy gray eyebrows lowered as Joseph's green eyes shifted uneasily. "Señora," he said in a voice barely above a whisper. "I offer you a bit of advice. No matter how well he treats you, never, ever forget that Castle Perote is a vile and loathsome prison. Horrible things go on beneath the floors of the fortress. Despicable." Madeline shivered as the door to her room closed behind him. The bathwater looked warm and welcoming, and she needed to chase the chill from her bones, as well as to wash away the dirt. As she settled into the luxuriant heat and slathered lavender soap over her skin, her thoughts dwelled on the man she had yet to meet.

The governor of this prison had not gone to the trouble to have her kidnapped and transported thousands of miles to allow her the pleasure of a scented bath and beautiful clothes. And although it may involve comforting luxuries, his plan—whatever it was—most certainly had ties to the devil.

Because as long as she lived, Madeline would never forget the sound of Brazos's voice as he repeated this man's name. *Salezan. Damasso Salezan.*

She tried to picture the man. Thick and swarthy, certainly. Probably with beady eyes and a hooked nose. He more than likely had lines of excess on his face and dirt beneath his fingernails. Well, she'd managed many men in her time. Salezan would be no different. "I'll simply have to escape before he can set his devilish schemes in motion." True, her attempts to flee had met with failure so far, but she wasn't about to quit trying.

"I never admit defeat," she declared, staring at a soap bubble hugging her knee. Well, except for Brazos. She'd given her very best efforts for those two weeks, and still he'd intended to leave. Defeat tasted bitter, but she took comfort in the fact that it took a man of Brazos Sinclair's caliber to manage the victory.

Splashing away the bubble, she swallowed the lump that had suddenly appeared in her throat. Maybe when this was all over, she could convince her game-loving husband to change the wager to the best two out of three. But that would have to wait. She had other troubles to deal with at the moment.

Quickly, she bathed and dressed, then spent the remainder of her hour gazing out the window, searching for a weakness in the battlements. Certainly, the prison appeared impregnable, but experience had taught her that few things in this world were totally secure. After all, she'd found a way into the earl of Wentworth's castle; surely she could find a way out of Damasso Salezan's.

Patience, Madeline, she told herself. It was one of the most valuable tools of any thief. That and careful study. Over the years, she'd spent many an hour preparing and watching, waiting for the precise moment to strike. The circumstances were no different here. Her moment would come. It had to come—she had a family now, and there was no way a devil named Salezan was going to take that away from her.

She repeated the words over and over as she left her room, prepared to meet her enemy. She almost tripped when she noticed the figure waiting at the foot of the staircase, a bright, welcoming smile playing across his face. He wore a dark blue soldier's uniform with gold stripes and fringe and gleaming gold buttons. In one hand, he held a single red rose, which he offered to her, saying in a cultured tone of voice, "Welcome,

Señora Sinclair. I have so looked forward to meeting you. My home is your home."

Damasso Salezan was the most handsome man Madeline had ever seen in her life. He all but took her breath away. As she stared at him, the single word that came to her mind was light. His hair was a burnished gold, his skin fair and without blemish. And his eyes— oh, his eyes were the blue of the sky on a crisp winter morning, only they twinkled like stars in the night. He could have introduced himself as the angel Gabriel, and Madeline would have believed him. "Mr. Salezan?" she asked, her voice sharp with disbelief. He smiled at her then, and had she been a lesser woman, she would have swooned at his feet. He was a god.

No, she reminded herself. He is a devil.

Salezan took her arm and escorted her into the dining room, where a long mahogany table was laid with Irish linen and silver of all shapes and sizes. Silver goblets, silver cutlery, silver serving platters. Silver vases held bouquets of roses, and even the paintings on the wall were encased in silver frames. The only items on the table not made of silver were the plates—they were made of gold.

Madeline's knees were feeling a bit weak, and she gratefully took her seat. Poteet was nowhere to be found. Retreating to the defense of good manners, she smoothed her napkin onto her lap and waited silently while her host sat down. Salezan nodded for dinner to be served, then said, "So, Señora Sinclair, I trust you found your room to your liking?"

His beautiful home, his gentlemanly manners, his exquisite smile; suddenly, she could stand no more. Straightening her spine, she lifted her chin and demanded, "Why have you brought me here? I demand to be told of your plans."

He lifted a single brow, and although his features remained schooled, a hard light entered his eyes. "Please, madam, we do our best to maintain a sense of civility while we dine. Business matters can wait until after our meal. Now, try the soup. I'm certain you shall find it delightful."

Business matters, Madeline silently repeated, her stomach churning to such an extent, she'd have thought she was back aboard ship. *Patience, Madeline, remember.*

Salezan served a seven-course meal. He inquired about the political situation in France and the latest trends in fashion at the English Court. Little questions he asked betrayed an unsettling knowledge of how she'd occupied her time during the journey from Galveston to La Réunion.

She refused to allow herself to speculate about what he knew of her personally. It wouldn't do for him to be aware of her relationship to Rose or to Julian Desseau.

Madeline forced herself to eat. Having missed so many meals in her youth, she knew always to take advantage of such opportunities. Also, she practiced her patience, confident he'd get around to the topic of her interest in his own good time.

He told her about his years spent in England at Oxford. Madeline couldn't hide her surprise, something he took in stride and, in fact, laughed about. "My mother, you see, was English. It is from her that I get my coloring. However, it is the heritage of my father's family that has guided my life."

He paused, obviously waiting for Madeline to inquire about his father. She chose to sip her wine instead. These minor rebellions were dangerous, but necessary for her state of mind.

Salezan frowned, then said proudly, "My father was half Spanish, half Karankawa. It is a fine and noble heritage. Are you at all familiar with the Karankawa, Señora Sinclair?"

"No, I am not."

A demonic light entered his eyes, and he sliced a bite of his beefsteak, speared it with his fork, and brought it to his mouth. "Funny, your husband is well versed in the history and practices of the Karankawa peoples. In fact, one might say he has an intimate knowledge." He put the meat into his mouth and chewed it, smiling. Not understanding why, Madeline shuddered as she sipped her wine.

At the end of the meal, Salezan rose from the table and said, "We could adjourn to the parlor for coffee if you so desire, Señora Sinclair. But you do appear rather anxious, and it might aid your digestion if we attend to our business immediately. It's entirely your decision, my dear."

With precise movements, Madeline set aside her napkin and said, "I prefer to learn of what you have planned for me."

Anticipation shone brightly in his brilliant blue eyes. "To my study, then." He led her toward a room a few doors down the central hallway. Madeline smiled weakly as they walked past Joseph, who watched her with a pitying gleam in his eyes. At that moment, she wanted nothing more than to rush through the front door and flee whatever awaited her in Salezan's study.

The governor turned a silver doorknob, paused, and gestured for Madeline to enter before him. She walked into the room, then stopped abruptly and gasped aloud as she beheld the life-size and very lifelike painting that dominated the room.

The tall, well-muscled, barbaric man was depicted stark naked, but not unadorned. Pieces of cane perforated the nipple of each breast and his lower lip. A tattoo stretched from shoulder to hip, and in one hand he carried a bow as long as he was tall. But it was the object held in the other hand that at once attracted and repelled the eyes. It looked to be a human arm, hacked off above the elbow, bleeding and dripping into a pool of red at the savage's feet.

Madeline turned her head and focused on the pottery vessel sitting atop a table against the wall as Salezan said, "Magnificent, isn't he? He is Capoques, painted from the description in Cabeza de Vaca's journal. I commissioned the painting myself." Salezan took his seat behind his desk and motioned for Madeline to sit in the red leather armchair opposite him. As she did so, he opened the lid of a silver box and withdrew a cheroot. He lit it, took a drag, then leaned back in his chair and exhaled a stream of woodsy-scented smoke. "Señora Sinclair, I am in your debt. Feel free to make any request, and it shall be granted to you—within reason, of course."

"Release me."

"Now, my dear, I did say within reason. The debt I owe is substantial, but not without limits."

Madeline's fingernails nervously scratched the leather upholstery. She drew a deep breath and said, "I don't understand."

"Your husband stole something from me," Salezan said, frowning at the lit end of his cheroot. "An object of great value."

"Brazos stole something?" Madeline didn't believe it—not after all of the grief he'd given her.

Salezan's hand lifted to rub his upper arm. He said, "Yes. He absconded with my wife. I believe you have met her? My Juanita Marie?"

For a moment, Madeline drew a blank. Then she matched the Spanish pronunciation with the Texan drawl she'd grown accustomed to and thought, Juanita Marie. Juanita. Brazos's Nita was Salezan's wife. "Oh, my," she breathed.

His chuckle soured the air. "Yes. Oh, my." He took another drag on his cheroot. "You see, Madeline—I may call you Madeline, may I not?—a confrontation between your husband and myself has been inevitable, but it has taken on a certain élan with you as part of the drama." He gestured toward a sheet of paper lying on his desk. Madeline could see Brazos's signature scrawled across the bottom. "Your husband has sent me an invitation to join him at a certain silver mine in South Central Texas, but I prefer to do my business from here. You are my lure, Madeline. He will come for you."

Immediately, Madeline began to shake her head. She stifled a hysterical laugh and said, "No, no, he won't. You misunderstand our relationship, Governor Salezan. Brazos intends to divorce me. He'll not bother with chasing after me."

Shrugging as though he were unconcerned, Salezan said, "I know Sinclair. He will come. You are his wife. He is responsible for you."

"No." Madeline stated it crisply and decisively. If there was one great truth in life, it was that Brazos Sinclair would never return to Perote. What man embraces a trip into hell for the sake of a person for whom he feels only lust? Not Brazos. Why, even if he had the slightest inclination to do so, he'd never make it aboard a ship to sail here. No, Brazos wouldn't come for her.

But Julian Desseau would. Her father had traveled the Atlantic for Rose; he'd surely sail the Gulf of Mexico for a daughter he'd only recently discovered. All she had to do was wait and perhaps make initial efforts toward an escape attempt. Of course, the waiting might not be easy. Salezan had yet to mention just what he had planned for her while waiting for Brazos to arrive. Her stomach churned, and she almost groaned aloud when a new thought hit her.

Almost everyone believed that Brazos and Juanita had been lovers. Certainly, the Mexican beauty's husband would think no differently.

Salezan chuckled again, drawing her gaze. He was all brightness and light; beautiful. She wondered absently if perhaps Satan had been the same before being banished from heaven. Softly, she asked, "What did you do to him?"

"Sinclair?"

She nodded. Her hands twisted nervously in her lap as Salezan extinguished his cheroot in a silver ashtray and smirked. "He does not relish returning to Perote, eh? I cannot understand, he was treated in such a special manner during his stay with us. Tell me, madam, what has he told you of Perote?"

"Nothing," Madeline snapped. "He says nothing. But he dreams—" She broke off, the glimmer in Salezan's eyes indicating his pleasure in her information.

"Dreams?" Damasso repeated after a moment. "He suffers nightmares, perhaps?" He leaned back in his chair and grinned maliciously. His voice was a smooth, seductive purr when he asked, "Tell me, my dear, does he scream in his sleep? Break out in a sweat?

Perhaps"—his eyes took on an unholy gleam—"perhaps he has hurt you?"

Fury misplaced any sense of caution she possessed. "You, Governor Salezan, are a beast."

He laughed loudly, clapping his hands and rubbing them gleefully. "No, señora, don't you see. It's your husband. It always has been. He is the *bestia,* and he returns. Our games will resume. I find I cannot wait.

"The *bestia* has always been my favorite."

THE STEAMER *LUCKY Linda* chugged south along the coast of Mexico, carrying a skeleton crew and a handful of passengers. Just days ago, she'd been docked at the wharves in Galveston waiting to take on passengers for the biweekly run to New Orleans. But in the dead of a moonless night, the new owner escorted aboard four silent passengers and established them in the finest of cabins before ordering the lines cast off. The captain was told to set a course for Vera Cruz, Mexico.

On the afternoon of the first day out, the steamer's twin stacks belched smoke as black as Brazos's mood into the pristine sky above the Gulf of Mexico. He paced the texas deck, halting on occasion to stare blankly at the streamers of soot trailing behind the boat, as he envisioned his future. "There are times in a man's life when the idea of dyin' has a certain undeniable appeal."

"You are not going to die," Tyler Sinclair said, coming up behind him and holding a glass of blended whiskey in each hand. Passing one to his brother, he said, "If you up and did something dumb like that, then *I'd* be the one stuck with unloading this boat you purchased for an exorbitantly high price. Surely, if you'd taken a little more time, you could have conceived a better plan for making the trip to Mexico. Really, buying a boat to transport four people."

"Five," Brazos replied. "Don't forget Rose." He sipped his whiskey, then shut his eyes to enjoy the false warmth stealing through his icy heart. He added, "I've plenty of money, Ty. What I don't have is time. Besides, like they say, you can't take it with you."

Tyler swallowed his drink, then reared back and flung the empty glass out over the gray gulf waters. "If you get yourself killed during this little excursion, I'll never forgive you, Brazos. In fact, I'll make you a promise—right now. Knowing how much you enjoy ocean travel, if you go do something stupid, I won't rest until I've retrieved your carcass. Then I'll do like the Vikings used to do. I'll lay you out right here aboard the *Lucky Linda*, stoke up the fire, and send you sailing off into eternity instead of burying you beneath solid ground."

"You're all heart, brother," Brazos replied dryly.

"Stop bickering, you two," Sister Cecilia called from a deck chair, where she sat holding Rose on her lap. "If Mother could hear you, she'd slap you both. We are in a dangerous situation here, and it is no joking matter. I'm growing weary of this senseless quarreling. The whole idea of this trip terrifies me."

The brothers exchanged looks of chagrin, then Brazos handed Tyler his empty glass and sauntered over to his sister. Leaning down, he pressed a kiss to her cheek and said, "Don't worry, Sister Sis. I promise that you're not in any danger aboard the *Lucky Linda*. That's one reason I bought her in Galveston. Salezan has an army in Texas, but I don't think he's scraped together a navy—yet, anyway. For him to have learned about Madeline, I figure he had spies on us along the trail. With you and Rose here, I don't have to worry about you."

"It's not me I'm worried about, Brazos. It's you. I'm frightened to death at the thought of your returning to that place." She touched his arm. "Are you sure, Brazos? Isn't there some other way you could help Madeline without going back. Besides, how can you be sure she's still . . . still . . ."

"Madeline will be all right." Brazos spoke through gritted teeth, his gaze leaving his sister's concerned countenance and seeking out the man at her side. Julian Desseau's face was ashen. The man had aged twenty

years right before Brazos's eyes since he'd listened to
Brazos's expurgated version of his dealings with Damasso Salezan. "She will," Brazos insisted. "Maddie will
be fine. She's a survivor."

Sister Cecilia murmured platitudes, but Desseau
simply stared at Brazos, fear adding a hard edge to his
brown eyes. Eyes so much like Madeline's.

Brazos muttered a curse, then abruptly turned
away and tramped down the stairway to the hurricane
deck. Stopping beneath a gingerbread arch, he wedged
his boot between two spools on the railing and stared
out at the water. "She *is* a survivor," he repeated. But the
chill that had haunted him since returning to the cabin
to find Madeline missing grew colder with every puff of
black smoke rising from the *Lucky Linda*'s smoke-
stacks.

He was scared witless at the thought of what
Damasso Salezan might do to his wife.

MADELINE SNUGGLED beneath the downy
comforter, sipped her chocolate from a china cup, and
opened the novel to the last page she'd read before
Joseph had knocked on the door to retrieve the bathtub
from its place before the fire. After a week as Governor
Salezan's guest, Madeline sought refuge in fiction because it made more sense than did reality.

Something was going to happen—it was only a
question of what and when. Every day, she expected
Salezan to make his move. Every day, she was assaulted
with luxurious pampering and nothing else. Each night
after she was bathed, powdered, and perfumed, she
heard Salezan's footsteps approach her door. She would
reach beneath her mattress for the silver letter opener
she'd lifted from the study, and she'd tuck it beneath the
covers. He had yet to turn the knob.

Would he attempt to take her? Did he intend to
draw the parallel between Brazos and Juanita, himself
and her? The idea of that angelic-appearing devil's
hands upon her made Madeline ill, but in her heart she

admitted, letter opener or no, here in his realm, Damasso Salezan could do whatever he pleased. Therefore, her only option was to escape the kingdom.

Madeline had devised a plan, one she believed offered a good chance of success. She'd already stolen the stable boy's clothing, and the cache of gold and silver coins she'd swiped could probably buy her passage to China if she desired to travel there. But the problem holding her back was Julian. She felt certain he would come after her, and she was afraid to leave because of it. Wasn't it just her luck that after all these years, when she *finally* has a real family of her own, it ends up creating problems for her?

She sighed. "I'll bet Brazos would have a pithy saying appropriate for the situation." Wouldn't she love to hear one of his little bits of Texan wisdom right now. She missed him so.

Deep in reverie, she'd also missed hearing the sounds of Salezan's footsteps, so when he entered her room through a side door previously kept locked, she jumped, sloshing chocolate from her cup to stain the bright white covering of her down comforter. "Oh," she said with a squeak.

Casually, he tossed a sheet of parchment onto the bed at her feet. "Good evening, Madeline. You must be more careful; I would hate to see you burned." Though his smile reflected concern, his eyes glimmered with amusement. Salezan wore no coat. The buttons of his shirt were undone, and the placket lay open to display a tuft of yellow hair on his chest. His fingers removed the silver links from his cuffs as he walked farther into her room and remarked, "It appears I startled you. I apologize. Perhaps it is because I am so accustomed to entering this room without knocking—it was my wife's room, you realize."

Stealthily, Madeline's hand edged down the side of the mattress, and her fingers felt for the cool surface of her weapon. She palmed it and stowed it beneath her sheets as he placed his cuff links on the table beside the bed. Madeline swallowed hard and gripped the letter opener hard when he sat down beside her and trailed a finger across her cheek.

"What sort of lover is your husband, Madeline?" he asked. "Is he gentle with you, does he linger over you and savor you? Or is he perhaps rough, sometimes even violent in his lovemaking?"

He cupped her breast, and Madeline had had enough. "I'll not give in without a fight," she declared, jerking away from his touch and scooting across the bed, out of his reach.

Salezan laughed. "Ah, you are a hellcat, Señora Sinclair. How much pleasure you shall bring me over the next few days."

She looked at him then, questions in her eyes. He lifted the paper and handed it to her, saying, "I have sent him my reply. Rest well, my dear. The games begin tomorrow."

Grabbing her hair, he yanked her toward him and lowered a bruising kiss upon her lips. At the same time, his free hand found the weapon and wrenched it from her hand. "Such a hellcat," he repeated, rising and leaving the room without a backward glance.

Madeline stared at the door until she heard the lock click, then lowered her gaze to the paper. Her eyes went wide, and she gasped as she read the words: "You win. Me for her. Hurt her, and I'll kill you." The note was signed "Brazos Sinclair."

"Oh, Brazos, no!" Madeline reeled in shock. He'd come for her. Here, to Perote. "No, I don't believe it."

But she held the proof in her hands. Brazos Sinclair had actually returned to this place, where all his nightmares had begun. For her! And he had offered himself up to his enemy in exchange for her freedom. Why? Why would he do such a foolish, stupid thing?

Her heart began to pound as a hazy thought took shape. Could it be that she'd succeeded in stealing his heart?

Salezan's words echoed in her mind. *The games begin tomorrow.* "No." She couldn't allow that to happen. She had to escape now—tonight. Before Brazos could do such a crazy, wonderful thing as to sacrifice himself. Besides, she'd a question she couldn't wait to ask. Had Brazos come to love her?

Madeline scrambled from her bed and flew to the wardrobe, where behind and beneath Juanita Salezan's multitude of dresses, she'd hidden her disguise. Quickly and silently, she donned the boy's shirt, trousers, and boots. Grabbing the pouch of coins, she stuffed it down her chemise before tiptoeing to the window and easing it open.

The hinges creaked, sounding like a cannon shot in the night. She held her breath and listened. Nothing out of the ordinary—somewhere, someone was strumming a guitar; and the faint sound of laughter could be heard from the soldiers' quarters. She peered into the darkness. The shadows were deep, but all was still.

Madeline released her breath in a silent whoosh. Stepping to her bed, she reached way under the mattress for the rope she had hidden there three days earlier. After tying one end around her bedpost, she fed it through the window, where it dangled against the ivy-covered wall.

Careful, Madeline, she told herself. This was the most dangerous part. She kept her gaze glued to the door connecting her room and Salezan's as she climbed onto the windowsill and eased her way over the edge. The rope burned her hands when she slipped a bit, her foot becoming tangled in the ivy vine, her knee scraping against the rough brick. She ran out of rope some ten feet above ground, so she held her breath and jumped.

"Bloody hell." The angry oath escaped her lips as she landed with a thud on her behind. Standing, she dusted herself off and glanced up toward Salezan's window, praying he'd not heard either the noise of her crash into the bushes or her curse.

No sounds of stirring upstairs. Although her heart was pounding, as she turned to go, she wore a half smile upon her face. It died abruptly when two figures stepped from the shadows into the moonlight.

"You win, Poteet," Damasso Salezan said, his voice colored with amusement. "I believed it would take her at least thirty minutes."

"Nope," the Texan answered. "Less than half that, just as I predicted. Of course, I have more experience with Mrs. Sinclair's escape attempts. After all, she tried it at least twice a day the whole way down here from Dallas."

Madeline heard the clink of coins as Salezan tossed Poteet a pouch. Both men laughed, and had she had a gun, she'd have shot them both dead right then and there. Angry and filled with despair, she held herself rigid as Salezan escorted her back to her room. She'd failed him; she'd failed Brazos. This defeat was more than she could bear.

Calling for Joseph to stand as her guard, the governor tied her to her bed, trailing his hands familiarly across her breasts and thighs. Madeline clenched her teeth, more angry than afraid. Silently, she swore, I won't bear it. I won't admit defeat. Somehow, I'll find a way. I refuse to leave Brazos to Salezan's mercy.

"Such expressive eyes you have, Señora Sinclair," Salezan jeered, his lips twisting in a savage smile. Then he twisted her nipple viciously and slapped her hard across the face.

Madeline was quite proud of herself for holding back her tears until after Salezan exited the room.

Joseph pulled a handkerchief from his pocket and wiped the wetness from her cheek before dabbing at the blood dribbling from the side of her mouth. Madeline stared at the bright red stain on pristine linen and asked, "What will he do to my husband, Joseph? What does he have planned?"

The servant shook his head. "Don't, madam. You cannot affect it, so there is no need to add to the worry. The governor has planned this confrontation for years. He has kept the priest alive for this moment alone."

Madeline tugged against the rope that bound her. "What priest?" she asked.

"Padre Alcortez." A frown creased deep wrinkles in Joseph's brow. He sat in a rocking chair and folded his hands, saying, "If you must worry, Mrs. Sinclair, concern yourself for the good father. He is a good man, a true man of God. For many years, I have seen to his comfort, and it pains me to know the fate he is facing."

Madeline's eyes had rounded. "Padre Alcortez? Is his name Miguel? Is it Miguel Alcortez?"

"Yes," Joseph confirmed. "He and your husband arrived at Perote together some six years ago. He has taught me much over that time."

"Brazos believes he is dead."

Joseph shrugged. "Your husband is premature in his beliefs, but not by much. Salezan will kill the priest once he recovers the El Regalo de Dios armband."

Madeline pictured the piece of silver jewelry and the man who wore it. "I don't understand. What do you mean?"

"The governor has kept Padre Alcortez alive to translate the etchings on the band. Once that has been accomplished, Salezan plans to send the priest to his reward."

Madeline shut her eyes and asked, "And Brazos? What of my husband? Tell me, Joseph. What does Salezan intend to do with my husband?" The only reply was the yawning creak of the rocking chair. "Joseph, please!" she insisted.

The old man sighed heavily and said, "He is the *bestia*, madam. He is the governor's closest friend."

Chapter 19

Brazos led Julian to a sheltered area in an outcropping of rock some five miles from Perote Prison, and there they made camp. The weather was colder than Julian had anticipated, it being the summer months and so far south. But they were high in the mountains, and rain had fallen for a good portion of the day, drenching the area with a bone-chilling drizzle. Shortly before dark, the sky cleared and a quarter moon rose to bathe the area in a shadowed, silver light.

"A rustler's moon," Sinclair said with satisfaction.

Julian stacked brush and twigs for a campfire and asked, "Why a rustler's moon?"

"A moon like this provides both enough light for cattle thieves to see and enough shadows to conceal them," Brazos replied. He gestured toward the pile of leaves. "We can't built a campfire this close to the prison, Desseau. Salezan undoubtedly knows I'm here, but I'd just as soon not show him exactly where."

Julian tugged a woolen blanket around his shoulders and watched as Brazos stood tossing a ball from hand to hand as he gazed toward the east. Toward Perote Prison. From the moment he had returned to his La Réunion home and discovered his wife missing, Brazos had been a force to be reckoned with. Resourceful, determined, relentless—he'd blasted his way through any obstacle set in his path. Yet, tonight an air of hopelessness clung to him, and it left Julian with an uncomfortable question. What devils did Sinclair expect to face on the morrow?

The Frenchman had been told but a portion of the story about what had happened between his son-in-law and Damasso Salezan. He'd discussed the subject with Tyler while aboard the *Lucky Linda* and learned that even Brazos's brother knew only bits and pieces of what had occurred behind Perote's walls. But here in the talons of the night as he observed the silent, brooding figure, Julian knew a sinking in his stomach. He recognized the presence that surrounded the Texan like a velvet cloak./

Death. Death draped the shoulders of Brazos Sinclair. He wore it knowingly and with a calm acceptance, and Julian realized then that Brazos believed a return to Perote Prison meant his death. But he was going anyway.

Mon Dieu, Julian thought. "So great must be his love for my daughter. "Sinclair?" The Frenchman's voice cut through the shadows of the night. "It is not too late to halt this scheme. We could proceed with your brother's idea. I could attempt to infiltrate the prison and free Madeline from the inside."

Brazos shook his head. "Nothing has changed, Desseau. I won't put her at further risk, and I won't leave her in Salezan's clutches for a minute longer than necessary. We'll continue as planned. Tyler has made some powerful connections in Mexico City since my last visit to this country, and I feel certain he'll be able to get me sprung lickety-split."

Julian gave Brazos a searching look before quietly saying, "I'm certain your brother will give the venture his greatest efforts." Silently, Julian added, But you're not counting on him, are you, Sinclair? You believe that nothing can save you.

Maybe the Texan had good reason for such pessimism. Maybe death did await him at the prison, or perhaps something worse than death. Julian accepted Brazos's decision and his right to make it. But if returning to Perote meant certain death for Brazos Sinclair, then all care should be taken that his sacrifice not be made in vain.

With that in mind, Julian voiced the worry that had plagued him since Salezan's man arrived at the *Lucky Linda* with a reply to their message. "There is one potential problem we have not discussed, Sinclair. In truth, I've been afraid to bring it up. It is obvious from Salezan's answer to your message that he suspects you of rescuing his wife. He demands that she be returned to him tomorrow. Have you considered that once you tell him his wife is dead, he might return the favor? He might well kill her, Sinclair. He might kill Madeline."

Brazos stepped back and hurled the ball he held into the darkness. As he spun around, his voice ripped the night. "Don't you think I've thought about that? Don't you realize that it tears me to pieces to know I might be puttin' her in more danger than she's already facin'? Goddammit man, it's all *my fault*! She's there because of *me*. And I want her out of that hellhole and safe more than I've ever wanted anything in my life."

His head fell forward, and he raked both hands through his hair. When he spoke again, his tone was both bitter and determined. "The stakes of this game are higher than any I've played before, Desseau. I've considered all the angles. I know what cards Salezan's holdin', and I know the different ways he might choose to play 'em. I think you're right; he might consider killin' Maddie. But I can figure no other way than to gamble that he wants me and the silver mine more than he'll want to make an innocent woman pay for Juanita's 'death.' Pray that I'm right, Julian, 'cause if I'm not . . ."

"She's my daughter," Julian said, pushing angrily to his feet. How could he express what those words meant to him? The child he'd lost, miraculously returned, then cruelly stolen once again, before he'd so much as embraced her. She must be saved, at all costs. "Is there not anything I can do to help in this, Sinclair?"

"Just do as we've planned. Get her to the boat safe and sound." Sauntering over to his bedroll, Brazos tugged at the leather ties, then kicked it out flat. "That's the most important thing—it's the only important thing. I want Maddie safe."

Lying down, Brazos stretched out and covered his eyes with his hat. Julian opened his mouth to argue that although Madeline's safety was paramount, other considerations did exist—little things like the Texan's life. But he stopped himself before voicing a word. What use was there? Sinclair's decision had been made during a single long minute upon his return to La Réunion with Señora Salezan in tow. Julian himself had witnessed the emotions that had rolled across his son-in-law's face, betraying but an inkling of what demons lurked within the man. But once Sinclair had declared his intentions, he'd never faltered.

Brazos Sinclair had made the decision to sacrifice himself for Julian's daughter.

The Texan said in a weary voice, "Best get some sleep, Desseau. You've a long trip ahead of you tomorrow. I want to feel secure that Maddie's safe and sound aboard the *Lucky Linda* before the sun sets on this godforsaken land tomorrow night. You'll make sure of that, won't you?"

"You have my word."

Neither man slept very well, but they exchanged no more words before dawn. The sun was a fingernail on the horizon when they mounted their horses to cover the last few miles to Perote Prison. Before they left their camp, Julian asked one last time, "Sinclair, are you certain of what you do?"

Brazos nodded and said, "My pa's got a sayin': What you can't duck, welcome. Well, I've been duckin' this long enough. It's time that I gave Damasso Salezan a good ol' Sinclair welcome."

• • •

BRAZOS COULD HAVE been a knight of old come to lay siege to a castle and rescue the damsel in distress. He rode a fine steed purchased in Vera Cruz from a French diplomat and carried a sword—a knife, actually—forged from the finest steel. The armor he wore as he approached Perote Prison, though, encased not his body but his heart.

The morning possessed a surrealistic quality. Brazos envisioned the road stretching toward the fortress walls as a winding ribbon of bleached bones. Black mountains clawed at a blood red sky, and he knew that he was seeing something that did not exist. But he didn't care.

Every so often, Desseau would attempt a conversation, and Brazos would simply turn his head and stare at him silently. He couldn't afford to speak. He couldn't afford to feel. If he did, he might just turn his horse around and run.

God, he was scared. But as he and Desseau approached the drawbridge to Castle Perote, Brazos searched the ramparts for any sight of Maddie and allowed himself one regret. For a knight, his lance was a might rusty; it was too damned bad he'd not have the opportunity to polish it one more time before battling the dragon.

The odor hit him first. Pungent and pervading, it cast him years into the past and brought home as nothing else the fact of his return to this hell on earth. Wood groaned and chains rattled as the bridge lowered over the moat's dark water. Then, suddenly, she was there, standing at the other end, her long, blond hair hanging free and blowing like a golden standard. Madeline wore a high-waisted gown of sapphire blue silk, and she stood stiff and proud. Fury burned in her eyes, and Brazos vaguely wondered how Salezan would fare beneath her stare. Hell, Maddie, he thought. You're no damsel in distress. You're the blessed dragon. A smile tugged at his lips, and he murmured, "I'm surprised Salezan's not burned to a crisp by now."

Winston Poteet stood on one side of Madeline, Damasso Salezan on the other. The governor's hand grasped her upper arm, and Brazos inwardly seethed that the bastard so much as touched her. Salezan broke the silence. "I've brought your woman, Sinclair. Where is mine?"

For just a moment, Brazos hesitated. His fingers rested lightly on the hilt of the Colt revolver holstered at his side, and he mentally pictured drawing and firing at Salezan if the man even hinted at making a threatening move toward Maddie. Please, Lord, protect her, he prayed. Then he said flatly, "I don't have her, Salezan. I was too late. Your man, Cuellar, had already had his fun with Juanita by the time I tracked them down. She was dead. He is, too, now."

Brazos stood motionless, prepared to go for his gun as he watched Salezan's face blanch. In the periphery of his vision, he saw a smile flit across Poteet's face before the man schooled his expression into a scowl and spat a vile curse. "I warned that boy not to touch her. Damn, I should have killed him myself."

In a steel-edged voice, Salezan called, "I suspected you to attempt some nonsense such as this. It was quite daring of you actually, Sinclair. Don't you worry I might harm your woman, having caught you in your lie? My wife is not dead—you seek to trick me, weakly at that. None of my men would dare to touch my Juanita. Really, Sinclair, could you not concoct a better tale?"

"I have proof," Brazos answered.

"Proof?" Poteet and Salezan asked in unison.

Brazos nodded. "Juanita was a beautiful woman, and those of us who knew her couldn't help being aware of her greatest vanity." He gestured to the bag at his feet. "Here's my proof, Salezan. Look at it, and know that your wife is dead. And while you're at it, don't be forgettin' that it was *your* man who did the deed."

"What sort of trick is this?"

"Look in the bag, Governor."

Salezan shook his head. "You. You show me."

Brazos shrugged, then stooped and lifted the bag. Untying the flap, he reached inside and grabbed hold of his "proof," then let the bag fall to the ground. As it fell, it displayed a long, thick, shining rope of blue-black hair.

"Son of a bitch!" Poteet exclaimed.

Salezan swayed drunkenly. "*Hijo de la madre,*" he cursed.

Madeline spoke for the first time. "Oh, Brazos, no. She *is* dead." For just a moment, the only sound to be heard was the caw of a crow from its perch atop one of the stone statues.

They'd bought it. Brazos could see it in their expressions. Just as he'd hoped, anyone familiar with Juanita knew that her hair was her greatest vanity. No one would believe she'd willingly allow those knee-length tresses to be cut were she still alive. Of course, no one else knew Nita as he did. All he'd had to do was ask, and the deed had been done.

Actually, she'd been even more beautiful with ringlets framing her face, although eyes red and puffy from tears had distracted from the effect.

His hand holding his dear friend's rope of hair, Brazos fixed a hard stare on Salezan and said, "I figured I'd need to prove it to you, and she was beyond carin' about it at this point."

Salezan's handsome face turned ugly. To Madeline, he said, "I'm sorry, señora, I had hoped it would not come to this. Lieutenant Poteet, kill her."

From behind him, Brazos heard a rifle cock as Julian shouted, "No!" Quickly, Brazos said, "Do it, and you'll never learn where the silver is. I've hidden the armband, Salezan. If you want the mine, you must let Madeline go free." Poteet looked questioningly at the governor, his gun pressed to Madeline's temple. Along the castle wall, no fewer than fifty guns were trained on Brazos, and a similar number pointed behind him toward Madeline's father.

"My wife is dead," Salezan said. "Why should yours not join her?"

"Well," Brazos drawled. "The way I figure it, I'm a dead man no matter what. You've lost your wife, so it kinda seems more even that Madeline lose only her husband, instead of both her husband and her life. Besides, I know you want the silver mine. And I've a pretty good idea that you're lookin' forward to takin' me back down to your little playroom beneath the castle."

Salezan trailed a finger down Madeline's cheek. "Maybe I'll take you both to my chambers below."

Though rage coursed through his veins, Brazos forced his expression to remain impassive. "Let her go, Governor. I'll give you me; I'll give you the mine." He palmed the knife hidden beneath his shirt and brought it up to his neck. "If you don't let her go, I die right here and take the secret of the mine *and* the amusements you have planned for me right along to hell with me."

"You are not a man to kill yourself," Salezan scoffed.

"Hell, it was suicide for me to come back to this hell on earth, so that decision's already been made," Brazos answered with a shrug. "How it gets done is another matter. You're the one who has a choice here, Salezan."

Brazos held his breath. Every word he'd said was true. He knew he'd meet his end at Perote, and he'd made his peace with the fact. Of course, he wasn't gonna slit his own throat. If Salezan made the wrong decision, Brazos would point it out in a most fatal manner. Sure, the sharpshooters on the wall would get him, but he'd get Salezan first. And if everything went right, Desseau would take down Poteet before he could hurt Maddie, and father and daughter could escape in the confusion.

Nice plan, if a little ambitious. Brazos bit back a grown. Hell, Maddie wouldn't stand a chance. *Please, Lord, let me have figured Salezan right.* He watched Salezan's eyes and braced himself when the Mexican opened his mouth.

"Wait just one minute," Madeline demanded, slapping the gun away from her face. "I'm sick and tired of men thinking they can make all the decisions concerning my life. One thinks he wants to kill me, another wants to divorce me, and I've yet to hear how my father managed to lose me when I was but a baby."

Salezan and Poteet stared at her with wide eyes. Brazos mouthed a vicious curse and warned, "Maddie!"

She put her hands on her hips. "I'm done with it, do you hear? I'm going home. To Europe. I shall find a cloister of nuns where men are forbidden to come within a mile, and I'll spend the rest of my days in peace. You gentlemen can stand here and argue till your tongues fall out for all I care, but leave me out of it. I'm going home!" Tossing her head, she took a wide, determined step onto the drawbridge, and when nothing felled her from behind, she kept on going.

"Boss?" Poteet questioned.

Salezan grinned and shook his head. "A hellcat, just like I said. Let her go. All right, Sinclair. I guess I've made my decision. Pitch that knife of yours into the water, and join us on this side of the bridge."

Brazos closed his eyes and sighed with relief as he tossed the knife into the moat.

Madeline's temper exploded as she heard it plop into the water. "You bloody fool," she raged, advancing on him like the ball from a cannon. "I didn't need you to save me, you know. I'd have saved myself. I've been doing it all my life." Watching Brazos's eyes narrow, she could hear Salezan laughing behind her. Her mind worked furiously. Although things had gone well so far, she doubted the governor would allow her and her husband to stand in the middle of the drawbridge and plot an escape. Plus she needed a chance to slip Brazos a weapon; it might be a while before she could return to the prison to help him break out. But Brazos's hands were as slow as cold honey compared with hers, and she feared he'd fumble and give her away. She decided to take the risk.

"Maddie," Brazos said, scowling fiercely. "Shut your mouth and get your fanny out of here."

She screamed at him, "Gladly." Drawing back her hand, she hissed at him, "Fall with me." Then, staring meaningfully into his eyes, she hit him. Hard.

He simply stood there, looking furious, and the next time she hit him, she wanted to. She managed to stumble into him and grab his shirt. "Fall, damn you."

"Hell," he muttered, and they tumbled over the side of the bridge.

The water was dark, rank, and chillingly cold. Madeline shuddered even as she fumbled for the knife strapped to her leg. She felt Brazos's arms come around her, and quickly she shoved the handle of the weapon into his hand. As their heads broke the surface, their gazes, met, and Madeline's heart swelled at the admiration reflected in Brazos's eyes. But she had no time to bask in the glory; she had to pretend to drown.

"Help," she cried loudly. "I can't swim. Save me!" She flailed in the water, pushing and pulling at Brazos as they both turned to look at Salezan, who leaned over the bridge and called, "One false move and I'll kill you both, Sinclair."

"Thanks, Beauty," he murmured in her ear. "I'm proud to have you on my side. Head on out—"

Beneath the cover of the water, she pinched him to get his attention. "Listen to me, Brazos. You stay alive in there. I don't care what that monster does, you stay alive, or I'll kill you."

Brazos spat out a mouthful of water. "Somehow, that makes sense to me."

"We'll come back for you," she continued.

"No! You go home with your daddy, you hear?"

Madeline ignored him. They were almost to the bank, and she had so much to say, so many questions she wanted answered. Questions like, Why had he come for her? Her feet brushed solid ground, and she knew she'd run out of time. Instead of asking a question, she whispered, "Don't give him the armband, Brazos, or the priest will die."

Then hands reached down and grabbed her, lifting her from the water. Soldiers stood between her and Brazos. They pushed at her, blocking her view of her husband as other soldiers led him back across the bridge. A sob built within her, and as warm, gentle arms wrapped themselves around her, the sound escaped.

"Ah, *cheri*, don't cry. Please. It will be fine. His brother will help him."

Madeline looked up into her father's troubled face

and said softly, sadly, "I didn't get to tell him that I love him."

THROUGHOUT HER LIFE, Madeline had often dreamed of finding her father. The fantasy always involved a conversation in which father and daughter exchanged words of love and regret, of joy and thankfulness and hope for the future. Never had she imagined that their first tête-à-tête would be a vociferous argument that all but scared their horses into bolting.

The debate had begun less than a mile from the prison walls, when Madeline led her horse off the road and up a small embankment. She'd wanted to study the fortifications from that perspective.

"I will not hear of it," Julian said, twisting in his saddle to glower at Madeline.

She glared right back. "I'm not leaving without him."

"You are not going back to that prison, *ma fille.*"

She blinked in amazement. Julian Desseau looked and sounded exactly like an exasperated father. His chest was puffed out, his brow was furrowed, and he all but roared as he spat out his orders. It made her feel all warm inside.

But no matter how much she enjoyed being on the receiving end of parental demands, Madeline had been making decisions for too many years to blithely allow any man to take the power from her. She smiled and said, "Yes I am, Papa. I appreciate your concern—in fact, I think it's wonderful. But I'm afraid I cannot allow you to dictate to me at this late date. At least, not about something as important as this. If you would like, perhaps we could give it a try after we've rescued Brazos."

"Madeline . . ." Julian began.

"Don't worry!" she said, turning her face into the steady, warm breeze. How good to feel the sun and wind after so much time indoors. Freedom kissed her skin, and she reveled in it. "All we need is a plan." Leather creaked as she dismounted, and she paused to pat the bay mare's neck before stepping forward for a better view of Perote. "I'm quite experienced at devising plans," she continued. "Good at it, too. Over the years, I've developed a number of schemes for finding my way into places. In fact, I've a head start on the problem, because I spent a good portion of my time at Perote figuring a way *out* of there."

"Even if I agreed to this ridiculous notion," Julian countered, swinging from the saddle, "which, of course, will never happen, it would be just as impossible to break into that prison as to escape from it. Look at the place, Madeline." He stood beside her and waved toward the castle. "It's impregnable. It would take an army to breach those walls."

"I don't intend to breach them, Father. I'm going to sneak by them. I have this idea—"

"That's enough!" Julian snapped. "Listen to me, child. Even your husband realized such an effort would be futile. That's why he chose to offer himself up like a human sacrifice!"

"I did something similar about five years ago," Madeline continued as though he'd never spoken. "There has to be a convent or a monastery near here someplace. We'll get some robes and—"

Julian raked his hands through his hair. "It's over with, Madeline. More than likely, the man is already dead. He expected as much. Stop this foolishness, please!" Reaching out, he took her hand and said, "Don't allow his sacrifice to be in vain. Come now. I promised him I'd take you home. Let me do that. It was what he wanted."

She stared down at the hand gripping hers. "He is not dead. He's not. And I told him I'd be back for him, and I intend to be. Brazos escaped from Perote Prison once before; he'll do it again."

A harsh, evil laugh split the air. "I wouldn't count on it, sweetheart," Winston Poteet said, his Colt revolver aimed at Madeline's heart. "You see, Juanita Salezan was around to help him back then." The Texan spit a stream of tobacco juice at her father's feet and added maliciously, "I'm afraid you'll be otherwise occupied."

"What is this?" Julian demanded, stepping in front of Madeline.

Poteet's smile was ugly. "You foreigners are just plain stupid people. Did you actually think Governor Salezan would allow you to go free? Hell, as soon as your backs were turned, he sent me after you." The light in Poteet's eyes took on a sinister gleam as he added, "He's got a quiver in his liver at the idea of having Mrs. Sinclair participate in the entertainment he has planned for her husband."

Chapter 20

Smell the moldy odor of sodden walls in a darkness brilliant in its totality. My lungs expand and fill with the fragrance. My lair, my castle, my home. Sinclair, the Weak One, fights me yet. He struggles, and I play with him. It amuses me.

My hunger grows, but the time of my satisfaction is near. The Weak One will feed upon the truth, and it will kill him.

I shall live forever.

BRAZOS WOKE SLOWLY, clinging to the oblivion of sleep like a child clutching the ragged crib blanket that was his talisman. With awareness came pain—the raw burn of skin scraped bloody by iron manacles; the throbbing of muscles beaten and bruised; the hollow, aching acknowledgment of all he had lost.

He was chained to the wall in the dungeons of Perote Prison. How long he'd been there—days; weeks;

hell, it felt like years—he couldn't tell. Salezan kept him in the dark, literally. Only when the guard entered The Hole carrying a torch and a cup of water did Brazos see anything, and then the light nearly blinded him. It was one of those cruel mercies that they kept him thirsty enough so it happened only on occasion.

So far, the one good thing about his stay beneath the castle was that he'd managed to defeat the terror that had plagued him for years upon occasions infinitely less threatening than this. He'd fully anticipated losing his senses the moment he set his foot on the first of the crumbling stone steps leading down into the dungeon. But he hadn't, and although at times he felt that awful fear rumbling around inside him, he managed to hold it at bay. Mostly by thinking of Madeline—imagining where she must be by now, remembering how she looked, the rosy fragrance she wore, how she tasted, how tight she—

"Damn," he sighed into the darkness. Maybe he had lost his senses after all, thinking of such things under these circumstances. The rate he was going, he'd die of frustration before Salezan ever got to him. "Might not be such a bad way to do it. Wouldn't that just fry his bacon."

Salezan was already pretty damned angry, Brazos thought, and despite the physical pain of doing so, he grinned. Neither the governor nor his lackey lieutenant had been happy when they'd whipped the location of the armband out of him. Heading into this situation and not knowing just what was in store, Brazos had wanted to make the band available, but not too easy for Salezan's people to retrieve. So he'd left the piece with the monks at St. Francis Monastery with explicit instructions as to how it could be used. The holy men were to keep it for one year, after which time they would be free to sell the jewelry and use the proceeds as they saw fit.

Such provisions would not prevent Salezan from obtaining the armband, but it would delay the inevitable. Even a man as powerful as Damasso Salezan would find it difficult to fight the Catholic church in

Mexico. He'd win eventually, but those monks would give him a fight.

Monks. Priests. Brazos's thoughts wandered to the last words Maddie had whispered in his ear. *Don't give him the armband, Brazos, or the priest will die.* How had she known about the monks? Sure, the woman was a talented thief, but he didn't think she'd advanced to stealing his thoughts. How had she known he'd left the armband with a bunch of priests? And if that wasn't what she'd meant, what in the hell had she been talking about?

Was there a priest somewhere out there who would lose his life once Salezan recovered the armband?

Brazos wondered about the possibility off and on for the next few hours until a nagging thirst became a raging need. Apparently, Salezan had added a new depravity to his games. He must have decided that starvation was taking too long.

A thought—a truth—niggled at the edges of his brain. Something about thirst, about being hungry. About his last time at Perote. Then he felt the thing that lived inside him breathe a breath, and Brazos slammed shut the door in his mind. Instead, he tried to remember the last time the guard had arrived with water and released his chains to allow him the use of the fetid bucket in one corner of the cell. But his thoughts glimmered only in fractured, frustrating images. Seeking respite, he slept until a bright light and music pulled him back to reality.

Or was it reality? Torches lined the walls, lighting even the farthest, darkest, corners of the cell. Brazos winced, his eyes throbbing at the assault. On a round, marble-topped table set against one wall, a ribbon-wrapped package sat beside a music box that played a tinkling minuet. But what captured his attention wasn't the sight, or the sound, or even the sensation of freedom that resulted from the release of his wrists from their manacles. What brought him away from the wall and straining against the iron collar around his neck was the aroma of roasted meat arising from the table set for one in the middle of the small room.

Droplets of water beaded on the surface of a silver pitcher, a few of them dribbling down its side in a slow, seductive trickle. Brazos's tongue felt too big for his mouth, and his throat ached to taste what his eyes feasted upon. Hell, he was thirsty.

Oh, Lord, he was hungry.

"Well, well, my friend, I see you have finally awakened." Brazos tore his gaze away from the table to see Damasso Salezan standing beside the closed cell door, a derringer held casually in his hand. The governor of Perote Prison wore a ruffled, white linen shirt beneath a vest of royal blue satin and a black frock coat. Polished silver buttons flashed in the torchlight, and silver spurs spun on the heels of his black leather boots as he stepped across the stone floor toward Brazos.

A chill crawled up the Texan's spine at the look in Salezan's eyes. This was it, then. The end. But only the beginning of the end, God help him. Just let me die like a man, Brazos prayed.

And let me take Salezan with me.

The governor gestured toward Brazos's neck. "The bolt has been loosened. You may remove your necklace should you so desire. I would caution you to remain circumspect in your motions, however. Any aggressive movements you might consider would be dealt with harshly."

Forcing his raw and stiffened fingers to maneuver, Brazos removed the iron from his neck. He squared his shoulders and straightened his back. The scent of food and drink called out to him, but he ignored it, concentrating instead on the man whose dark gaze raked him with an anticipatory gleam. When Salezan's stare fastened upon the old scar on Brazos's left breast and heated with a glowing, sexual light, Brazos felt a sickening in his gut and the stirring of the monster within himself.

Was this the truth he'd been running from for years? The event that had given life to the overpowering fear that ruled him?

Had he been raped?

Cold crawled across his skin like a slow-moving

fog. His mind was a blank; he couldn't remember a goddamned thing. Salezan motioned for him to take a seat at the table, and slowly, the chain binding his ankles together clanking against the cold stone floor, he complied. With a nonchalance he did not feel, he lifted a goblet to his mouth and sipped. The water was sweet and cool, and if it was drugged, he could not tell. He drained the vessel as Salezan took a seat opposite him.

Salezan lifted the silver pitcher and refilled Brazos's goblet, saying, "You must be terribly thirsty. I'm afraid I quite forgot to send a man with your water for the past few days. My apologies."

Although hunger was a sharp pang in Brazos's belly, his gaze shied away from the juicy hunks of meat sliced into bite-size pieces on the plate in front of him. Salezan caught the look and grinned knowingly. "Help yourself, Brazos. I'm certain you must be starved. You'll forgive the breach of etiquette in serving your meat already cut, I trust? After your little foray with the knife last week, I thought it best to limit your access to sharp objects. Two of those men almost died."

Brazos lifted his fork and speared a chunk of fried potato. He fought to keep his hand from trembling as he brought it to his mouth. Cooked in bacon grease and seasoned with onion, the potato was both heavenly-tasting and too much for a stomach so long empty. Slowly, Brazos finished the potatoes, ate the green beans, the carrots, the rolls, and the baked apple.

But he didn't want to eat the steak. And although he could not have said why, he knew it was because of more than a heavy hand with the seasonings.

Amusement twinkled in Salezan's eyes. He said nothing, just watched, his gaze never once leaving Brazos's face. When Brazos, his hunger finally assuaged, laid down his fork, Salezan began to chuckle. "What is the matter, *mi amigo*? Is the meat not cooked to your taste? Perhaps it is too rare? Or, more likely, too well done? I seem to remember that you like your meat almost raw."

Brazos's gut clenched. I must've eaten too fast, he told himself. But he didn't believe it. Something else caused the nauseated feeling inside him, and suddenly he'd had enough. "What kind of game are you playing, Salezan?"

"A game? Why, *you* are the master game player, Sinclair, not I," Salezan protested. "Don't you remember all the tricks you used to play on me during your last visit to my home?" One corner of his mouth lifted in an insolent grin. "Maybe not, hmm? Then dreams, perhaps? Your dear wife did suggest you suffer from nightmares of your time here at Perote. Now, why is that, do you suppose? If you'd like, I'd find it a pleasure to refresh your recollections."

Brazos's hand clenched around the stem of a goblet filled with red wine. He'd wanted to know, hadn't he? He'd thought to confront Salezan at the mine and wrestle the information out of him, hoping to rid himself of the fear that slithered around inside him. Hope. That's what his entire plan had been about, and since that was the case, why should he worry about learning the truth now?

Did he really want to learn that he'd been buggered by Damasso Salezan years ago? "You so much as touch me, and I'll kick your *cajones* up under your ears."

Salezan's brows lifted. "So, that's the way of it? You think I fucked you?" He burst into laughter and rose from his chair. Walking to the small table set against the wall, he lifted the music box and rewound the key. Music once again filled the small cell; only this time, the airy notes reminded Brazos of a dirge. "True, I enjoy a wide variety of sexual experiences, Sinclair, but I am not a man lover. I like women. In fact"—he tilted his head and gave Brazos a measuring look—"I considered taking a woman—one particular woman—here on this floor while you watched. I thought it just might be enjoyable. But I'm afraid the anticipation of offering you my gift has overwhelmed me. I've waited for so long. I can wait no more. Eat your meat, Sinclair."

One particular woman. Brazos set his wine down abruptly. "What woman?" he demanded.

"Eat," Salezan said, gesturing toward the plate with his gun. "Eat, and I will tell you."

"Damn you, Salezan." Brazos speared the smallest piece of meat with his fork and shoved it into his mouth. He all but gagged at the taste, and inside him, the terror rose. Forcing himself to swallow, he said, "All right, I ate. Let's hear it, Salezan."

The music ended. The governor's eyes shone with a fiendish light. He lifted the ribboned box from the round table and walked toward Brazos, his boots clicking hollowly against the stone. "Open my gift, Sinclair, and you'll know everything."

Kill him now, Brazos told himself. Why wait any longer? He's bluffing about a woman. Juanita's back in Texas, and Maddie—well, Maddie had to be safe. Desseau protected her. She's his daughter; he wouldn't allow her to be harmed.

Brazos didn't want to see what was inside the box.

I'll hit him in the nose, he thought. Shove it up under his eyebrows. That'll kill a man if you do it right.

He *had* to see what was in that box.

Salezan stretched out his arm and offered Brazos the gift. "You did enjoy your steak, didn't you? I had it specially prepared. My father's recipe, you know. Remember us talking about my father? About the Karankawa?"

Brazos went for him. With his left hand, he slapped away the box. He slammed the heel of his right, palm flat, toward Salezan's face, intending to catch the bastard's nose and drive it up into his brain. But the derringer went off, catching Brazos in the shoulder, and his blow succeeded only in bloodying his enemy's nose.

"*Pinche cabron,*" Salezan cursed as Brazos came at him again, losing blood and quickly growing weak. They struggled for the gun, and with a last surge of effort, Brazos wrenched it from the governor's hand. Breathing heavily, he backed away and took aim for Salezan's head.

"Look," Salezan shouted, kicking the box at his feet.

In his weakened state, Brazos looked for just an

instant. But an instant was all that it took. A long coil of gold spilled from the box. A braid. Madeline's braid.

Brazos remembered. Brazos died.

The Beast roared to life.

"Ah, *bestia*," Salezan said, panting for breath. "My favorite has returned."

THE SOUND OF chains dragging across the stone floor intruded upon Madeline's sleep. Not opening her eyes, she tugged the threadbare blanket up over her head and burrowed into the minimal comfort of her thin, lumpy mattress. Her papa was pacing again. The man worried entirely too much. He simply wouldn't accept her assurances that all would be well.

Of course, she'd feel better about it herself if her luck in finding the entrance to Salezan's secret dungeon would improve. The governor had played right into her talented hands when he'd incarcerated them in a remote, seldom utilized section of the prison. No one was around to see her pick the lock on her cell door, using the hat pin she always carried in her petticoat.

One other person shared their wing of the prison, Brazos's friend Father Miguel Alcortez. After so many years as Damasso Salezan's guest, the priest was able to provide Madeline with all sorts of details concerning prison life. He knew when the guards were likely to pay a visit, and from whom she could steal clothing for an effective disguise. The one thing he didn't know, however, was where Brazos was being held. That a dungeon called The Hole existed at Perote was common knowledge, but its exact location was an ugly secret.

"I spent a couple of months in The Hole, Madeline," Father Miguel had said. "But I'm afraid I was unconscious both upon entering and when leaving. All I remember is a sliding panel—a secret door—that led to a staircase that winds down into total darkness." Madeline had begun an immediate and clandestine search for that hidden doorway and her husband. So far, her efforts had been fruitless.

The hazy sunlight of dawn filtered through the single, rectangular window carved in the stone high on the outside wall. In the distance, a cock crowed, while from the parade ground came the sounds of soldiers gathering for the morning review. Madeline stifled a groan as she sat up. As soon as they were all safe, she swore, she'd find a soft bed and sleep for a week. These nighttime excursions were beginning to wear on her body. Almost as much as they appeared to be wearing on her father's mind.

The poor man continued to pace. Madeline slipped her feet into her shoes and walked to the door. She peeked into the dark hallway, then listened for sounds. Nothing. Each day, breakfast—or the watery gruel that served as such—was offered to the three prisoners in the isolated wing of Perote after the general population had eaten. Barring an unexpected change in routine, Madeline knew she had a good two hours before a guard would appear nearby.

So she picked the lock on her cell door and visited her worried father. At the sight of her outside his door, Julian lifted his eyes to heaven and said, "I'll die of heart failure if she continues this way." The first time she'd popped over, after he'd recovered from the shock of learning that his eldest daughter knew how to pick a lock, Julian had tried to convince her to escape immediately, without even attempting to free Brazos. He hadn't listened to her then, and he wasn't listening to her now.

"Please, Madeline," Julian begged, waving away her assurances that all would be well. "Save yourself. The man sacrificed himself for you. Don't allow it all to go for naught."

By now, the argument was tired. "Sir," she said sharply, "you dishonor me with such talk. Yes, my husband put his life at risk in an attempt to rescue me. But am I less of a woman than he is a man? Brazos has never once claimed love for me, and still he faced his own worst fears by returning here for my sake." She braced her hands on her hips and continued, "I, on the other hand, have declared my love for him—shouted it to anyone who would listen. What kind of a person would I be if I just walked away and left him?"

"You'd be a *living* person!" Julian replied, throwing his arms wide. "Madeline, your reasoning is faulty. For goodness' sake, you're only a woman!"

She almost hit him then. "Only a woman? Only a woman!" She inhaled a deep, calming breath, then said, "The thought crosses my mind that it may have been a good thing for both of us that I did not grow up under your control." Throwing him a frustrated glare, she returned to her cell.

Gentle laugher spilled from the room across the narrow hallway. "Ah, Madeline, you do so liven up this old jail," Father Miguel said. "In my solitude over these past years, I've forgotten just how entertaining people can be."

"Hush, Father Miguel," Madeline said, retreating to her cot. "Any more from either one of you, and I'm liable to leave you both behind when Brazos and I escape."

The priest was still chuckling, Julian fuming, and Madeline sulking when Joseph arrived with breakfast. Madeline took one look at the contents of the bowl and said in a rueful voice, "You know, Joseph, I find I enjoyed the soufflé you served me a couple of weeks ago more enjoyable."

Salezan's butler sniffed, "Now, Madame Sinclair, I would not complain were I you. This is much better than your poor husband is receiving these days."

"Brazos, you've seen Brazos?" Madeline asked, clutching his sleeve. "How is he? He *is* alive, right? He's well?"

Joseph winced and backed away a step, looking everywhere but at her face. "I spoke out of turn. I am sorry. It's just that he's so . . . he can't . . ." Joseph pursed his lips into a frown and said, "He is not the same man you have known." With that, he beat a hasty retreat from her room. He failed to speak at all to Julian, but when he opened Miguel's cell, he brought both food and a basin of steaming water. Watching through the window in her door, Madeline saw Miguel's eyebrows lift in surprise. "What is this?" he asked.

Frowning, Joseph showed him a bar of soap and a towel. "The governor will see you in an hour. You would prefer to be clean, I am certain."

"Why does he want to see me?" Miguel asked.

Madeline's hands gripped the two iron bars in the window of her cell door and said fearfully, "The armband."

Joseph nodded. "I'll see that a clean cassock is sent for you, Padre," he said as he closed and locked the door. His steps rang hollowly down the long hallway.

Madeline's thoughts whirled. Brazos *was* still alive! But Miguel wouldn't be alive for long; Salezan was in possession of the armband. Brazos was in some sort of trouble. What had Joseph meant *not the same man*? "I must find that entrance," she declared. "Today. Now! I haven't mentioned this before, Father Miguel, but when I was here the first time, Joseph told me something. He said that as soon as—"

"As soon as Salezan recovered the armband, he'd kill me. This is not news, my dear. He has told me the same thing almost daily since Brazos escaped."

"But why? I don't understand? What is so special about a piece of silver jewelry?"

"Ah, Madeline," the padre said with a smile in his voice, "it is more—much more than jewelry. The band is one hundred fifty years old, and I found it buried in a box of old church records. It is a map to riches beyond your wildest imaginings."

"A map?"

"For one familiar with both the area of Texas in question and the symbols and teachings of the Catholic church, the engravings show the way to the El Regalo de Dios."

"Silver," Madeline said, thinking back to her time in Salezan's home, where silver objects adorned every room. "But he already has so much of it. Maybe he already knows about the mine."

"Mm," Miguel said reverently. The sound of water splashing spread across the narrow hallway as he

added, "I'd forgotten what a pleasure hot water can be.
No, Madeline. The secret of El Regalo de Dios has been
lost for over one hundred years. Your husband and I had
just begun to explore the puzzle when we were captured
and brought to Perote."

Madeline told him, "I've seen the silver—a portion
of it, anyway. Brazos told me a bit of the story." She
heard the sound of rustling cloth as the priest continued
speaking.

"Using the papers I had discovered, Brazos and I
were able to find a cache of buried silver bars—a small
portion of the wealth that had been prepared for
transfer to Mexico. When the Franciscans began battling with the Jesuits, they hid all evidence of the mine.
They didn't want to lose control to the more powerful
order, you see. Before any more was done, the Lipan-
Apaches attacked, and the secret of the mine was lost."

"Until you discovered it."

"Yes."

Julian, listening to the conversation at his own cell
door, said, "But I don't understand. I was of the opinion
that you and Sinclair were friends. If he had the map all
this time, why didn't he use it to bargain for your
freedom?"

"Brazos doesn't know the band holds the key. The
church documents showed us the way to the cache. Only
after I was interred here in these pleasant surroundings
did I, for lack of anything better to do, study the
etchings and put the facts together. Salezan overheard
my musings and took the armband. But he was unable
to decipher the designs. He moved me into a separate
area of the dungeon and went to work on forcing the
information from my lips. He was close to succeeding
when Brazos escaped and for some reason—I believe a
message from God—took the armband with him. It's
what's kept me alive these past years."

Julian asked, "Why did he leave you behind? That
doesn't appear to be the act of a friend."

"Brazos thinks you are dead," Madeline said
immediately, bristling at her father for daring to think
poorly of Brazos. "He doesn't speak of it, but his

brother told me. Tyler believes that it was your death that made Brazos so . . . so . . . well, he suffers." She smiled and added, "I can't wait for him to see that you are alive."

"Which brings us back to the beginning of this discussion. The armband is back at Perote. And I'm afraid, my friends, that my tolerance for torture has never approached Brazos's talents in that regard. I fear I shall not keep the armband's secret for very long."

"Then we shall escape today," Madeline declared. "No more tiptoeing around; we'll find Brazos somehow. Papa, how are your eyes? Will you be able to travel?"

"The swelling has receded; I am much improved. I'll help you search for Sinclair today."

"Good. I'd still like to find a way to make Poteet pay for hurting you." Madeline pursed her lips and said, "We must develop a plan. Father Miguel, how do you suppose Salezan will attempt to gain your information?"

The priest approached the window on his cell door. "Promise me, Madeline, that after the escape, you will scheme me up a hot spring in which to bathe." He hung his damp towel through the bars of the window and sent her a wistful look.

She smiled and said, "I promise."

"I think that the governor will offer me freedom in exchange for information. Freedom he has no intention of allowing me."

"Will he put you in The Hole with Brazos?"

Father Miguel lifted his shoulders. "I don't know. He's done it before. The man derives a sick pleasure from torture, especially while another prisoner observes. Salezan is an animal." Frowning, Father Miguel tapped his mouth with his index finger. After a moment, he said, "I believe I could convince him to take me to his library at the manor house. I could say I required a book—the Bible, perhaps—to correctly interpret the message on the armband."

"That's a wonderful idea!" Madeline exclaimed. "I already know an easy way out of the manor house.

Now, next we must—" She broke off as the sound of footsteps coming down the hallway reached her ears.

It was Joseph. He carried a priest's robe over his arms. Unlocking Father Miguel's cell, he handed over the cassock and lifted the basin of water. "I'll take this down to the *bestia*," he said, "and then I'll be back for you, Padre. The governor is anxious to begin."

"I imagine so," Miguel said wryly.

Madeline scowled. Something Joseph said bothered her, but she couldn't quite figure out what. She shrugged and turned her attention toward her search. As soon as Father Miguel left with Joseph, she'd release her father, and then they could begin to explore. She'd send Julian to the south tower; she'd not examined it yet. She'd head toward the west wall and—

She froze. *Not the same man you have known,* Joseph had said. She remembered Brazos in the *Uriel's* hold. The *bestia*. Joseph was taking the dirty water to the *bestia*. "It's him!" She rushed to her door and quickly picked the lock.

"Madeline?" Julian asked.

"Joseph, he knows," she said in a rush. "He's going to Brazos now. I have to follow Joseph. When he comes back, make sure he doesn't look in my cell."

"But your disguise!" her father replied. "You're in a dress, Madeline. You'll be recognized."

"I've no time to change. I'll be careful, Papa." Quickly, she tripped the lock on her father's cell, saying, "But just in case I run into trouble, you can come save me again."

"God go with you, Madeline," Father Miguel said, the window in the door to his cell framing an expression filled with concern.

She paused for just a moment outside his door, her hand lifting to the shorn edges of her hair. "You know my husband well, Father Miguel. Will he hate my hair? Will he think I'm ugly?"

His gentle voice followed her down the hall. "I do know him well, my dear. There's no doubt in my mind that he'll recognize you as the beauty you are."

• • •

IN THE SOUTH corner tower, Joseph set the basin of warm, though dirty, water on a cane chair. He pulled twice on a wall sconce, then bent down and pushed on a stone three rows up from the floor. From behind him came a distinctive click as a lock released.

Madeline, peering around the tower door, yanked her head back and stood flush against the wall, her heart pounding so fiercely, she feared it could be heard. Elation cut through her fear as she realized she'd been right. Joseph *was* going to Brazos. She'd found the secret entrance to The Hole.

Joseph pressed a plain section of wall with his shoulder, and a doorway appeared. Leaning inside, he grabbed a torch, then crossed the small, circular room to the hearth, where a fire burned. After lighting the torch, he lifted his pan of water and disappeared into the inky darkness. Madeline was halfway across the room when the door slammed shut.

"Bloody hell," she murmured, hoping she'd witnessed all the required movements to release the lock. She decided to wait a few minutes before trying. She hoped he'd be far enough away by then not to notice the opening of the door. Joseph's words came back to her as she lingered. *He is not the same man.* What did that mean? What had happened to Brazos?

Having decided enough time had passed, she pulled the sconce and pushed the stone. The hidden door swung open. Madeline wiped her sweaty palms on her dress, took a deep breath, and stepped down onto the first wedge-shaped stone step. Using an old burglar's trick, she counted each step as she descended into the darkness. Torches hung every fifteenth step or so, their flames flickering, casting a fog of smoke that hung just above Madeline's head. The circles of light illuminated streaks of mold growing on the walls and the occasional crumbling edge of a neglected step. From far below, Madeline heard the scrape of metal against stone. It must be Brazos's chains, she thought.

Then came another sound. Footsteps headed her
way. Fast. Bounding up the stairs.

Her heart pounded. There was nowhere to run.
She'd no weapon. He was almost upon her. She climbed
three steps, placing herself between the torches where
the light was haziest. She pressed back against the wall.
And prayed.

Joseph ran right past her, so close that she could
feel the water dripping from his shirt and smell the scent
of coffee on his breath as he cursed the one he called the
bestia. Then, a few feet above her, he stopped.

"He's made me so angry, I forgot," he muttered.
Joseph turned and descended the stairs, brushing by her
again. She was gripping the wall so hard that the rough
stone cut her fingers. Stay still and quiet, Madeline, she
told herself. You've done this before. Remember the earl
of Peckingham's dining room? Still and quiet, like all
good thieves.

The scant light beneath her began to disappear,
and Madeline realized that Joseph was extinguishing the
torches. She felt more than saw him pass by the second
time, and within moments, she was plunged into total
darkness. She'd never been so frightened in her life.

Cautiously feeling her way, Madeline descended
the stairs one by one. She counted as she went, and on
seventy-three, she caught a glimpse of light beneath her.

Sweat trickled down her neck as she finally
reached the dungeon floor. The small glow was a beacon
that both summoned and repelled. For a moment, she
stood frozen, unable to move. But then she heard a
sound, a rumbling growl of pain, and it drew her
forward.

There was a single cell at the end of the corridor. It
seemed to have been carved out of solid stone, a cave
more than a cell—a large, well-lit cave, at that. Vertical
iron bars placed but inches apart formed a wall through
which the interior of the cell was clearly visible. A large
chair resembling a throne sat outside, and Madeline had
a sudden picture of the royals visiting the London zoo.

The basin Joseph had carried downstairs lay over-
turned just outside the door. Slowly, quietly, she ap-

proached. A fire burned in a brazier, and torches hung on the wall, providing light for all but the farthest corner of the room. She tilted her head, staring into the darkness toward the dusky shape she detected there. "Brazos?" she asked, gripping the back of the chair.

The shadowed shape moved, stretched. Stood and walked into the light. Madeline gasped, her eyes flying wide at the sight before her.

It was the man in the painting in Salezan's study. Tall and naked. Painted pictures done in black and blood red of animals with teeth that dripped. An angry gash, half healed, ran from his shoulder to his right breast, a companion to the puckered scar from long ago on his left. Inserted into the skin was a length of beaded cane. But it was his face that made her tremble, caused her knees to weaken. She sank into the chair and stared at the thing in the cage that was a nightmare come to life.

He smiled gruesomely. His eyes flashed with power and madness and the secrets of hell. He was the painting in Salezan's study.

He was Brazos Sinclair.

"Well," came the gravelly, rumbling voice. "If it isn't the Weak One's bitch-woman. I am the Night. Welcome to my lair."

Chapter 21

Like a caged tiger, he paced the cell. From wall to wall, in and out of shadow, he constantly moved, his predator's gaze never wavering. When he spoke, he used a serpent's hiss. "So, you are not dead."

"Dead?" Madeline squeaked. Her heart pounded as she sank deeper into the chair, and despite the bars and lock on the door between them, she felt threatened as never before. Brazos was no longer Brazos, but an animal of barbaric strength with a rabid glow in his eyes.

A frisson of fear brought prickles to her skin at the idea of being alone with him in this secret dungeon. He was not what she had expected to discover. She'd anticipated finding Brazos in wretched shape—broken bones and wounds, perhaps starved and lying in filth. This creature had been beaten, but the bruises were yellowed and fading and blended naturally into the painted tattoos adorning his skin. He had been shot; the wound high on his shoulder was recent, but showed signs of treatment. He stood tall and healthy and strong.

And out of his mind.

Suddenly, he stopped his pacing. He faced her, his hands braced on his hips, and his gaze skimmed her indifferently before locking on her face. He studied her, tilting his head and frowning. After a moment, a smile touched his lips, slowly growing until he broke into an amused chuckle. "My master has been up to his tricks again, I see." He pointed toward her and said, "Your hair."

Madeline's hand lifted to finger the blunt ends of the chin-length locks. She felt a wash of shame amid the riot of feelings coursing through her—confusion, concern, terror.

He smirked. "'Twas a nice touch, using you to kill the Weak One. That's what did it, you know, the sight of your long, golden braid at his supper table."

Madeline stared at him, her mouth paper dry as she strained to make sense of his words. Concentrate, she told herself. Think. "What are you talking about?" she asked. "Who has been killed?"

He wrapped his fists around two of the iron bars and watched her through hooded eyes. "The Weak One is gone. The one you called husband. He's dead. Just as I predicted, the truth killed him. He was weak; now, I shall live forever."

Madeline lifted her hands and steepled them over her mouth. "My God," she softly said. She stared at him, studying him as thoroughly as he had her just moments ago. Tears welled up inside her as she realized the extent of his madness. "Brazos, what has he done to you?"

His roar echoed off the stone walls. "Do not use that name. I am the Night. The Weak One is dead." The bars rattled as he shook them and shouted, "Dead!"

Madeline whimpered, huddled in the chair like a child hiding from the monsters beneath her bed. Only this monster stood right before her eyes, and he was not a figment of her imagination. He was real. Oh, God, the beast was real.

Unable to watch the insanity in his eyes, Madeline's gaze snagged on his breast's ornamentation. She shuddered at the thought of cane puncturing a nipple. Then her scrutiny drifted lower, and she noted his flaccid sex. That, too, brought home the fact that this creature was not her husband. She flirted with hysteria as the thought occurred that although she'd seen Brazos Sinclair naked a number of times, she'd never seen him like this.

The Night's mouth twisted in a sneer. "You are a typical bitch. You wish my male-part transformed, do you not? You want my body to come to yours and gift you with my essence." Madeline saw his knuckles whiten as his fists clenched. "But then I would be as the Weak One, and that I cannot allow."

"The Weak One," she repeated. "You mean Brazos?"

He pounded the iron bars. "Do not use that word!" His features hardened in an ugly scowl. "Now, leave. You have no place here."

At that moment, Madeline wanted nothing more than to flee up the steps into the sunshine, away from this dark dungeon nightmare. That feeling gave her an idea. She remembered the instance in the *Uriel*'s hold, and how he'd snapped out of his spell when they'd climbed up into sunlight. She thought of the time in the well and sunlight's restorative effect. The obvious first step to saving Brazos was to convince this beast to climb the winding staircase out of the dungeon.

Inhaling a deep, steadying breath, she said, "But Braz . . . I mean, Mr. Night, I cannot leave alone. I've come to release you, to give you your freedom." Pushing herself from the chair, she took a step toward the cell door, imploring, "You must leave with me now, before someone arrives to check on you." After sending a brief prayer of thanks for her professional skills, Madeline went to work on the lock, muttering, "The next time Brazos grouses about my being a thief, I'm going to remind him that it was my abilities that got him out of prison."

The beast backed away, scoffing at her. "Why

should I wish to leave? This is my home. I have everything I need here. I am—" and he emphasized the words "—*well fed.*" He turned away and added coals to the brazier that sat against the back wall, providing heat and adding light to the cell.

The lock clicked open. The door scraped against the stone floor as she pulled it open. A rat darted through the open doorway, and Madeline shuddered.

Turning his head slowly and with control, the beast pinned her with a narrow, fiery stare. "What do you dare?" he hissed. "I dislike your efforts to test me." He pointed toward the door and roared, "Go, bitch, before I decide to make a meal of you." His nostrils flared as he breathed a heavy breath before adding, "Bony as you are, 'twould hardly be worth the effort."

Madeline didn't move, she couldn't. An idea flickered at the edges of her mind, something his words had sparked to life. She struggled to grasp it even as his gaze swept her body and he pensively said, "Of course, I've never had a woman. I wonder if you would be different than the priest? Perhaps your meat would be more sweet."

No, Madeline denied as she began to back away, he didn't say what I think he said. She gagged at the idea. Should I get out? she asked herself. This was more than she'd bargained for. Obviously, Brazos's problems involved more than physical torture. Perhaps she should give herself time to determine how she should deal with problems of the mind. Besides, this beast was dangerous.

But before she could move more than a few steps, he pounced. Grabbing her arm, he yanked her inside the cell, then slammed the door behind him. "What's the matter, bitch? Are you not strong-hearted? Are you not my enemy, giving aid to the Weak One as you have in the past?"

Shaking like a tree in a gale, she forced herself to think. Instead of answering his question, she asked one of her own as the vague idea still hovering at the edge of her consciousness took a hazy shape. "What . . . what priest?"

He approached her, the smile on his face a grotesque caricature of mirth. His savage laugh made her stomach clench. Gripping her arm mercilessly, he pulled her across the room and threw her on his cot. His arms folded, he stared down at her. His blue eyes glowed with malevolence as he answered, "Father Miguel Alcortez. He was the Weak One's friend and therefore my enemy."

A band of hope squeezed her chest, and she strained to draw a breath as the idea burst full-bodied across her mind. Was this it, the secret Brazos had buried so deep inside of him, the source of all his pain? A truth so horrifying that he couldn't live with it?

A truth that was a lie.

"What happened to your enemy, to Father Miguel?" she asked, watching his eyes closely.

"It is the way of the Karankawa, the manner in which one captures the strength and destroys the soul of one's enemy." His smile made her shudder. "My master and I shared his flesh."

Madeline knew it was a lie, but hearing him put it into words still made her feel nauseated. Then he lowered his voice to a purr and repeated the question he'd asked earlier. "Are you strong-hearted, woman? I know you are my enemy. I shall enjoy destroying your soul." He touched her cheek, and she jumped from the bed, dashing for the slop bucket, where she vomited.

"My master must have planned this for me," the animal called Night mused. "I should have guessed when he gave me your braid. At the time, I thought the purpose was to kill the Weak One, but now I see my master intended to offer you as my gift."

Madeline rinsed her mouth with water, and tears pooled in her eyes, spilling slowly down her cheeks. That bastard Salezan merited a slow and tortured death. She decided then and there to do her best to see that he got what he deserved. "Oh, Brazos," she said quietly. "It's a wonder you survived at all."

He began to growl and retreated to one corner of
the cell as she stepped toward him. "Salezan lied to
you," she said, advancing slowly. "Father Miguel Alcortez is not dead. I spoke with him just before I came
down here. He's upstairs, alive and healthy. Governor
Salezan *lied* to you."

"Quiet!" the beast roared. He came out of the
shadows a vicious animal, eyes flashing, fists clenched
and raised as weapons.

Madeline stood with her spine stiff and chin
uplifted, facing him fearlessly as he moved close. "I tell
you the truth, Mr. Night. You must accept it. Why, my
very presence here is proof. You said, 'So, you are not
dead.' You said that Salezan used me to kill Brazos
Sinclair—my golden braid at his dinner table. Did
Salezan serve Brazos meat and then tell him it was me?
Is that why he retreated and allowed you to come
forth?"

"Bitch!" It was a feral scream of rage that echoed
through the dungeon and shook Madeline to the core.
He grabbed her shoulders and shook her violently.
"Why do you do this! I'll kill, don't you see? Why are
you foolish enough to come into my lair and anger me?"

Then he lowered his mouth and kissed her.

*PAIN EXPLODES THROUGH my body. I'd
thought the Weak One dead, but he is here, battling me.
Winning. He senses the source of his power within reach
and attacks. Where I, like the Karankawa of long ago,
draw my power from the heart and body of mine enemy,
the Weak One siphons his strength from the force
within the Woman. I must stop it. I must separate from
her.*

*But he is strong. Even now, he moves my hand and
brings it to her waist, feels the curve of her hip. "No,"
I cry, and I tear the hand away so that my arm hangs
limply at my side. But her lips, her kiss, it is strong. I
struggle against it. Pull away, pull away.*

I cannot.

He moves my lips. She whimpers, and it is an arrow to my heart. I feel him building inside me, strengthening. Pressure swells. Pulses. It begins as a groan deep in the hollow of my soul. I close my throat, but it, he, is too strong.

"MADDIE," BRAZOS murmured against her lips.

She pulled back and gazed into lucid blue eyes. "Brazos! Oh, Brazos, thank God."

NO! I SHALL NOT allow it. I summon my energy for one great effort. My hands—not his—lift to her waist and shove her away.

She falls back, tripping on a chair leg and sprawling on the cold stone floor. We are separate; the pain within me lessens. I march toward the door, shut yet still unlocked, and I slam it with the palm of my hand. It swings open, banging against the corridor's stone wall. The sound echoes like a death knell.

"Out," I shout, my hands fisting at my sides. She must leave immediately. The Weak One has touched her, grown potent. He nearly defeated me.

The woman is my greatest danger. I should kill her.

SITTING UP, MADELINE threw a proud, undefeated glare at the naked beast standing beside the door and bit hard on her lip to stifle a sob. She'd been so close. Brazos had been there. He'd spoken. For a moment, she'd thought the spell of mindlessness that held him prisoner had been broken with their kiss. Like in the nursery stories told by the brothers Grimm.

Well, obviously, life was no fairy tale.

"You're being a fool, Madeline," she murmured

climbing to her feet and dusting herself off. Sunlight and fresh air were what he needed. Her being womanish about this business was helping neither one of them. "Listen, mister," she said. "I don't care how many people you think you've made meals of. I don't care if you want to call yourself Night or Sinclair or the bloody king of this castle, for that matter—I've risked my life to come after you. I hounded my father to risk his life on your behalf. I could have rescued Father Miguel a week ago if I hadn't been searching for you. Now, surely you've a loincloth or something lying around this cell. Put it on and come with me at once! We've wasted too much time as it is. Someone even crazier than you might be on his way down those stairs even as we speak."

Turning her back on him, she stepped to the small cot and rifled through the bedding. No clothing there. She bent over and peered beneath it. She couldn't see very well, so she got down on her hands and knees, then ducked her head beneath the bed and felt around on the floor, sneezing as the layer of dust she disturbed clouded around her head. Her knees caught in her petticoat, so she stretched and wiggled, trying to work the fabric around to give her more room to move.

An almost tortured groan met her ears, and she jumped, banging her head before scooting out from under the cot. "Bloody hell," she muttered, rubbing the tender spot on her head. She'd found nothing more than well-worn leather boots beneath the bed. "Really, you must have some sort of covering around here. Surely you get cold sometimes and—" She glanced over her shoulder and stopped.

He still had the beastly look about his eyes, but the man staring with rapt attention at her backside displayed a certain physical endowment that was patently Brazos Sinclair.

Delayed reaction, she thought, suddenly full of hope. Maybe it takes a few moments for the spell to be broken. Or maybe in real life, it took more than just a little kiss to get the job done. Maybe it took extra effort.

Madeline was good at extra effort.

She rose to her feet with feline grace. Pouting, she put a hand behind her head and said, "Ouch. I bumped my head. It hurts. In fact, I think it's bleeding. I think—oh." Her knees buckled, and she fell in a faint upon the bed.

Quite realistically, too, she thought.

"Woman," he snapped. When she remained silent, he repeated, "Woman!"

She lay on her back with her arm flung across her brow, effectively shielding her eyes so that she could peek without his seeing. He was scowling at her, looking more vicious than at any time since she'd entered his prison room. She risked a low, pain-filled groan.

The scowl transformed to a look of concern, and he took a hesitant step forward. Such a beast you are, Madeline silently scoffed. For a man who supposedly eats people, he certainly was a soft touch.

Speaking of soft, that wasn't quite the effect she wanted. She'd better see to getting him over here, fast. Before the effects of her kiss and wiggles wore off.

Madeline stirred and whined loudly, "Oh, I'm burning. I'm hot," she said as she tore at the buttons of her bodice, opening her dress and exposing a thin chemise.

He took another step forward. She sneaked a furtive glance at his loins and thought, Now, that's the Brazos Sinclair I know. But it was the one calling himself Night who leaned over the bed and spoke to her. "Woman, I give you warning. I am going to kill you."

Madeline suffered a moment of doubt as his fingers wrapped around her throat. Had she misjudged his capability for hurting her?

She opened her eyes and looked up into his furious, insane gaze, searching for a sign of the man she loved. There, past the anger and the madness, lay a plea for help, an appeal for salvation. Softly, she said, "You won't hurt me."

"I'll choke the life from your body," he hissed, putting a knee on the cot, then straddling her. "I'll rip out your heart and feast upon it before it has ceased to beat." The fingers around her throat tightened.

"No, you won't," she rasped. As she watched the struggle in his face, she knew what she must do. "I love you, Brazos Sinclair," she said.

He flinched as though it were a physical blow. Quickly, she repeated, "I love you. And I know that you won't hurt me because you love me, too."

He wrenched himself off the bed. He stood with his back to her, his chest heaving with the heavy breaths he took. "Go," he rumbled. "Go now, while I am weak enough to allow it. Take your lies and leave me."

"I'm not lying." She rolled off the cot and stood, laying a hand against his back. "I love you, no matter what name you choose to call yourself. Even if you had done what Salezan claimed, I'd love you still. You are my friend." She wrapped her arms around his waist. "My husband." She pressed herself against him. "My lover. I love you, all of you."

He stood frozen like the stone effigies guarding the entrance to the prison. Madeline circled to his front, her hands continuing to touch him, never breaking the connection. Lifting her face, she pulled his head down toward hers. "I love you," she repeated softly, and then she kissed him. And the kiss went on and on and on.

LOVE. A WEAPON *without equal. A force more powerful than any other. She has gifted the Weak One with its might, and he has become Strength.*

I yield to the power of Love.

FOR BRAZOS, IT was an epiphany. A brilliant, rapturous instant in which the memories of the past and truths about the present exploded onto his consciousness. But one thought transcended all others and warmed him like a tot of French brandy.

Madeline loved him. Really loved him. Enough to challenge the monster inside him. Enough to defeat the beast. Damn, but she was some special kind of woman.

And he loved her, with a heart now whole and a soul redeemed. He loved her so much, the tumbleweed in his blood had gone to dust. He only wished he had time to love her with that other part of himself that had found new life.

He broke off the kiss, took her face in his hands, and staring solemnly into her eyes, said, "I love you too, Beauty. But if you ever try another stunt as dumb as this one—and by that I mean everything from returning to Perote to daring to enter this cell—if you *ever* pull something like this again, I'll plumb dust your feathers."

A radiant smile lit Madeline's face. "Oh, Brazos, you can dust my feathers anytime you want."

He couldn't resist. He took her mouth in a long, wet, sense-stealing kiss and surrendered to the need to do a little groping. "Aw, hell, Maddie," he said when he finally found the strength to pull away. "Stop doing this to me. A man gets extra thirsty when he can't get to water, and I doubt we've time to do any divinin' right now. Tell me what's goin' on up above."

Madeline shook herself, and Brazos witnessed the joy drain from her expression. One more thing to hold Salezan accountable for, he thought.

She nibbled worriedly at her lower lip before asking, "How long have I been down here, ten minutes or so?"

"Honey, you're askin' the wrong person. For all I know, I've been in this hellhole for a year."

"Two weeks," she answered, her mind obviously on another subject. "Probably by now Joseph has taken—" She stopped in midsentence and looked at him. "Brazos, do you remember? Do you know what happened to you down here?"

For a long moment, he remained silent. Oh, he remembered, all right, and he even thought he knew the truth. Obviously, Madeline was alive and well; Salezan had used Brazos's own ploy against him. He tilted his head and looked at her. "You look kinda cute with your hair short, Maddie."

The look she gave him was a mixture of pleasure and vulnerability. Briefly, he considered telling her that the rest of her hair was underneath his mattress, but then he figured it'd probably just set her to crying. He hated it when she cried. He summoned the courage to ask, "Is what you said earlier true, Madeline? Is Miguel still alive?"

"Yes, he is," Madeline answered, laying a comforting hand upon him. "He's been here at Perote all this time. Salezan kept him alive because Father Miguel could decipher the map that is etched on the silver armband you took. It's a map to the—"

"El Regalo de Dios silver mine," Brazos interrupted, feeling as if the weight of Texas had been lifted from his shoulders. Savoring the words on his lips, he repeated, "Miguel is alive."

"Um, Brazos," she said, "about that armband. Salezan's men brought it to the prison this morning. He's sent for Father Miguel to decipher the map. Remember what I told you on the bridge? Salezan has threatened to kill Father Miguel once his usefulness is over. I think perhaps we should hurry."

He muttered a curse. "Wouldn't that be just my luck—to manage to get him killed just when I've learned he's still livin'. Do you know where Salezan planned to take Miguel?"

"His library. Father Miguel was going to insist that he needed the Bible to interpret the markings."

Brazos nodded once and gestured toward the open cell door. "Let's get out of here. Do you think you could find me some clothes someplace? I imagine I'd be less conspicuous—oh, shit."

Damasso Salezan stood just outside the barrier of iron bars with a gun leveled at Father Miguel Alcortez's head. "Well, well, Mr. Sinclair," he said, sneering. "I thought we'd seen the last of you." He gave a mighty shove to the priest's back and sent him sprawling into the cell. Father Miguel climbed slowly to his feet, brushing the straw that covered the cell floor from his cassock. The door clanged shut, and the lock clicked into place.

Salezan turned his attention to Madeline, saying, "You, however, I am not at all surprised to find here in my dungeon. You've quite a talent for wriggling your way out of places I've put you."

Brazos dismissed Salezan with a scornful look before clasping Father Miguel by the shoulders. The two friends stared at one another, taking measure, communicating their pleasure at each other's presence with nuances of expression long familiar. "Damn, I'm glad you're alive," Brazos said.

"And I you," the priest replied. "However, I'd have preferred that this meeting occur under different circumstances."

"Yeah, well, I can't argue with that. It does appear that we're plowin' in a bad row of stumps."

Madeline looked at Brazos, "Plowing in a bad row of stumps? You do have a problem with languages, don't you, dear?"

He shook his head. "I've a problem with sadistic Mexicans who try to drive me insane. Watcha gonna do now, Salezan, see if you can get us *all* believin' your lies? Only problem is, who you gonna say's been eatin' who? We're all here."

Brazos lifted a brow as he noticed the slight shake of Madeline's head. So, they had allies above them somewhere. Who? Desseau most likely, maybe even Tyler. Brazos didn't know whether to be relieved or more concerned at that thought.

Salezan took his seat, looking every bit the king he liked to believe he was. "Actually," he said, pouring himself a goblet of wine from the decanter kept ever at the ready beside the throne, "I've decided that this is the perfect opportunity to indulge in another scenario I've fancied in the past. In fact, I find the thought so delicious, I all but tremble with anticipation. My lone problem is to decide who should go first. Me or the good priest, there."

"What are you talking about?" Madeline demanded impatiently.

Something ugly slithered around Brazos's mind, and as Salezan opened his mouth, Brazos knew what he was going to say.

"I find such symbolism in the idea of the priest. A man of my heritage sets great store in ritual and symbols. Yes, the priest will be first. Once I have taken my revenge for the loss of my wife, there may be nothing left for the holy man to make use of."

From the horror spreading across her face, Brazos knew that Madeline had caught on, too. She said, "You . . . you mean—"

Salezan smiled a devil's grin. "The priest will have you first. Then I shall take my turn. Now, lock your husband into the manacles on the wall. I'll shoot him dead if you attempt any foolishness."

Brazos nodded at Madeline, whose eyes rounded in fear. Then he shared a long look with Miguel. He didn't quite have it all figured out yet, but he damn well knew Salezan wasn't gonna get his way this time. Nor would the bastard leave the pits of Perote alive.

He turned his back toward the governor and walked toward the dangling chains. He whispered to Maddie, "Julian?"

"Yes."

"Anyone else?"

She shook her head. "I left Papa in an unlocked cell. He may be on his way."

"We may not have the time. I won't allow anyone to hurt you. Are you any good at manacles, Maddie?"

She lifted her chin and sniffed before saying beneath her breath, "I've never met a lock I can't pick."

"Wrists and ankles, my dear," Salezan said. "And be quick. I find I'm growing impatient."

As Madeline bound his hands to the cold stone wall, Brazos whispered in her ear. "See the bottle of moonshine on the table, Maddie? Get one of the blanket scraps and plug it into the bottle's neck. Tell Miguel to get a torch, light it, and throw it at Salezan."

The governor called out, "Move away from your husband, Madeline. Turn toward the priest as you remove your dress. I'm certain that after so many years of celibacy, our padre will enjoy the sight of such luscious bounty. Now, he made need a little time, a little inducement. Or perhaps"—he turned an evil grin toward Father Miguel—"he'll need no coaxing whatsoever. Tell us, holy man, is your cock hard? Are you already lusting after your friend's wife? Have you dreamed of pumping yourself into her, of spilling your seed in the heat of her body?"

"I pray God sends you to hell," Miguel Alcortez said, his gaze vibrant with fury.

"Ah, hah," Salezan laughed. "You do want her! Woman, move more quickly. I want to see the good father's eyes when they glimpse those lovely *chi chonas*."

Madeline threw Brazos a desperate look. "It's all right, Beauty," he said. "Do what he says." Brazos felt her embarrassment, saw her shame. But then she stiffened, squared her shoulders, and lifted her head high. Turning her head toward Salezan, she pushed her dress from her shoulders, looking down her nose at him as though she were a queen and he nothing but a lowly stable boy.

Watching her, Brazos was filled with pride. She was an amazing woman, and Salezan was too stupid to see it. The governor's gaze was fastened on the thin lawn of the chemise she wore beneath her gown; he actually licked his lips. Brazos wanted to rip the chains from the wall and kill the bastard with his bare hands.

"Beautiful, my dear," Salezan said as the dress dropped to the floor. "See, priest, just like I promised. And think in just a few minutes you'll be inside her, wrapped in her velvet sheath. Of course, she will need a little stimulus. Are you Catholic, Mrs. Sinclair? Have you fantasized about fucking a priest? Well, your dreams are soon to come true. Take off the cassock, holy man. Let's see how you lust after your best friend's woman. Give her a glimpse of your hard cock. She'll get wet for you, I'm certain."

Blood surged through Brazos's veins so hard and fast, he thought he just might explode. He was going to wipe the floor with Salezan before he killed him. Madeline looked ready to cry, and Miguel—*Oh, hell,* Brazos thought.

Miguel was a man of God. A good man. A pious man. But he was still a man. And by the look on his face, he'd not been unaffected by Madeline's body. Brazos didn't like it, but he understood it. And he knew damn well that Father Miguel would be mortified if his uncontrollable reaction was made visible to all here in the dungeon. His friend had suffered enough. It was gonna end here and now. "Madeline," he said, "you go tell Father Miguel that there's nothing to worry about." He caught her puzzled gaze, then darted a significant look at the wall torch.

Madeline reached for Father Miguel's hand and whispered to him. The man nodded, but only Brazos saw his relief. "Salezan," Brazos said, "if I'm gonna have to watch this little opera you're orchestratin', do you think I could at least have Madeline give me a swig of that home brew your soldiers make to help get me through it?"

Salezan crossed his arms and leaned back in his chair. "Why not?" he said expansively. "I find if you mingle the senses—taste, sight, touch—it does increase one's pleasure. Give your husband a drink, Madeline. Fondle him a moment. Maybe he'll enjoy this as much as the good father and I."

"Oh, I think I'll enjoy this a whole hell of a lot. Now," he said. And it took only seconds.

Miguel pivoted and swept the burning torch from the wall while Madeline poured liquor over the blanket scrap before shoving it into the bottle. As the priest took the bottle and set it alight, Madeline hurried to her husband and went to work on the locks. Miguel slipped the makeshift bomb through the bars and tossed it at Salezan's feet.

"No!" Salezan screamed as the bottle exploded. Shattered glass pinged against the stone as blue flames flared at the feet of the king and his throne. Then, in little more than an instant, Salezan's clothing caught fire, engulfing him in a blaze. His screams echoed off the walls.

With two of the manacles undone, Madeline shuddered, grimacing at the sounds the governor made. The fire spread, consuming the dry straw scattered through the passageway. A breath-stealing fog of smoke rose and hung along the low-ceilinged corridor.

"It's spreading," Father Miguel cried, beating at the flames that had inched their way inside the cell.

Madeline had but a single shackle to loosen to free Brazos from the wall. He watched her hands tremble, saw how the heat from the fire scorched her skin, how the smoke burned her eyes. She blinked hard to see through the watery film. She pulled on the manacle. It held. "Damn," she cried.

Brazos's voice was calm and soothing even as the table inside the cell went up in flames, the crackle and pop of burning pine causing her to jump. "It's all right, Beauty," he said. "You're doing fine."

The flames were gaining on Miguel. Gray smoke engulfed the cell, so thick, Brazos could no longer see the door. He realized that if they didn't escape now, they'd all perish. "I can do this one, Maddie. Go get the door. Open the cell door and help Miguel out of here. I'll be right behind you."

"No," she cried. "I'm not leaving you behind. I can do this. I'm a thief! I do this all the time." She pulled at the iron cuff. Nothing. "Oh, God, help us," she wailed.

"Go, Madeline, now! I order you! Save yourself, dammit. Miguel, come get her. We've run out of time."

She looked up at him and shouted, "Bloody hell, Sinclair, are you going to go to your grave still trying to order me around? Haven't you learned anything over the last months?" She bent herself to her task with renewed determination, and soon came the gratifying click of a lock being released.

Brazos wrenched his ankle from the iron and

grabbed Madeline's arm, tugging her in the direction of the door. "Watch your skirts, honey." Flames licked his bare feet as he crossed the room, and he knew that if he was still alive tomorrow, he'd suffer from the burns. "Miguel!" he called, staring through the smoke to find his friend. "Miguel!"

Father Miguel didn't answer, but as Brazos reached the cell door, he found his friend, weakened by years spent in prison, gasping for air. Hell, Brazos wondered, had they run out of time?

"Sinclair?" an excited voice called from the other side of the door.

"Here!"

Julian Desseau drew a penknife from his pocket and quickly tripped the lock. Pushing open the door, he waved them toward the stairs, asking, "Madeline are you all right?"

Coughing, Madeline managed to say, "Yes, but the padre . . ." She stopped to pull on Miguel Alcortez's arm.

"Go, Maddie," Brazos hollered, pushing her at the same time he tried to lift Miguel.

Julian shoved him aside, saying, "Sinclair, get her out of here. I'll help the priest."

"Papa, you saved us," Madeline said. "But how did you get the door—"

"Later, *cheri*. Up those stairs while we're still able to breathe. The smoke is rising; take small breaths."

She ran for the stairs, Brazos right behind her. Something caught him around the ankles, and he pitched forward, falling on the smoldering body of Damasso Salezan. The governor's face was black and crusted, but his eyes were open and alive. Pleading. Brazos stood and wiped his hands on his trousers. He hesitated.

Salezan deserved nothing better than to die here in the bowels of Perote Prison, where he had played his sadistic, horrific games. Here, where he had created the animal that had dwelt inside Brazos for so long—the beast that had been defeated by the pure, unbounded love of the beauty waiting to climb to freedom with him.

Heedless of the heat against his own skin, Brazos bent and lifted his enemy into his arms. Silently, he carried the dying man up the stairs and away from the flaming corridors of Brazos's personal hell.

Chapter 22

The escape from Perote Castle proved to be easier than Madeline had hoped. Stepping into the tower room after climbing the dungeon staircase, she discovered Joseph, pistol in hand, anxiously pacing the room. After taking one look at the agony etched across Salezan's disfigured face, Joseph asked Brazos to lay the governor on the floor. Then the servant provided one last service to his master. He put the pistol to Salezan's temple and shot him.

Joseph displayed little emotion as he provided each of the ragtag band of prisoners a set of clothing before escorting them to Perote's front gate. Only when he offered the reins of a beautiful black gelding to Father Miguel did the butler betray his true feelings. He said, "I ask your forgiveness, Padre. I am ashamed for the part I played in keeping you here at Perote."

Father Miguel offered the man a gentle smile and said, "You need not be ashamed, my friend. You found a balance between your familial duties and your moral ones. Without your assistance, Joseph, I don't doubt that I'd have died years ago." The priest placed his hands on the servant's shoulders. "Don't question God. Everything happens for a reason. You're free now. Go and pursue your calling."

The rocky road shimmered with heat as they rode away from the castle. Brazos wiped his brow with a kerchief and asked Father Miguel, "Familial responsibilities?"

"Joseph was Salezan's half-brother."

"His brother!" Madeline exclaimed, twisting in her saddle to look at the priest. "Why, Salezan treated him terribly. What made Joseph tolerate such abuse?"

"He had made a promise to their mother."

"Hard to imagine Salezan havin' a mother," Brazos commented, slowly shaking his head. "So Joseph was his brother. Well, I'll be damned."

"I suspect so, unless you change your ways, my friend," Father Miguel replied dryly.

"Wait just one minute," Madeline interrupted. "Brazos is a very good man."

The two friends looked at one another and laughed. "It's an old joke, Maddie. Don't take him seriously," Brazos told her. "For a priest, Miguel is a terrible tease."

She sniffed disdainfully and gigged her horse, catching up with her father. They rode silently side by side, and were it not for the questions plaguing her, Madeline would have enjoyed the freedom of the ride.

She worried about the future. So far, Brazos hadn't said a word about it, and she didn't have a clue as to what he was thinking. She settled for asking her father how he managed to open the lock on the dungeon cell door.

Julian offered her a sheepish look and confessed, "While searching for you, I stole a penknife from Salezan's study. I'm afraid I'm quite proficient at locks; 'tis a knack I discovered during my youth."

A warm surge of pleasure engulfed Madeline upon hearing his words. Obviously, she'd inherited her talent from him. She couldn't wait to explore other family connections. Most of all, she couldn't wait to hold Rose in her arms once again.

As Brazos led them to the coastal site where they would rendezvous with the *Lucky Linda,* she determinedly pushed her worries from her mind. For now, she wouldn't concern herself with the likelihood that her father would wish to take her sister back to France. She refused to fret any longer about whether Brazos would want her to join them or not.

Dusk cast a shadowed glaze over the water as the steamer paddled its way toward them. Madeline recognized Tyler's shout and Sister Cecilia's joyful squeal as the stern-wheeler drew close enough for all to see one another. It seemed to take forever to get aboard, and although Rose was already asleep in her bed, Madeline couldn't resist picking the child up.

An hour later, following the reunions and explanations, Brazos ducked into his sister's stateroom and found Madeline sitting on the bunk with tears streaming down her cheeks as she rocked the sleeping toddler. "Aw, Maddie, don't cry. You know I hate it when you cry. What's the matter, Beauty?"

What could she tell him? How could she possibly explain what was in her heart? All her life she'd been searching for a dream, and now it was within her grasp. She had a family, a father and a sister, and a beautiful home to return to. In France.

That was a long way from Texas and Brazos Sinclair.

One time, he'd told her he loved her. Once, down in that dungeon cell, where the possibility of their leaving alive appeared slim. He'd not mentioned the word *love* again, and Madeline wondered if he ever would. Drying her tears, she sighed and said simply, "I missed Rose."

A shuttered look came over Brazos's face. "I know, Maddie." He shut the cabin door and leaned against it, his arms folded, the toe of one boot softly tapping the floor. Silence yawned between them so that every rumble and clang from the engine sounded like a roar.

Tension mounted to such a pitch that Madeline wanted to scream.

When Brazos opened his mouth to speak, she knew by the noncommittal look in his eyes that she wouldn't like what he had to say. "Your father says he's taking the first ship out of Galveston bound for Europe." Brazos hesitated for just a moment before he said, "Guess you'll be goin' with him and Rose."

No words had ever hurt more. It was all she could do not to clutch at her stomach and moan aloud. But since acting was one of the numerous skills every good thief possessed, Madeline pasted a smile on her face and replied, "I guess so."

Brazos pushed away from the door. He paced the room, its space limitations and his size requiring he pivot every four steps, and the more he walked, the more he grimaced. Madeline watched him closely, and the fiercer his scowl, the more she began to hope. "Since the day we met, all you've talked about was wantin' a home and family," he said, shoving his hands in the pockets of his pants. "Well, you've got what you want."

Madeline returned Rose to her crib, then turned to face her husband. She searched her mind for the right words to say, the words that would make him see what was in her heart, what had always been in her heart. "I've never belonged before, Brazos. Not to anyone or anyplace. That's what I've wanted, to belong and to have someone belong to me."

He stopped. Twice he opened his mouth to speak, twice he snapped it shut without uttering a word. Brazos stared at her, anguish reflected in his eyes. She answered him by allowing love to shine her own.

"Well, hell." He lifted his gaze to the ceiling. "I tried, Maddie, I truly did. But I reckon I've damn well used up my share of nobility."

Her heart pounded, and her knees felt weak as she asked, "What do you mean, Brazos?"

He flashed her a crooked grin that was rueful, unabashed, and downright wicked all at the same time. "I'm afraid I'm through with bein' nice about this. You're not leavin' me. I'm not givin' you up."

"You're not?" Madeline asked, a fierce elation bursting within her like fireworks on a summer sky.

"I'm not."

She wanted to fling herself into his arms, but she knew she shouldn't. It wouldn't do for the man to think he could order her around. So she said, "What makes you think you can stop me?"

He moved as swiftly as the wind, grabbed her hand, and tugged her out of the stateroom and into the one next door. She saw his saddlebags on the table beside the bed and realized this was his room. His bed.

"Why do I think I can stop you?" he repeated, advancing on her like a predator after his prey. "Because I love you. Because, amazing as it may be, you love me, too." He stroked her cheek with a gentle finger, and Madeline shuddered as a wave of desire swept through her.

Brazos pulled her into his arms, holding her firmly, but gently. "Because, Madeline Sinclair, you don't belong to your father and your sister. You belong to me. I belong to you. I'm never letting you go, and I'll be damned before I allow you to let loose of me." He brushed kisses against her forehead, her eyelids, her cheeks. Just before he lowered his mouth to hers, he swore, "Hell, I'll go to France. I'll go wherever you want to go. I'll live wherever you want to live. I'll be happy as a 'coon in a corncrib as long as we're together. I love you, Beauty."

And then he kissed her, a deep, passionate, arousing kiss. Madeline thrilled at the rough, erotic touch of his tongue against hers. She exalted in the proof of his hunger pressing hotly against her and answered it with a slow roll of her hips.

Somehow, through the haze of desire, his words drummed into her senses. "No, Brazos," she said, pulling away.

"No?"

She nodded. "Yes. 'No.'"

His words sounded hoarse as he asked, "Why the hell not?"

"Because I don't want to."

"You don't want to," he repeated scornfully. "Well, honey, that's not what your body was tellin' me a second ago."

"Not that," Madeline said, waving away his comment. "France. I don't want to go to France. I want to stay here in Texas, Brazos. I'm a Sinclair, and all the Sinclairs live in Texas, right?"

Brazos scowled. "All but for Aunt Penelope. She travels with a circus in Europe, so I would have family over there, too."

"Circus?" Madeline tilted her head and looked at him. "High-wire act?"

"Bearded lady. She's actually an aunt by marriage, so you needn't worry about our daughters, Maddie."

"That's a relief."

Brazos sat on the edge of his bed and rubbed his chin with his palm. "You really don't want to return to France?" She nodded, and he said, "What about Julian, Maddie? And Rose? Hell, I don't know that I could stand to live without Rose bein' in our lives."

Suddenly, a sense of peace and purpose settled over Madeline. She sat beside Brazos and took his hand in hers. "We'll work it out, Brazos. I know we will. I'm good at schemes, remember?"

"Oh, I remember all right." He lay back against the mattress and pulled her down beside him. "Seems like we never finished that fight we were havin' a good time back. Schemes and stealin'. We need to talk about that, Maddie."

"Later," she said, kissing the hollow at the base of his neck.

"Later," he agreed, rolling to his side and sweeping his hands beneath her skirts.

For some hours after that, they did all their conversing with their bodies.

BRAZOS GRUNTED AS Madeline's elbow caught him in the ribs. "Wake up, Sinclair. You're been asleep for ages, and there's planning to be done."

Slowly, he opened one eye and tried to glare. But he felt too good to glare, so it turned out more as a leer. She gouged him with her elbow again. "Ouch, Maddie." He lifted his head up and this time managed a respectable glower. "What the hell did you do that for?"

"I've an idea."

"Wonderful," he said glumly.

She snuggled against him, smiling like a cat who'd knocked the lid off the butter churn. "We'll convince my papa to stay in Texas. He can join the La Réunion colony, and he and Rose can live—"

"Hold it right there, wife. That dog won't hunt," Brazos said, gripping her arms and moving her away from him. "I'm not livin' and raisin' my children among a bunch of people who intend to establish something called a Court of Love whose leaders are referred to as fairies, fakirs, and genies."

"Why is it you only remember the parts of Fourier's teachings that deal with sex, Brazos?"

He ignored her. He'd do just about anything for Madeline, but a man had to draw a line somewhere. Living at La Réunion was his line. "Now, I know that they're all not amoral—folks like the Brunets are good people—but I don't liken to the idea of all those men lookin' at you with community in their eyes."

Madeline giggled. "Brazos, I've told you before that La Réunion is not entirely committed to all of Fourier's theories. But I don't have to live there. Maybe we could move across the river to Dallas."

"Hell, no." Brazos lay back down and pulled her on top of him. "That's too close to that pretty-boy wagon master. I don't want you within a hundred miles of him."

"Do you mean Ben Litty?" Madeline asked innocently.

He pinched her bottom. "You are wicked, Mrs. Sinclair. Yes, I mean Ben Litty."

She nibbled at his ear and whispered, "You needn't worry about Ben. I told him long ago that I was in love with you, and that I wasn't giving up on our marriage."

"Damn, Maddie. You told him before you told me?"

"*He* was ready to hear it."

"Oh, well, I guess I can't argue with that."

"No, you can't." Madeline's teeth nipped at his lower lip as she added, "I don't really want to live in Dallas, anyway. That's too close to your dear friend Juanita."

Brazos licked Madeline's neck and said, "Not unless you call an ocean away close. The day your pa and I left La Réunion, Monsieur Bureau was fixin' to take Juanita with him back to Paris. I suspect they're halfway there by now."

"Juanita in France? Well, if nothing else could convince me to stay in Texas . . ." Her fingers trailed up his thigh.

"Don't tempt me, Maddie. You plumb wore me out last night. Give me a chance to build my strength back up."

She bit his ear. "Yeow," he cried, but he grinned while he did it.

She rolled off him and nestled against his side. "Where will we live, Brazos? Near your parents?"

"I own a bit of land along the Brazos River," he told her, his fingers playing with the ends of her hair. "It's pretty—lots of oak, rolling hills, good farmland. It's near the orphanage, too. If you've a mind to, we could settle there. I'd even be willin' to spend a month or two at La Réunion helpin' those folks prepare for their first winter. I'm tellin' you, Maddie, unless they change their ways, that colony doesn't stand a snowball's chance in hell of survivin'."

"If we go back, I could tell the colonists good-bye. The Brunets could move in to our house. Lillibet likes it so much more than those the colonists are building," Madeline absently mused. She was remembering when Sister Cecilia told her about the plantation Brazos had purchased all those years ago. The place where he'd intended to build a home and raise a family. "The land you own sounds like a lovely place to live, Brazos."

Brazos smiled and tenderly kissed the top of her

head. "You think there's a chance we could convince Julian to stay?"

"I've learned to believe that anything I wish for can come true."

"That reminds me," Brazos said. He rolled over and pulled open the drawer beneath the bed. "Close your eyes."

"Why?"

"Just do as I say, Beauty."

"That'll be the day."

"Don't I know it." He laid three items in her lap. Madeline lifted the first, a sheet of paper, and read the writing upon it. "What is this?"

"Recipes. My sister wrote them down for me. I want you to pick which one I should bake." She stared at him in confusion, and he sighed. "Maddie, I once told you that the day you became my equal was the day I tied on an apron—"

"—and baked a cake," she finished. "Why, Brazos Sinclair."

"You asked for chocolate. I figure it's long over-due. Show me which one you want."

Laughter bubbled up inside her. "I don't care about the cake. It's the apron I want to see. I've one at La Réunion that has a lace collar and flowers . . ."

"Don't press your luck, woman."

Smiling, she picked up the second item, the blue velvet bag that had contained all of her stolen articles. The third was her magical mirror. Brazos said, "I left La Réunion in a pretty big hurry, but I figured you'd be wantin' this stuff, so I tucked it in my saddlebags."

"Oh, Brazos," Madeline sighed, her heart swelling with love. She pulled open the bag and peered inside. Frowning, she dumped out the contents. "Some things are missing."

"They were mine to start with, Maddie. It's only right I took 'em back."

"Your watch and your gun I understand." She lifted her brows in a silent question.

His voice held a note of defensiveness as he

answered, "That golf ball really is special to me, Maddie."

Smiling, she shook her head and lifted her mirror. Her fingers traced the gems and filigree on the back; then ever so slowly, she turned the it over and gazed into the glass. Tears of joy trickled down her cheeks as she saw reflected in her mirror a new image, one she'd never dreamed before.

A two-story brick house stood on the rise of a hill within calling distance of a slow-moving river. A wooden veranda painted white stretched along three sides, and in the yard, a rope swing hung from the branch of an ancient oak tree. Children played on the lawn. Rose, perhaps nine or ten, pushed a younger child, a girl with gleaming blond hair and sparkling blue eyes, in the swing. Two boys played marbles while another boy stood beside Brazos, an older Brazos, but even more handsome with a touch of gray at his temples. Brazos was showing the boy how to swing a golf club while Julian Desseau waved at an approaching carriage carrying André and Lillibet Brunet and three boys.

Madeline didn't see herself in the picture, but she knew she was there because she could hear her own laughter at the antics of a toddler chasing a golf ball on the grass.

"What is it, Beauty?" Brazos asked, wrapping his hand around hers, the one that held the enchanted mirror.

"It's wonderful, Brazos," she told him softly. "Obviously, we all will live happily ever after."

ABOUT THE AUTHOR

After growing up in a home on Alamo Drive in Wichita Falls, Texas, GERALYN DAWSON was destined to write about Texas history. In addition to twice being a Romance Writers of America Golden Heart semi-finalist, she has won numerous writing awards. Today she lives in Fort Worth, Texas, with her husband and three children.

Don't miss these fabulous Bantam women's fiction titles

now on sale

• NOTORIOUS

by Patricia Potter, author of *RENEGADE*

Long ago, Catalina Hilliard had vowed never to give away her heart, but she hadn't counted on the spark of desire that flared between her and her business rival, Marsh Canton. Now that desire is about to spin Cat's carefully orchestrated life out of control.
_____56225-8 $5.50/6.50 in Canada

• PRINCESS OF THIEVES

by Katherine O'Neal, author of *THE LAST HIGHWAYMAN*

Mace Blackwood was a daring rogue—the greatest con artist in the world. Saranda Sherwin was a master thief who used her wits and wiles to make tough men weak. And when Saranda's latest charade leads to tragedy and sends her fleeing for her life, Mace is compelled to follow, no matter what the cost.
_____56066-2 $5.50/$6.50 in Canada

• CAPTURE THE NIGHT

by Geralyn Dawson

In this "Once Upon a Time" Romance with "Beauty and the Beast" at its heart, Geralyn Dawson weaves the love story of a runaway beauty, the Texan who rescues her, and their precious stolen "Rose."
_____56176-6 $4.99/5.99 in Canada

Ask for these books at your local bookstore or use this page to order.

❑ Please send me the books I have checked above. I am enclosing $ _____ (add $2.50 to cover postage and handling). Send check or money order, no cash or C. O. D.'s please.

Name _____

Address _____

City/ State/ Zip _____

Send order to: Bantam Books, Dept. FN123, 2451 S. Wolf Rd., Des Plaines, IL 60018
Allow four to six weeks for delivery.
Prices and availability subject to change without notice.

The Very Best in Historical Women's Fiction

Rosanne Bittner

_____	28599-8 EMBERS OF THE HEART ..	$5.99/$6.99 in Canada
_____	28319-7 MONTANA WOMAN	$4.99/5.99
_____	29033-9 IN THE SHADOW OF THE MOUNTAINS	$5.50/6.99
_____	29014-2 SONG OF THE WOLF	$4.99/5.99
_____	29015-0 THUNDER ON THE PLAINS	$5.99/6.99
_____	29807-0 OUTLAW HEARTS	$5.99/6.99

Iris Johansen

_____	28855-5 THE WIND DANCER	$4.95/5.95
_____	29032-0 STORM WINDS	$4.99/5.99
_____	29244-7 REAP THE WIND	$4.99/5.99
_____	29604-3 THE GOLDEN BARBARIAN	$4.99/5.99
_____	29944-1 THE MAGNIFICENT ROGUE	$5.99/6.99
_____	29968-9 THE TIGER PRINCE	$5.50/6.50
_____	29871-0 LAST BRIDGE HOME	$4.50/5.50

Susan Johnson

_____	29125-4 FORBIDDEN	$4.99/5.99
_____	29312-5 SINFUL	$4.99/5.99
_____	29957-3 BLAZE	$5.50/6.50
_____	29959-X SILVER FLAME	$5.50/6.50
_____	29955-7 OUTLAW	$5.50/6.50

Teresa Medeiros

_____	29407-5 HEATHER AND VELVET	$4.99/5.99
_____	29409-1 ONCE AN ANGEL	$5.50/6.50
_____	29408-3 A WHISPER OF ROSES	$5.50/6.50

Patricia Potter

_____	29070-3 LIGHTNING	$4.99/5.99
_____	29071-1 LAWLESS	$4.99/5.99
_____	29069-X RAINBOW	$5.50/6.50
_____	56199-5 RENEGADE	$5.50/6.50
_____	56225-8 NOTORIOUS	$5.50/6.50

Deborah Smith

_____	28759-1 THE BELOVED WOMAN	$4.50/5.50
_____	29092-4 FOLLOW THE SUN	$4.99/5.99
_____	29107-6 MIRACLE	$4.50/5.50
_____	29690-6 BLUE WILLOW	$5.50/6.50

Ask for these titles at your bookstore or use this page to order.

Please send me the books I have checked above. I am enclosing $ _____ (add $2.50 to cover postage and handling). Send check or money order, no cash or C. O. D.'s please.

Mr./ Ms. _____

Address _____

City/ State/ Zip _____

Send order to: Bantam Books, Dept. FN 17, 2451 S. Wolf Road, Des Plaines, IL 60018

Please allow four to six weeks for delivery.

Prices and availability subject to change without notice.